Angelo

...“You want to know the ground rules is what you mean?”

“Yeah, that’s what I mean. The ground rules.”

Angelo brought the empty pillow back a little to his lap, and Jamie stopped his pour midway and looked at him.

“All right. That’s easy enough. First, this is a one shot deal. This pillow will work, Jamie,” Angelo looked down at the unstuffed pillow in his hand, and then back at Jamie, “but it only works once. And only for you.”

Jamie nodded his head. “Okay.”

Angelo nodded his head too. “Secondly, you pick whatever dream it is that you want to dream.”

“I don’t get it.” Jamie kept one knee on the carpet and brought his other knee up so he could set the bowl on it. “How do yuh mean?”

“It’s the dream of your choice, Jamie. Whatever it is you want to experience in those seventeen and a half seconds is up to you—although you do have to run it by me before you walk away with this. But it’s basically that easy…you provide the framework and the pillow will do the rest.”

“I pick the dream.” Jamie said it more to himself than back to Angelo. Like repeating it would sketch it somewhere on his brain so he would remember these couple of rules.

“When you leave with this and you tuck it beside the pillow you sleep on or somewhere in the sheets or wherever you decide, and you fall asleep with it there, the dream,” Angelo held the empty pillow out to him again, “is yours.”

Jamie just sat there, steadyin’ the bowl on his knee.

“Oh. And it’s real, too. Everything that happens will be a reality.” Angelo smiled...

Also by Louis J. Fagan
NEW BOOTS

Angelo

Angelo

LOUIS J. FAGAN

A-Peak Publishing

$\mathcal{A}$-Peak Publishing
Johnstown, NY

Printed in the United States of America

Cover art by Maria Masucci
Cover design by Jennie O. Collura
Layout by Chad C. Fleck

Fagan, Louis John, 1971-
    Angelo / by Louis J. Fagan. -- 1st ed.
    p. cm.
    LCCN: 00-102451
    ISBN: 0-9667407-6-9

    1. Dreams—Fiction. 2. Friendship—Fiction.
3. Modern-day Fairy Tale—Fiction. 4. Small
Town Life—Fiction. 5. High School Life—Fiction.
6. Inspiration—Fiction. I. Title.

PS3556.A3263A54 2000   813.6
                                   QBI00-435

To
the muse
who whispered this idea
in my ear one night
when I got up to take
a leak

Angelo

I remember when he came in that day after school and sat down and told me.

I remember a lot about that afternoon, but as strange as it seems, one of the things I remember most is how I felt those few seconds before he knocked on my open door.

My back was to him and I was at my desk, and I had the feeling that someone was standing there and debating whether or not to knock. I felt his hesitancy in my gut before I heard his three quick taps that sounded to me something like "What the hell, I got nothin' to lose." A feeling closest to what I'm not quite sure—a flash of stage fright or homesickness or even relieved dread— pinched through my stomach and disappeared across my chest. It was a feeling I had just once before when I sat in front of a fortune-teller who was about to predict something...something strange and significant, something strangely significant and significantly strange. It was a feeling that signaled truth.

I'm not sure why he told me. Some people aren't at all about lying, if you know what I mean, and he's one of them, so maybe he just knew that I'd believe him. I doubt, though, that he even had one exact reason why he told me, so I don't worry or wonder or think that much on it. And I don't think you should either. Just know that what I'm about to tell you is true.

All you can really do is believe it because it is true.

His truth. The truth of a fifteen-year-old, small town kid who met this guy named Angelo. I'll keep as close as I can to what he said, use the words he used, tell you what it was for him and how he felt it. And who knows, maybe you're like me. Maybe somewhere in his story—his truth—you'll find a truth of your own...

3

Chapter One

———

CHEETOS. THE really hard baked kind, not the puffy kind. A miniature bag for thirty-five cents. Them and a soda. Sprite usually, sometimes Coke or somethin' if they were out. That was his lunch for under a buck.

Today the goddamn Cheetos were stale. He reached in his side pocket and pulled another one from the bag he had put in there, and moved the shriveled-up thing to his mouth. His hands were cold and chapped, but he couldn't eat and hold a soda can if he was wearin' his gloves. 'Cause those things were puffy. Too puffy. His mom had bought 'em for him for Christmas, and they didn't really match his gray winter jacket, but they were warm and he tried to appreciate 'em for what it was worth. He had stuck them in his other pocket with the fat fingers stickin' out like someone was sorta squished inside there and reachin' out.

He had had to wait in line at Ray's. Some random customer. An old lady usin' loose change to buy a frozen Pepperidge Farm cake. He'd never seen her in there before and she was usin' up his lunchtime on her Wednesday afternoon, sweet tooth cravin'. He thought about the minute or two she had eaten away while she was shufflin' around in her shoulder bag, lookin' for the last three exact coins that would spare her from gettin' more change. She told the man behind the counter she thought he could use the change and that she hoped she could get a paper bag, not a plastic one. The handles always rip on those and she had a ways to walk.

Jamie stepped through the snow. Man, she was sorta pathetic, in a sad way. He took a swig of Sprite. Like she didn't have any grandkids or anything. Just her and maybe *The Price Is Right* to keep her company. You know, she was the kinda lady who spent too much time at the OTB. Her coffee table probably even had some of those stubby blue pencils from the place, and she used them to do her word-finds. But her knit hat looked like one his own grandmother would have made—not really stylin', but a handy piece of work. Strange, yuh know.

The snow was deep and still fallin', and the sky was gray…yeah, actually almost the same crappy gray color his jacket was. And Coformon Falls was smack in the middle of a snowstorm. Not a totally unbearable and harsh snowstorm, but cold enough and with big, wadded flakes—flakes as big and as light as feathers, "angels shakin' their behinds" his dad woulda said to him when he was a kid, or somethin' stupid like that—flakes that dropped all hellbent to bury the already covered ground even more.

His prints were the only ones there in the risin' layer that hid the sidewalk, and his sneakers were wet to his socks from his way up to the corner store, even the cuffs of his jeans were startin' to starch with crusts of snow. His ears felt the cold too and he knew the red of their rims probably matched the red of his nose right about then.

He sniffed and ate another lousy Cheeto.

It wasn't that he didn't want to be late for the first bell or for sixth period. He usually made it. Truth was, he didn't want to end up walkin' directly in front of or directly behind these three guys that always came out of one of the houses at the bottom of the hill before you turn onto Rea Street, the road the high school sat in the middle of. Usually he timed it so that he was a good distance from them. He'd be kiddy-cornerin' somebody's lawn when he'd hear them laughin' and talkin' while they came out from across the street. On the rare occasion they came out before him, he'd slow his pace some, take shorter steps and put some extra space between them and him. He'd been late for class doin' that before. But that was no big deal.

This end of Main Street still had Christmas decorations up. Green all-purpose garland, like ball field turf cut into strips, wrapped around streetlight poles, and under the curved neck of the lamps hung huge gold, eight-pointed snowflakes. All of it was weathered with salt and snow slop, and a little out of place now, yuh know. You could say it didn't have any of the "spirit" in it that it had just a couple weeks ago. And it was just danglin' instead of decoratin'. Just somethin' else for the snow to dump itself on.

They had never said anything in particular to him or picked on him or anything. Those guys. And, shit, he could care less what they thought anyway, but every day this past fall, he left the school about a minute or two after them for lunch break. His school did that, let you leave for lunch if you wanted to. Those guys walked up the block to one of their houses. He walked to Ray's. They wore polo shirts in the fall, and on Fridays they would wear their jerseys when there was an away game. A couple times he'd seen Number 10—that's what he called the one with the dark hair shaved above his ears because he didn't know his name—turn around and look at him. Maybe the kid's first name was Rich, he thought it mighta been Rich. Jamie would pretend to be lookin' at the speed bump he was crossin' over, when Number 10, or Rich, turned around and looked. The other two turned too, after Rich said somethin' to them. Then they just kept walkin'. That was only a couple times that that had happened. But every day he saw them on his way to Ray's.

Jamie passed the house. Rich's or one of Rich's friend's house. It was big. Off-yellow. Bone yellow, if there is such a color. Two stories and a front porch with twisty black metal railings. Nothing fancy, but not bad either. A lot like the house to its left and to its right. And the houses next to them.

He was cold. Because it was gettin' colder. Maybe the roads would get worse and the school would close early—now that they'd stayed open long enough to get their state aid or whatever it was that they worried about gettin'. He finished his can of Sprite and went to cross the street. There was no sidewalk on the other side, but he'd only walk a few feet and then he could cut the guy's lawn that he always cut. The street was a lot like the sidewalk, a snowplow had gone through earlier but it hadn't done much good. A few cars had left their marks too, but the fallen snow, for some reason, reminded him of a bakin' cake—up it was gonna go, unless someone slammed the kitchen door...

Jamie sorta slid across the street. He tried crammin' his empty

8

can in his pocket, the one with his gloves, when he heard them.

"The cold made it expand." One of them kicked the screen door shut, and you could hear the aluminum dent and the door meet its frame.

Jamie's Sprite can had found itself some room, and he zipped his coat up a little more and got to the other side of the street.

"You idiot, heat expands shit, not cold."

"Whatever. Don't kick my parents' door."

Jamie didn't turn around. He was liftin' his feet through the snow, workin' his way onto the lawn on the corner lot. He felt the wet of a snowflake find its way to the skin on the back of his neck, where his hairline and his collar left a half inch wide open when he looked down to step the hidden curb.

As he made his way across the big white lawn, he saw the guy who owned it. He was on a ladder, his back towards Jamie, takin' down Christmas lights that were wrapped around his house's eaves. In a goddamn snowstorm, the guy was takin' down lights? Jamie almost shrugged. He raised the corner of his lip and lowered his brow a second, sayin' "Whatever does it for yuh" without sayin' anything. He fisted his stiff, wet hands just then and stuck them in his pockets. Shit.

"Somebody's glove."

"Just leave it."

"In the middle of the road?"

"Just leave it, retard."

They lowered their voices just a little then. Got less rowdy, maybe better said. Like the curtains of the fallin' snow would drown out what they were sayin' or somethin'.

"Maybe it's his."

They crossed onto the lawn.

Jamie was crossin' off. His hands were tight in his pockets and he watched his step. There were a couple Cheetos left, and one had somehow escaped from its bag and burrowed in the corner of the pocket's leftover space. It sat against his knuckle and was wet now too. Jamie felt some of the orangy artificial cheese spray that Cheetos are sprayed with there on his knuckle.

"Who? Friendless."

They laughed. A slap your buddy's back or punch your pal's shoulder unison kinda laugh.

"Friendless." One of them repeated the other.

"Shut up, dick. He's gonna hear yuh."

"Boys, square that corner, please."

Jamie looked up. Not behind him. Up, as if it would help him hear better.

"It's that I'll have a muddied footpath straight across my lawn when spring comes if you boys don't square the corner."

Jamie pretended to be lookin' at the sky. He kept walkin'. Behind or above the snow comin' down, he could filter past the gray. He had to squint. Musta been the guy who owned that corner house talkin'.

"Yeah, no problem." Probably Number 10 who yelled back.

"Thanks boys."

"Yeah. No problem."

Jamie got a little more distance in those couple of seconds. He could still hear 'em tee-hee'in'. Callin' that guy an old prick and stuff, but they weren't right up his ass, like he felt like they were just a minute ago. He crossed by the patch of woods and over the culvert, both of them kind of the dividin' line between town and school property. Yeah, it sorta marked where school property started. Or ended, maybe? You couldn't see it today because of all the snow, but there was a little brook or stream or whatever you wanted to call it, that Rea went over. He doubted that it was even frozen over underneath all the snow, well, maybe a thin sheet on it under there, but it took really cold freezin' weather to freeze it up. People said it came straight from the mountain and that was why. But who knows. He looked down at it real quick while he was walkin', just 'cause yuh do that sometimes when you're thinkin' about somethin', even though you know you're not gonna see it. Just snow there though, that filled up even with the sides of the ditch. Like nature's booby trap floor or somethin'. Yeah, Coformon Falls quicksand. You'd think you're walkin' on level ground and then BAMM! you'd be up to your ears in snow and your feet would be standin' in ice-cold mountain water. That'd sure as hell wake somebody up.

He looked back up and his eyes even felt a little cold, like snowflakes were meltin' or stickin' to his lashes. The cage was right there on his left, and he knew he'd rather be walkin' in six feet of snow than be stuck in—hmm? The cage?

Well, the tennis courts sat directly behind Coformon Falls High School. C.F.H.S. had a team. They weren't any good, and the people who ordinarily cared about stuff like that didn't care anyway. You can guess why if yuh want. Before the school instituted an open lunch, when everyone finished eating, you were herded into the fenced-in courts—the cage it started gettin' called. The janitors wanted to clean the tables and clear the halls, and they ruled for a while, so everybody ended up in the cage no matter how long you tried to take eatin'.

Across the street from the courts was a makeshift football field where the kids played flag football for gym class from mid-October to mid-November. The coaches would throw on one of their championship jackets with the blue and silver dragon stuck on the front, where somebody would stick a name tag if they worked at McDonald's, yuh know, sorta over the heart, and then the year that the soccer or wrestling team or whoever had made state finals or somethin' would be pasted on the back. Quilt lining, not shabby at all. Meanwhile, the guys in his class would be runnin' around in shorts, maybe a sweatshirt, and a goofus belt with two plastic flags velcroed to the sides of it. Some of 'em runnin' around really gettin' into it, yellin' numbers and "hutt, hutt" and shit like that, while most of 'em were freezin' balls and waitin' to hear the seven minute change bell.

The field was a water puddle in the spring, and most of the winter you could barely tell it was there. Only sign of its half existence was the short set of bleachers that kids sat on when they forgot their gym clothes or some excuse. Just a snow mound with the back and ribs of aluminum, the sleeping blue and silver Coformon Falls HS dragon on sabbatical.

Jamie passed between the field and the court, and he planned on usin' the back doors, like he always did. There was a stack of stairs that led up to 'em that widened at the bottom and narrowed at the top and whose rise-over-run seemed a little off. They looked like a sad attempt at some stairs on some Egyptian temple or somethin'.

No one was around. Really quiet. Snow has a sound though when it falls and Jamie listened to that, and he was conscious of his body's in and out of the storm air, too, the sound his movin' body made as it breathed January's honest air. Man, he knew he was a country kid. Honest air and storm air and all that stuff.

He started to walk down the short grade of the back parking lot. Cars to his left and right, tires covered in the white wash, lookin' like they had somehow sunk beneath the earth's new surface or somethin'.

He wouldn't have seen him if he hadn't turned his head to the noise of a school bus comin' from the other end of Rea. The squeak of its overused brakes and bounce of its worn shocks was hollerin' that beneath all the snow still laid a yellow painted speed bump the driver should remember was there before he turned onto the traffic loop and parked in front of the school. Closer to him though was a side door to the school, usually with an open-from-the-inside and locked-from-the-outside mentality. Sittin' in front of it was that kid in the wheelchair. Ben.

Jamie kept walkin'. Okay, so Ben was sittin' outside the side door, that was the entrance most accessible, with ramps and stuff. Jamie looked further off again, the bus rocked really clumsy-like over the speed bump, and under its wheels some snow shot up and spit out. Spurts of snow from the wet, black treads. Jamie's stomach bounced a little off the bottom of his ribs when his brain clued him in. He looked then at the wheels of Ben's wheelchair, and they weren't even half as entombed as the parked cars' tires, or spewin' snow from them like the bus's were or anything like that. But they were there. In the snow. Snow that had piled up on the sidewalk after a once-over with a snow blower. Maybe half as deep as the snow Jamie'd just plowed through, but deep enough. Deep enough for wheels that looked like bicycle tires, minus the thin wiry spokes, but with five or so thick plastic ones extendin' from their centers instead. And clutched to the tops of 'em—the wheels—were Ben's hands. He had some ski gloves on, and he was sorta pushing and turning the wheels. Shiftin' his body some, slidin' his left hand forward on the left tire and lockin' it in front of a thick plastic spoke and then, with a quick backwards thrust, stiffening his upper body and spinnin' the wheel in reverse. Jamie saw that the back of his shoulders was beginnin' to form a yoke of snow, and his hair was wet.

Ben bein' in a wheelchair didn't bother Jamie, didn't phase him…or make him uncomfortable, that's the word, it didn't make him uncomfortable the way some people might feel when they hold the elevator door for somebody in a wheelchair, or when they hear somebody in a wheelchair ask if the restrooms are handicapped accessible, or if the dance floor at a wedding has a person in a wheelchair on it. Even Ben bein' out in the snow in his wheelchair with wet hair and beginnin' to look like a snowman didn't make Jamie feel that way.

Jamie started to walk towards him, and his stomach shot another jab at the bottom of his lungs for a different reason.

He had known Ben when they were six. They had been sort of friends. Tuesday and Thursday afternoons at the YMCA. For swimming lessons. Ben could walk then and, man, he was like some kinda amphibian back then. They'd sit on the edge of the pool in their wet swimsuits and dangle their feet in that mega-chlorinated water they used to have in that pool. You'd have to wait behind the others while the two instructors—one who was a real bastard, this nineteen-year-old kid who took it way too seriously—took the next in line and swam the kid across the short length of the pool. That's how he met Ben. Ben always ended up bein' the kid in front of Jamie. Maybe they finished changin' into their bathing suits at the same time or somethin', couldn't tell yuh, but there Ben was in the line of kids and always in front of Jamie. When it was Ben's turn, Jamie'd watch, most of the kids would, because Ben, if he happened to be paired up with prick boy instructor, he would do somethin' unpredictable, like dive in and swim across underwater or stop halfway across and do an underwater somersault and go the rest of the way. He never needed either of those instructors' arms or help or anything. He liked horsin' around a lot, on the diving board during free-swim at the end of class and stuff, doin' all sorts of crazy shit, like a cartwheel off the thing or jackknifin' it, and he'd conquered the butterfly stroke pretty early on too. He didn't belong in the tadpole group at all, yuh know.

Anyway, Jamie and him got to know each other a little that year, but they were from different elementary schools and only saw each other twice a week. Yuh don't really build friendships when you're six on two hours a week. So when Ben got in a car accident, that was pretty much it. Jamie really didn't see him after that.

Sort of knew each other better than just knowing someone, and sort of knew each other less, a lot less, than how friends know each other. That's how they were now. Sorta strange though, right? Don't people wish they'd rather not know somebody at all than to have that feeling of "Should I look up and say hi? Is the other guy gonna say hi?" when they see them?

"Hi."

Ben's body jerked and he looked towards Jamie.

Jamie took his right hand from his pocket and lifted it to the back of his neck for a second. He was still a distance off from Ben when he spoke. He had come a little closer and stood now a couple feet from him. He noticed Ben's hair was wet with more than just snow and that his chest was risin' and sinkin' at the rate of someone who had just been workin' out. "Sorry. I didn't mean to startle yuh."

Ben smiled. "Hey, what's up." He looked at his left wheel. "Would yuh believe I've been sittin' here about a half hour?"

"Yuh have?" Jamie looked down at the wheel, too.

"Yeah. They got me signed up for bowlin' for gym class." He looked at Jamie and then thumbed towards Rea Street. "The driver was a sub and he brought me back, dumped my ass, and took off."

Jamie closed the distance between the door and himself. His toes were cold in his sneakers. He pushed on the long bar handle. "Yeah, this thing is always locked from the outside." He pushed on it again and then turned to face Ben.

"Yeah, I usually have a stop in it, but one of the janitors musta taken it out, worryin' that the snow'd blow in or somethin'." Ben fisted his right hand and tapped it lightly into the palm of his left a couple times. He wore ski gloves, and their lining bulged. Some threads had busted in places where they had been in constant contact with the wheels, bein' Ben maneuvered himself all over the place with them on in the winter. "It's gettin' cold."

"Jesus, you're right." The cold climbed up Jamie's back and scattered a chill across his scalp when Ben said that. He bounced up and down on the balls of his feet and folded his arms across his chest. He looked down at Ben's left wheel and kinda studied

16

it for a second. Maybe there was a layer of thin ice beneath it. He didn't know. "Listen, can I give you a hand or somethin'?"

"A couple of legs I could walk on would be a lot better."

Jamie looked up quick.

Ben was smilin', lookin' at him, and he kinda laughed a little.

Jamie's lips formed upward, a little higher on one side than the other, and his laugh was more like some kinda not sure exhale.

Ben laughed again. "Yeah, maybe you can wheel me around front—if you don't mind. The snow's too deep for me to wheel myself."

"Sure. I can do that." Jamie moved behind Ben's chair. He gripped the two black handles that stuck out from the back of the chair about at the height of Ben's lower shoulders.

There was an embroidered patch with streaking silver letters in the left corner on the back pad that gave away the brand of the wheelchair. Jamie read it to himself: *Mercury-Mover.*

Ben's hands were back on the wheels. "Okay. Pull back a little." While Jamie did, Ben turned his right wheel towards Jamie. "One more time." Both of 'em workin' together worked, and the chair pointed towards the front of the school. "All right. Now, if yuh could just kinda push me through this—but not too hard 'cause if we hit a bump, you'll see me take a flyer."

Jamie braced his sneakers in the snow some and started to push.

Ben kept his hands on the wheels, pushin' them forward too at the right times and hesitatin' with one or the other to keep a steady course.

They were making progress.

"Aren't you in my English class?" Ben looked sideways and

up as they cornered the front of the school.

"Yeah, second period, right?" In the back with him, three rows over.

The bus had parked in front of the school, and its exhaust shot from behind it. You could smell the crappy stuff as they got closer to the line of front doors.

"Francis is a flake."

"He's all right, I guess."

"Yuh think?" Ben cleared his throat, turned his head, and hocked a luggie over the snow bank by the wooden fence that separated the walk from the front lawn of the school. "Sorry. Had to do that."

Jamie watched the snotty spit launch the good span of six or seven feet and disappear in the snow. He couldn't help the corner of his mouth from raisin' again.

Ben turned his head and looked up and behind him the best he could. He had cracked himself up a little, too.

Short laughs came from both of 'em.

"Umm. Yeah. I mean, a lotta people give him a hard time and stuff because he's kinda the new guy, but I like to write and he usually gives me pretty good grades, so I can't complain."

They had reached the doors, and Jamie moved from behind the chair and pulled one open.

"Yeah? I guess you're right, he's not really too bad of a guy." Ben sat in his chair. About two feet from the open door. He wheeled himself a little closer until the door could stay open because of how the chair was positioned. He moved his right hand from the wheel to the door. "Okay. I got this if you wanna just push me through."

Jamie left Ben with the door, and he got back behind the chair and pushed him over the door's frame.

They were inside.

The lobby's brown tiled floor clung muddied snow. Puddles of street sand and snow. The mats were still sopped from the morning's traffic. Heat blasted from a radiator and the low ceiling didn't let it go anywhere. Students were all over the place. Freshman, sophomores. Seniors, juniors. Everybody talkin' at once and some of 'em sayin' nothin' at all. Some were carryin' books and notebooks and folders at their sides and in bags, headin' for class already. Some of 'em stood in groups and talked with their hands and talked with their mouths, waitin' for the warning bell. A bunch were standin' by the trophy case. There were pictures—black and white to the most recent ones— in there, and tall trophies galore. Harrison Farlow's all-county MVP tennis trophy was even in there.

"Benny." One of the guys yelled from the group over there.

Ben was takin' off his gloves when he heard his name called. He looked up and set the pair on his lap. He brushed some of the snow off his arms.

"Oh, my God, Benjamin." Nicole Fraker had followed Ron Dychett's words across the lobby to Ben.

Jamie stuck his hands in his pockets and his right hand found the one glove still pushed down in there. The radiator was too goddamn hot in this school. He unzipped his coat a little, and took a step back from Ben's chair and started to head to his locker.

Nicole Fraker and a couple of her girlfriends and Ron Dychett began to cut through passing people.

Jamie felt a pull at his coat sleeve.

19

"Thanks."

"No problem."

"Benny, what the hell happened to you?" Ron led his posse and was talkin' to Ben before they were standing in front of him. Jamie bent. Ben's glove had slid off his lap and laid palm side up in a wet spot on the floor. "Hey, your glove."

"Holy shit, Ben. You must be freezing." Nicole's best friend Rachel Stappuck had finished a nose length in front of Ron in gettin' to Ben and was talkin' now and movin' to the opposite side of the chair that Jamie was on.

She was right in Ben's ear, with her hand on his shoulder and then her other arm stretched across the back of the wheelchair. "Where have you been, Ben? You're soaked." Rachel licked her lips after everything she said. Maybe it was her lip-gloss that made her do it, she was always puttin' that on in class. Didn't matter because her lips were always so freakin' chapped, you could tell. She wasn't a cheerleader or anything but most of her friends were, and her parents were out of town a lot.

"Not a big deal," Ben started to say. He sensed the motion on his lap as Jamie was puttin' his glove there, and he interrupted himself by turnin' towards it. He glanced up at Jamie and gave a quick nod. "Than—"

"Dude, you are so wet." Ron Dychett was beside Rachel now.

"We wondered when you weren't at lunch if the van broke down or something or it went off the road because of the storm." Rachel tucked a kinked curl behind her ear.

Jamie turned then. He didn't hear how Ben explained things. He had watched Ben's hand secure his glove on his lap and hold it near the other one. Then he turned around. He unzipped his jacket the rest of the way and headed down the hall. He passed a few more of the front doors, there were a line of 'em. A door then a long window then a door and a couple more. He looked out the windows as he passed 'em. Really he looked in the direction of outside the whole walk towards his locker, just the doors blocked his view half of the time.

He saw that another bus had pulled up behind the earlier one. They sat there with fumes pourin' out of 'em and their doors open a little. And the two drivers had gotten out of their buses and were standin' there talkin' to one another. One of 'em was a guy and he had a bushy beard. He had on rubber boots and a flannel, and was slidin' one of his palms across his other palm that was turned upwards. The other driver, a lady, was shakin' her head back and forth. She was short with a pixie haircut, and she just kept shakin' her head.

Jamie could see 'em through the snow and he looked away when he saw a third bus come up to the front speed bump.

The two drivers looked that way too.

His hair was wet, thawin' out. It was a little longer than most guys at school, not like ponytail long or anything but it fell over his ears a little. He ran his hand from the front of his forehead to the back of his head and took some of his longer strands with it. Snow-turned-water dripped down between his dark brows and shot down his kinda short nose. He felt it mix with a drip of his runny nose and he used the back of his hand to soak it off.

A fourth bus came up behind the third one makin' its way over the bump.

Jamie didn't let his inside shed across his lips.

School was gettin' out early.

Chapter Two

WHEN THE three of them had completely crossed the lawn, he stopped fidgeting with the lights. He left them alone and he climbed down the ladder. He had thrown on his pair of golashes, but he hadn't buckled them. He watched his step and his feet as he moved down each wooden rung. The snow sort of whirled down and around him and his breath rose to the sky in vapor form, passing the gray whiskers of his mustache along its way. He didn't have his bifocals on either, they were in on the desk. By the cardboard boxes where he had left them. But he made it down and he left the lights and the ladder where they were, and went into his house.

Fun. When they were kids they'd ask each other, "What one word would you use to describe your life?" He'd always say fun. He had grown up, and old, and way past old really, and he'd still say fun. He thought about that, or that thought was about him as he put boot toe to boot heel and slipped one off just on the inside of his front door. He always hated using the tip of his sock to toe off the heel of his other boot, his wet, snowy boot, because you'd always end up with a wet sock, or wet tip of a sock…but he did it anyway. His gray mustache was connected to a nicely trimmed gray beard, not annoyingly nicely trimmed, but kept well-trimmed and, the two, in cahoots or something, always seemed to make it look like his lips were just slightly turned up all the time. But maybe they were, he did still think he had it fun.

He unbuttoned his pea coat and hung it on a brass hanger. It was dim where he kept his coat and his boots, and the dimness seeped down a short hall to another door. A planked door with an arched top. He passed down the hall and passed through it.

His house was quiet. But his clock sat on a shelf just as you walked in and it greeted him with the purr of a cat. It read 5:59, and its long gold second hand pulsated on one of the small lines between VIII and IX. Didn't tick forward, didn't seem to want to. The face's numbers were in Roman numerals and wrapped in vegetable vines painted bright green. It was a harvest clock, encased in a fine wood and with a planting calendar under the timepiece and behind the glass. The way the animated moon sat half-hidden behind a mountain and a leaping cow positioned itself over it, a fair young maiden stood next to a blue and silver stream and looked towards the two. Her hands were on her hips, and she was smiling, like whoever had crafted her face had taken the time to make sure she smiled with a real confident and sincere smile, not like on some of the lawn ornaments you see around of Dutch girls being chased by little Dutch boys. And next to her mouth, a phrase would slip into an open slot. Today it was "Today is a good day to plant a seed."

He reached behind the clock and wound it and then straightened it a little on its shelf.

The room seemed to yawn, with its walls stretching and ceilings puffing out like a chest, high and rounding towards the center. Spacious, and like it was just waking up from a winter's nap. His carpet was more a garden of golden yellow grass that was close to needing a good mow. It lit up the room though, and there really didn't seem to be a need for any lamps because of the soft glow it seemed to give off. Even the warmth of the room could have had something to do with that shagged rug.

He found a seat in his favorite chair after he picked up his bifocals from the rolltop desk. He didn't want to be the kind of old man who wore those half glasses that sat at the end of his mildly long nose. He had left things sorta scattered about when he rushed off in such a hurry. One of the cardboard boxes had been stuffed and was ready to mail. Going to a woman in Northern Quebec, she had needed one and had written him.

He never sent one out unless the receiver had the right combination. He called it "the combination." Some people would never get one in their lifetime because they never found the combination. That wasn't a bad thing, it just meant that they weren't ready for it right then, that's all. (Heck, he'd even been one of those people himself.) But the woman in Northern Quebec was ready, and now she was getting one. He smiled then in his chair and picked up the one he was working on for the other box.

He looked up from time to time, never missing a stitch though, and looked into the dining room. You could see the dining room table and the painting on the dining room wall from where he sat. Sometimes, he'd look up to glance at the painting, play a sort of game with himself. Was there anything there in the oils that he'd missed? He loved looking at it, but he wanted to know its every detail, and he believed he did, but the game gave him an excuse to look, too. He just loved to see it. The flying buttresses and the bed of white, rounded clouds they reached from. The carved and curved stone that extended into air, not really going anywhere, but with a look of supporting something above it. The hundred different hues of the blue evening sky and the thousands of strands of moonlight through the arches, and ripples of the clouds. And stars that looked back at you. Every one different with bright golds and flickering borders. He knew every curve and color and star that shined in that painting.

His business was beneath it. Spread across the surface of the dining room table. The table had its two leafs in and still crowded everything. Cloth, some on rolls, stacked. All calico, green. A baby scale. Scissors. A stack of letters, not fifty or anything. But a stack of envelopes with opened seals and return addresses from all over. And glass jars. Thirty or more, some with their lids off, some closed. Old canning jars being put to good use. Filled with all sorts of things. Buttons, cloves, pine needles, dried rose petals, even hops and bear root. Pencil eraser shavings. Who knows what some of that stuff was, besides him. Some jars with hand-written labels on their clear, thick walls, some without any sticker on 'em. There was one jar that sat close to the baby scales, whatever jars sat in that vicinity were always in heavy use and this one sat empty. There were a few crumbs at the very bottom of it if you tipped it upside down or somethin', but it was empty. He knew he was out of them. There was a label on it and in black fine-tip marker he had written "MARIGOLD LEAVES."

Chapter Three

JAMIE CARRIED the 100-pound bag of oats across the cement supply room floor. It was chilly back there and he had on a flannel, and sweatshirt over that, and he had his cap on backwards. He was the only one back there. Usually was, except on delivery day. The ceilings were crazy high for tall stacks of feed and grain and stuff like that. And it smelled like bagged feed back there too. A good smell.

It was quiet, too. Just the sound of his boots—yeah, sneaks at school, boots here. He had a pair of workboots for good, yuh know how some guys wear 'em when they go places and stuff, but he didn't really wear his. They just kinda laid around on his bedroom floor, waitin' for somethin', or somethin'. Who knows. But he did wear his work pair—yuh had good stuff and yuh had work stuff in Coformon Falls—and that's all you could hear on the cement floor of the supply room when he was back there alone. Maybe some old bag had broken and some stray seed or

26

corn was there to crunch under his feet, but for the most part you could just hear his footsteps. And maybe the settling sound of a rafter echoed through once in a while too. But that was it.

It was kinda nice that way in there.

He walked through the swinging doors and offed the bag from his left shoulder and propped it onto a skid at the edge of the counter that the cash register sat on.

"Thanks, Jamie."

"He's lookin' more like James every day, Mary, with those dark brown eyes of his. Gonna be a looker. How are the girls, kid?"

"All right, I guess."

The town plow plowed their driveway and the store lot. His mom knew Barry, the county highway head crewman. They all used to run in the same circle in the day. His dad had been good friends with Barry. And now Jamie's mom traded a couple bags of grain or oats during the winter for Barry's kids' horses for the plowin' thing. That'd explain the huge plow truck that sat outside Augers' Feedstore and Pet Supplies. In case, you'd wondered whose it was.

Barry just laughed. He always had a pack of hard box Marlboros in his quilted flannel pocket, and even if they weren't there, when he laughed you'da known he smoked 'em like mad. He moved to the counter and hugged the bag and threw it on his shoulder. He looked at Jamie again and winked. "Don't forget, Jamesie, you finish high school and don't feel like helpin' your mom out here, I'll put a good word in for yuh at the Highway Department." He took his free hand and patted Jamie's shoulder.

Jamie's mom looked at Jamie, too.

"Thanks, Barry, I, I—"

Barry just laughed again. "Take care, Mary."

"We appreciate it, Barry."

"No trouble." Barry liked to plow. He liked it to storm in Coformon Falls. He got overtime when it did.

Jamie had gotten home almost the same time he would have gotten home on any regular day. The bus ride had taken just about two and a half times longer than it usually did because of the snow. And his house was just about the last on the route. He really lived in the town of Coformon Falls, not the city of.

"See yuh, Barry," Jamie said to him.

"Stay outa trouble, Jamesie," Barry said over his shoulder as he went through the door.

The strand of bells Jamie's mom had put on the door jingled, and Barry was gone with his bag of oats.

Jamie's mom—and him, you could say too—kept the feedstore goin'. She ran a pretty big petting zoo in the summer months besides. The animals didn't go away in the winter—like goats, a buncha them, some llamas, a couple of miniature ponies, some regular-sized horses, geese, chickens, pet pigs—and Jamie took care of 'em. Man, he used to be embarrassed to admit that. Every one of his teachers in elementary school and most of the kids he had went to grade school with knew he lived on a petting zoo and feedstore farm. They sold some fresh vegetables and sweet corn in the summer, too, and most everybody's parents bought from them mainly 'cause their prices were so cheap.

Jamie was halfway to the swinging doors already, and his mother had reached under the counter for the clipboard. They were like that. Picked up where they had left off, before Barry had come in.

Jamie had taken care of the animals in the back barn, made sure it was warm enough, given hay to the ones that had needed it, cleaned the horses' stalls and put some dry chaff for bedding under 'em. Stuff like that. Fed the birds and cleaned their coops. That job sucked, cleanin' those chicken coops, enough said on that though. Visual probably isn't necessary. He crossed through the snow and knew his mom wanted to get orders set—the store wouldn't be busy with it snowin' the way it was, so they could take care of gettin' orders ready for the regular customers. Mary did deliveries on Thursdays. When he came through the back door of the feedstore, he had heard Barry, said hey, and went and got the bag of oats.

All about business now. It was late afternoon. Mary probably could have turned the open sign to closed, but she didn't for some reason.

Sometimes it seemed strange to have his mom back there. He knew somebody had to be doin' this kinda stuff while he was at school, and, most likely if his cousin wasn't around and his mom was busy with somethin', she'd bring whatever customer back there to get his own stuff. But the back storeroom seemed like his turf somehow, yuh know. He knew where everything was. How high the stacks of bags should go. What rafter was weak and how much snow on the roof would crack it. He even knew where the mice holes were and what bags they tried to chew through. He knew when a rat found its way in there too, and how to get rid of him. But, whatever. It didn't mean he didn't like his mom or anyone else back there. It was just strange, that's all.

"Three bags of cottonseed."

"He feeds that stuff to his cows? Brings new meaning to

cottonmouth, I guess." He'd carry the bags to the loading dock, and his cousin, Will, would come in and help his mom load the orders on the delivery truck tomorrow. Willy did some part-time work for 'em, except in the summers when Jamie was home to do it. "Better order another five, Mom."

Mary clicked the pen's tip and wrote it down on the sheet under the one she was reading from. "How was school?" She was following Jamie.

Jamie came to the low stack of burlap bags. "Why?" He grabbed one of the bags and carried it with both of his arms in front of him. It was bulky and heavy.

"I don't know. Just thought I'd ask." Mary tucked the pen behind her ear and set the clipboard down on a stack of grain bags next to the cottonseed. She bent to grab a bag.

Jamie was hobbling along to the loading dock. He looked behind him. "Mom, I've got it."

"No, I've got it." Mary put her arms around the bag.

"Mom, I've got it. Don't lift that, go get the salt block."

"No, all I have to do is get..." Mary wedged her hands underneath the bag on both sides of it and lifted. She wedged her hands a little more and lifted again.

Jamie dropped his bag by the delivery door and headed for the second one.

His mom had gotten her hands around the bag, and had gotten it off the stack. She'd taken two steps and was squat-walking with it on her lap. She managed another step.

When Jamie saw her, he started laughing. "Mom, what are yuh doin'?" He was laughing.

Mary tried not to laugh, but she did. She lifted her foot and moved forward an inch, and dropped the bag. "That's heavy."

Jamie came closer. "What are yuh doin'?" He still had a laugh smile goin'.

"I thought I could get it." Mary and him sorta looked alike when they smiled.

He bent at his knees and lifted the bag.

"I'll get the salt block."

They headed for separate ends of the place.

"Sooooo." She yelled from over by the salt and mineral blocks.

"Yeah." Jamie answered back, over his shoulder. He plopped the second bag on the first by the loading dock.

"How was school?" She locked her hands around the medium size salt block and lifted.

"Okay. But, you never ask about school?"

They passed each other, each of 'em headin' in different directions again.

Mary had her hair in a big barrette behind her head, and a piece of her hair sorta flopped up and down with the awkward steps you make when you carry somethin' sorta heavy in front of you. "I know, but Barry mentioned gi—"

"Mom. Just. That's all right. Don't worry about it." Jamie was pickin' up the last bag of cottonseed they needed for the Everets's order. Talkin' loud enough so she could hear him. He hated it when his mother felt like she had to be his best buddy about guy things. Parents don't do that shit anyway, but his mom was ultra-conscious of it because his dad wasn't there to do it.

Mary put the salt block beside the pile of bags Jamie had started. She was heading back for her clipboard and they passed each other again. "I don't worry. I mean you never say anything about anything, school. Do you like anyone?"

She wasn't letting it go. Jamie set the third bag on the other two. "It's fine." He glanced up at the half-huge warehouse's ceiling, which was just the belly of the roof really. It had frost formin' there on the aluminum. He went back towards the center of the building.

His mom had gotten her clipboard and was waitin' for him. "What's next?"

She bobbed her head a little towards him. To get his attention. He had looked back up at the rafters.

"What's next, Mom?" He looked at her.

She looked down at the paper and pulled the pen from her ear. "Umm. One 50-pound bag of limestone." She checked it off.

Jamie started towards the end with the swinging doors.

"I just mean I don't worry. I wonder. You spend all day there and —"

"Mom, give it a rest, would yuh. Jesus." She was startin' to piss him off, not in a bad way, just the way mothers do sometimes when they won't drop somethin' because they start gettin' concerned. The limestone bags were made of two layers of heavy paper and they were always gritty when he pulled one off of the stack. Gritty, like make the tips of your teeth feel gritty, gritty. That feelin'.

"And it seems like you'd wanna say something about it. To someone. That's all I'm gonna say." She drew a little squiggle on the delivery list.

"Thanks. I don't though." He lifted the bag of limestone. It was smaller than the cottonseed bags were but heavier. Yeah, strange. Like, which weighs more, a ton of feathers or a ton of bricks sorta thing.

Jingling came from the store door.

Mary looked up.

"Who the hell'd be out in this?" Jamie settled the heavy bag in his arms and was cradling it like a concrete baby sorta, the best way to carry bags like that without throwing them on your shoulder. "Unless you're Barry." He started for the loading dock, not really expectin' an answer from his mother.

"I'll bet it's that man who wants his marigold leaves." Mary took a step to the doors. "He's called a couple times this week for 'em, and said he'd be in today."

"Sounds like a freak. Or Frank Purdue. Isn't that what he feeds his chickens?" Jamie was talkin' over his shoulder now.

"Did you put that UPS box that came this morning under the counter?"

"Yup."

The swinging doors scuffed on the concrete floor.

Louder and tryin' to beat the swish of their closing, "Leave the clipboard."

He heard the clipboard's flat back find the stack of limestone bags. And then the pen tapped down, too.

He heard his mom take on her customer service voice even before the doors swung all the way open. "Hi there. Heckofa storm out there..."

He could get the other stuff while she waited on the guy out front. He would lean the limestone against the wall by the loading area. Easy to get at it that way. He wondered what they were havin' for supper.

He was almost halfway to the landing, and the doors scraped on one another a couple times before completely closin'.

"It sure is—"

Swish.

"—thought I'd pick up—"

Swish.

They almost clicked each other shut when they stopped, but not really, not like they were locked or anything. There was always a little space they left.

He had his fingers locked around the belly of the bag while he was walkin' to the landing.

Some of the muffled conversation interrupted the sound of his boots on the concrete. He lost that damn glove today.

Chapter Four

THE NEXT day, or it mighta been a couple days later. Who knows, school does that to yuh. A lotta the days blur into one, one long day, and June finally decides to come and ten months are shot. Man, like seven hours a day, five days a week for ten months are somebody else's. And then multiply that by twelve years. That's just not right. Not even the work, but the stupid shit, like the janitor chasin' kids outa the lunchroom to wipe down the tables when lunch isn't even over. Or not bein' able to eat with your friends because you have split lunches and you're in Lunch A and they're in Lunch B. Listenin' to someone plug the Honor Society in homeroom. Three-minute bells and lav passes. Stalls in the john without any walls. Just cans. Group projects and long-term assignments. Subscriptions to *The New York Times* when some kids can't even afford toilet paper to wipe their asses. Little belts with Velcro plastic strips. Shirts and skins. Basketball tournaments in gym class. Pep rallies and assemblies honoring the football team for just missing the big one. Hour bus rides when you live ten minutes from school. Bus rides that pick up the inside-the-city kids last and drop them off first. Yuh know? It's like when they think you don't have your head screwed on straight because you're not into that crap, and you almost start to believe 'em. Maybe nobody ever stops to think, yuh know.

But anyway, it probably mighta been a few days later, when Jamie was sittin' in back of his English class. The teacher, Mr. Francis, hadn't come in yet. Because he was the newer guy on staff, that meant he didn't have his own room and had to briefcase it all over the new wing. There was like a minute and a half until the bell went off.

"So you want the 3:30 to 4." Denise Coler was in the aisle, movin' down Jamie's row.

"Yeah. Who's working with me?"

"Rachel."

"Cool."

Denise penned in Rob Hatteulle's name in the 3:30 to 4 o'clock slot on the sheet. Her pen cap was all chewed up. She was sophomore class treasurer. Into school, classes, advanced math. She belonged to a lotta clubs, too, international club—they sold egg rolls once, besides that couldn't tell yuh what went on in that club—she belonged to the chess club, science club, S.A.D.D., M.A.D.D., and Keep Your Hands Outa Your Pants Club. Who the hell knows what other clubs she belonged to. She was on the inside, hung out with the big clique. Her dad was in local politics and maybe he inspired her or somethin'. Doubt he knew she'd given head to Ron Dychett in their basement. But that even seeped down to the people on bottom, so maybe he did know. "Are you doin' it?" She was talkin' to Sandy Khatz.

"I'll do it if I can do it before those guys. Rachel and Robby'll fuck the change all up and who's ever after 'em will have to deal."

"Whatever." Rob looked up from his initials that he was bubble-lettering on his desk.

"Okay. How about 3 to 3:30. You're gonna be with Kelly Wester though."

"Who?"

"Kelly Wester. Short girl, kinda…" Denise spread her hands a little and puffed her cheeks.

"Fat. And smells like B.O. Eww. No. Why's she doin' it? She'll eat all the candy we're tryin' to sell and the class'll be poorer than we already are."

Rob looked up again, and the three of 'em laughed.

"I was in art class recruiting this morning and left the sheet on the counter while I was washing some brushes out, and when I came back she musta signed her name there."

"Yuh think?"

"I guess."

"No, somebody was probably fuckin' around. Isn't Renee in there with you, too?"

"Yeah, actually, she is. Whatta bitch." Still smilin', Denise leaned over and used Sandy's desk to write on. She scribbled out Kelly Wester and put down Sandy.

Jamie sat behind Sandy. He was bent over his open notebook and was writin' down some stuff in his journal. Free-write, don't censor yourself journal, keep the pen goin' stuff that Francis assigned once a week. Separate notebook for this stuff journal.

"You wanna work alone, Sandy?"

"Yeah. Doesn't matter. Maybe Aaron will. I'll ask him tonight."

Denise stood up. She stood a second and put her pen in her mouth, cap end first. She bit on it a couple times and then took it outa her mouth. "You wanna work the concession stand at the game next week, Jamie?"

Jamie looked up. His pen was still in his hand, his was a click Bic, black ink.

Denise's was already back in her mouth. She was standin' there with her sign-up sheet in one hand and her other hand holdin' the pen in her mouth.

"No. I gotta work."

The bell rang and Francis walked in, he always made the bell.

"Oh. Okay." She turned and left the back of the room and took her seat in the front row.

When you're in high school, nothing really happens in class during class. Unless the teacher leaves the room, then all hell might break loose. Today though, Francis didn't have to leave the room to make copies or to talk with another teacher who stuck their head in the door and said somethin' like "Sorry to interrupt. Dave, can I see you a second?" He stayed the whole 43 minutes and talked about *Of Mice and Men*. You know the story. The details about Lenny and George and the significance of Curly's glove…Francis didn't even squirm when he talked about that. He told it like it was.

Jamie tuned in, took notes. He liked to write better than read, even just notes. Black ink on a crummy white sheet of notebook paper. Not Mead, so the light blue lines were really light and the paper was a little thinner. But if yuh think about these marks all over a paper that mean somethin', or you givin' meaning to 'em, that's what sorta struck him. Even a freakin' doodle, yuh know. He had some of 'em in the margins. Lines with blotches of ink. Shapes and shaded curves. Even those meant somethin'. Somebody like a teacher or principal might think they meant that you weren't payin' attention or you were bored. Jamie kinda thought that extra lines along with some notes meant just the opposite, there was somethin' still goin' on up there that no one had gotten to yet. Uncharted territory.

Some people's notebooks hardly had any notes. That wasn't uncharted territory, that was a lobotomy case. He half-looked over Sandy's shoulder. T.L.A.'s all over the place and hearts with arrows stickin' out the sides—some with a little curve line where the arrow stuck in and came out. Clever, right. And inside 'em Sandy + Aaron. She was furiously puttin' a feathery tail on one of her arrows.

Jamie wrote down how Steinbeck was using his book as a social commentary as well. He wrote "as well" because Francis always used "as well" when he talked.

He hadn't talked to Ben since that day, the other day when he helped him in the school. Hadn't really seen him or whatever. It almost seems strange to say anything about him because that happens, see someone, talk or say somethin', and then you might not see or talk to him for the rest of high school. No kiddin'. Not that Coformon Falls had a big sophomore class or anything, because it didn't, but that's just the way it worked. You talked to who you hung out with.

39

Ben was there though, in class today, three rows over, sittin' there. His wheelchair was sorta folded up and parked in back of him by the radiator. And he was at a desk, bent over probably takin' the same goddamn note Jamie just wrote down. Jamie was sorta surveyin' notebooks on the thought he had had and Ben's was the next closest. Maybe that's why he noticed Ben today. Because the two kids were absent that sat between them.

Ben's notebook didn't have doodles. His notes were pretty neat. He used an Erasermate. Jamie looked quick to some of the scribbled out words he had on his sheet of notebook paper. He looked back to Ben and his notebook while Ben seemed to be finishin' up his sentence. Jamie could see he used the margins too. That pink line didn't even have a pen trace down it.

"Listen. I have your essays." Mr. Francis always did that. He'd lecture and then. BOOM. He'd just start with somethin' else. Today, he wanted to end class by passin' out papers. Jamie looked up front. Francis was pullin' the papers from his briefcase.

Ben dotted his sentence at the end and closed his notebook. And Jamie caught the motion with his eye and looked again towards him. The notebook cover was as clean as the day he probably bought it from Rite Aid. Yeah, it had the Mead symbol and bar code stuff, but no marks or anything. It was just a red notebook cover with the word "English" written on the top.

Ben looked up front, too, and put the cap back on his Erasermate. He musta felt Jamie lookin' because he looked to his left, at Jamie. He kinda tipped his head forward a little.

Jamie looked back down at this notebook and closed it. His cover was covered. Doodles, words, assignments, a buncha crap. Beat to hell besides.

Francis was handin' out the papers. Some kids were like "Yes!" Makin' it real obvious what they got and bein' like "Look at me." Some people were even like "Yes! C–." Rob was like that, but he put his arms in the air, too.

The assignment was on "Rip Van Winkle." Francis was big into that stuff, he did a whole couple weeks on writers from the Catskills, bein' that the town was right there in 'em. They had to take one of the scenes and expand on it. Using sensory detail, yuh know, details that awakened your reader's senses, incorporatin' some of the story's main ideas, too. Like they were watchin' a play of it. That sorta stuff.

Francis always handed papers face down to kids. The grade was usually in the top margin with a buncha comments before yuh got to it. Most of the time you could never read what he wrote anyway. He walked up and down the rows, reachin' over kids, handin' the papers back. Kids were already startin' to talk. They'd look at their papers and then stuff 'em in their folders or somethin'.

There was like a minute left of class.

"Continue with the novel. Continue with the — Listen people."

Kids were packin' their books in their bags and stuff, shufflin' in their seats, talkin' and stuff.

Francis walked back to Jamie's desk. He handed him his paper. "Nice job," he said kinda quiet. Didn't look at Jamie, already had his eyes on the kid's name on the next paper in his stack. "Read the next two chapters. Quiz tomorrow."

Everybody was listen' then. "Aww, c'mon." "Tsst." "Quiz?" Jamie turned his paper over.

Good work here. Well-written, well-organized. Nice detail.

41

Good understanding of material, as well—you seemed to like this one. A.

"*A.*" in a circle.

The bell rang.

"Remember you can revise these and turn them back in. Some of you need to improve your grade. So take advantage of this opportunity."

Everyone got up from their seats in a hurry. They really didn't care about revisions or turnin' their papers back in. They'd just given Francis his 43 minutes and the next three were theirs, at least they thought it was, startin' five seconds ago. Except for those kids who were still waitin' for their papers. They were the damned.

Jamie took his pen and stuck it in his journal notebook that he had left open on his desk underneath his notebook that was his regular notebook notebook, in case anything struck him while he was in class. He closed that notebook and then stuck his paper in the back of his regular notebook with the others that he'd gotten back since the school year started. Their edges were all ragged from hangin' out the side, and this paper would be too in about two days. He set both his notebooks on his other books and other notebooks. You couldn't stop to your locker between classes, so he had to carry all his morning classes' crap around with him.

Mr. Francis walked up the aisle three over, havin' just handed Ben his, and handed the last paper to the kid in the front seat.

"Shit."

Jamie looked over while he was gettin' up. He had his books and stuff under his arm already. He looked over at Ben.

Ben was sittin' there. He had his paper in his hand and he

was lookin' at it. "Shit." He looked over at Jamie. "I got a friggin' C-. Again."

Jamie sorta straightened his arm. *Of Mice and Men* was a smaller book and was kinda slippin' out. "Really. What'd he say?"

"Uhhhh, he said…lacks focus. I can hardly read what he has here. Need to recon…need to reconsider essence of story and setting to create your scene. Comma-splices." Ben put the paper in a manila folder he had on his desk. He kept the rest of his books in a gym bag that was on the floor. He looked back at Jamie. "How'd you do?"

"B+."

Ben took his bag from under his desk and put his folder and his *Of Mice and Men* book and notebook in it. He stuck his Erasermate behind his ear. Then he started movin' out of his seat, kinda givin' his legs a shove to move with him. He reached for his chair behind him and pushed on the seat and it unfolded to like a wheelchair again.

Jamie just kinda watched. Then, he looked at some of the people leavin' the room.

He looked at Harold Forrests and Mr. Francis. Harold Forrests was talkin' about his paper with Mr. Francis at the front desk. Harold was a premature balder that everybody called Rabbit. Don't know where the nickname came from. Maybe 'cause he had a little twitch sometimes just below his eye? Who knows. He had quite a few friends, didn't seem to hurt him in that department. Mostly jock friends who busted on him a lot, but what are yuh gonna do? Even the gym coach called him that. Rabbit. Mr. Martin was from Brooklyn and moved up here in the fifties and probably taught every sophomore's older brother and even their dad in gym. He was takin' attendance one day in gym class and he got to Forrests, and he was like "Forrests. Forrests, where is he?" Yuh know, clipboard in hand and lookin' at a bunch of guys sittin' on the gym floor. Harold had his arm raised and Mr. Martin finally saw him and said, "Jesus, Rabbit"—in his Brooklyn accent, he went—"Jesus, Rabbit, you're goin' bald." Unbelievable. The kid just sat there. Some of the guys laughed hard. And some of 'em sittin' next to or behind him rubbed his head and laughed. Man, that has to suck.

Jamie looked back towards Ben.

Ben was settin' his wheelchair sorta at an angle from the desk he sat at and he swiveled the chair's arm over. He slid quick, liftin' himself some with his arms, and clicked the wheelchair's arm back in place. It all took maybe ten seconds. Like the way we put our clothes on in the morning. "B+. That's cool. You think you could help me revise mine?"

Jamie had half thought the conversation was over. "What's that?"

Ben's bag was already on his lap and he was rollin' himself forward. He stopped to push a desk back in line that sorta blocked his way. Jamie stepped over his own desk and then the next row's desk. There was only a row between him and Ben now. Jamie pulled at the desk Ben was shovin' out of his way.

"Thanks." Ben started forward again. "I said 'Yuh think you could help me revise my paper?'" He looked towards Jamie and kept turnin' his wheels. The aisle was still a little narrow in places, and the metal on the wheels banged a dull bang against the metal of the desk legs.

"Yeah. I could help yuh if you wanted."

They were at the front of the room now. "See yuh Mr. Francis," Ben said while he and Jamie were goin' by.

Harold stopped mid-sentence. He and Mr. Francis looked up from the paper.

"See you tomorrow, guys." Mr. Francis included Jamie in his see-yuh. He was just that kinda guy, yuh know.

Some people thought he was a little weird, like Ben had said, but it was just because he got so into what he was teachin' sometimes. All excited about a book or play or somethin', or when a kid got some question right that he had asked and no one else seemed to have a clue or care or whatever. Jamie didn't see that as flaky at all, you're suppose to like your job, yuh know, and Francis did. Besides, the guy looked like he had a life besides what he did. Not like the other tenth grade English teacher they coulda been stuck with, Mrs. Optaight, who did look like she taught English, a lady who you know diagrammed sentences on Friday nights for fun. Francis was thirty-somethin', he had to be, probably listened to Springsteen too, and was still lookin' for his Jane Eyre or Mrs. Right For a Lifetime, you could just tell. Jamie hadn't really ever had a teacher that was a person and a teacher, yuh know. And like right now, Harold was drivin' him crazy— even though you couldn't tell at all by lookin' at Francis—and Francis was tryin' to be all patient with him and stuff. The guy deserved a medal.

But anyway, Harold Forrests just stood there—when Jamie and Ben went by—he had his mouth a little open, and he was gapin' at Ben. Some people are really stupid like that, and Harold was one of 'em.

"See yuh," Jamie said to Mr. Francis. Like Mr. Francis sorta knew him through his papers and it was kinda strange for Jamie.

Mr. Francis nodded and smiled, and Harold took that as a signal and started talkin' again and pointin' to a sentence on his paper. "I'm not sure what you mean I need to use a colon here. Is that the thing with the two dots? Errr...?"

The room had an empty room feelin' to it now, like everybody had left it when just thirty seconds ago it was filled with a buncha voices talkin' at once, but the hall was cram-packed. Kids goin', no lanes or anything, all of 'em weavin' in and out of each other. Some had already parked their books in their next class and were standin' outside the classroom door. That was cool if you did that. You'd put your hands behind your back and bend your leg and prop the bottom of your Nike against the wall and watch other kids go by. Say hey to your friends. Maybe stand next to another friend that was doin' the same thing the same way. That was the cool thing to do.

"Whatta yuh have this period?"

Jamie and Ben were goin' down the hall.

"I got a study hall."

They went around a corner and Mark Terrence was flyin' around it and nearly went into Ben's lap. "Sorry, Ben." He sorta patted Ben's shoulder and took off again. The kid had legs like an ostrich. Big, tall kid. A junior.

"So do I. You got work, orrr..." Ben looked up at Jamie. Sorta like when somebody is drivin' and talkin' to somebody beside 'em at the same time.

"Umm." Jamie thought about the biology assignment he'd gotten first period. The store woulda got a shipment of grain bags today, too, to take care of tonight. "No. You wanna work on it?"

Ben stopped short at Room 12. It was the room his study hall was in. "Yeah, if you can. I'd really appreciate it." He lifted his arm to give a slap me five sorta handshake.

Jamie gave him one back.

"Okay, so we can get library passes and meet there?"

"Sounds good." Jamie never really did that. He mostly stayed in his study hall room and did work. Some of the clowns always had a library pass. Yuh got one if one of your buddies had a study hall same period, different room, and you wanted to go to the library and shoot the shit. Find a corner and talk pretty quiet all period. Some of 'em would get sent back by the librarian, Mrs. Carson, because they were outa control or somethin'. Banned from the place.

Ben wheeled a little forward. "Hey. Thanks a lot."

"Sure." Jamie tucked his books under his arm better, gettin' ready to go. "See yuh in a few minutes." His study hall was on the other side of the school.

The hall was filterin' out. It was startin' to give off that same feeling that the English classroom had given off when they left.

"Okay. See yuh." Ben rolled more towards the door and then he re-turned his wheelchair some to the way Jamie had started to walk. "Hey. Jamie."

Jamie turned. He started to take short steps backwards.

Ben was sittin' in the doorway. "If you get there before I do, try and get the table in the map room. Mrs. Carson never goes in there."

"All right." Jamie nodded and gave a smile back at Ben.

A completely involuntary smile.

When he turned around, he really was about the only one left in the hall. There weren't really any classrooms in this hall except for the one at the end that Ben was going into. The water fountain hummed, and the gray-green lockers that lined both walls breathed through the three slits at the top of them. They breathed high school. The round combination locks that closed 'em, and what was inside 'em, and their little beat-to-hell silver plates with numbers on them. High school.

Jamie walked down the hall. He looked down. His Levi's were gettin' pretty faded at the knees. Almost ready to rip really. He looked back up then and passed the cement wall that broke the lockers into two sections on the left side of him. It was like a billboard. Strictly for promo. This week it advertised class rings. There was a poster that was taped in the four corners with masking tape, and someone had hung it crooked-like on purpose. It was pretty big. Jamie sorta looked at it as he went by. Couldn't help it, you know how your eyes do that sometimes, just look at whatever's there. There were five huge rings stacked around one another or like someone had tossed them onto this shiny wooden table surface, and gotten real close to 'em and snapped a picture. They all had these huge stones in 'em and they all were thick banded like class rings usually are. The year was there an' all, but the company who made the rings wanted you to see the fine craftsmanship that went into the image they etched into the sides of the bands. One had those happy and sad mask things, one had two baseball bats crisscrossed with the ball in the middle, one had this paintbrush with a swirl of paint comin' from its tip, one had a bugle or whatever instrument that is, and the one sorta on top had a buncha books with a rolled-up diploma beside 'em. Under them in big letters it went—*Something for everyone!* And under that in the white part that they leave for schools to write in whatever they want to write, someone had used a thick black marker and wrote in all caps—*DON'T FORGET TO ORDER EARLY.* Only they used two exclamation points after *EARLY. DON'T FORGET TO ORDER EARLY!!*

Jamie walked down the hall and turned down the main one.

The hall behind him was empty. The water fountain clunked off, and the thick-glassed lights in the white Spackle-paneled ceiling gave a fake feel to the green-gray lockers and the thin carpet in the new wing. It was quiet. Quiet and empty. Seemed kinda stupid then, after you were gone. Somethin' for everyone and the black marker block letters and two exclamation points— DON'T FORGET TO ORDER EARLY!!

Chapter Five

IF THIS was a movie or somethin', the camera woulda panned on that whole hallway when he left it. Then it woulda moved slowly towards that goddamn poster and got real close to those big black letters and their message and it woulda blurred them, and when it refocused it'd be on the same message "Don't forget to order early." But instead of marker block letters, they'd be cursive and the two corny exclamation points would be replaced by ellipses or dot dot dot in case you aren't sure what ellipses is, or are. And the *"Don't forget to order early..."* would be at the top of a different poster.

You gotta realize that things are all connected like that sorta. 'Course, Jamie didn't know it at the time either, so why should you.

Anyway, this poster'd be above one of the windows at the Coformon Falls Post Office. It'd have a really majestic angel on it all decked out in a long white gown and lookin' like she was straight from Bethlehem. And she'd be on a stamp, and someone somewhere woulda wanted you to order her early. She must notta been a big seller, though, if they left the poster up, because the post office usually isn't like that. Leavin' posters up for stamps they don't have in stock after the holiday—they musta had a few left over. Quite a few.

"Good morning, Angelo." She looked at her watch and then up again. "Or would you say it's afternoon?" She made herself laugh. Not a crack yourself up laugh, but a person behind the counter who laughs at small talk laugh. "I never know what to call this time of day. Good late morning to you, I guess." She smacked her hands down on the counter and laughed again. She was that kinda lady. She was old. Well, not old, but an older lady with big glasses that had the chain that draped from the bows and rested on her shoulder and disappeared behind her head and set hair. She dyed her hair auburn and wore her postal pastel blue with dignity. That navy sweater too. Took her job with serious pleasure or with a pleasured seriousness. She looked like she'd come with the place.

Coformon Falls's post office was pretty old. It was small and there were only two windows. They looked like the old varnished windows you'd see in an old bank in a Western movie. Minus the bars, and the guy with the mustache and visor and little thing on his head he'd use to look at the nuggets of gold that people would bring in.

Lilly knew everyone who came in a lot. She knew Angelo.

"Good morning, Lilly." Angelo smiled back. "How are you this late morning?" He was like that, always knew exactly what to say.

Lilly smiled. She liked Angelo. She liked his beard and his pea coat. He reminded her of an exotic sea captain or somethin'. A world traveler from another time and place. Or the guy in Mrs. Paul's commercials. Or both. Who knows what made a lady like Lilly tick. She just liked him.

He set a few medium or smaller sized boxes on the counter, and unbuttoned his top coat button.

Lilly was all business then, pulling them closer to her.

She took the box on top and set it on the scale and began to punch the zip code into the computer. "Mailing some more dreams today, Angelo?" She kept her head down, facin' the keyboard, but you could tell that she was sorta lookin' out of the corner of her eye at Joan, the lady workin' the counter beside her. Joan was sittin' there on a stool and waitin' for her next customer.

It wasn't like Lilly was makin' fun of Angelo or sharin' some inside joke with Joan about him or anything, and Angelo wouldn't have cared, anyway. He woulda and did tell anybody that mighta asked what was in those boxes. And she'd asked once before what he was always mailin', so he'd told her.

"Lilly. I've told you that I don't make the dream, I really just open the door for it." Angelo tapped one of the boxes in the stack of four or five. "With these." He smiled again.

Joan came around the counter that jutted out and divided her space from Lilly's. Almost caught her thigh on it. She had a black and blue or two from flyin' around it when she was in a hurry. Joan couldn't stand bein' left out on one of Angelo's mailings.

"Hello, Angelo." Joan was cut from the same mold as Lilly was. Only she wore a turtleneck under her post office shirt. Bad circulation.

"Hello, Joan. How are you today?" Angelo smiled and a buncha skinny lines fanned from the corners of his eyes and dipped around his cheeks.

"Just fine, Angelo." Joan was pulling the meter sticker from the machine. Helpin' Lilly out a little. She took the box off the scales and read the zip.

Just so yuh know, post office workers always read where you're sendin' whatever you're sendin'. They're curious. They almost *need* to know.

"For heaven's sake. Quebec." She looked at Lilly who was already putting the next box on the scale.

"That's nothin' Joannie, this one's goin' to South Africa." She started to punch in the zip code.

They weren't flirtin' with him or anything. Angelo and his boxes just gave them a charge.

"Angelo, you really should get a mail meter and you could postage these yourself." Lilly was always tryin' to sell Angelo on a postal meter machine, like for people who own their own business.

The machine spit out another sticker and Joan took care of it and stuck it on the top of the box in the corner. "Then you wouldn't have to put up with us." She gave her best post office laugh. Gave Lilly a good run for her money too.

"Where would the fun be then, Joan." Angelo took the next box and handed it to Lilly.

That made both of 'em laugh.

Maybe there was a little flirtin' goin' on. Not heavy-duty though.

When the last box got postage, Joan took the stack and went

to put 'em in a U.S. mail crate. They look like a laundry basket with the words "U.S. MAIL" on the sides of 'em.

"How do you know they come true, Angelo? The dreams you open doorways for." Lilly punched in a couple of more numbers and was about to run a receipt. Although Angelo really didn't need one, it wasn't like he paid taxes or anything.

Angelo thumbed past one more of the bills in his open wallet that he was holding. He looked up while he pulled out a twenty.

Joan was on her mission, but her head spun quick when she heard Lilly's question. She wore those shoes that tied on the side of them and they squeaked when she stopped short at the laundry basket and dumped the boxes in. She came back to the counter, and rested her elbows on the divider and then her head on her hands. The glasses she wore sorta magnified her eyes a little because they were kinda thick, and she looked at Angelo with these big blue eyes.

Angelo handed the twenty to Lilly. Even though Lilly had asked the question, it was really Joan's reaction that got to her. After she turned around and saw Joan bent like that at the divider counter, she got sorta interested in what Angelo was gonna say, too. She took the twenty from Angelo pretty slow and looked at him for an answer. She'd almost forgotten what she'd asked him to begin with. Her interest had sorta disguised itself behind kidding and postal politeness, and she didn't even know it.

There was a transistor radio in the back of the post office that was always on when you went in. AM-station turned on real low. Like everything stopped a second and all you could hear was the announcer givin' the station's number so listeners could call in and play some trivia.

Angelo smiled and reached in his pants pocket. "Twenty sixty-seven today, Lilly?"

The announcer was talkin' about the gift certificate he'd give to the fifth caller with the right answer.

Lilly looked down to the screen facing her. "Twenty sixty-seven." She still had the twenty in her hand and looked back to Angelo.

Angelo brought his hand out of his pocket. He held some coins out to Lilly, and sorta nodded his head a little, still smiling.

Lilly held the twenty in one hand and cupped her other out. With the look of a kid watchin' the flyin' trapeze or somethin'.

"Have a good day, ladies," Angelo said and dropped the coins in Lilly's hand. He turned around and walked out the door.

Joan didn't wait until the door closed behind him. She came up behind Lilly and looked over her shoulder.

The Supremes or somebody came over the radio.

Joan and Lilly both looked down. Into the palm of Lilly's hand.

Two quarters, a dime, and a nickel. And two pennies.

Chapter Six

"NICE. VERY nice."

Jamie was sittin' at the only table in the room. He looked up from his journal notebook when he heard Ben. He laid his pen in it and closed it and set it on his stack of books. Ben had been right about the map room. It was towards the back of the library and was glass encased like a fish tank. Except for the back wall that was shelf upon shelf of maps. Carson could see into the room from the front desk, like she was the big fish. She could look straight through the stacks, down the distance to the room if she wanted. But it was kinda like your own study room and it basically belonged to whoever was usin' it because, even though she was always at the front desk, she was stampin' books or doin' somethin'. "Yeah. I had to ask Mrs. Carson to unlock it though."

"Sorry. I thought you knew that." Ben wheeled himself in the room and got past the door and then swung it shut. It was one of those big heavy doors that didn't need a stop but could stay open by itself and swing shut by itself if you gave it a push. Ben did. He pulled up to the table and put his bag on it. "Yeah, she usually gives people a hard time about anything. She give yuh a hassle?" He unzipped his bag.

"Naw, it was no big deal."

Ben took out his manila folder. "Man, thanks again. I've got nothing but C's and D's since I started this class and my folks are startin' in on me. He pushed his bag to the further side of the table and opened the folder. His "Rip Van Winkle" paper was there on top. He handed it to Jamie.

Jamie looked at it. "What scene did you pick?" He felt kinda strange at first because he knew his own papers. He knew that readin' an English paper was sorta like reading somebody's diary. Doesn't matter what the subject, Rip Van Winkle or Curly's glove or the three witches in *MacBeth*, you somehow say somethin' about yourself in there, too. Whether you like it or not. Ben's paper was in his hands, though, and if you've ever had someone hand you their diary, no matter how well or not well you know them, you start readin'. Human nature.

"I picked the scene when Rip Van Winkle woke up and he went back to the amphitheater thingy in the mountains and it had turned into that huge waterfall."

Jamie read the first few lines while Ben was talking.

Washington Irving is one of America's great writers, he wrote "Rip Van Winkle" and "The Legend of Sleepy Hallow", as well. One scene from "Rip Van Winkle" was of particular interest to me.

Ben's penmanship was perfect. Blue pen, distinct letters. Print, not cursive. Even the small a's had that little cap on top. He used *as well* too, that killed Jamie. Christ, Francis had started a trend with that. His little pencil marks were all over Ben's introduction though. Francis was like that, he didn't mess around. *Comma inside quotes. Don't divide two independent clauses with a comma. Could you lead more directly into the body of your paper?* A buncha stuff like that. He'd write yuh somethin' and distinctly spell out the first couple letters and squiggle the rest of the word, like he was signin' an autograph or somethin'.

Jamie read through the rest of the paper and Ben had wheeled away from the table. He went over to the map wall and looked up it. He pulled out a pretty big atlas and flipped through it and looked to see if Jamie had finished yet.

Jamie had flipped the paper and was reading the back. His lips moved a little when he read. He'd done that since he was a kid, didn't know why.

Ben put the book back on the shelf and ran his finger over the thick binding of another one, *A Global History* or somethin' it was called. His finger left a streak in the dust that had settled on it, and the tip of his finger was sooted. Well, not sooted, but it had some dust on it. Ben blew on it. Some of it flew off, and the rest he wiped on his pant leg. "You listen to Dylan?"

"Huh?" Jamie was readin' the last line of Ben's essay.

"Bob Dylan?"

"Not really." This kid was like a kaleidoscope. Jamie could tell already. In Technicolor, but man, his essay, it was like, sorta, like Francis woulda called it, vague, nothin' solid to it.

"C'mon, really? Evvverybody mus' get stoned." Ben sang and bobbed his head a little like he was Dylan doin' it and then he wheeled back over next to Jamie. "What'd yuh think?"

58

Shit. "I think yuh got some good ideas. You just need to…" Jamie opened his notebook and took his pen out and ripped a sheet of paper out.

"Okay. Grammar stuff aside. First, describe it to me." Jamie took his Bic black fine point, clicked it, and put its point to the page.

He waited.

"I dunno. What'd I put?" Ben reached for his essay that Jamie had set down.

"Naw. Describe it again." Jamie kept his pen to the paper, like he was all ready to write. All poised-like, sorta into it, like a runner at the starting line, most people'd say. He thought that was a pretty clichéd sorta comparison though, so he refigured himself to be all poised-like, sorta into it, like one of those writers with the big quill for a pen and crazy-ass goatee and floppy white shirt, one about to embark on a work that would change the world. He probably came off as sort of a geeker though more than anything, but right about then, he seemed to be the only one noticin' if he was.

Ben sorta changed his reach and took his pen from behind his ear. His Erasermate. He kinda started to tap it on the edge of the table. "Umm…there's water."

Jamie began to write. "Okay, keep goin'."

"There's water annnnd it's running." Ben sorta laughed and tapped his Erasermate a little faster on the table. "I dunno." He shrugged his shoulders.

Jamie was still writing *it's running*. He finished and kept his pen on the paper still. "Describe it like you were Dylan."

Ben really laughed then. Out loud.

Jamie's ears got a little red, visibly red. And his shoulders that were all arched over the paper slumped a little.

It's not a big deal, but it kinda sucks when you're just bein' yourself and somebody does that. That's how he felt. No big deal though, he hardly knew the kid.

But Ben noticed. Like immediately. "No. Jamie." He took the cap off his Erasermate and stuck it on the other end of it. "I'm not laughin' like thaaat. It's like—that's good. Like Dylan, I mean." Ben sorta straightened himself in his chair and sat up some. "Okay. It's runnin' and the waterfall is huge."

Jamie began to write.

"It's crazy huge, gushing clear mountain water. You can hear it."

"How can you hear it?" Jamie didn't look up when he asked. He kept on writing.

"How?" Ben's eyebrows asked the question too. "It's like this rumble of water. I can't describe it."

"Try."

"Um. It's like pa-chuuuuu." Ben let the sound creep out of his vibratin' lips. "Chuuuuuuu." He got a little louder. "Yuh writin' that?" He leaned a little to Jamie's paper.

"Yeah, keep goin'. What else?" Jamie had a couple lines of the paper filled already.

"It's clear like you wouldn't believe when it goes over and at the bottom there's whirls and whirls of white water. Probably fish in there. They like that kinda water. And the pool it turns into is big, big enough so that it gets real calm by the time you're a little ways from the falls. And it's cold water, shrink your scroat up cold, this bring you back to life cold. It's deep too. You can jump from the falls and have plenty of water to jump into."

Jamie was tryin' to keep up. *...bring you back...*

Ben was sorta usin' his Erasermate as a pointer. "Irving said there's a dark shadow. And there is. Around it. The trees shadow across some of the water, but for shadow there's gotta be sun. Right?"

Jamie looked up a second. "Yeah."

"Yeah, that's what I figured, but Irving doesn't mention that. Sun's pouring down, too. Bright, like it's noon in July or somethin'. Man, you can feel its rays if you're swimmin' in the water and come up for air or somethin'." Ben stopped.

Jamie wrote a few more seconds, gettin' it all. His hand slowed down a little when he got towards the end of what Ben had said. Maybe because Ben had stopped. Maybe not though. *...in the water...* He finished and looked up.

Ben pulled his pen cap off and stuck it back on the tip end. "What kind of a name is Rip anyway, really?"

"I dunno. Norwegian?"

"Norwegian." Ben stuck his pen behind his ear.

They started laughin'. Jamie was holdin' his pen in his hand and he sat back in his chair. Just laughin'. And Ben was there in his wheelchair, his shoulders bobbin' up and down.

Tap tap tap tap tap tap. Rapid fire of a finger on the glass wall made 'em turn their heads.

Mrs. Carson was standin' there in her navy pantsuit and waggin' her finger. She had an armload of books in one arm and used her free hand to shake at Ben and Jamie. She mouthed to them, "If you can't behave, you can leave."

Jamie and Ben nodded their heads.

She turned around and walked two aisles down to shelf some books about Communism or somethin' like that that someone had checked out for a paper and returned that mornin'.

Jamie and Ben looked at each other and cracked up again.

"Man, that's funny." Ben was still laughin' a little when he talked. He looked at his watch, not like he was lookin' for the time, but more like a habit thing. But the digits did sorta bring him back. "Shit, what time's this period end?"

"Five after. What time is it?" Jamie sat back up, he was still laughin' a little too. "Norwegian."

Ben started crackin' up again. "Quarter of."

"Oh shit, all right." Jamie got ready to write again. "All right, umm, all we really have to do is get somethin' down about the story itself, kinda mix it in with our scene."

"Okay." Ben left his pen behind his ear and he was lookin' at Jamie.

"Sooo…"

Ben lifted his blond eyebrows.

"What'd yuh think of the story?"

"Oh." Ben took his Erasermate from behind his ear and held it. "It was all right. He was dreamin', right? I kept expectin' him to wake up and be back on the mountain and learn some lesson or somethin'. So I guess I don't really know."

"Well, he fell asleep, but I don't think it was a dream, he woke up and it was like fifty years or whenever later, and that was it, yuh know."

"That's just crazy. That's what I think. Imagine fallin' asleep and then—" Ben fisted his pen in his hand and then popped his fist into his other open palm, "shit, your life is totally different.

Totally."

"Yeah, I know." Jamie wrote Ben's idea down for him. He handed the sheet of paper to Ben. "All you really have to do is tie what you just said to me into that scene you described, and you have your paper."

"Yuh think?" Ben took the paper and looked at it and then back at Jamie.

"Yeah." He ripped out another sheet from his open notebook and set the blank paper in front of Ben. "Mess around with it, and then I'll help yuh with some grammar, if yuh want."

"Yeah, thanks. I don't know what a comma-splice is." Ben took the sheet Jamie had been writin' on and put it beside the blank sheet. He uncapped his Erasermate and started to write somethin'.

Jamie really didn't see what. He flipped back to the last line in his journal notebook and jotted down somethin' of his own that he'd just thought of. He did it quick and then closed the notebook. He looked over at Ben.

Ben was pulled close up to the table and was bent over writin'.

Jamie pulled his biology book from the bottom of his pile and started his assignment.

The ameba is a living-breathing creature, just like you and me...

Chapter Seven

IT HADN'T really been too bad of a day so far. Jamie rarely let himself think that, though, because the second yuh did, something really shitty would happen and blow it all to hell. It was actually kinda warm out first of all. As warm as it can get in January. The midst of a January thaw.

In case you don't live around Coformon Falls or in Upstate New York, January thaw is like a couple days in January when the weather breaks. The cold, the wind, the freakin' snow give up for a couple days and the sun comes out, and you can actually feel it. Forty-five degrees feels like 80. It's like a dick tease—sorry, but it is—that lets you know spring is still a season. It's sorta false hope. Because you live it up for the four days that everything thaws and then it's back to sub-zero and burn your lungs cold.

Jamie was walkin' down Rea. Lunch. Headin' for Ray's Cornerstore. When you're in school, it's like that. One minute you're doin' somethin' and blink twice and there you are again doin' the same goddamn thing. Today though, the sun was out and the snow that had been dumped in the last storm was all packy and sloshy and wet. Some kid had tried making a snowman on the front lawn of one of the houses on the street, and the thing was all sorta slanted and kinda had some dead leaves and grass and some dirt in it.

The road had little streams of water runnin' all over it. All of it headin' for some plugged street drain. You really couldn't help but catch spring fever. It was sloppy walkin' on the road, but Jamie didn't care. He unzipped his jacket and looked up at the sun. He squinted, but he felt it on his face. Shit. It was like he was happy for a second. You can smell sunlight, maybe he had that disease where you go crazy if you don't get sunlight. That lack of Vitamin D disease. He thought about summer and workin' outdoors and havin' no school and stuff like that.

The street was so wet it was like his sneakers coulda hydroplaned. Not really hydroplaned, but there was that thick layer of moving water all over it. That's how warm it had gotten.

He was about halfway up Rea Street. Walkin'. Thinkin' stupid stuff that you think about when you're by yourself. Ben was a pretty cool kid. Number 10 and his merry men weren't around today. He'd finish that biology after he unloaded the grain bags and ate supper. Barry, remember the guy who snowplowed, he had to be pretty disappointed the snow was fadin'. Barry was a good guy. If you had a county job like Barry, you were doin' pretty well for yourself in Coformon Falls. Eight to four, benefits, weekends off. He was just lookin' out for Jamie, sayin' what he said the other day, Barry had been a good friend of his dad, that's why he said stuff like that.

Jamie heard a couple of birds goin' nuts in a bare tree on somebody's lawn that he walked by. He looked and he saw this jet red cardinal bein' chased around by this blue jay. Blue jays are like that. He watched 'em a second, while he kept walkin'. Their colors were almost like fake they were so bright. The cardinal took off and the blue jay just hung out there. Somebody musta had a feeder somewhere. That was kinda funny because chances were pretty good the feed came from the store, Jamie's store.

The store and the animals weren't bad. He liked it and them. Really. He could see himself doin' that, yuh know, keepin' it goin'. That's what you did in Coformon Falls, you did what your parents did or you got a county job.

He was just about to the corner and ready to cross the street and then cut the lawn to get onto Main—or square the corner actually, he had been since that guy told the three stooges to the other day.

The sun was really warm. Nice on your face.

He heard music. Loud, rock and roll where you really can't understand what the singer is sayin'. Somebody had their window down. Comin' from school. Jamie didn't look behind him, he kept walkin' and would cross after they passed.

Who knows when stuff like that happens, he didn't look behind him, he just kept walkin'. Whatever. Some kid had a new stereo and a dose of spring fever like him, yuh know. Jamie moved a little more to the side of the road, but he kept walkin'. The car or the music came up behind him quick. They were goin' pretty fast. Somebody whaled on the horn. Like a few long honks. You could hear 'em over the music. That's when he looked behind him, instinct, yuh know.

This blue car was flyin' down the street. Water and shitty street sand flyin' underneath its tires. That really wasn't Jamie's thought though. Or what he was worried about. He had about two seconds to get off the road.

He turned back around and stepped for the melted dirty snow bank.

One and a half seconds.

The music and the spray and the car flyin' by. A longneck bottle of Bud, too. Nearly caught him in the head. One last good blow of the horn, too. Jamie's chest caught that sound and tucked it inside of him and then let it explode. That freakin' horn. He didn't dive, it was more like he fell sideways. Over halfa snow bank onto somebody's lawn in the wet snow.

That was it. Over like that.

He heard the music as it got further down Rea Street and the car stopped for the stop sign. And then the song faded up the street.

Jamie had went sideways but landed front first. His hands out, like he was gonna do some pushups or somethin'. The snow was like crystaly, like it gets when its wet and it turns sorta icy. Yeah, like the consistency of a Slush Puppie. His palms dug into it and they instantly stung when it ground into 'em. He tried to keep his face clear of the snow, but it was like somebody had shoved him hard and all he could do was turn his head. So one side of his face smashed into the snow, too. Some got in his mouth. And he just let it melt on his lips, he didn't try to spit it out at first.

The little grinds of snow were gonna leave indents on the

side of his face. And he pictured himself as if he was somebody else watchin' and he thought about what he looked like when he flew flat on his face.

It wasn't like he laid there a second.

"Are you all right?"

Jamie pushed himself up on his knees when he heard the voice behind him. He looked down at himself. Snow was on his button-down shirt and had went down the front of his collar because his jacket was open. He brushed off his shirt and shook it. Some snow fell out. He looked at the palms of his hands. Blotchy red, and he had to rub 'em together to get the rest of the snow off 'em that had sorta grooved into 'em. Damn, that hurts when yuh do that.

"Can I give you a hand?"

Standin' on his knees on somebody's lawn. He ran the tip of his fingers down the side of his face that he'd just buried in the snow. He thought he'd scraped it.

He heard snow crunchin' behind him, and that's when he turned.

"Are you okay?"

"Yeah." Jamie stood up then.

The guy moved a little to him—to like help him up—puttin' his hand sorta out for him, but Jamie kinda leaned a little away and stood up.

"Where the—where'd you come from?" Jamie looked straight at the guy then.

"My name is Angelo. I live across the street. I was on my way back from town."

"Oh." Jamie looked across the street to the house. It was that crazy bastard who was takin' down the Christmas lights in the snowstorm. He squinted. Strands of tiny different colored bulbs still hung around the eaves and window frames. "Nice to meet you." His head hurt like when you jar your teeth hard.

"I got the license plate on that car." Angelo looked toward Main Street if you were headin' for town. The direction the car had went.

Oh, man. "Really, that's all right." Jamie started to walk away. He took a step. His left ankle was throbbin' so bad he felt it in his throat, under the friggin' Adam's Apple he woke up with one day last year. He stopped to zip up his jacket. When he got it to his chin, he looked back at the guy. Angelo. The guy was lookin' at him like he was lookin' at a guinea pig in an aquarium or somethin'. Jamie put his hands in his pockets. "They were my friends."

"Oh." This guy Angelo had some pretty big gray eyebrows goin' and he kinda raised 'em a second when Jamie said that.

"I mean, I'm sure I know them." Jamie put his hands in his pockets.

"Yes. I'm sure you do." Angelo sorta looked around him a couple times and patted his hands on his coat pockets, like somebody would if they were lookin' for their keys or somethin'. "All right, then. As long as you're all right."

"Yeah, I am. Thanks." Jamie took a step. He didn't limp, not in front of this guy. It didn't really hurt that bad to limp anyway.

Angelo nodded his head. "Take care."

Jamie smiled like you do to your dental hygienist when she says see yuh in six months. "Yeah, you too."

They both started over the snow bank. Both of 'em were

lookin' down, watchin' their steps. Jamie had his hands in his pockets, but Angelo was sorta keepin' his footing with his arms spread out a little. There was nobody around and the blue jay had takin' off too and had stopped screechin', so it was pretty quiet. Just Jamie and Angelo steppin' outa the snow was all you could hear. When they got on the road, they both stomped hard a couple times and shook the snow off their shoes. Well, sneaks and...Jamie looked over to Angelo's. He had golashes on. The ones with the funny buckles. Like rubber golashes old guys wear.

Angelo had stomped a couple times and the snow from his boots plopped to the wet of the road and melted into it. He looked to cross the street, towards the school. Jamie was on that side of him. He smiled. Didn't really avoid Jamie's face or anything when he did. "Enjoy the day."

"Yeah. You too." Jamie noticed Angelo's pea coat was unbuttoned and open when he said that.

Angelo looked the other way and then crossed the street to his house. He looked like an older guy with those golashes and pea coat and gray whiskers and hair and stuff, but the way he walked, it was like he was one of those guys you couldn't quite guess his age, like somewhere between forty and seventy. And he kept his face into the sun, too. Like he knew about January thaw maybe. Or not though.

Jamie just stood there a second. His hands in his pockets when it wasn't even cold. His sneakers surrounded by movin' wet snow over asphalt that Barry Buchanan probably paved last summer. He took one of his hands out of his pocket and touched his face to see again if there were any marks, and then he looked at his hand when he took it away to see if there was any blood on it. Nothin'. He was all right. No big deal at all.

He started to walk again, towards Ray's store. Favorin' his left ankle a little. He musta looked like an idiot when he flew over that bank. A complete idiot...

Chapter Eight

"JAMIE."

He had heard the quiet knock and the squeak of his door bein' opened a crack. He was a light sleeper like that. But he was asleep. Had just fallen asleep really.

"Jamie." His mom whispered again.

He rolled onto his other side. His sheet had come off the corner of his bed by his pillow when he did, and he could feel the scratchy material of his mattress against his arm. He didn't care. He was asleep.

"Jamie." The door opened a little further and his mom's voice got a little louder. Still in whisper mode though. "Jamie."

"What." Jamie opened his eyes and looked into the dark and into the wall that his bed was by.

"I'm sorry, Jamie," his mom was almost talking in her everyday voice now. She turned the light on that hung by his door. "I wouldn't get you up if I could help it. Titania's having

72

her baby and I don't know what's wrong, I can't do it by myself. Can you please come out?"

Titania was one of their horses. She was a young mare, maybe about three-years-old. His mom's favorite. Dark brown with a black mane, lifted her front hoof when you told her to shake, rode yuh all over in the fields behind the barn. His mom knew her animals — Tite, that's what Jamie called her — was an awesome horse. She was havin' her first foal.

"Get out so I can get dressed."

"I'll be in the barn."

He heard his mom goin' down the stairs.

He turned back over on his other side and laid there just a second with a layer of warm blankets up to his neck, and his eyes open. His room had clothes coverin' the floor, and most of his walls were covered with posters. Rock groups, movies, and some nature stuff too like mountain scenes or a buncha horses. He had left his biology book open on his desk, too.

He pulled the blankets off. The house was always cold at night. They ran the furnace on low and had a wood stove goin' downstairs, but even with both of 'em, it was still January cold.

All he had on was a pair of long underwear, and his bare skin was like a cold air magnet. He put his bare feet on his rug and he sorta folded his arms across his chest. His ankle felt a little better, but he'd knocked his shoulder pretty hard on the door of the shipping rig when he was unloadin' an oat bag that afternoon. He let one of his hands move up his other arm to it and rub it a little. A little stiff, that was all. He yawned and he opened his eyes some more and looked at his alarm clock on his night stand.

Bright red digits. 12:47. He knew what the scenario had

73

been. His mom had probably finished watchin' *Letterman* or had woken up from fallin' asleep in front of *Letterman*, and had went out to check the barn. Yuh do that when you have animals. Go out, walk through, make sure everything is okay before yuh go to bed for the night.

He heard the front door open and close.

He was awake. He reached down on the floor for a sweatshirt, got one, and pulled it over his head.

* ✦ *

Their barn wasn't bad. Some barns outside Coformon Falls were pretty shot. Like with saggin' roofs from the snowstorms, and zero paint job left from the coat they got in the fifties. Their barn wasn't that bad off, but it was no Saratoga stable with little silver nameplates by the horses' stalls either. It was old, and there were some drafts, but it kept the animals pretty warm in the winter and it was a barn. Barns just have that feel no matter if they're beat to hell or owned by people who wear derby hats and goofy boots that they tuck their pants in when they ride their horses. Barns are long and there are big wooden sliding doors in front usually that roll on a track. And when you go inside, there's the line of windows on both sides and some bales of hay stacked on some of the walls. And you smell it, the dry, cut grass, and you smell the animals and, of course, their crap, but that's a barn for yuh. It's what a barn is suppose to smell like.

If yuh haven't been in one a lot, yuh probably wouldn't get it. But when Jamie slid the big door shut and walked into the front part of the barn and then through another couple of doors into the actual stable part, it was kinda warm in there and his mom hadn't turned all the lights on, so it was sorta dim and the animals were lyin' in their pens or their stalls. Sleepin' or nosin' at and chewin' on their leftover hay from feedin' time earlier. It was quiet and warm and just sorta left the January night out where it belonged.

He used to check the barn at night with his dad when he was little and didn't have school the next day. They had a buncha cows and stuff back then. He stopped and bent down and lifted one of his pant legs. He had slipped into his boots and hadn't tied them when he was in the house. He tied one up and then the other. And then he walked down to Tite's stall.

The horses, the regular ones, not the miniature ones, had pretty descent stalls that they could walk around in. Not tied up or anything. They were at the other end of the barn. Jamie's mom had had an extension put onto the barn, so it looked sorta like an "L," and the horse stables were the added on part.

Some of the animals lifted their heads when Jamie went by. A few of the small horses in the pens untucked their noses from their sides to look. A couple of the goats even stood up and arched their backs like they thought they were wakin' up for mornin' and they walked over to the boards of their pens and stuck their heads through. Jamie pet one behind the ears when he walked by. He kinda thought their loyalty only went as far as the bucket of grain he brought 'em twice a day, but yuh can't help but pet one behind its droopy ears when you see it. The thing tried to nibble at his flannel sleeve when he did. Goats'll try to eat anything.

There was a post where a bunch of twine from the bales of hay got hung when they were taken off. Jamie took a couple off the nail and wadded 'em and stuck 'em in the back pocket of his jeans.

They had quite a few horses. Nine. His mom wanted to raise more. Maybe sell 'em. He didn't picture her doin' that though. She always got so friggin' attached to anything that had four legs and fur. She saved five baby skunks whose mother had gotten killed in the road a couple of years ago. Sorta fed 'em for a while until they could fend for themselves. She let 'em go, but she probably woulda turned 'em into house cats if she coulda found a good enough reason to. She was like that.

She wouldn't get rid of Tite's foal though. Because Jamie's dad had given her the horse as an anniversary present.

The latch was undone to Tite's stall, and Jamie pulled the door the rest of the way open and walked in. His mom was on her knees on the stall floor with the horse. Jamie had bedded the stall with a bunch of straw that afternoon, more than usual, because he knew she'd be havin' her baby any day. Some of it was soaked and a little bloody from the horse's water breakin'. Tite was all sprawled out. Her legs were stiff and stretched out. It always looks worse than it is with animals, especially when it's their first. Tite had her halter on, but she wasn't chained up or anything. She swung her head up to see who was comin' in. Her eyes were dark brown and they weren't wild or anything. It looked like she just wondered, yuh know.

"Easy, girl." Jamie kneeled down beside his mom behind the horse. "Did you call the vet?" He ran his hand down Tite's back leg. Her coat was a little clammy. Like she'd been tryin' to do this by herself for a while. Horses can usually do that, have babies by themselves. But somethin' was up here with Tite.

"I called him before I got you up." Mary had some rubber boots on, and an old, thick flannel shirt over her nightgown. She had this winter hat on, too. One of those ones without a pom-pom on it or anything. Christ, it was like she was Ma Ingalls or somethin'. Her voice was shakin' a little. She never really got like this. She had delivered so many animals in her life, but she loved this horse, Titania, so goddamn much because it was really the last thing that Jamie's dad had given her. She had let that get the best of her tonight, she'd be the first to say it when everything was over. Plus yuh know how when you wake up at night and sometimes things seem worse than they are. You're still half asleep or somethin'. "You know how long it takes for him to get here from Richfield though."

"Mom, just relax first of all. Christ." Jamie looked closer at the horse. One of the foal's hooves was stickin' out. If everything is okay, most of the time the two front hooves stick out and you pull the thing out, yuh know with some help from the mother and stuff. He felt Tite's side to see if the baby was movin' around in there or anything. The foal was right there, sloshin' around. He didn't hate doin' stuff like what he was about to do, but you still think about it just for a half a second before you do it.

He took off his flannel and tossed it to the side. Then he shoved up his sweatshirt sleeve and put his hand inside of the horse. Man, there is no nice way to put it and it really isn't that big of a deal, yuh know. You do what you have to. He followed with his hand up the leg of the foal that was stickin' out and found where it connected to body and then he found the other leg. He looked towards his mom. "It's twisted, Mom. That's all." He worked his hand to the hoof and grabbed onto it and tried to straighten it and line it up with the other leg. That took some work. Tite was lyin' there, and Jamie's mom was strokin' her side and calmin' her. Jamie could feel the foal movin' around. He had to get the leg, it was tucked funny or somethin'. It took a few minutes, he was startin' to sweat, that's how much it takes to do shit like that.

He reached with his other arm for his back pocket and pulled out the two ropes he'd gotten and handed 'em to his mother. He pulled the other hoof out while he did that. He sorta sat back then and shook his arm. Steam was rollin' off it and it was sorta messy. With placenta and stuff. His chest was goin' in and out, and he caught his breath while his mom did her thing.

She shifted to where Jamie had been sittin', and she was like the paramedic now or somethin'. She took each of the strings and looped them around the foal's legs, just above its soft hooves, that's the way they are when somethin' is first born.

Jamie came a little closer and he was back on his knees beside his mom. She took the ends of the ropes and tied them together, so it was like one rope now with the other ends on each of the hooves. Her hands were in the center where she had tied them. Jamie put his hands there, too.

Animals aren't like people, they do things on instinct. The second Tite felt everything was okay she started to push, or have her contractions or whatever you'd say, and Jamie and his mom pulled. The legs started to come out. They were white, covered with goop, yuh know, but you could tell it was gonna have white legs. "Hold up," Jamie told his mom. They let off the rope some and let Tite rest.

Tite's body was still all tensed up and everything. All her

muscles were tight and she was breathin' hard. But she needed a second.

It was quiet in there, with the three of them breathin' the way they were. Straw is golden-colored and soft, and it kinda muted every move any of 'em made. It warmed things too, like the lower parts of Jamie's legs pressed against it.

Tite pushed, and Jamie and his mom could just make out the tip of the foal's nose. "Okay," Jamie said without lookin' at his mom.

They pulled. Not jerky or anything. It was like when you're doin' tug-a-war and you just sorta dig your body into the ground and pull with a strong, steady pull. The ropes were tight, but they were connected to two long white legs with bulky round knees. The foal's head was comin'. They kept the strings taunt, and Tite was really doing the work now. Her body could do what it had to now with the foal's legs in their right position.

First you could see the nose. The tip of it was white like the legs. The head was the worst part, but once they got past that, the foal would pretty much slide out. You still had to pull it, but it would come out easier than what was comin' out right now. Tite wasn't goin' nuts but she wasn't likin' it at all. Her nostrils were big and flared and she kept lookin' behind her every couple minutes, like she was sayin' "What the hell are you doin'?" Her ears were pricked up straight, too.

Jamie moved from on his knees to on his feet. He scuffed some of the straw hay away with his boots to get to the boards of the stable floor. He stayed sorta squatted when he did, and he kept his hands on the rope beside his mom's and didn't take his weight off it.

The foal's tongue was like danglin' out and it was covered with slimy stuff. You could see the small nostrils now. The foal was gonna have a white mouth and nose. The head widened, but it took some time, yuh know. The arch of the nose started to work its way out.

Jamie's and his mom's hands were wrapped tight around the rope, and they were leanin' with their weight away from Tite and you could see Tite bracin' herself and her body pushin'.

The foal was gonna have one of those strips of white that ran from between its ears to the tip of its nose.

"A little more," Jamie's mom said under her breath, to herself really.

Her words registered though, and both her and Jaime moved their bodies together with Tite's contractions and the difference was there. The wide of the head slipped and it was out. Jamie stood up then, not completely straight up, but almost. And his mom stayed on her knees. They kept the pullin' out sorta balanced this way.

It was still work, but easier now. Tite's job was sorta over. They pulled and the foal's front shoulders and chest came. It was gonna be big, you could tell by its chest. There was so much length to it. They kept up pullin' and the back end came. Jamie and his mom gave another pull so the foal's back thighs could come, and the back legs followed without any too much work.

Jamie let go of the rope and stood all the way up. He stepped back. He still had the one sleeve of his sweatshirt up, and he pulled it back over his bare arm. He stood there and caught his breath. His arms were sorta out, and he was gonna rest his hands on his hips, but he looked down at 'em and they were pretty wet.

So he just stood there like that while his mom got the strings off the foal.

Mary was still on her knees and she took the strings off the foal's legs and handed 'em to Jamie to take care of 'em. She peeled the sack and stuff out and away from the foal's mouth so it could breathe better. Its tongue wasn't danglin' out anymore and it was already tryin' to lift its head or it was just gettin' used to bein' alive, sorta shakin' sense into itself. "Thanks, Jamie. I probably coulda done it. I just..." She was peelin' away the sack from the foal's body now, and didn't plan on finishin' her sentence.

Jamie took a step forward and bent down. "Doesn't matter." He held the wet strings in one hand and cleaned the foal's mouth out a little more with his other. Really stickin' his fingers in its mouth. Just makin' sure it was okay. It was. He sorta scratched the foal's head between its ears. It was all wet and its coat was matted. It was still shiny though, like anything newborn is. "Look at those legs." He ran his hand down the leg that had been crimped. It looked all right.

Its legs were long and they looked even longer than they really were because they were so white. And its knees were exaggerated balls right now. Like it'd have to grow into 'em. Jamie moved around to the back end of the foal and lifted a back leg.

"Girl?" His mom was restin' now, still on her knees. She'd taken her hat off and stuck it in her flannel pocket. Her hair was in a ponytail and pressed down and a few strands stuck up and out from static.

"Nope, a boy."

"He's big."

The colt—that's pretty much the same thing as a foal, just a boy though—was already trying to sit up instead of layin' there all sprawled out like it was. Tite was comin' down too. She had drawn her legs in and was layin' there like you'd normally see a horse layin' down. She shook her head a couple times like to wake herself from a dream or somethin', then looked behind her to see if it was real. She stood up then.

"I guess she's okay." Mary stood up too.

Tite turned and moved towards her new kid. She sniffed it up.

The colt sorta raised its head to check out its mother.

It had a really dark brown coat except for its legs and the streak down its face and nose. And it had Tite's eyes, maybe even a darker brown than hers by the looks of 'em.

Jamie and his mom stood there a second and watched the two. The colt already wanted to nurse and woulda stood if it could have. It was thrashin' a little lyin' there, already tryin' to get up.

Jamie looked at the wet ropes in his hands. His mom's eyes caught his movement and she looked over at him. His hair was stickin' up in places.

"I got it now, Jamie. If you wanna go back to bed."

It had to be 1:30. He got up early to do barn work before he went to school. "Do you want me to see if I can catch the vet before he gets here?" Vets cost a lot of money. Especially when you call 'em in the middle of the night.

Mary smiled. "Yeah, if you could. I think everything's okay. Don't you?"

Tite was already up and the colt was fine too. "Yeah, they're fine."

Jamie looked down at the colt again. It had wiggled around

enough so that its legs were stretched straight out in front of it now and it had already learned how to keep its head up. "Yuh keepin' it?" He looked at his mom.

She had looked down at it too. "Puck." She looked at it a second longer and then at Jamie.

"I guess so." He knew without askin' anyway. "Keepin' Dad's Shakespeare thing goin'." He moved to Tite and patted her neck. Her coat was bright from her sweat, and her body was back to normal already. He stopped quick and turned to his mom. "I'm goin' back to bed."

✦ ✦ ✦

They had a bathroom upstairs and downstairs. His room was upstairs and his mom's was downstairs, so it was like he had his own space or place a lot of the time. He had called the vet, gotten his wife outa bed—for a second time that night. But she was probably used to it. Maybe. She said she'd get in touch with Bill. CB or cell phone or somethin'.

Jamie stood there in his jeans in front of the mirror. He had taken his boots off in the kitchen and he had taken his sweatshirt off too and thrown that right in the washer downstairs. He had the bathroom door shut, and the water runnin' was already changin' the air of the small room. Their bathroom was pretty ordinary, there was no duck theme goin' or anything. No basket of potpourri sittin' on the back of the toilet. Not even a can of Glade. He wanted to take a shower. He would take one tomorrow mornin' anyway after he finished in the barn and before he got the bus, but he wanted one now, too.

He stood in front of the mirror a second while the water warmed up. He sorta looked at himself. He had a pretty built frame started, for a fifteen-year-old. 'Course, when he saw himself he saw this ganglin' kid who was more kid than man. He had only been in bed maybe 45 minutes, but his hair looked like he'd slept on his head all night. He had dark circles under his eyes and he was a little pale. He thought he looked like hell. He wasn't really a night person yet. The night seemed short when you were in school. A long day, and then time to yourself was like the flick of a channel. Mornin' came, you feel like you slept maybe twenty minutes, and the remote was in somebody else's or everybody else's hands again. That made his stomach tighten. He didn't feel like goin' to school in seven hours or whatever. His biology book was still open on his desk, and people like Number 10 and Denise Coler and her basketball sheet came in his head…and that car today and whoever was in that car blowin' their horn and playin' their music. He didn't even have a face to go with them, just a feelin' and that fuckin' horn all in his chest.

Random though.

That whole thing had to be random.

His hair was gettin' dark above his lip. Not bad, but he was just startin' to get whiskers. Puberty, adolescence, whatever yuh wanna call it. He had had hair under his arms already now for a while, and on his, yuh know, too. He made eye contact with himself. Have you ever done that? Looked yourself right in the eye. He tried it sometimes. Try it, see how long you look at yourself. He had kinda long eyelashes, not like a girl or anything, but long, and his eyes were dark brown. Like his dad's. He looked away, and unbuttoned his jeans and unzipped 'em part way.

He went over to the tub and stuck his hand under the runnin' water. It was hot, too hot. He turned the cold water knob on a little more and stuck his hand under the water again. He did that a couple times until it was just hot enough so you could stand it. He pulled up the shower plug, and water started to shoot out the showerhead. Water has a certain sound when it first starts up and it runs into an empty tub. A hollow sound, it echoes. He pulled the curtain across so none of the stray water would splatter out. Doin' that sorta muffled the sound.

He pulled off his gray winter socks and then unzipped his jeans all the way. He took them and his long johns off sorta at the same time. The stuff laid outside the bathtub and he got a towel out of the drawer and set it on the toilet beside the tub.

It was chilly and he got in. He worked his way under the hot water. First an outstretched arm and then slowly his shoulder of that arm and then his whole body. The water poured over his back and rolled down his body. He stood there with his arms folded across his chest at first. The air still a little cold. Then his body was all wet and his muscles loosened, and the shower was a shower. He stood there when that happened. He kinda rubbed the water on his arms, cleanin' the one off he'd put inside of Tite. He'd use the bar of soap in a minute. Right now he just let the hot water clean him. Their shower wasn't a knock you over shower, where the water almost feels sharp when it hits your body because there's so much pressure behind it, instead theirs poured out on you. He backed up a little and the water crept up his neck and head, and his hair and face got some of it.

He closed his eyes a little when it ran over the top of his head and dripped down and found a way into 'em. The hot water ran all over him and washed what was left on his arm that he used to straighten Puck's leg.

Puck. Jesus.

It had to be a random thing, had to.

He kept his eyes shut and lifted his hands up to them. He pressed his fingertips into 'em and rubbed 'em. He stepped into the water more. He was right under the stream of it now. He brought his fingertips from his eyes and slid the bottom of his palms there in their place. He pressed into the soft tender part between the bone around his eyes. He pressed hard, but that never helps. He left 'em there though because the bottom of the palms of his hands fit there and he kept 'em there. He kept his eyes closed and put his head down, and he kept his jaw and his lips as tight as he could.

It didn't matter though. His shoulders jerked once, real quick, and he felt the warm water on his face.

+ ✦ +

The clock sat on a shelf. About five or six hardcover books were on one side of it. They were sorta at a slant with no bookends or anything holdin' 'em up. It was one of those shelves that was built right in the wall, and the books went from small to big, so the bigger, thicker books were propped against the wall and sorta standin' up straight with their own weight and the smaller ones leaned into 'em. Some were books about dreams and stuff and some were like readin' books, yuh know like novels that looked like they were first bound editions or somethin'. On the other side of the clock was a small statue of a Hawaiian girl in a grass skirt whose hips wiggled on a spring every time somebody walked by. The clock was there in the middle and set sorta at an angle so he could reach behind it and wind it like he did most of the time when he walked by it. Its hands still read 5:59, but the vines that had wrapped themselves up and around the Roman numerals had little buds on 'em now. The second hand that clicked somewhere between the VIII and IX had unstuck itself from there. It ticked right on the IX now.

The moon had come up from behind the mountains and it was sittin' on their peaks. It was smilin', not creepy or anything, it had a man on the moon face and its eyes were lookin' at the cow that was jumpin' over it.

The woman in the dress and apron and braids wasn't standin' either. She was bent on her knees and had moved away from the blue and silver stream. It flowed and rippled behind her now. She was in her garden and you could make out the rows of things she had planted. Nothing was up, but the ground was darker in lines where she had planted rows. Her face was determined, her cheeks were all rosy and that stuff still, but you could tell she was gonna make whatever it was that she'd planted grow. She was bent over and waterin' it with a tin waterin' can, and she'd moved away from the slot where the phrase slipped in, but it was still suppose to be her talkin'. It was just above her head and it read "Feed the seed."

✦ ✦ ✦

Chapter Nine

THE NEXT time Jamie saw Angelo was a few days later. He was on his way back to school from Ray's, and Angelo was up on his ladder, messin' around with his Christmas lights—again. This time a couple of strands were danglin'. Some from the eaves, some from his ladder, and he was workin' at another one. Jamie didn't see Angelo turn his head and look at him because his head was down and he squared the corner now, like Angelo had told those other guys to do. He was in the street about to turn onto Rea. He'd seen the back of Angelo and really began to doubt the guy's sanity. What was his obsession with the lights?

It was a warm day and Angelo didn't have a jacket on. Neither did Jamie, he'd left his in his locker. It was more like sweater weather. Angelo had on a white wool rollneck sweater, and Jamie had on a T-shirt and a flannel buttoned over it. Jamie was really a little underdressed, but kids do that the second the sun shines a little and the air warms up. Some of 'em had worn shorts today, but even Jamie thought that was a little too much.

Angelo wasn't sly or anything when he sorta turned to see Jamie comin' down the street. The other three guys passed about five minutes ago when Angelo had looked out his window, so he was expectin' him.

Jamie had finished his bag of Fritos, he'd switched since the day he'd gotten the stale Cheetos. He had stuffed the empty bag into his jeans pocket and he had a can of Sprite in his hand. He took a swig just before he got to the corner. When he saw Angelo out there, he felt a little weird. From the other day, yuh know. He walked around the corner and figured he just wouldn't look that way.

Man, it was like spring. Lawns were sloppy brown like swamps and some of the grass was turnin' green. The snow banks were low mounds of dirty snow and the streets were dry. There was a big maple tree on one of the lawns on Rea and about a hundred black birds, or some kinda bird like them, had landed there and they were whistlin' really loud all at once, like an audience before a show or somethin', lovin' the sunshine, too. It sucked though in a way. All a false alarm, the thaw was just a little longer than it usually was.

"Beautiful day, isn't it?"

Jamie was just about to pass Angelo's driveway. He looked up and Angelo was on the ladder and stretched out and reachin' for some lights. "Yeah. It is." Jamie sorta smiled and kept walkin'. He didn't want to talk to the guy. He saw Angelo smile and stretch a little more for a strand of lights that was danglin' from the eaves.

Angelo stretched a little more and moved his feet to the edge of the ladder rung he was standin' on. He looked at his feet when he did and then back at the lights. He had his golashes on. They were buckled up, but golashes are always like clodhoppers, yuh know. Impossible for a job like he was doin', tryin' to keep his balance and everything. He stretched a little more, and the lights were at his fingertips. The strand sorta swayed in the light breeze. And he touched 'em but couldn't get his fingers around 'em. And it started to slide. The ladder did. It started to slide towards the strand he was after.

"Hey, careful." Jamie pointed with his hand the soda can was in. "Your ladder's slippin'." Jamie stopped in front of Angelo's driveway when he said that. Angelo was at the top of his ladder, yuh know, he was pretty high up, and it was slippin' now.

Once it started though and Angelo kept reachin', it didn't stop. Jamie dropped his soda can at the end of the driveway and kinda ran up the blacktop to stop it, but it wasn't gonna do any good. The ladder scuffed against the edge of the roof and Angelo was goin' with it, his arm was still out, like if he grabbed onto the strand of lights, it'd be like a rescue rope or somethin'. Didn't matter because his hand completely missed the lights and he fell with the ladder. It was one of those adjustable aluminum ones and it scratched and screeched when it rubbed against the edge of the roof. It missed the side of the house, good thing because it looked like Angelo had just had it re-sided or somethin'. The ladder and Angelo were midair for about two seconds. He held onto it and his weight musta shifted it out a little bit and away from the house.

The two were on the ground before Jamie got there. The ladder didn't crash or anything, after it slid from the edge of the roof and missed the side of the house, it just thumped onto Angelo's lawn.

The aluminum clanked a little, like where it was loose where the two parts adjusted together, but really it just thudded when it hit the ground. If it was one of your friends or somethin', or in a movie or somethin', you mighta laughed, but not some old guy.

"Are you okay?" Jamie went over to him and looked down at him. He'd ran pretty fast over there to try to catch the ladder and he bent over and put his hands on his knees and caught his breath and talked to Angelo.

Angelo's one side of his sweater was muddy and wet from the lawn. One of his golashes had slipped half off even though it was buckled up, and his foot was sorta stuck in between two rungs and some strands of lights he had hung on the ladder. His hair was standin' up, and he was lyin' on his back, lookin' up. The top button on his trousers had popped off on the way down and his fly was a little down and Jamie could see the top of his underwear. Boxers. Jamie looked back at Angelo's face. His lips were sorta curved up.

Angelo shifted his eyes from the sky to Jamie's face. He smiled like Jamie was at the checkout. "I'm fine." He started to get up. Jamie sorta took a step back and looked around. Like lettin' him do his own thing.

Angelo unwrapped his foot from the ladder first. He sorta tried to sit himself up. He kinda groaned, too. "Ooohhh." He ran his hand from his forehead to the back of his head and made his hair stand up even more.

"Are you sure you're okay?" Jamie took a step back towards Angelo. "Should I call 911 or somethin'?"

Jamie didn't know what to do, he squatted down beside Angelo. "Here. Do you want some help?" Jamie hated when people asked him that after he'd done somethin' like fallen or cut himself. He usually just wanted to help himself. Maybe this guy wasn't like that though.

Angelo put one of his arms out and Jamie took hold of it. Angelo bent his legs and started to stand up. "Ooohh."

When Jamie saw Angelo makin' to get up, he sorta put his hands around the arm Angelo had put out for him and heaved him up. The guy was heavy, solid weight, and he wasn't helpin' much. Jamie lifted, and Angelo pushed himself with his other hand on the ground.

"Oooohh."

They made progress and Angelo was standin', feet sorta spread apart and arms out, like he'd just gotten off the merry-go-round or roller-coaster or somethin'.

"Ooohh."

With those ooohhs, c'mon. "You think you broke anything? Maybe I should call somebody." Jamie was standin' beside Angelo and he wasn't touchin' him but he sorta kept his hands out a little, like when you steady somebody.

"No, that's all right. Maybe—" Angelo sorta turned towards his house. He put his hand on his lower back and winced. "Maybe if you could just help me inside, so I could sit down."

Jamie looked to the house, too. He did *not* want to go into this guy's house. "Umm."

Angelo took a step towards his house. "Oh." He rubbed his lower back.

This guy was probably like a molester or somethin'. Jamie moved to the other side of him.

Angelo took that as an "Okay," and they started to walk

forward. "I can't thank you enough."

"No problem."

Angelo reached down and pulled up his pants a little, they were startin' to slide down from the lost button. Then he put one of his hands back on his back. "You're a student at the high school?"

They were on the short walk now that led to Angelo's front door. It was made of little bricks and had room for flowers on each side. Jamie looked down and some tulip buds were just stickin' through. You know when people have wood chips around their shrubs or flowers, well, they were pokin' through some of those wood chips. Angelo had a pretty nice house.

"Yeah."

"What year?"

This guy was just old and lonely. Jamie had him pegged with that question. When he worked the counter on Saturday afternoons for his mom, old people came in just to come in. They'd check somethin' out, like a bag of birdseed or somethin' and find somethin' to talk about in the meantime, especially if no one else was in the store. Like how the neighbor's cat always was after their birds and did he happen to know what kinda bird whistled with that short little whup, whup, whup whistle and they'd demonstrate and did he have a cat and they remember when everyone in Coformon Falls had cats or they'd talk about somethin' like that. They were just lonely though and if they weren't crabby or anything, he'd end up bein' like that sounds like a so and so bird or try puttin' your bird feeder up higher or whatever. "I'm a sophomore."

They stepped the couple steps to Angelo's front door. Angelo opened it and he went in first. There was a big knocker on the front with a crescent moon danglin' from it.

Jamie hesitated at the front door a second.

Angelo moved forward in the hall to make room for Jamie. He moaned again when he bent to unbuckle his golashes. "If you could just get me to my chair, I won't trouble you any further." He didn't look up at Jamie when he talked, he just undid his boots.

Jamie went in and closed the door. He wiped his feet on the mat. It had one of those half-sun half-moon faces on it—kind of a cool lookin' thing for an old guy to be havin' on his door mat, but who knows, yuh know.

Angelo had gotten out of his boots and led Jamie down the short hall. Jamie wasn't scared or anything, well, maybe of bein' trapped by an old guy who had no one to talk to, but he wasn't creeped out or anything. He'd get him in his chair and take off.

Angelo opened the big wooden door. It reminded Jamie of a door in a castle. They walked through and it was like summertime in there. Summer about seven o'clock at night. You expected to look out the window and see the sun on its way down and a shit load of purples across the sky. Summer sunsets are always purple. It was warm, too, not like heater warm, but warm warm, and bright. And it smelled like a mild brand of a novelty potpourri or somethin'.

Angelo closed the door behind 'em, and Jamie sorta looked around. You know how you go into someone's house and you don't wanna be rude but you just sorta look around at things. That's what Jamie did. It looked a lot bigger on the inside than the outside. The room in front of 'em was the living room and the dining room was past that. There was a buncha crap on the dining room table and a baby scale. What'd this guy deal drugs or somethin'? His eyes caught the huge picture just past the table and hangin' above it, man, it was—he heard the door shut and it brought his attention back to where they were standin'. There was a shelf with a clock on it. Jamie looked at the girl on her knees and then at the clock's hands.

The time was completely off, like at six o'clock or somethin', and Jamie's face probably registered his thought because Angelo had came around beside him and said, "That's been around for quite a while." He walked the two steps to it and stuck his hand behind it and wound it. "I always say 'Even though it seems off, it's really keeping the right time somewhere else.'"

Jamie watched Angelo wind it and straighten it a little back on the shelf. He really didn't know what to say. "It's a nice clock."

The Hawaiian girl was shakin' her grass skirt on the other side of it because Angelo's arm had sorta jarred it and its movement caught Jamie's eye. He looked at it a second and then he looked to the other side and saw the books.

Angelo was still standin' there admirin' his clock with his left hand on his back, so Jamie started to look at the bindings of the books. Most of 'em looked like they had been around awhile. A little beat-up, faded covers, yuh know. There were some ones on stars, like one called *Stars and Beyond*, and more than a few on sleep like *Common Sleep Patterns* and *The Dreamful Sleeper*, just to name a couple. Most of 'em were out there stuff like that. The smallest book though, closest to the clock, was a really bright red, it looked older too, but pretty well-kept, and not even realizin' it, Jamie bent a little closer to look at the title. Gold letters running down it: *A Midsummer Night's Dream*. When he

saw that, his spine tingled a second at the bottom of his neck. He
didn't have a poker face on, either.

"You like Shakespeare." Angelo was pullin' the small book
from the shelf before Jamie could say anything.

"Oh. No, not really." He straightened back up. He didn't
really wanna tell Angelo, but he felt like he had to explain why
all of a sudden he looked the way he did. "It's just that that was
my dad's favorite book."

Angelo had finally taken his hand off his back and he opened
the book and held it like two feet from his face and looked down
at it and sorta flipped through the pages. "One of the greats."

"Yeah, my dad thought so, too, but I can't understand half of
what they're talkin' about."

Angelo looked up at him and smiled. "Wellll, Shakespeare
takes time. Anything of worth does."

Jamie had to read *MacBeth* last year. Instead of makin' the
class read it, Mrs. Vastune had brought in this old record and they
followed along with it in their books. It was horrible. The player
was from the fifties and the record sounded like it had been used
as a Frisbee more than a couple times. Jamie got into it some, but
he had so much other homework in his classes he couldn't spend
that much time with it, like readin' over the scenes again like he
was suppose to when he got home. He ended up buyin' the *Cliffs
Notes* for it. "Yeah, I guess you're right."

Angelo closed the book. "You're welcome to borrow this
and give him another try." He put his one hand back on his back
and kinda stuck the book out to Jamie with his other one.

"That's okay." Jamie started to put one of his hands in his
pocket. He felt the wadded up Fritos bag. "It looks like a pretty

old book, I wouldn't want to lose it or anything. Thanks though."
He looked down at the book and then at Angelo.

"Not to worry. In fact, it's all the more reason to take it — if
you lose it, I'll have an excuse to get a newer copy." Angelo
stood there holdin' the book and his face looked like it had a big
question mark on it. His head was sorta tipped a little and his
eyebrows were raised. He woulda made a good insurance
salesman at the moment or somethin'.

Jamie woulda stuck his hand further down in his jeans
pocket, but instead he was reachin' for the book. Yuh know when
you do that. Like you know when someone isn't gonna take no
for an answer.

When Jamie had the book in his hand, Angelo headed from
the small foyer thingy they were standin' in and into the living
room.

Jamie looked at the book and knew he wouldn't get it.
Thee's and thou's and all that shit. He wasn't into Shakespeare
at all. He opened it and looked at a line: "'If we shadows have
offended,/Think but this, and all is mended,/That you have but
slumbered here/While these visions did appear./And this weak
and idle theme...'" See, told yuh. He closed the book and just
sorta followed Angelo over to his chair. Set him down and then
go. "Are you sure I can't call someone for you? I really gotta
go..." This guy had to live alone.

Angelo pulled his pants up again and turned and sat in his
chair. Big cushy chair, the kind you can pull a lever and you can
put your feet up. There was a sewing basket beside it with stuff
stickin' out, but Jamie didn't stare. Or he thought he didn't. Just,
you know, an old guy that lived alone, or seemed to live alone,

with a sewing basket. Strange.

Angelo sat a little forward. Probably because his sweater was all crappy on his arm and on his back from fallin'.

Jamie looked back at him. He had taken a pretty bad spill an' all, but Jamie really had to go. "...back to school."

Angelo looked beside his chair, down at the basket.

Shit.

"Ahh, my dream pillows." He leaned to his side a little and pulled out a small pillow that didn't look soft at all and had a needle and thread hangin' from it. There were a couple more in the basket and some scissors and some scrap cloth and stuff like that.

"Oh. It's nice." Dream pillow? Jamie really wasn't lookin' for an explanation, and he coulda kicked his own ass for lookin' at the freakin' basket like it was filled with gold or somethin'. He had a book in his hand that he didn't want and now he was givin' this guy more of an excuse to keep talkin'. But even still, "Dream pillow?"

Sorry, but you wouldn't let it pass either.

Angelo talked like he'd known Jamie since he was born. "I'm not surprised you've never heard of them." Angelo sort of turned it in his hand and looked at it. The pillow was about the size of a freezer bag, and it was half open at the end that the needle and thread hung from. "You put one under your pillow or hang it on your bed's headboard and—"

Angelo looked up at Jamie.

Jamie was just standin' there with the book in his hand and one of his eyebrows raised.

"—and the dream you have is real." Angelo brought the pillow to his nose and sniffed it.

It dawned on Jamie that that was what smelled like a big incense stick or bathtub full of potpourri. This guy had to deal hash or somethin' and he probably smoked it, too.

"Of course, the dream is up to you."

"Oh. That's…interesting." Jamie's eyebrow went from bein' raised, to both of 'em makin' room for his forehead. "I really should go." He turned for the door.

Angelo wasn't worried, but he knew he had to start workin' on Jamie. He only had 15 seconds or so. That part made sense to Jamie when all of it was over. "You don't believe me."

Jamie stopped and smiled. "No. I believe you, I just, I'm gonna be late for class." Then he turned to go again.

Angelo took hold of the dangling needle. "Better get my glasses," he said under his breath. He looked to his side and back into the basket. He had left his bifocals in there today and he let go of the needle and reached for them. He kinda flipped the loose, floppy arms of 'em out with his hand and then stuck 'em on his face. He took the needle again and started to stitch. He'd finish this one as long as he was sittin' here and then he'd go change his sweater and pants. "I'll tell you this." He stuck the needle through the cloth. "People always think they have the right combination, and then one day the same old lock they use every day won't open and the world requires that they come up with a different one. Or a different way." He sorta pinched the cloth together and then pulled the needle and thread through the two sides of the pillow.

What a fu—"Take care." Jamie half turned when he said "Take care," and he walked towards the door.

"You too, Jamie." Angelo was lookin' down at this pillow

and gettin' ready to make another stitch.

Jamie just stopped. His hand was on the door and he was by the shelf and the clock and the books and the little statue from Hawaii. He turned around and looked back into the living room. Angelo was sittin' there sewin' on his dream pillow or whatever you call 'em.

"How do you know my name?"

Angelo looked up and smiled. "You told me the other day, remember."

Jamie stood there a second and looked at Angelo. He stood there a second and then he left. He left with that goddamn book in his hand.

Chapter Ten

RAVIOLI WAS pretty big, and subs were always an everyday hot seller. Today, a couple of the cafeteria ladies had big spoons in their hands and they were puttin' ravioli onto trays. They'd dip into the metal basin thing and scoop up some and then put 'em in the big rectangle on the tray. You know they were countin' how many raviolis they were puttin' on each tray. Because if they put more than seven on there, they'd pretend to get you more sauce but take the extra two they'd just given you and lose 'em back in the basin. You could have that and some fries in a Styrofoam soup bowl. Kind of strange, get your four food groups lunch, but kids ate it and the school served it.

The line had wrapped down the counter and out the door and into the hallway today. Kids usually shot out of their fifth period class to be the first in line. There were a couple reasons for that. The line got long enough sometimes that you might end up waitin' half of the lunch period if you weren't on the top end of it. You'd get your tray and sit if you were one of the unfortunate, and two minutes later, Mr. Powers would be at your table ready to wipe it down with his ammonia-based bucket of water and a rag. But really you were lucky if you even got a tray when you were one of the last ones in line. Sometimes the lunch ladies miscalculated and they wouldn't even make enough whatever, and you'd end up with a selection of bologna subs wrapped in yesterday's plastic. Bologna.

Bag lunches reduced the risk, but food that sat in a bag in a locker had its downside too. A sandwich that was all warm that wasn't supposed to be warm sucked too, and you probably had to get in line for a milk anyway, unless you brought a juice box, which was so uncool in high school.

The lunchroom smelled like hospital food, and it had about as much atmosphere as a hospital. A big square room painted light blue. That soothing, in case you go into shock, surgeon's scrubs blue. Fake-wooded, round tables with multi-colored plastic chairs. The art students had painted a big dragon above a line of windows that divided the main hall from the lunchroom. It was suppose to look all intimidating with silver and blue scaly skin and fire shootin' out of its nostrils, and with its body stretchin' the length of the windows and its pointed tail hangin' over the last of 'em and down the wall. But the art students who had painted it fucked up, and it was like they'd given the thing a little smirk or somethin'. So there it was breathin' fire at yuh, but smilin' like it didn't know any better.

It was like everyone had unofficial assigned seats in the lunchroom, too. If you went in there, you'd see the same people sittin' at the same table with the other same people on any given day. There were a few table roamers and they messed up the synchronicity of the dining experience for a few kids. There was one kid who had a hearing problem and he didn't have any one set of friends and he'd sit at a random table every day. Throw people for a loop when Alan sat at your table. Some people would talk to him, some kids acted like he wasn't even there. He'd always bring an egg salad sandwich that would stink like ass and gross people out when he opened the Handi-Wrap it was wrapped in. But other than a few people like him, the tables coulda had name tags at 'em reservin' the seats for whoever.

The table closest to the row of windows and the Coformon Falls dragon mural was where Ben Callihan sat. He usually pulled his wheelchair up on the side of the table that he could look out into the main hall and people watch. He did that a lot. When his friends at the table started talkin' about somethin' he wasn't into, like football, NFL kinda football or whatever, he'd drink his chocolate milk and watch people walk by or run by. He always drank his milk last. He'd eat his sandwich, usually deli ham or somethin' with Gulden's—he brought a bag, some chips that he'd brought from home or whatever, and an apple. He didn't have his mom buy any single serving stuff, like pudding cups or Jell-O cups or Little Debbies or Granola Bars.

Today he wadded his plastic wrap up and stuck it in his bag and crushed that up between his hands. He shook his milk and separated the carton's lip and took a sip.

The lunchroom was clearin' out some, but Mr. Powers wasn't in today, this past year he'd been out a couple times with some serious arthritis in his hands. He only worked because he couldn't retire yet, he was like a fixture at C.F.H.S. anyway, a lot of the staff was.

Ben always sat with Ron Dychett, Rachel Stappuck, Nicole Fraker, Aaron delConceed—Sandy Khatz's boyfriend, her, and Rob Hatteulle. There were a few other kids like Denise Coler or Amanda Wrule or Don Neggito that might sit with 'em, but those were pretty much the regulars. The table was pretty full today even though the period was windin' down. Kids were roamin' around the halls and the lunchroom. There were some strays left at other tables in the room like at Ben's table. All you could hear was people talkin' and the lunch ladies cleanin' up the mess behind the lunch counter. Bangin' big trays and scrapin' ravioli sauce that had stuck to the bottom of the pan.

Most everyone had finished their lunch at Ben's table and had dumped their tray. They were hangin' out, takin' full advantage of Powers's absence. Ron Dychett had a Ping-Pong ball and he was sittin' there with his chair pulled away from the table and snappin' the ball against the floor while he talked. Rachel had a hand mirror out and was reapplyin' some watermelon lip-gloss. Everybody else sorta had a conversation with the person right next to 'em or somethin'.

"What's up for the weekend?" Ron looked up from his Ping-Pong fest.

Rob Hatteulle was usually weekend coordinator. "Rachel, are your folks in town?"

Rachel kept her eyes in the mirror. She was swipin' her bottom lip. "Yeah. My dad has some meeting that he has to be at in Tarrytown on Saturday, so no Ski Windham for them this weekend."

"What good are yuh?"

She looked up at Rob with her mouth gapin' and her lip smacker in her hand. She rubbed her lips together and capped the stick. "Benny's parents are goin' somewhere, aren't they?" She looked over at Ben.

It was rare his parents went away. But his mom's mother lived further upstate and they were goin' there for the weekend. He'd thrown a couple of parties so far in his high school career and they weren't any big deal. Nothin' outa hand or anything. People usually had a good time, but he didn't let things get outa control. A few cases of beer. Leave by midnight. That sorta thing.

Ben really hadn't been listenin' until he heard his name. He was drinkin' his milk and starin' out the glass into the hall. The conversation most of the lunch had revolved around this guy Nicole had fallen madly for. He played soccer at one of the schools next to Coformon Falls. He was a senior and she'd met him at a party last weekend. He was on a couple of his mom's Valium at the party, and that bothered her a little, but he was sooo hot she had to overlook that.

More than one lunch conversation had revolved around Nicole in some way. Sometimes she even sat there cryin' if she'd messed up her progress report or if some guy took her out and then wouldn't talk to her the next Monday. She liked to write notes in class and pass 'em in the hall between classes. She was still talkin' about Mike Whatever to Sandy and Aaron.

Ben swallowed his sip of milk. "Yeah, they are."

"There we have it, novelty-seekers." Ron cupped his Ping-Pong ball in his hand when it bounced back up to him. He was tryin' to get the table's attention by addressin' them as a group.

Aaron was the first who wasn't involved in the weekend conversation to look over and get roped into it. He'd heard enough about the buff soccer player who created insurmountable dilemmas in Nicole Fraker's sophomore life.

"Party at Benny's tonight."

"Party at your house, Ben?" Aaron looked at Ben.

"Sure, I guess. Very low key though." Ben had half a carton of milk left and he took another sip.

Aaron poked Sandy, and she looked at and listened to Nicole until Nicole finished her sentence, and then she held up her finger and cut Nicole off. They both looked at Aaron. "Party at Benny's tonight."

"Party at your house, Ben?" Sandy said.

That's what you do in high school. Always ask that confirmation question. Take whatever has just been stated to you and put a question mark at the end of it. Test tomorrow in European history. Test tomorrow in European history? Party at Ben's. Party at Ben's?

"Can I ask Mike?" Nicole crossed her legs and put her elbow on her knee and then her chin in her hand. She leaned towards Ben.

"He's a fuckin' pharmacist's nightmare, Nicole." Ron went back to his Ping-Pong ball. He and Nicole had a thing goin' on and off and he hated it when she got really crazy about other guys. Sure, he'd gotten head from Denise Coler, but that was like eons ago or somethin' to him and Nicole.

"Whatever, Ron. Like you're drug free."

"I am." He was lookin' at that Ping-Pong ball on its way up.

"Right."

"Benny said low key, Nicole." Aaron always played peacekeeper between those two.

Nicole took her head off her hand and she sorta twisted her hand so she could chew on the corner of her pinkie's cuticle. She bit and looked down at it and grabbed hold of it with her teeth again and chomped it again. She musta got it because she stuck her tongue out a little and pulled the tip of it with her fingers, wiped it clean and then flicked the thing at Ron.

Nicole laughed pretty hard at that one.

Ron leaned sideways in his chair to avoid the flyin' piece of skin, and his Ping-Pong ball went crazy and bounced away from him. He got up to chase it.

Ben turned in his chair some and watched Ron go after it, then he turned back to Nicole. "Bring whoever, Nicole. Ron brought that fuckin' stripper to the last party Rachel had." Ben killed his milk, and everybody cracked up.

"Oh, my God, you're so right." Rachel licked her lips and unwrapped a lollipop she had gotten out after she'd done her beauty makeover.

Ron came back over and turned his chair around and sat so the back of it was between his legs. "What the hell's so funny." He thought everyone was appreciatin' his little Ping-Pong run.

"You still get it from Bonnie Morrison?" Aaron had a huge smile on his face. His parents had hooked him up with braces when he was in junior high, and he smiled half the time like he was in a Dentyne commercial because he knew they looked good. His parents weren't from money or anything, but his dad had a foreman job at one of the leather mills in town and his mom worked in a lawyer's office doin' somethin', so they could take a trip to Florida in the spring and buy their kid braces when they had to.

"Who?" Ron held his Ping-Pong ball up ready to bounce it.

"The stripper chic." Rachel stuck her Tootsie Pop in her mouth.

Everybody at the table laughed, except Ron. He was still holdin' up his Ping-Pong ball and his face was like Huh? Then it was like somebody flicked the TV on or the toast popped up or the alarm clock just blasted music on, and he smiled. "Shut the fuck up." He started with the Ping-Pong ball again.

Bam, bam, bam and everyone at Ben's table, includin' Ben, turned towards the glass. They were all still laughin' and looked when they heard somebody poundin' on the glass from the hall.

Rich Passellow, yuh know, Number 10, was pressin' his face up against it and his mouth was open and it looked like a big crevice with a lizard's tongue flickin' against it. Derik Brine and Wayne Bowenht were with him, and they came on both sides of him and did the same thing.

Everyone at the table saw them and laughed. The girls were like "Eww" and "That's mad-ass nasty," but they were laughin' too.

Ben laughed but he stopped a while before everyone else did, and squeezed his empty milk carton. Rich Passellow was kind of a wise-ass. He was funny, but he was a wise-ass.

The three of 'em brought their faces from the glass, and Ron signaled 'em to come around and come in.

"Passell's a freak," Sandy said. She looked at Rachel. "Can I get a licka that?"

Rachel took the lollipop from where she had stuck it inside

her cheek and handed it to Sandy, and Sandy started to lick it.

Rich and Derik and Wayne had went down the hall and then went around the corner and came through the double doors into the lunchroom. They came up to the table. Ben turned some to like acknowledge that they were there because he was in his wheelchair and his back was to 'em. Rich and the other guys got chairs from an empty table and pulled 'em up around where everyone was sittin'.

Rich patted Ben's back and sat his chair next to him. "What's up?" He addressed the whole table.

"Hey, Passell."

"What's going on?"

Derik and Wayne found some empty space too or everybody shifted their chair a little so they all could fit.

"Hey."

"What's up."

Nobody uses hi.

"You guys need serious help." Sandy passed the grape lollipop back to Rachel.

The three of 'em laughed.

"Look at the fuckin' window, it's covered with slobber."

Everyone looked back at the glass when Rob said that and the thing had three wet, breathed-on marks on it. They all laughed.

"You guys were at Wayne's?" Ron couldn't stop with the friggin' Ping-Pong ball. He pushed his chair back a little more so he had room and started up again.

Derik was the closest one to him, so he answered. "Yeah, dude, it's like 60 out there. You would not believe it."

The first warning bell rang.

"Is that the first bell?" Wayne asked.

Somebody nodded.

"Where's the beer tonight? Rachel's." Rich Passellow loved to party. He looked at Rachel.

She took the lollipop out of her mouth, and pointed with it. "Benny's."

"Niiice." Rich put his hand up to hi-five Ben.

Ben gave him one. "Cases, Passell. No keg." Whatever party went on, Rich Passellow always felt like he had to round up a keg or two. He was the one who always hooked up the beer.

"Oh, shit, Passy, look quick." Derik jerked his head toward the hallway.

Rich took his arm down and looked out to the hall. So did everyone else.

The warning bell had sent the little swarm of electrons on the move. Again. Some kids were startin' to make their move. The warning bell had the Pavlovian effect on some of 'em. The closer it got to sixth period, the more of 'em would appear and the faster they would move.

But Derik wasn't pointin' at just anyone.

Jamie had come through the back door like he always did. He had to pass through the main hall to get to his locker and he passed the lunchroom on his way. *Midsummer Night's Dream* was small enough and he had stuck it in the back pocket of his jeans. He walked past the lunchroom.

Yuh know when you feel a buncha people watchin' you, and you turn your head? Jamie was walkin' past the glass and he turned his head. He saw the table full of kids lookin' at him. He saw Ben front and center stage.

Ben saw him see him. He sorta tipped his head forward.

Jamie just sorta looked away or down or somethin'. There were like ten people watchin' him go by. He just kept walkin' and turned the corner away from the lunchroom and to the side hall his locker was in.

"It's that kid." Rich had a big smile on his face and he looked at Derik.

Wayne wanted in on the inside joke. "You guys. The other day, me and Passellow and Derik did a liquid lunch." He was addressin' the group. "We were in Danny Skinner's car, and Skinner was bein' a complete psycho like he always is and he sent that kid flyin' for a snow bank." He was laughin'.

"Really?" One of the audience members answered. Confirmation call.

"We were on Rea, leavin' for the sandpits, and Passy unrolled his window and nearly corked him in the head with a Bud bottle and when Danny swerved at him, he flew, you guys." Wayne stretched his arms up like he was divin'.

"Jay-may."

"That's pretty funny."

"Danny Skinner's an idiot."

Derik and Rich Passellow and Wayne were laughin' like they had just thought of a funny part of a movie that no one else at the table had seen.

Everyone else smiled or laughed a little. Yuh know, tryin' to appreciate it, and they did, just not as much as the guys who were actually there. Everyone except Ben.

The second bell rang.

"I gotta go." Ben picked up his garbage and his crushed milk carton, and he started to back his wheelchair away from the table.

"What's up, Benny? You got time." Ron finally was puttin' his Ping-Pong ball in the front pocket of his shirt.

The guys were still laughin', but they cut it short when they noticed Ben pullin' away.

"Naw, I need to finish that Course II homework before class."

"What time tonight, Benjamin?" All about confirmation. Rich was askin'. But someone else, probably Rob, woulda if he hadn't.

"Whenever." Ben had to set his crumpled-up bag on his lap because he couldn't really maneuver with it in his hand. He still had his milk carton in his other, that was small enough not to deal with. He started towards the line of plastic garbage pails.

"Yuh want some help, Ben?" Aaron asked.

"No thanks. Later guys." Ben was movin' away from 'em now.

"Is he okay?" Nicole asked. Pull the possible drama alarm.

"Ben's overly sensitive, he doesn't like it when we bust on people," Rich thought he was the psychologist, "he's done that before. Gotten all uptight when we were just fuckin' around."

"Man, we got loaded though."

"What time is everyone goin' over to Ben's?"

"Nine?"

"What time is the beer gettin' there?"

Some of 'em started standin'. Gettin' ready to go.

"You gettin' a keg, Passy?"

"Ben would kill you."

Passy just smiled.

Chapter Eleven

THE HALL that Jamie's locker was in was like a side street. A dead-end side street. There were like only ten or twelve or fifteen other lockers down it and no one really came down the hall unless you had a locker there or you were goin' to the German classroom. And there were no German classes in the afternoon, so there wasn't anybody down it when Jamie got there.

Even though the heat was blastin' from a vent in the ceiling, the hall seemed almost chilly because the sun was a different kinda heat, and Jamie got goose bumps on his arms.

He walked up to his locker and put his hand on his lock.

It was one of those combination padlocks that you bought for three-fifty at the beginnin' of your junior high years and hoped you didn't lose it or get it stolen or forget your com over the summer. But you always did forget it or lose it or somethin', and you ended up buyin' at least two or three before you graduated.

You know how it goes, turn the knob a couple of times to

clear it.

Jamie used his thumb.

Turn it right. First number.

One complete turn left, past your second number.

Then land on your second number.

Then right again to your last number. And, voilà…

Jamie tugged at the lock. Okay. He gave the knob another couple of random spins. First number, one past, second number, third number and.

He pulled again and the lock didn't open. Goddamn it.

Traffic was gettin' noisier and heavier. Sixth period settin' in. A couple people who had lockers in Jamie's hall turned in to get their books. He looked up at 'em.

"Hey."

"Hey."

He looked back down at his lock. He took his other hand and held it and used his other hand to do the turnin'. Thumb and pointer finger—more precision. Maybe he wasn't exactly on the numbers. Locks sometimes won't open unless you hit the numbers exactly on their little lines.

Okay. He was even bent over a little. Random spins. 25. He stopped on the thick long line. Past 33, one complete turn. On 33. 33 didn't have a thick long line. Short and thin 33. Last number 11. Another short thin line. He lined the mark up with 11's short thin line and pulled.

"Sonofabitch." Jamie looked from his lock to the two girls that had come down the hall. One of the girls had a locker and she had hers open and was gettin' some books out. She had perfectly covered textbooks, like she had given them all new grocery paper bag covers over Christmas break or somethin'. She had label maker stickers on 'em too. Red strips with bumpy white letters.

They were lookin' at him when he said that.

"Hey." Jamie sorta smiled a quick smile.

"Hey."

He sorta just pulled at the lock again and spun the dial until the girl had finished gettin' her books and the two of them had left. He didn't really know them. That girl had been in his homeroom and had a locker a few feet down from him since seventh grade and that's as far as their conversation had ever gotten. "Hey." "Hey." Jamie knew why too. He was the type of guy who said "Sonofabitch" when he couldn't get his locker open and she was the type of girl who recovered her books over Christmas break.

He kneeled on one knee. His eyes were closer to the lock. And he turned with the turns of a surgeon.

25. Exactly 25.

33. Exactly 33.

Short turn to 11. He slowed down. Exactly 11.

He pulled.

"What the fuck?"

"What's up?"

Jamie turned his head quick. He still had a hand on the lock and was on one knee.

Ben was wheelin' himself closer. "Sorry, didn't mean to startle yuh."

"You didn't." Jamie didn't wanna talk to Ben. He thought of Ben's little head nod hello.

Ben looked around the short hall like he'd never been down it or somethin'. Or like he had just wheeled into Jamie's house.

Jamie looked back at his lock. He tried again. He was no more accurate or off than he had been the first ten times. He pulled. No click. He stood up, ready to kick the goddamn thing.

Ben looked back at Jamie when he stood. "You can't get your lock?"

"No. I've only tried like six times."

"Let me give it a shot." Ben put his hands on his wheels.

Jamie took a second. Then he stepped out of the way, so Ben could get closer.

"What's the com?" Ben maneuvered himself so he was in front of Jamie's locker and he put the lock in his hands.

Jamie was behind him. He looked down at the padded back of Ben's chair.

Mercury-mover.

"25-33-11." He looked over Ben's shoulder.

Ben did the erase turns. 25. 33. 11. He pulled.

Click.

Ben took his hands from the lock, and the round part dangled from the arch that looped through the locker.

Ben looked over his shoulder up at Jamie. "These things are pains in the asses. Mine never opens either." He put his hands back on his wheels.

Jamie stepped back so Ben could pull out.

Ben backed up and turned his chair a little toward Jamie.

"Thanks."

"Sure." There was another second when Ben felt like lookin' around the hall like he should compliment Jamie on it or somethin'. "Listen."

Jamie was steppin' towards his locker.

"Yuh got a study hall this afternoon?"

Jamie slipped the lock from the locker door and opened it and then put the lock back in the slot it hung from. He turned to face Ben. "Tuesday Thursday week?"

(Gym was a one-credit course at C.F.H.S., so yuh had it two times a week and every other Friday. It was a real pain in the ass to remember what week you were on—a T Th week or a M W week—and who had gym that Friday.)

Ben shifted his eyes to the ceiling a second and then nodded.

"Yeah, I got gym today." Jamie turned and opened the locker door all the way. All his books were at the bottom and he squatted down to get at 'em.

"What period?"

"Last."

"I got a study hall. You feel like helpin' me do some kayaking?"

Ben had moved to the side of Jamie, and Jamie looked at him. "Kayaking?"

"Yeah, Coach Martin lets me do it once in a while in the pool. I need some help with it though, so I could maybe see if he'll let you…come in, if yuh want."

"I dunno, Ben." Jamie started to see where his Social Studies book was.

"What are you guys doin' in gym?"

Jamie found his book and pulled it out. "Monster ball tourney."

They sat there and then they cracked up.

"That sucks."

"Yeah it does."

"So help me with the kayak."

"Martin's not gonna go for it."

"Sure he will. Trust me on it."

Jamie grabbed his notebooks and his Course II book. He had math in the afternoon too, not in Ben's class though. He got all his crap and a pen and stood up.

Ben backed his chair up a little.

Jamie held his books under his arm and stuck his pen through the spiral of one of his notebooks and banged the locker door shut with his other free hand. He snapped the lock shut, and looked at Ben. "All right."

"You wanna then?"

"Yeah, okay."

"I'll tell Martin before your class. Then when you get there just stop in his office so he doesn't mark you absent, and come to the pool."

"All right, I'll meet yuh there."

"I'll be in the locker room." The last warning bell rang while Ben was talkin' and he looked at his watch. "Shit, I gotta get my books." He started to run his wheels. "See yuh eighth."

"See yuh."

Ben was like a slow movin' vehicle pullin' into heavy traffic. People were flyin' down the hall. But he held his own.

Jamie looked down at his books, makin' sure he had what he needed.

Another kid came down the hall to get into his locker.

"Hey."

"Hey."

Jamie started to head out of the hall and behind him he heard the kid click his lock open. He stopped short, and felt his back pocket with his hand. He just shook his head and then walked out into the swarm of kids.

Chapter Twelve

BEN HAD been right. Jamie had walked into Mr. Martin's office and Mr. Martin—or Coach Martin, whatever yuh wanted to call him—was the one to say it. Jamie was gonna be like, "Mr. Martin, I'm not sure if Ben Callihan told you or not—" and whatever, but Martin was on top of it. He was sittin' with his legs stretched up onto his desk. His feet were crossed and his Nikes were like a normal teacher's elbows. They were right at home on the mound of papers and shit that was all over his desk. He was talkin' a *Sports Illustrated* article with one of the other coaches when Jamie came in.

There were two doors. One goin' into the gym, the other comin' from the boys' locker room. (Not the one Ben was in, the pool had a separate changin' room.) Jamie came from the boys' locker room. Dirty socks, moldy tiles, sweaty armpits from the fifties to today embedded in the walls and benches. Everything echoed in there and guys were changin' and some of 'em were goin' nuts already.

The other coach was leanin' against a filing cabinet and sorta moved so Jamie could come in the office. Tight squeeze in there. Desk, filing cabinet, two coaches and a kid pretty much did it for a gym teacher's office. Couple of those pennant things on the wall and a trophy or two on top of the cabinet, too. Martin took his feet off the desk and was movin' for his attendance *slash* grade book as soon as he saw Jamie. Gym class is all about attendance and gettin' dressed. That's how Jamie pulled a 90 in gym, it sure as hell wasn't about skill or enthusiasm, at least not when it came to him, anyway.

"Augustus Augey Auger, you're kayakin' with Callihan the Man today," Martin had said to him. Two things about gym teachers. They're always loud. On the gym floor, in the hall, in their office, even if you see 'em in the grocery store. Loud talkers. And two, they've always got a nickname for yuh. Augustus Augey Auger. Callihan the Man. Doesn't matter if you suck at gym or you're in a wheelchair or if you're the all-star, you got a nickname freshman year.

Martin opened his book, put a check mark in it. "Augey, suit up in there, I'll be over to look in on you guys" and that was it.

Jamie walked into the room the pool was in through the double doors at the opposite end from the changin' rooms. It was empty. They had already done their swimming section of gym class, and none of the elementary schools came to use it this late in the day. The room was huge, well, it had to be, there was a huge in-ground pool in it. But the ceiling was way high too and like half of it was clear plastic or somethin'. Solar energy, who knows. Muggy too. Fake muggy. Heaters blastin' heat and the moisture from the water. The chlorine could knock yuh on your ass, too.

Jamie walked the length of the pool. The surface of the water was calm but it still sloshed steady over the edges and onto the floor. It poured into the grates that went all around it. And that's mostly what you could hear in there. Talk about echo in there too. Slosh...drain...slosh...drain.

Jamie set his books on the front row of the metal bleachers. No one was comin' in, so they'd be all right there.

He walked into the boys' locker room. "Ben?"

"In here."

Jamie grabbed one of the tight-ass blue bathing suits from the 28-30-32 "clean rack" shelf and walked the rest of the way into the room.

It was divided into three sections of lockers and Ben was in front of the first one. He had parked his wheelchair and taken his clothes off. They were in a pile on a bench beside him. He was just pullin' a bathing suit on when Jamie came around the corner. Ben was a pretty muscular kid, his legs were skinnier and all, but his chest and arms were pretty big for a kid his age. Because he used them so much. He sorta wobbled back and forth in his seat until the suit was up over his waist. He looked up. "You're puttin' a swimsuit on?" He pulled on the string of his own suit and tied it.

"Martin said he's comin' over to check on us."

"Oh, because I was gonna say all you really gotta do is get the boat for me and help me in it." Ben started to pull his wheelchair away from the locker section. "No swimmin' involved—unless I start to drown or somethin'. Picture that. The fuckin' boat tippin' over and I'm upside down in it thrashin' around like I'm in some movie or somethin'." That image really seemed to crack him up because he let out a good couple laughs after he said it.

Jamie sorta laughed too even though he didn't really get as much of a kick out of the thought as Ben did. He moved a little to the side, so Ben could get through.

Ben noticed Jamie couldn't really appreciate the humor. "Naw, I wear a lifejacket anyway. You aren't gonna have to jump in after me or anything." He started to wheel in the same direction Jamie had just come from. "There's a room on the other side of the pool where they keep all that crap and the kayak—I'll be in there diggin' out a vest."

"Okay." Jamie walked into the section and tossed his suit on the bench. He kicked off his sneakers beside Ben's stuff and took off the rest of his clothes. Flannel, T-shirt, socks, jeans, underwear. He was butt-ass naked for a second. Big difference when there wasn't twenty other guys all standin' around with towels dryin' their asses, and their balls hangin' out. Some guys didn't care, they were really into it, yuh know, showin' off their body and stuff. It didn't really bother Jamie to get naked, he didn't get a charge out of it in the locker room like some guys did, but he wasn't ultra-shy either. When you had swimming for a couple of weeks for class, didn't matter who you were, whoever the upper-classman was that was helpin' out made everybody— jock or no jock—toss his swimsuit into a big plastic bag and you had to stand there naked while he handed everyone a towel. You didn't take care of your bathing suit, you didn't get a towel. You stood there in this five by five space after you got out of the shower with a buncha naked guys waitin' to get a towel handed

124

to yuh. Bein' forced to stand there naked was a different story. But you sucked it up, yuh know. There was this one kid in Jamie's freshman year that refused to do it, not not take care of his bathing suit, but he refused to take it off before he got his towel, and the kid who was handin' them out was screamin' at him. The kid was still standin' there dripping wet when the period had ended and everybody else was leavin'. Jamie remembered walkin' past the huge mirror on the way out the door and seein' that kid in it still standin' there. Scrawny, little kid, his hair all flat and pasted to his head. And the senior, standin' sorta beside him, blockin' his way, all red in the face from screamin' at him, and not lettin' him go by to his locker and clothes until he got naked. Martin was somewhere in his gym office or somethin'. Some of the guys who knew the senior, Jamie didn't know the guy's name, they had tried to get him to quit it, yuh know, leave the kid alone, but he wouldn't let up on him. Sissy. Fairy. Faggot. Shit like that.

Jamie pulled the nylon skimpy—that's what it reminded him of—over him. He prayed the washman or woman or whoever had done their job. People got crabs from shit like that. Athlete's Feet lived and breathed on the floors of locker rooms, too. He hadn't fallen victim to either of 'em, and didn't plan on it any time soon.

He tied the drawstring and left. He wasn't gonna bother showerin' before he got in like they usually made yuh do. He walked out into the pool area and walked the short end with the diving board and deep water. They used to dive for pennies when they were in elementary school and they got bused up to swim for like an hour a day for three weeks in the school year. You liked shit like that when you were a kid, missin' school time, swimmin', divin' in twelve feet of water for pennies. The water pressure was crazy on your head and when you made it down there you'd be outa breath and the penny would never be where you reached for it because the water warped it. Everybody'd be watchin' and you'd look like a total loser if you came up empty-handed. It was worth it though back then.

The storeroom door was open and Jamie could hear Ben rummagin' around. He walked in and the place looked like anybody's storeroom. It was a glorified closet and a mess. Buoys, balls, Styrofoam float boards all over. Even some diving blocks—spare ones, who knows. A couple kayaks and paddles, either hangin' off the wall or propped up against it. There were lifejackets but they were in a crate buried beneath a pile of shit.

Ben had about a square foot to move his wheelchair around in, and he was pullin' a string of buoys off the top of the crate when Jamie walked in. He looked at him. "Blue's definitely your color."

"Yuh think so?" Jamie moved to take the string of buoys. "Here, I'll take 'em." He wadded them up some and set 'em over on a stack of float boards.

Ben practically lifted himself out of his chair. He stretched and reached into the crate and pulled out a lifejacket. Kids' size. He dropped it back in and pulled out another that looked big enough. They were the kind that were orange, this one was faded as hell from all the chlorine, and had the pad in back, and a couple down the front. Straps, the whole nine yards, you know. Ben landed back in his chair and had the jacket on his lap. "All right, I'm gonna get the hell outa here so you have room to get the boat." He started to turn himself around in the space, and Jamie kicked a couple of stray bathing caps out of his way.

"Either of 'em?" Jamie looked at the one hangin' on the wall and the one on the other side of the room leanin' against the wall.

"Naw, the one with the flat bottom, if yuh could, it's less tippy."

Jamie rummaged some himself, workin' his way between the pile of float boards and a diving block that had one of those long handled save your life rods leanin' across it. He moved it—the rod thingy—because it blocked his way, and he propped it against the wall. He got his hands on the one kayak Ben was talkin' about and pulled it towards him. It was sorta standin' on its end and he lifted. The thing wasn't too heavy, maybe 50 or 60 pounds, it was just a matter of gettin' it outa there without knockin' a buncha shit over. Jamie stepped toward the door and got a better grip on it. He lifted it completely off the floor and brought it over his head and bent and rested it on his back the best he could. He could feel the end behind him bangin' into whatever was there. He walked out with it over him like a turtle with a shell that's too big for him. He turned it over and set it by the edge of the pool. "Jesus."

Ben had his life vest on and wheeled closer to Jamie and the kayak. "Fun, right?"

"They keep that pretty straightened up in there." Jamie looked back towards the room.

"Tell me about it. And I'm a sorry dude to ask yuh for one more thing, but could you grab me a paddle?"

"Oh. Yeah. I think I saw one behind the door." Jamie went back in, and there were two crisscrossed and leanin' against the wall behind the door. Jamie stepped between four or five bags of bathing suits and bathing caps and got the double-ended oar paddle thing.

When Jamie came out, Ben had flipped one arm of his chair so it flopped loose out and he had lined and angled his chair up by the seat of the boat. He looked to Jamie. He was all about business. "Thanks. Now if you can just steady this I should be able to get in it." He nodded towards the kayak.

Jamie set the paddle down and he bent beside the end of the boat just behind the seat and tightened both his hands on it.

Ben lifted his one leg and then his other so his feet were in the hole. He made sure with his hands that his brakes were locked on his wheels, and he lifted and slid himself down at the same time. He sorta directed his legs in the hole on the way down and lowered himself in. He got comfortable, straightened his legs better, pushed them a little further in the hole and rocked a little until he was sittin' there like he wanted to be.

He was grinnin' like he just got strapped onto some crazy-ass ride at The Great Escape. (That's an amusement park upstate.) He looked at Jamie.

Jamie had loosened his grip some but he was still there beside the boat.

"Okay, all you gotta do is hand me that paddle and then shove me in."

Jamie stood up and got the paddle and handed it to Ben. Then he got on the end of the kayak that was away from the water and he dragged the thing so its front end would go straight into the pool. He bent down and pushed, and that was it. The bottom of the kayak sorta whooshed across the floor and sent an echo when it did, and before it was all the way slid into the water, Ben was already paddling.

"Whoa-whoo." Ben worked the paddle like a champ. You could tell he'd done it a lot before. He turned himself to face Jamie. "Thanks, man. What a pain in the ass, right."

"Naw, it wasn't bad." Jamie sorta had his thumbs tucked in the top of his suit and his hands on his waist. He walked to the edge of the pool and stuck his toes in.

"You gettin' in?" Ben was usin' his paddle and rockin' the kayak forward and backwards.

"Yeah. It's always that first gettin' wet part though." He dipped his foot a little more in the water.

Ben brought the one end of his paddle across the water, and a splash covered Jamie.

Jamie stepped back like he'd just gotten hit with a water balloon or somethin'.

Ben was laughin' hard. "Man, I didn't mean to get you that bad."

Jamie was wet, and he just looked down at himself and ran the two steps to the pool. He cannonballed in as close to Ben as he could.

Ben, on instinct, was tryin' to paddle away, but he didn't make it. He got soaked.

Jamie came to the surface and the two of 'em splashed the shit out of one another like they were in one of their own backyards and somebody woulda came out and said, "Stop it, you're gonna splash all the water out of the pool." Parents always worry that their kids are gonna splash all the water out of the pool.

They were goin' ape-shit, and they heard a whistle blow. Loud. Twice. It didn't really register with either of 'em the first time they heard it. When they stopped and looked the second time, Coach Martin was standin' there on the other side of the pool by the door Jamie had first come through. His whistle was still in his mouth and his hands were on his hips.

He let the whistle drop out of his mouth. It was tied to a string around his neck. "Callihan, Auger. I want you doin' laps, yuh got it." No nicknames, he was pissed.

"Yes, sir, Coach." Ben yelled back.

Martin just stood there a second, and gym teachers don't stay pissed long, the burnout rate would be too high. "I'll be back in before the period's over and you guys better be zippin' around the water like there's a crowd yellin' in the bleachers." He cupped his hands around his mouth. "Cal-i-han-the-Man. Aug-ie-Aug-er." Yuh know, like pronouncin' every syllable like a crowd was chantin'. "Cal-i-han-the-Man. Aug-ie-Aug-er." He just dropped his hands from his mouth and turned to walk out, like what he just did was totally normal behavior. "I'll be back in later, guys." He didn't turn around when he yelled that. He just walked out the door.

Jamie was sorta treadin' water the whole time, and him and Ben looked at each other when Martin left. They cracked up.

"He's a fuckin' number."

"Yeah, he is."

They laughed at it, but at the same time they both sorta started to play gym. Ben paddled and started to circle the pool. Jamie dove underwater one more time and when he came up he was doin' the long length of the pool freestyle.

That's what they did most of the period. Jamie went from freestyle to breaststroke after maybe like three laps and Ben slowed his pace some, too. But they were sorta into what they were doin'. The water was slappin' a littler harder against the edges of the pool from them, and the echo was a quiet echo like nobody was in there, and it was kinda cool.

Jamie had lost count what lap he was on, not like he had done fifty of them or somethin', but he really stopped thinkin' about it and just swam, yuh know. The water was warm and he was just swimmin'. He'd been stayin' towards the middle of the pool, so he was outa Ben's way. When he did stop and look up to the clock above the bleachers, the period was almost over.

He looked down and his books were still there. Not like they would've gotten up and walked away or anyone had even been in there with him and Ben, but he saw 'em sittin' there.

He looked around, and Ben was at the diving board end. He was paddlin' really steady. Long, easy paddling, but pushin' himself along, yuh know. He didn't see Jamie had stopped and looked, and it was one of those things where if he had, he would have—it woulda been like he woulda had that feelin' you get when you're doin' your job and you're all into it and then someone you sorta know walks in and sees you doin' your thing when they've never seen you do it before. And it's like if you have to wear a uniform or work clothes or somethin' and you're really into it, you're like naked in front of 'em or somethin' and they've just looked straight at you.

Maybe Ben wouldn't have felt that way. But Jamie would have.

Jamie breaststroked to the side of the pool about where he

had launched Ben forty minutes ago. He didn't get out of the water when he got there, he sorta put his back to the wall and stretched his arms across the edge, like he was sittin' in a hot tub or somethin'. He started to kick his feet, not crazy or anything, just below the surface of the water. Like he was doin' some sorta cool down exercise on an exercise show without knowin' he was.

Ben rounded the corner down by the diving boards, and he kept his pace until Jamie came into his line of vision. He slowed down and looked up at the clock. He came closer to Jamie and he used his paddle like you'd use your brakes on your bike. He circled out a little bit and pointed the nose of the kayak at the wall Jamie was leanin' against, then he dug into the water with the paddle like he was gonna oar himself onto shore. The kayak moved forward and Ben anchored a foot or two of its front on the edge of the pool a couple feet from Jamie.

Jamie watched him. The kid knew what he was doin' with the thing.

He laid his paddle across his lap and splashed some water on his face. "ESPN move."

"No kiddin', Ben. You got the moves with that thing."

Ben smiled. "I love doin' shit like this. You were gettin' a little Olympic, too, though."

Jamie smiled too. Sounds just like one big smilin' fest. But seriously, both of 'em were still breathin' pretty hard and there was just that feeling after you do somethin' like that and you're all high on adrenaline or somethin'. It's a cool feeling, and they both had it. "I was gettin' into it, to be honest."

"Yeah. Me too." Ben sorta laughed. Then he looked up at the time clock above the storage room.

Jamie looked across the pool and his eyes went up to the real clock on that wall again.

Ben's kayak sorta rocked in the water. All you heard for a second was the water sloshin' in the grates.

"You'd think—" "Don't yuh wish—"

"Sorry, go ahead."

Ben rolled the bar of his paddle a couple times across the top of his kayak. "No, go ahead. What were you gonna say?"

Jamie brought his feet just as close to the surface as he could without breakin' it. "Ah, I was just gonna say don't you wish every period went this fast?"

"Man, I totally do. Some classes you feel like you're in forever."

"Hey, thanks for gettin' me outa monster ball."

Ben sorta waved his hand. "No problem. I didn't think you'd have to do anything though."

"Didn't matter. This was kinda cool."

"Sometimes Passellow or Dychett help me, but they just hang out." Ben picked up his paddle and looked at the curves where you put your hands. "I guess because they got study hall this period and not gym."

Jamie's toes broke the surface, and he looked towards the starting blocks. Every one was a different color and all of 'em had a racing stripe across their sides.

Ben looked back over at him. "But whatever…"

The water was more like the ocean the way it washed over its edges.

"Hey, what are yuh doin' tonight?"

Jamie looked back to Ben.

Ben was sittin' there with the paddle in his hands.

"I dunno know. I gotta work."

"Really, where do you work?"

Jamie took one of his arms from the side of the pool, and he still attached the other one on it. He was still facin' Ben, but he had moved so he could tread water. Slow, yuh know, so you don't start to get cold. "My mom owns a feedstore. I help her out with it."

"Oh yeah?" Ben started to pretend to paddle like he was workin' hard at it. "Okay. Augers'. Right. That's cool."

"It's all right."

"What's your dad do? Are they split?"

"Naw..." Jamie locked his arm a little better on the side of the pool. "He died a couple years ago."

Ben stopped fake paddlin'. "Really. I'm sorry."

"Thanks." Jamie kinda nodded. "What do your folks do?"

"My mom works at a doctor's office. And my dad teaches English—go figure—for Taymum High."

Jamie smiled. "Yeah, how'd you do on that essay you rewrote?"

Ben laid the paddle back down and slanted his hands towards each other and put 'em together at his fingertips. He made a triangle with his arms and smiled.

"Nice."

"Yeah, man, you helped me out with that one big time."

"Cool, anytime."

"My dad sure as hell thought it was cool—hey listen, my folks aren't gonna be home tonight. I was gonna say if you weren't doin' anything, I'm havin' a party."

"Really."

"Yeah, if you feel like it, it's 1556 Frede Street. Right down from the elementary school."

"Oh, okay." Jamie brought his other arm to the side of the pool and lifted himself outa the water. He turned and sat on the edge. He mussed his hair up. It was sorta dryin' flat and stickin' to his head. "I sorta had plans but maybe."

"Yeah? Maybe try to make it. We'll drink some brews and I'll get the Dylan discs out for yuh." Ben looked over his shoulder to the clock. "Martin never came back."

Jamie looked up at the clock, too. "Shit, we better get this thing put back. I don't wanna miss my bus."

When you take the bus, whether you're in school or wherever you're takin' one, your life revolves around trying not to miss it.

Jamie stood up and pulled the kayak and Ben further onto the floor. Ben pulled off his lifejacket, and they were all about business…

◆ ✦ ◆

Helpin' Ben out of the kayak wasn't that hard.

Jamie let the hot water from the shower run over his hair. You took a shower even if they didn't make you because you were just about radioactive with chlorine when you got done swimmin' in the high school pool.

Ben had kinda propped himself on the back of the hole and Jamie swung the wheelchair around beside him. Ben had Jamie set it sorta at an angle so it was easier for him to get in, and Ben checked the locks on the wheels. Jamie got behind him and put his hands under Ben's arms. It was sorta on the count of three, and Jamie lifted and Ben pushed himself up. Ben was in it, gettin' comfortable, positionin' his legs with his hands, liftin' 'em so they weren't all twisted up. That was it. Then him and Ben took care of the other stuff. Puttin' the paddle and life vest and kayak away.

Jamie heard the change bell buzz. It was a buzzer when you were in the pool, not a bell. He turned off the shower, and tracked water into the locker room. He went past the section that him and Ben had put their stuff to get himself a towel. He walked past Ben's wheelchair. When he did, it dawned on him why Ben had to park on the outside of their section—because there wasn't enough room for his chair between the lockers and the bench.

Ben had gotten out of his chair though to get dressed, and he had slid himself a ways on the bench and was buttonin' his jeans—yeah, he wore button flies. He looked at Jamie when he walked by. "Hey, I got yuh one." He buttoned his top button and tossed a folded white towel that was sittin' next to him on the bench.

"Thanks." Jamie wiped his face off and walked into the locker section.

"So you gottta take the bus." Ben looked at his watch and then grabbed his shirt from the bench where he had left it.

"Yeah. What time is it?"

"Twenty-nine after, you got a few minutes." Ben had a button down, and he swung it over his shoulders and stuck his arms through.

"How 'bout you?" Jamie was towel dryin' his hair.

"I take that van-bus with the lift. It can be a drag sometimes.

136

You remember a couple weeks ago or whenever that was." Ben started to button his shirt. He started at the top so he didn't get to the bottom and see that he had missed a button and it was all crooked.

"Yeah." Jamie took his towel and did his chest and under his arms and part of his back. He always missed some of his back.

"I turn sixteen this summer though, and my parents are thinkin' about gettin' hand gears for the car, so maybe I'll get my permit."

"That's cool." Jamie wiped his legs and feet and dropped the towel on the floor and stood on it. He pushed his suit down and let it drop around his ankles. He stepped out of it. His crap was in a locker on the side to Ben's back. He opened it and pulled out his underwear. He pulled his jeans out too and he set 'em on the bench, kinda beside where Ben was sittin'. He started puttin' on his underwear and he heard somethin' clunk on the floor.

Ben looked down beside him. "You dropped somethin'." He leaned over, kinda holdin' himself with his one arm so he wouldn't fall off the bench, and he reached down to the floor with his other arm.

Jamie pulled his underwear all the way on and kinda looked over Ben's shoulder. He'd kinda forgotten what he'd stuck in his back pocket. Not really forgotten, but you know how somethin' is there, but it kinda gets shoved outa your mind if other crap is goin' on. He'd done that a couple times today already when it came to that book. He picked up his jeans.

Ben sat back up and looked at the title of the small book he had in his hands. "*A Midsummer Night's Dream.* William Shakespeare." He looked up at Jamie. "Dude, you really are into

English."

"Not really." Jamie pulled his pants on and then sat down on the bench beside Ben but facin' towards his own locker.

Ben handed him the book.

Jamie looked at it in his hand. He looked at the real red cover and the gold letters.

"What?"

Jamie looked at Ben. "Some old guy gave this to me today. You wouldn't believe it." Jamie opened the book and flipped a couple pages. "Really weird."

Ben ran his hands across the top of his head. He forgot a comb, hadn't really planned on gettin' wet today. "Really? What happened?"

"A lotta shit, I guess. But mostly he knew my name and I swear to God there's no way this guy could know my name."

"And he gave you a book?"

"Yeah, that was the weird part of it, too." Jamie set the book beside him and stood up to zip his jeans.

Ben picked it up and opened it.

Jamie scratched his shoulder. "My dad loved that book since he was a kid, and..."

Ben looked up. He had the opened book on his lap. "And?"

"And it was like this guy already knew that."

"So maybe he knew your dad or somethin', and you just never knew him."

"Yeah, I guess." Jamie reached in the locker for his T-shirt. "But it was like—it was like some sorta...it wasn't creepy or anything, but it was like it was some sorta déjà vu or somethin'." He stuck his hands in the T-shirt and found its tag and turned the back so the back was in back, and he pulled the thing over his head. "Well, I don't even know exactly what déjà vu means but you know what I mean."

"Yeah. I totally do. I've had that feeling before, like dream state or somethin'. I'm not kiddin', now that you said that— today," Ben closed the book and set it beside him and reached for one of his sneakers beside him. He had put them on the bench too with his clothes. He already had his socks on and he started to do his sneaker. "Before Martin came in and we were fuckin' around, yuh know." He looked at Jamie.

Jamie had gotten his flannel and was buttonin' a few buttons at the bottom of it. He looked up. "Yeah, when we were goin' ape-shit."

Ben kinda laughed. "Man, I haven't heard that word in a while. Ape-shit."

Jamie sorta laughed, too.

"Yeah, I had that feeling for like a second." He started to tie his sneaker.

Jamie sat down and the book was between them. He reached in his locker and got out a sock and put it on. "Yeah. It lasts for like a second. Exactly. And on top of it, with this guy, I mean—" He got his other sock and started to pull it on. "I dunno, like somethin' tells me I should go back and see him or somethin'."

Ben was just about dressed, too. He had set his other leg across his lap and he was lacing up his other sneaker. "Like a gut feeling."

Jamie got his sneakers out. "Yeah. A gut feeling." He dropped them on the floor and set up his right one and crammed his foot into it. He didn't bother untyin' the strings. He did the same with his left and stood up.

"Then seriously..." Ben had picked up his wet towel and bathing suit and bunched 'em up and put 'em on his lap. He was slidin' down the bench to get back into his wheelchair. The bell rang, well, buzzed in there, and Ben looked at his watch midway there, like he was makin' sure the school had rung it at the right time or somethin'.

Jamie picked up the book and looked over at Ben.

When he had gotten in his chair and got situated, Ben unlocked his brakes and put his hands on his wheels and sorta rocked his chair a couple times forwards and back. Real small, quick rocks. "Seriously, go with it then. I mean, I dunno."

"What?" Jamie stuck the book back in his back pocket.

Ben rocked his chair one more quick rock. He wasn't lookin' at Jamie, but he was sorta lookin' down at his lap, at his wadded up bathing suit and wet towel. "I mighta been a kid, but yuh know the day I got into that car—man, somethin' told me not to. Gut feeling. Whatever. I kicked my dad in the shin before he buckled me in the front seat." He looked up at Jamie and sorta laughed. "Whatever." He kinda tipped his head to the side. "I don't regret it or anything. Yuh know, live with it, right. I mean I wouldn't mind bein' able to take a fuckin' swim once in a while without havin' to worry about sinkin' like a stone, but you deal, yuh know." He played with his thumbnail a second with one of his fingers. "What I'm really sayin' though is you can't ignore that instinct or gut feeling or whatever you wanna call it." He put his hands on his wheels and rocked his chair one more time. "Hallelujah! Amen! Listen to that voice, my brother!" He used a shake of his head for his exclamation point, and that was it. His face changed expressions like that. And he laughed. "Oh shit. I forgot my fuckin' bag." He took the wet stuff he had on his lap, wadded it up a little more and took a shot for the big hamper cart just under the long mirror by the door.

He made it.

Jamie looked under the bench, and Ben's bag was there. He grabbed his swimsuit and towel off the floor and reached down and got it for him. "I got it."

"Thanks." Ben started to turn his wheelchair, just gettin' ready to leave while Jamie got his bag for him.

The bag was half zipped and Jamie went to zip it all the way. He saw Ben's books and notebooks in there. Like his Course II book and crap. And he saw a plastic bag, not like a Ziploc plastic bag but like a hospital medical plastic bag with a long tube connected to it. He looked up quick when he saw that. Ben was in the middle of maneuverin' his chair though, so he didn't see him see. Stuff like that you don't need to see when you first start hangin' out with a guy.

Jamie pulled the zipper the rest of the way shut and walked out of the locker section. He handed the bag to Ben.

Ben had a baby face, he was one of those guys who'd grow some whiskers when he got in college or somethin'. He wasn't wimpy lookin' or anything, he just looked like the same kid who tried to bounce as high as he could on the diving board at the Y. Maybe a couple years older or whatever—and in a wheelchair, but still the same kid.

"Thanks." Ben set the bag on his lap. "Hey, you gotta get your books too, don't yuh?"

"Oh shit, yeah. They're out there."

Ben started to wheel for the door and Jamie was behind him. Jamie saw himself in the mirror, and the thing was high so it only got some of Ben's head. When they got to it there was a door at each end of it. One went out into the hallway and one went back to the pool. Jamie dropped his wet shit into the canvas hamper on wheels.

Ben shifted his chair so he was facin' Jamie. "All right, man. 'Preciate it." He reached his arm out to him.

"Yeah. It was a good time. Take it easy." Jamie shook Ben's hand. Yuh know, not business, firm handshake, but a high school handshake.

"Yeah. You don't want me to wait for yuh?"

"Naw, I'll just go out the other door. My locker's right down that way anyway."

"All right. Catch yuh later then."

"All right. See yuh."

Ben turned his chair back towards the hallway door and Jamie started out the other door to get his books off the bleachers.

"Hey. Jamie."

Jamie turned and Ben was sittin' at the hallway door. He was holdin' it open, and you could hear it was Friday afternoon out there. "Try to make it tonight. 1556 Frede. Around 9—if you can."

"Yeah, thanks. I will."

Ben swung the door open some more and wheeled out.

Jamie walked down the bleachers and he heard the door close. He picked up his books, and looked up at the clock.

Then he walked out the door he had came in.

Chapter Thirteen

———

HIS MOTHER shook the two dice she had left in the plastic cup. She got all into it, puttin' her hand over the cup's mouth and shakin' it to her left and then her right.

"Just roll 'em." He was smilin'.

She was satisfied. She tossed the dice onto the little felty tray that comes with the game. "That's my last roll, right."

They watched the two dice land and roll and stop.

"Yeah. You're screwed." Jamie had the score pad in front of him and the little nubby pencil in his hand.

Mary was workin' on a large straight and she'd rolled a one and a two—both which she already had sittin' up there with a three she had rolled on her second shake.

"No I'm not. I'll take it as my ones."

"You already used your ones."

"All right. I'll use my chance." She started to add the total of the dice.

"You already used your chance too."

"Nooo."

Jamie pushed the pad towards her.

She looked. "Shit. All right. Cross off Yatzee."

Jamie drew an X in the Yatzee slot, and his mom picked up the five dice and put 'em in the cup for him.

"You don't roll for large straights, Mom. I told yuh, you just gotta let 'em happen."

If your family is anything like Jamie's was, it went through game phases. It was Monopoly when he was a kid. His grandma had bought it for him one Christmas and that's all him and his mom and dad did for the whole year. Park Place and the little green hotels, all that crap. His dad was always the cowboy and Jamie was the car and his mom was the hat. Sometimes Jamie and his dad would switch but that was usually how it went. When they did switch, one of 'em would start movin' the piece that they usually were and it got to be a pain, so they didn't switch that much. Then they shifted to cards—as far as games went. His mom taught him 500 Rummy and that was the big thing for a while. Then it was Spit. That's a card game, too. Him and his dad were really into that. Spit championships. Who held the title, who had the belt. It was like Solitary sorta for two and you had to be fast.

Then his dad died and they didn't really play games for a while. Obvious reasons.

But his mom got on a chair one day and opened the cabinet above the coat closet where they kept the photo albums and board games and shit like that and she pulled out Yatzee. Latest craze at the Auger house.

Jamie shook the dice. He wasn't as melodramatic as his

mom was. His Yatzee advice was his annoying tactic. He clunked 'em around and then dumped 'em on the tray.

They looked at 'em.

"Fives."

"Fives."

Jamie moved the two fives to the side of the tray into their holder, and picked up the other three dice and put 'em in the cup.

This was like their tenth game of Yatzee tonight. He never did homework on Friday nights. No matter how much he had. Always Sunday nights. So they'd started playin' after they finished supper and did the dishes. They cleared the kitchen table and were sittin' at one end of it. Farm families or country people always have big tables. There was just Jamie and his mom now, but they had a long table and a big kitchen.

Jamie saw his mom look over at the clock on the stove. He shook the cup and looked over to it too. It was almost 10.

"You're addicted to Lifetime."

"No I'm not." Mary took a sip of soda from her Pepsi can. "Just shake."

"You are to. You love bad Lifetime movies." He dumped the dice.

No fives.

"What's on tonight?" He put the dice back in the cup.

"Nothing, Jamie, it doesn't matter." Mary crossed her legs and started to bounce her foot.

He rattled the dice around. "Mom, I'm not gonna get my feelings hurt or anything if you wanna go watch a movie." He rolled and the dice bounced into the tray. "It's not like we haven't played fifty games tonight already."

They both looked down at the three and the one and the six.

"Shit." Jamie put ten in his five slot. That's bad, you need three of everything for your singles to get your bonus. "You won this one anyway." He had a can of Pepsi sittin' on the table too and he took a swig and killed it.

The digits turned 10 on the stove, and Mary looked at the clock on the wall. Sometimes the clock on the stove was fast, but the one on the wall said 10 too. "You don't care?"

"No, go ahead. I'm ready to go to bed, anyway." He yawned. Word association or somethin'.

His mom helped him put the stuff back in the box, and then lit for the living room. She took her can of Pepsi with her. "Good night."

"Night." Jamie left the game on the table in its box. He dropped his can in the recycle pail and headed upstairs to his bedroom.

His mom was already on the couch when he passed through the hall and she had the lights dim. Movie mode they called it. The TV's color was flashin' up the room though. She always kept it pretty quiet even though Jamie was upstairs.

He took the stairs two at a time.

Tonight on Lifetime. Dramatic pause. *Jacklyn Smith and Tab Hunter are two...*

He was at the top of the stairs and flicked on the upstairs hall lights. He headed for the bathroom—he had to brush his teeth and take a leak before he got in bed.

◆ ✦ ◆

The keg was in the tub. That's where they always end up. Or in the refrigerator with all the racks ripped out and sittin' in the kitchen sink. That's what they always did at Rachel Stappuck's house—put the keg in the refrigerator—because there was never any food in there and the bathroom was upstairs.

But Ben's refrigerator was chocked full of shit. His dad liked to cook. Was into the cooking channel or whatever. So there was always erotic or exotic vegetables or whatever in there along with a ton of leftovers. Ben's bathroom was centrally located too, not like Rachel's. He had a big one-floor house they moved into after the accident, so Ben didn't have to deal with stairs.

There were a lotta people there. People multiply like cancer cells when there's a party in high school. From just the kids at the lunch table which was what, seven or eight or somethin', there was like twenty-five or thirty now.

Some people were standin' in little groups, shootin' the bull, flirtin', whatever. Some of 'em were in the living room watchin' MTV with no volume on—the stereo was on instead. Some of 'em were sittin' at the dining room table and playin' Asshole (which is a card game where you drink a lot). Everybody had the same mission wherever they were. To get all fucked up. They'd only been there since a little after nine, but it doesn't take much when you're fifteen or sixteen. Plus some of 'em smoked up. Yuh know, like weed. All of 'em were drinkin' from cups from Ben's cupboards. Coffee mugs and glasses they used at dinner.

They had gotten a keg—Passellow and his crew—but they hadn't gone the extra buck fifty for plastic cups.

Somebody always plays DJ. Tonight it was Ron Dychett. He was tryin' to score with Nicole who hadn't brought Mike Soccer

Guy because the kid had some other party to go to and gave her the "give me the address and maybe I'll stop by" thing. So Ron was playin' a bunch of *Top 40* crap, Casey Casem shit from Ben's disc collection that his mom listened to, because Nicole loved that shit.

The stereo was in the dining room and it was almost like the lunchroom table had transplanted itself to Ben's dining room table. Clique.

"Your turn."

"I can't play."

"Drink."

"Go Ben."

"Skip Derik." Ben laid down a seven on top of somebody else's seven.

"Derik drink."

Asshole is all about drinkin'.

Ben was pushed up to the table and he wasn't rocked but he was feelin' it. He was pissed about the keg. One. And two, it was his house. Host can never get outa control. Rachel did when she threw parties and somethin' shitty always ended up happenin'. Like broken furniture or people hookin' up in her parents' bed. Crap like that.

"Dychett, get this shit outa here and put in one of my discs."

Ron had his back to the group and he was lookin' at the back of a disc for the songs that were on it. The stereo was so loud that he didn't hear Ben yell to him. Or he didn't wanna hear Ben yell to him.

Derik took his drink and finished his beer. He was drinkin' from a pint glass Ben's parents had picked up at the Celtic

Festival at Hunter Mountain last summer. "I'll tell him, Benny. I gotta get a refill anyway." He pushed his chair back. It was Ben's mom's chair at the dining room table. He pointed at Ben's glass. "You need another."

The glass was about half full. He was pacin' himself. "Naw, I'm good. Thanks."

Derik walked over to Ron on the way to the bathroom. He talked into his ear. Ron nodded and turned around to look at Ben. He had taken the disc out of its case, ready to put it in the player. He had that in one hand, and he gave Ben a thumbs-up with his other hand. He mouthed the words "After this one."

"Drink Benny," Passellow nudged him, and Ben picked up his glass and drank.

✦ ✦ ✦

Friday nights are strange. When you're young all you wanna do is go out. Doesn't matter where, you just think you should be out. Goin' out. The last thing anybody wants to do is to be sittin' home with his mother playin' Yatzee or goin' to bed at 10 o'clock. When you're fifteen, you think you should be out. There's somethin' wrong with yuh if you're not.

When Jamie finished in the bathroom, he hit the light switch in there and then the one in the hall. It was dark and he could just barely hear the dilemmas on the TV. He walked into his room and turned on the lamp by his door and then shut the door behind him.

He had thought about the party at 9 when he was sittin' in the kitchen with his mom. He tried to picture what was goin' on there while his mom was lookin' at the dice she had just rolled and she was tryin' to figure out what to keep and what to throw back in the cup for another shake. And then it was his turn and he marked down whatever she had decided and he kinda forgot about it.

His school clothes were hangin' off the back of his desk chair where he left 'em this afternoon when he got home, and Ben's party hadn't really gone anywhere because when he saw 'em it crawled back outa the back corner of his brain and sorta invaded his chest where things like that like to go when you're fifteen and you don't know where to feel them anywhere else. They'd sit like a dragon in a cave and wait in your head until somethin' went pokin' around—last time bein' the hands of the clock and this time some school clothes tossed over the back of a chair—and then they'd climb down and fill any spare space left over on top of your ribs. There wasn't a hell of a lotta space there, but it'd stretch itself all out and arch its back and spout fire from its nostrils.

Fuck it, let it.

He looked at the stack of books on his desk. Homework in just about every class.

He'd put the book that that guy Angelo had given him on top of 'em. He looked at it sittin' there and he reached to pick it up and then stopped himself.

He sat on the edge of his bed and all of a sudden it was last Friday and the one before that and next Friday and the next one and the next one.

He got undressed. He was gonna sleep in his underwear instead of his long johns because it was still pretty warm outdoors, had gotten a degree or two warmer every day. Really strange

150

because January thaw never lasted that long in Coformon Falls. They still kept a little fire goin' in the wood stove and that made it pretty warm in his room tonight. Besides he couldn't find his long johns. He had to pick up his room sometime in this lifetime.

His blankets and sheet and thick-ass gold-colored bedspread that he'd had since he was about 11 were a tangled mess, so he straightened them out some. Then he flicked on his light on his night stand by his bed and then turned off his other one. He walked the two steps and reached over his school clothes and the back of his chair pushed up to his desk, and picked up the book — *A Midsummer Night's Dream* — and he got in bed.

* ✦ *

Everybody was gettin' loaded. The music had to be turned down some because the Crandles lived next door and they were an old couple. They wouldn't tell on Ben or anything. He'd had parties before and they never seemed to know the difference, but he didn't wanna push his luck. Turned down is still pretty loud when you're fifteen or sixteen though. Besides, the kids watchin' MTV had turned the sound up on that, so noise level hadn't changed all that much. Ben was just makin' himself feel better when he wheeled over and clipped the disc a notch. Dylan had had a shot, and Ronny had stepped down and DJ was random. Somebody had put in one of Ben's dad's discs. It was this Motown compilation you can order off the TV for $19.95. There were a bunch of discs outa their cases on top of the stereo, and Ben didn't bother with 'em. He'd deal with it tomorrow.

Asshole had broken up. Nicole Fraker had hogged the

President position and abused it hardcore. When that happens everyone just gets all whacked, and the game has done its job. Ben had left the table, people were still sittin' around it, but he had to get a refill. He looked into the living room on his way. Kids were smokin' cigarettes and drinkin' beer, and some of 'em were standin' up kinda bouncin' up and down to the video that was on. There was only one light on in there, the one on the end stand by the couch, so the TV was flashin' onto the ceiling and walls. Some kids were sittin' on the couch, lookin' at the TV like it possessed them or they were talkin' like it wasn't even there. A girl and a guy were sittin' real close in Ben's dad's recliner where he read the paper every day after work. The guy moved in to kiss her and she wasn't sure if she was into it yet, so she backed her face up a little and took a sip from the cup she was holdin'. The guy did the same thing, took another drink. Every cup and glass musta been in use. The cupboards had to be empty. There were unclaimed ones sittin' around. Cups Ben had never seen before, that's how far back in the cabinet kids had went. Some of 'em empty or half full. He'd have to get them later too.

Most everybody was hangin' out in the dining room or living room and Ben passed a couple stray people on his way down the hall to the bathroom.

"What's up Ben."

"Cool party, Benny."

"Yuh got that Ben or yuh want some help?"

Handshakes or hi-fives.

He was pretty buzzed. Feelin' it. Nicole had demanded everyone with more than five cards in their hand had to chug their beers, you could do that when you were president. Ben was one of them and that seemed to be the glass that pushed him from sober host to sloppy drunk. He had his glass tucked beside one of his legs and the arm of the wheelchair. He turned into the bathroom and kinda caught his wheel on the door frame. He backed his chair up and ran his fingers down the wood. He was makin' sure he didn't take a chunk out of it or somethin'. That would be somethin' his mom would notice right off. He wheeled himself through with the extra caution and made it.

No one was in there and the keg was still standin' in a bunch of cold water and ice in the bathtub. They hadn't come close to kickin' it yet. Ben took hold of the tap. He pushed in the button and he tipped his glass so he wouldn't end up with a buncha foam.

The beer lined the cup and started to fill it.

Ben just sat there. They had a big tub with a fold-up seat for him when he took a shower. Directly across from where he sat in his wheelchair was a long metal bar bolted on the side of the shower wall. Most people wouldn't ever see one of 'em unless they came to the Callihans' house or they stayed in a hotel room that was handicapped accessible. Ben just sorta stared at that and kept his thumb on the beer tap button.

◆ ✦ ◆

That's why he didn't read before he went to bed. The second he opened the book and read the first page or so, he passed out. When he woke up, he was all sweaty. He had a ton of blankets on and the room was warm and stuffy and smelled like a fifteen-year-old guy's room. His back was wet and his hair was too. He rubbed a couple strands off from his forehead where they were stickin' to it, and he reached under the covers and fixed himself.

He rolled over and looked at the clock. It was 11:47. He was half asleep still. He felt around for the book and it was right beside him. He picked it up and set it on his night stand.

He had read some of it, but he didn't even remember what he had read. He had went through the cast of characters and he recognized some of the names, like Licander and Hermia and Oberon and of course Puck and Titania. His dad had tried to read it to him when he was younger but when you're that age—the age when your dad is readin' to yuh—you wanna have him read you *Clifford* or shit like that. Not Shakespeare. His dad would read a little of that though, probably more for his own sake, and then he would get real animated readin' somethin' else to him, like *Clifford* or a *Golden Book* or somethin'.

Jamie set the book down and reached and turned off his light. He rolled over and laid there with his eyes half shut and starin' at the wall. He always slept facin' that way. When he was a kid he was scared to face the other way because of the window across from his bed. The curtain had to be just so when he was a kid too, so no one could look in. Pretty stupid though, like wasted fear, yuh know, because he was on the second floor anyway.

His eyes adjusted to the dark, and he made out the light color of his wall. The scene had started out in a palace, in the play, and two people had taken a page or two to say what they had to say. Thesis and Hippo-somethin'. He blinked and speckles of leftover light were in his eyes. He was gonna give it his best shot. Readin' it. Like find time that weekend between workin' and other crap he did on weekends (which wasn't much besides work or ride horse or hang out with his mom or do homework on

Sunday night) to at least get through it. Maybe it'd be warm enough to read outside, behind the barn in one of the fields. He was gettin' used to this weather. Mother Nature was gonna pull the plug on 'em any day now though.

He stared another half minute at the wall. He was sweaty but his bare skin cooled off quick. The room was warm but January warm, so he kinda pulled the blankets back around him and shut his eyes. He had had a dream and it was somewhere in those times. Like Shakespeare times. Castle walls. Cold and gray stone walls with tapestries hangin' on 'em. And he couldn't remember what the dream was about. Not the details. He was there though and the guy who had given him the book was there too at a huge fuckin' table with all this food on it and he was hangin' out with his dad. Angelo was hangin' out with Jamie's dad. Yeah, and Jamie was watchin' them. They were talkin' and laughin' and there was a bunch of other people there too all dressed like they came from that time and like they were havin' a party. And then he was, Jamie was, in a courtyard or somethin'. Like that—with the snap of somebody's fingers. The sun was really warm and everything was green. There were sculpted shrubs all over the place and he was a ways from everyone and everything. He heard a fountain and he went to it and there was this girl in the pool by the fountains. Takin' a bath. Naked. He was half asleep and he shifted himself when he remembered that part and tried to picture it—her—better. Hey, he was fifteen. You woulda too.

✦ ✦ ✦

155

When you're in high school and you're out somewhere, that place clears out when it hits a certain hour. At Ben Callihan's that Friday night that hour was midnight. Nobody let their kid stay out much past midnight in Coformon Fall unless their kid wasn't a good kid. Then *those* little hoodlums walked the streets or dealt the drugs or tried to buy beer at Price Chopper and force it on the innocent. That was the scum of the earth that lived on the welfare street in town. Every town's got one of those streets, where the houses are all beat to hell and the tiny front lawn is dirt instead of grass, and the zero tolerance laws are really about that street and all the junk cars in their backyards that are eyesores. *Those* people had a buncha kids but they weren't good kids.

"Are you okay to drive?" S.A.D.D. Queen Denise Coler stood at Ben's door and asked people as they staggered out onto Ben's front porch. Most of 'em didn't have their license, but some of 'em did.

The keg was kicked. Floatin' sideways in the tub. And it was almost 12. It looked like a movie had just let out.

Yeah, so and so is drivin' or I just gotta walk to such and such a place. People who really didn't know Denise kinda just looked down at their sneakers when they left instead of answerin' her. Passenger, driver, or pedestrian—nobody left sober. That's just a fact. Kids are sponges around beer. Yuh know, slurpin' it up as fast as they can...like puppies at a bowl of warm milk.

Psycho Dan had come to the party. He'd came late, but he was there. He was sittin' at Ben's table smokin' a Camel and buttin' his ashes into a half-filled cup of beer when just about everyone had left and Denise came back down the hall. "Let's go out to Richfield. To the Grill." Dan had a brown leather jacket he wore like a good eight months of the school year so his parents would smell it and not whatever he was smokin'. He had it on tonight.

"Too far." Passellow spoke for the group.

Aaron, Sandy, Rob, all of 'em sorta bobbed their heads in agreement.

"Tsst. You're fuckin' wussies." Dan took a Heineken he had stuffed in his leather jacket. Had saved it for the moment that happens at every party. When the beer is gone and everyone is completely hammered and no one wants to drink another drop anyway, and he is still ridin' high. He used his lighter and popped the cap off and drank.

No one cared. Everybody was quiet. Kinda in their own world for a minute.

Ron had his hand on Nicole's thigh and he was rubbin' it under the table. They were goin' some place and it wasn't Richfield. She had tried to call her newest bad boy when Ron wasn't around. Like when he was switchin' discs or somethin'. But he wasn't answerin' her beeps — he probably didn't recognize Ben's number when she punched it in, that's all, that's what she whispered to Sandy when she came back. Yeah, right.

Rachel had thrown up already and her stomach was throwin' punches while she sat there. She rinsed a cup out and filled it with ice water. She took sips and then swallowed hard and licked her lips. It was like a process. She'd breathe hard once in a while in there too.

Wayne Bowenht was practically passed out, and other buddy Derik had picked up the beer cap Dan had flicked and he was turnin' it across his knuckles. Tryin' to, but he kept droppin' it.

Passellow had started buildin' a card house and Don

Neggito—one of the lunch table extras—was watchin' him.

The stereo was still on but it was really low. Someone had put in an Abba disc for the hell of it, and "Fernando" mighta been playin'.

Ben was sittin' there, too. He was restin' his arms on the arms of his wheelchair. He was drunk. Not to the degree everyone else was, but drunk. His eyes were open and they didn't have a sheet of glass over 'em. Maybe a layer of syran wrap but not a sheet of glass. After he filled his own cup, he had slowed down some.

"Let's go."

"I wanna help Benny clean up."

"I got it."

"No, we'll come over tomorrow, Ben, and help yuh. That's what Passy and I did last time." Ron had stood up. He was ready to move everyone outa Ben's house because he was ready to make his move on Nicole. They were gonna wait 'til everyone left and then they would use the guest room off the kitchen. He'd done that the last time with some other chic—he couldn't remember her name right then—when Ben had a party.

"Yeah, definitely." Rich Passellow stood up too. He looked at Psycho Dan. "Yuh give us a ride?"

Dan was swiggin' his Heineken. He swallowed his beer and then looked to see how much was left. "Yeah. Let's go." He stood up. "Turn this off?" He kinda turned to the disc player behind him.

"Yeah, thanks."

Dan stopped the disc and pushed OFF and you could hear the disc stop spinnin' and then shut down.

"Anybody's welcome to stay over, if yuh want."

The rest of 'em stood up while Ben was extendin' the invite.

"Naw. Thanks though Ben, I'll be over with Ron tomorrow mornin' and we'll get that keg, too."

"Thanks, Benny."

"Yeah, thanks, Ben."

"Later, Ben."

Rachel gave Ben a "See yuh, Benny." It was a quiet, painful "See yuh" and when she bent to kiss his cheek, Ben could tell she had had pepperoni on her pizza for supper.

Everyone was filin' out. Psycho Dan would pack 'em in his car or some of 'em would start walkin' and he'd drop the others off and come back and pick them up.

Ron was hangin' towards the back of the parade and he'd sorta taken Nicole's hand. They were standin' by the dining room table when Ben got behind everyone to sorta see 'em all to the door and lock it when they left.

"You don't mind if we stick around a few, Benny, do yuh?"

Nicole was lookin' at her Nikes.

"I'm goin' to bed, Ron. You guys can do what yuh want, just hit the lights when you crash or lock the door if yuh leave."

"Yeah. Yeah. Definitely."

Ben got everybody to the door.

Hi-fives. Handshakes. Laters. Be careful.

Rich was already gettin' his second wind and he was askin' Danny how long he thought it'd take him if they went out to the Richfield Grill, and did he think he'd get carded. Dan was all over that shit, real supportive and sayin' "Only about twenty minutes, man" and "All you need is hair on your nuts out at the Grill" and stuff like that.

Ben closed the door behind them. He wheeled himself into the bathroom and started to do his bathroom stuff. He was in there maybe almost a half hour, brushin' his teeth and takin' a crap and stuff like that. He had heard Ron and Nicole shut off the dining room light and make their move to the guest room when he was puttin' his toothbrush back in the holder.

He finished and flicked the light off in the bathroom and he checked the hall door again. The house smelled like smoke and that was okay because his mom smoked. It probably smelled like beer too, but he couldn't tell. He'd Glade it tomorrow anyway. They weren't suppose to be home until afternoon. He liked it when they left him alone. Not because of parties or anything. It just gave him two minutes to himself. His mom got all nervous and stuff about him bein' there alone so it was a rare thing, but his dad was all on his side. For some reason his dad knew that yuh never got that two minutes when you were in a wheelchair and everyone was always askin' yuh "Can I get that for yuh?" or "Need some help?" or "Yuh got that okay?"

Yeah, it seemed good, those two minutes did.

He wheeled past the doorway of the kitchen. Ron and Nicole had hit the light in there on their way into the guest room—that was off the kitchen. The guest room door was closed, and Ben could hear them makin' out or makin' it already. His room was far away from them, off the living room. But he could still hear the bed start to squeak when he turned the light off on the end stand in the living room. That bed in the guest room was pretty old but it really hadn't seen a lot of action.

It was dark in the house then when he hit the light, but the living room always seemed a little lit from the moon. Or maybe

160

the street lights. There was a big window facin' the street and it let in the light from the outside. His mom had some nice curtains up, thin lacy ones or somethin' and they let the light through. Ben wheeled across the living room to his bedroom. There was almost a track grooved in the carpet from where he'd done it a million times before.

His room was pitch black. There was a small window in there, but it faced another house beside it. No light, during the day or at night, really got in through it. He closed his door behind him.

He wheeled himself closer to his bed and started to unbutton his shirt. He hit the light switch by the head of his bed when he got closer to it, and he squinted when it came on.

He was unbuttonin' his pants when he heard 'em leave. The floor gave it away. No matter how soft anybody walked out there, you were gonna hear 'em. He heard 'em unlock the door and open it and then re-lock the lock. They were talkin' when they got on the front porch, but Ben didn't hear what they were sayin', he didn't really want to. The door closed behind 'em and the house was quiet.

Ben finished undressin'. He did what he had to do with his catheter, too, and he parked his chair by his bed and transferred himself onto his mattress. He reached around and onto his pillow and got the T-shirt he wore to bed and put it on. He got in bed and reached up and flicked the light off.

The room went pitch black again.

Some nights yuh wanna just get into your bed. Between the sheets and under the covers. It seems like the safest place. The only place that's yours. That's how Ben felt tonight, lookin' up at his ceiling.

Chapter Fourteen

"GOOD TO see you."

"Hi."

"Would you like to come in?"

"Umm. Okay, only for a minute though."

When Angelo answered the door, he didn't look surprised or anything. It was like he'd invited Jamie and Jamie mighta been a few minutes late, but he was there now, standin' on the doorsteps.

Jamie wasn't holdin' the book like it was a stick of dynamite or anything, but he didn't have it pressed to his chest like he was totin' the Bible either. It was there in his hands like kinda out, so it was obvious and all that that was why he was standin' there. He didn't know what he was gonna say to the guy, but sorta like a doctor at the doctor's office, Angelo led the way in and then opened the inside door and let Jamie walk in before him.

The clock's hands were still stuck at just about 6—well,

Jamie squinted—5:59 to be exact, and maybe the second hand had moved a second or two, but he couldn't really tell. The short phrase had switched though, he did know that. He hadn't paid too much attention to it the last time he had been there but it had said somethin' about feedin' a seed or somethin', and now it said, "Know life can only first sprout beneath the soil's surface." Okay, yeah, it was all a little strange, but maybe that was part of why he just waited there anyway, beside the bookshelf, while Angelo closed the door behind them.

"Come in and sit down." Angelo took the lead again.

When they moved into the living room, Jamie noticed another chair in there. It was an old chair that had been kept really well, or had been redone. It had a velvety back and a seat with carved wood trim and legs. It was a dining room chair or somethin' from somebody's house who used to be important. A mini-throne. Yeah, that was probably the only way Jamie coulda described it. Where you'd put the back of your head there was a foot in a shoe like Robin Hood woulda worn or somethin' and it had a feathery wing attached to its side.

"Could I get you something to drink? Maybe a Coke or something warm?"

"No. Thanks, though." Jamie sat. The chair was directly across from the chair Angelo had sat in the other day. It wasn't on top of it or anything, but it was sittin' a ways from it so whoever sat in it was facin' whoever sat in the other one.

Angelo sat in that one. "How did the book go?"

"Oh. Good." Jamie got up and walked the couple steps and handed it to Angelo and then sat back down. "Well, all right, I guess. I read it all this weekend so I could get it back to you.

Thanks for the loan."

"No need to hurry with it. Would you like to keep it longer?" Angelo held it out and smiled. He always seemed to have at least a small smile. Not like he was retarded or somethin' and didn't have any clue but like he was—like he was the bearer of good news or somethin'. He gave off the feeling that behind his smile, everything that was goin' on was pretty important—in a good way.

"No. That's okay. I liked it and everything, but I got a lot of homework and work and stuff, so I probably wouldn't get to it again for a while." Jamie leaned forward and was gonna put his elbows on his knees. The chair didn't have any arms. He sat back up though and put his foot across his knee. You know. The way guys cross their legs. He held his foot with his hands. He smiled back at Angelo. "Thanks, though."

Even though the clock didn't seem to keep the right time, you could still hear its tickin' when you didn't say anything for a minute. It wasn't library quiet in there or quiet like when the doctor is writing something in your folder about you quiet. Angelo took the book and put it in his basket and traded it for a pillow.

Jesus, those freakin' pillows. Jamie looked up at the ceiling. He hadn't noticed before, how it kinda poofed up. It was a cool setup in there. The rug and the lights and the ceiling. It was homey. Naw, better than that, there was only one other place Jamie felt like how he felt at that second. Where the hell was it?

Angelo started to pull at the needle and do some of his handiwork. "I thought you might have a little more to say about the play." He didn't sound disappointed or anything, just makin' conversation.

"A lot of it was hard to understand. The way they talk and

you have to keep stoppin' and lookin' at the footnotes. So I probably missed out on some of it."

"You're right. If you get lost in Shakespeare's words, you sink. Without a doubt." Angelo was lookin' down. He kept stitchin' and he nodded. "Every one of his words count. They're like building blocks, but you can't look at every brick in a house to see what makes it stand the way it does, at least not until you get good at it, or you'll go cross-eyed. You'll just about make yourself sick, right?" He tugged at the needle and looked up. He had had his glasses on since he answered the door, and they had slipped down a little on his nose from him lookin' down. He smiled and propped 'em back up with the back of his finger.

"Yeah. That's true."

Angelo looked back down and looked at his stitching. It was pretty good. Straight. Close together. He put his needle to the cloth and poked it through. "What made you come back here, Jamie?"

"I wanted to bring you back the book." Jamie took his foot off his knee and took his other foot and put it up. His sneaker had come unlaced so he tied it. What kinda question was that?

"Really?"

"Yeah, really."

"That's it?"

"That's it." Jamie pulled the string tight. He used to double knot his sneakers when he was in junior high. He didn't anymore.

Angelo just held the two edges of the pillow together and stitched away.

Jamie looked at the pillow. He looked in at all the crap on the

165

dining room table. The table probably belonged with the chair he was sittin' on. Its legs were sorta swirly and carved too. And the whole thing was very *tres grandeur* (*deux* years of *francais*, they made yuh take it if you wanted a Regents diploma). There was a white plastic bag with somethin' in it leanin' against one of the legs. It had red letters on it, the bag did. Thanks for shopping at Augers', it said.

Jamie looked back at Angelo when he saw that.

Angelo had stopped stitchin' and was lookin' at Jamie when Jamie turned his head to look at him. "That's how you know my name."

"No. That's not how I know your name."

Jamie took his foot off his lap. Both his sneakers were on the carpet. "Then how do you know my name?"

"I'll tell you how I know your name, if you tell me why you really came back here." Angelo went back to his goddamn pillow.

"I told you why I came back here, because I wanted to give you the book back."

Angelo found the exact place he wanted to stitch and made one.

Jamie looked back at the bag leanin' against the dining room table leg. He got up and walked over to it. Then he looked back at Angelo.

Angelo didn't give a shit.

Jamie bent down and he looked in the bag. There was a UPS box opened at one end. There was a buncha little dried leaves in it. Special order...special order..."The day of that storm. That was you." Jamie stood up and walked back to his chair and sat down. "You came in for flower leaves." He half snapped his fingers a couple times and looked up at the ceiling. "Uhhh, rose petals, lily—no. Daffodil. Marigold leaves." He pointed and looked at Angelo. "That's how you know my name." Jamie brought his foot back up to his lap and nodded his head a couple times.

Angelo just kept workin'. He stopped a second to study the last stitch he'd made because it may have been just a hair off, but he ran his thumb over it and then started back up again. Because he knew the next one he made would line it directly back up with the whole scheme of things. "And the reason you came?"

Tick. Tick. Tick. That's all you heard for a second or two.

"I don't know why I came back here. I—I don't know why."

Angelo pulled his thread tight and he had been right. He looked up. "Yes you do."

Jamie shook his head slow. "I really don't, I—I just thought I should. Like I was suppose to or somethin'. I can't explain it."

"That's the reason then. That's why. You listened to something most people don't even know they have." Angelo set his pillow that he was workin' on back down in his basket. He got up. "That voice. Your intuition, that's the first part of it. Come here." He walked into the dining room.

"First part of what?" Jamie got up and followed him into the dining room.

Angelo stopped in front of the table and was standin' there, and Jamie came up beside him. The table's top hadn't changed much from the other day when Jamie had first seen it. Still covered with crap, but this time the scale had a blue, clear glass bowl on it. It wasn't a big bowl, maybe the size of a medium-sized mixing bowl. The glass seemed to glow, it was that kinda blue. Jamie looked down into it and there really didn't seem to be anything there except maybe a couple pieces of dust balls that you'd find under your bed danglin' from your box springs. Yuh know, dust bunnies.

"This. It." Angelo looked across the table at everything on it. The glass jars and all that stuff. Then he looked at Jamie. "I know your name, Jamie, because there's a dream here for you. Well, a dream's way, really." He smiled like he had just confirmed a flight reservation for someone. "And everyone who gets one needs the right combination before his dream becomes reality."

Jamie just stood there. He was listenin' to Angelo and everything, but he didn't know what to do with his hands. He went to put 'em in his jeans pockets, then he was gonna fold his arms across his chest. He ran one of 'em down the back of his head, too. "I don't know what you're talkin' about." His hands said the same thing his mouth just did and he hooked his thumbs in his side pockets. "I don't know what you're talkin' about."

"Once you have the right combination—I need to be sure you're right for all of this, and with you, I am. It's just a formality. But once you give me the combination—"

"Angelo." That was the first time he used his name, and he felt his cheeks flush a little. Did you ever really think about when you use somebody's name to his face? Have you ever really thought about when you don't and then you finally do? "What are you talkin' about, combination?" Jamie caught a look at the huge painting on the wall right then when he said that, and he did a glance once and a glance twice at it. Somethin' better known as a double-take, except for here in Coformon Falls.

Angelo had stepped a little away from him and he reached for one of the jars and a set of tablespoons that were hooked together on a loop and were layin' somewhere in the mess. "Let me see—" He picked up a jar with a lid on it. Jamie couldn't see what the label said, but the jar looked like it was filled with some sorta sand. Gold sand. "There's a combination, parts to the key that opens the path, your dream's path. Your path." He reached between two other jars and a stack of letters and came up with the spoons. "And you've found the first part." He was holdin' the spoons and the jar and lifted the metal part that held the lid in place. His hands were full but you could tell he had done it this way a million times before. "Well, half of the first part, but the other part of the first part comes easy enough."

Jamie watched Angelo take the lid and set it down and fan out the spoons until he came to the smallest one, probably the teaspoon. Angelo got better hold of the spoon and dipped it into the sand and tapped it on the edge of the jar's rim. A few grains dropped back into the jar, but Angelo still had a heapin' spoon full, as heaping as a teaspoon can get. He set the jar down and stretched his arm to the blue bowl and dumped the sand in there. He tapped the spoon against the bowl's edge. "Very good. Would you like a cup of tea or soda? Or anything?" He set the set of spoons down and looked at Jamie. "Don't look so serious, Jamie."

Jamie had followed Angelo's hand over to the bowl and he was still lookin' that way. Dust bunnies and gold sand. Okay. This guy had to be on crack. "Yeah. Sure." He looked at Angelo.

Angelo smiled. Again. And then he turned and walked for a

swinging door off the dining room. Probably goin' into the kitchen.

Jamie leaned over the table a little more. Like lookin' directly into the bowl was gonna give him the answer or somethin'. Not even the answer. He didn't know what the hell he was lookin' for. He could hear Angelo whistlin' some tune from the kitchen. Heard the refrigerator door and the rattle of a can across the wiry shelf of the fridge. He looked towards the swinging door and then back to the bowl.

Some of the grains of sand sat on top of the dust bunnies and some of 'em had dropped to the bottom of the bowl. It was like the stuff had multiplied though and the teaspoon Angelo had dumped in there had turned into a couple tablespoons. It was brighter, too. Bright gold in a blue bowl. Along with a wad of lint and hair and dust from underneath somebody's bed. Jamie just sorta shook his head. What the hell?

The soda can—that's what Jamie had guessed it was—bein' cracked open made him turn his head again toward the kitchen. A second later, Angelo came walkin' out with a Sprite in his hand. "I hope Sprite is okay." Angelo handed the can to him.

Sprite. All of this was a little too strange, right?

The can was cold. "Yeah. Thanks." Jamie took a swig. The room was a sleepy warm and the soda was a cool cold goin' down his throat. He took another swig. He looked at the dining room table and all the crap on it, and he didn't wanna stare. He looked up again at the painting on the wall. "I don't get it." The gold of some of the stars almost—it sounds stupid—but it was like whoever had painted them did it so they almost seemed to twinkle or shimmer or somethin'. Jamie just kinda looked at 'em and then looked at Angelo.

"Don't try to figure it out too much, Jamie. There's something you want to do and you need to do. Part of your purpose, you could say, and what I'm here for and what this is here for," Angelo put his hand out to the table and the jars and the bowl and stuff, "what this is all for is to set you on your way, that's all."

"Don't try to figure it out? Somebody I don't even know who mixes sand and dust, and sews pillows—" Jamie nodded his soda can towards the living room, "and knows my name without me tellin' him it. I don't think I can just—I mean, not to be a—" he wanted to say dick, "rude or anything, but this is crazy, I don't even know why I'm standin' here."

"Jamie, just like the reason you came in here, you've got a reason why you're standing here." Angelo was lookin' over the jars on the table, like he was tryin' to find a particular one. "Start getting to the real reasons why you do what you do. Don't settle for 'I don't know why I's.'" He looked up and smiled and then turned back to searchin'.

Jamie didn't say anything for a second. He took another swallow of his soda. He looked towards the painting again. It was like the stars in it had gold and silver and white in 'em. They really looked real, the whole thing looked real. He looked at Angelo again and then he walked to the other side of the table and stood facin' the painting.

It was big, maybe 7x7, if you're into dimensions, or like bigger, a lot bigger, than the top of a card table if you have a hard time judgin' feet.

The painting had dimension too. Like whoever had painted

it had made it so it seemed you could reach into it. It was strange. Jamie got these tingles up his spine and down his head and the back of his neck. Like when someone pretends to crack an egg over your head and they put their hands real close to you but don't touch you and they move their hands slowly down your head. Like an egg is oozin' over it and you get all tingly and shit. That's what standin' in front of that painting did to Jamie. It was strange. But even just as weird was this cool air—this was really nuts. The picture definitely was of night, and when Jamie stood there it was like, almost like he could feel this cool air. To tell yuh the truth, he looked down and then up to see if there was a small vent blowin' air on him. There wasn't and he knew there wasn't. It wasn't like fake air, like house air. It felt like he was standin' in one of his fields behind the barn and it was a summer night and there was a cool warm breeze blowin'.

He drank some more soda and looked over his shoulder behind him. Angelo had a jar in his hand. Its top was off and he was reachin' in it and pullin' out what looked like a sun-dried tomato. He didn't look at Jamie, he was all into what he was doin', but he talked to him. "I play a little game with myself with that painting when I'm working here or in my chair." He had the shriveled-up red thing in his one hand, and he bounced it there, like he was judgin' real roughly how much it weighed or somethin'. "I look at it from time to time, and I try to see something there that I didn't before." He dropped the thing in the bowl, and bent a little to read the number and line the baby scale's needle was pointin' at.

Jamie had turned back around and was lookin' back at the painting. But if he hadn't of, he woulda saw this powder-blue puff of smoke rise from the bowl when Angelo tossed that mutant-lookin' tomato in. It was all right and everything, it was suppose to do that.

Angelo set the jar down and sorta flapped his hands over the bowl. And he glanced over at Jamie's back. "What do you see?"

It wasn't so much what Jamie saw. It was more like about what he felt standin' there. But he didn't wanna say anything about the breeze or anything. So he looked at the painting a little more. "Everything's alive. Even this stone on these buttresses." He lifted the hand he was holdin' the can in and he followed one of the arches with his pointin' finger. "It's like you're lookin' out a huge open window of like an old stone church or castle or some place sacred or somethin'. Like whoever painted it, put this border around it because they wanted you to feel like you were inside lookin' out." Just on the inside of the frame was exactly what Jamie had tried to describe, like a painted-in stone frame, real thin, but there. He looked sorta to the side, like he was lookin' behind the frame, like the picture went on beyond it. He took a drink, and looked at it again. He pointed to the lower part of the picture. "Yeah, like you're in this holy place in—" he couldn't think of the country where they have those domed roofs and people turn and bend and pray like six times a day, "in Tibet or somethin' and these like vague things here are the Himalaya Mountains or somethin'." Jamie hadn't heard any movement behind him. Like jars clankin' or Angelo's weight crackin' the floor as he moved doin' whatever he was doin', so he turned around because he didn't wanna feel like he was just talkin' to himself.

Angelo had capped the one jar he was holdin' and he set it

down. Truth was, he was listenin' to Jamie, sorta lookin' at the painting with him. And when Jamie turned around, he saw Angelo standin' there with his arms kinda folded across his chest and studyin' the picture. Angelo really didn't look like he saw Jamie turn around to him, that's how into the painting he was. He snapped out of it like in a second, like someone had snapped their fingers in his face. But he stood there a second and then snapped out of it and looked at Jamie. When he did, he took his arms from his chest and started to come around the table for a better look. "Window frame, hmm?" he said while he walked around the side of the table.

"Yeah." Jamie pointed at a part of it next to the real frame. "Right here." He moved his hand up the frame a little, tracin' the painted frame for Angelo.

"Right, right. The frame." Angelo tipped his head up and followed the frame a ways. "And the mountains on the horizon."

"Yeah, they're back here." Jamie pointed across, between a couple different buttresses.

Angelo bent a little on his knees and held a bow of his glasses. "Um-hmm. Mountains."

Jamie looked at the silvery silhouettes of the distant mountains a second more. Then he kinda shook his soda can. It was almost empty and he finished it off. "I should really go, Angelo."

He used his name again. And it still felt kinda strange, but not like as much as before.

Angelo stood straight and looked a second more at the mountains. "Your lunch break is almost over?"

"Yeah. I think I might even be late." Jamie looked at the can in his hand and then around the room a little. For somethin' to toss it in.

"Here. Let me take that for you, and I'll show you out."

"No, that's okay." Jamie handed the empty Sprite can to him. "I mean you don't have to show me out. I mean. I mean you've done enough already, yuh know. Thanks for the soda and stuff."

"Certainly."

Jamie kinda smiled.

"And the least I can do is walk you part of the way out." Angelo started around the table. He set the soda can on the corner of it as he passed.

Jamie followed him and they walked through the living room.

"You'll come back tomorrow?" They reached the door and Angelo opened it for him.

Jamie stood there, in that little place between the hall out to the front door and Angelo's living room.

Tick. Tick. Tick.

He looked over at the clock and the lady in her garden. Then back at Angelo. "I guess so."

"Jamie, you already have the first part of the combination. How can you say 'I guess so'?"

"I thought you said I only had part of the first part." Yuh know when you say things, and you can't believe you say 'em but you are sayin' 'em. That's how Jamie felt when he started talkin' about parts of parts. He took a couple steps for the door.

"The other half comes easy. It's why you were standing there when you said you didn't know why you were. It's why I'll see you tomorrow."

"I still don't know." Jamie stopped in the doorway.

"Yes you do. You know what it feels like, you just don't have the word for it."

Oh, Christ. "I really gotta go."

Angelo looked at the clock, and he looked at it like it told the right time. They were a little pressed for time—not as far as lunch went, but thinkin' about the big picture.

Jamie looked behind him and sorta followed Angelo's eyes over to it. Forget it. "Yeah. Okay. I'll see yuh tomorrow." He turned and started to leave.

Angelo just ignored him, and leaned against the door's edge. He rested one of his arms across his stomach and then he put his other elbow on that arm, settin' himself up so he could stroke the whiskers on his chin with his thumb and pointer finger. "You remind me a lot of Pandora, Jamie. And who can blame you." He shook his head a couple times, not in a bad, sad way or anything, but like he was, like he was—yuh know, like when you wait to do a long-range assignment until the night before it's due, and one of your folks walk in on their way to bed at like 10:30 and you're like halfway done. You look all freaked out, with the scissors in your hand, clippin' articles about the Middle East or somethin', and old newspapers are all over your room. They just sorta stand in your doorway and sorta shake their head with "I told yuh not to wait" on the tip of their tongue. That was how Angelo had just shook his head.

Jamie stopped in the hall and looked at him.

"The world we live in will do that to anybody. But Pandora looked at the bottom of her box and that's what you do. It separates you and a few others from the rest."

"Pandora."

"Um-hmm."

"Oh, right. Right. Pandora."

Angelo was still leanin' against the door, rubbin' his beard and lookin' off somewhere. But then he stood straight again, all quick-like, like they had just cleared it all up. "Very well, then. Take care, Jamie. I'll see you tomorrow."

Jamie kinda stood there in the hall between the door into the house and the front door. He kinda stood there with a look on his face like nothin' had been cleared up. "Yeah. See yuh."

Angelo smiled and closed the door.

It clicked shut and the hall was quiet.

"Pandora?" Jamie was askin' himself now. Yuh know, kinda under his breath. He stood there a second more and stared at a knot in one of the planks on the door. Angelo didn't mean Endora, did he?—Samantha's mom on *Bewitched?*

He turned and walked the couple feet to the front door and went out. He stood there on Angelo's porch for a second when he got outside, and yuh won't believe it, but the January noon sun was bright and warm on his face and he had to squint a little. He walked down the steps and was pretty far down Angelo's walk before he answered himself.

Naw. Not Endora. Pandora. Angelo had said Pandora.

✦ ✦ ✦

Angelo wouldn't of heard Jamie leave. He had already walked his way, well, kinda scurried his way across his living room and into his dining room. He had went around his dining room table

177

and stood in front of his painting.

He stood there now, holdin' his glasses again to his face. "Window frame," he sorta said out loud to himself. He traced the line of painted silvery gray stone just inside the picture frame with his eyes and then he looked for the mountains Jamie had spotted. He found 'em there, and he shook his head. He shook it in a good way, like when you walk in the kitchen the next morning and your kid is half asleep eatin' their Lucky Charms but their long-range assignment is there on the table. Completed. And you know they'll get an A on it. He smiled again, even though it seemed like he always was, and he felt the cool night breeze of a warm summer night and he looked out the window of…and he smiled an even broader smile then…some place sacred.

Chapter Fifteen

LIBRARIES ARE strange places. A wealth of written knowledge in 'em. Well, not necessarily in Coformon Falls High School Library though. Very limited there. You wanted anything beyond a certain point, ol' Mrs. Carson would be pullin' out an inner or intra or whatever library loan slip and sendin' it off to another friggin' library for the book yuh needed. Eight to ten days, she'd tell yuh. It really took fourteen, or sometimes even longer, and by the time the library got it, your paper was due anyway, so you wrote it with the crappy references you could pull from the shelf here.

Jamie went to the library for study hall that afternoon. He never went to the library for study hall. You know that already. Today he did though. He couldn't help thinkin' about Angelo's house, the stuff he said and all that. It was strange, it wasn't like he'd become obsessed with it or anything, he just felt different. That shit about dreams or whatever, it was probably a buncha crap. But what if it was real—just for a second while he was sittin' in math and Mr. Dairnott was rattlin' off at the blackboard about derivatives of x or y or somethin'—he thought, what if it was real?

He ended up here at the library. When he walked in the double doors, it was pretty loud in there. He saw Miss Fultoon, she was the European History teacher. She was herdin' must be one of her classes into this audio-visual room hooked onto the library. Jamie hung a right right when he walked through the doors and found a cubicle tucked in and along the wall towards the back where there was nothin' but books stacked on shelves. There were a couple cubicles like that in the library. They were punishment cubicles. If you were at a table with your friends and you kept shootin' the bull and you got told like six times to shut up by Carson, then she usually banned you to a cubicle somewhere in the stacks if she didn't throw you out or if you begged her really hard to stay or somethin'. You'd get sat there. By yourself.

Jamie set his crap in the cubicle, but he separated out his one notebook, remember the one Francis had 'em use as a journal. He took that and his pen. He wasn't gonna really use his notebook, well, he'd probably write some stuff down in it about what he was gonna look up, but he was gonna bring whatever book he found back to the desk. He took it 'cause there was a lotta stuff in that notebook. Not like personal, well, some of it, but it just had a lot of his own stuff in there and he didn't care if people stole his math notebook or book even or whatever, he just was a little paranoid about his journal.

Instead of headin' for the computer by the front counter you used to look up the number of the book you were lookin' for, he went to the far corner of the library. The computer usually had a line of people, because the library only had one. So they kept the old card catalog around, stuck it in the back corner. Probably didn't even update it or anything, but it was there in case the line was too long or the computer wasn't workin'. Card catalog? It was this long-legged wooden thing and it was filled with cards. You could look up your subject, or title or…or like your author or somethin' and flip through and find a card with what you needed on it and then you could get the number off the corner of it and find your book. If it was in. Out of all the goddamn books in the library there's nothin' that pisses you off more than to go to the shelf and have the one damn book you want to be out.

Jamie was thinkin' that, when he set his notebook on top of the card catalog. He looked down at the little slips of paper on front of the drawers. He found the P-Q drawer and pulled it open. These drawers were long, like *Alice in Wonderland* long. He was gonna have to look it up by subject. He started flippin' through the cards. *Subject: Pennsylvania Dutch Country.* Too far. He flipped a couple cards back towards the front of the drawer. *Subject: Penis.* Christ, somebody wrote a book about that. And over the call number in the top right-hand corner, some kid musta pulled the card and they penciled in a graphic. Complete with pubes and all. That's what kids in high school do. Not even just high school, Jamie flipped a few more cards towards the front, when he was in elementary school, there would be a huge-ass dictionary on a round swivel tray and kids would look up "vagina" and circle it with their nubby red, thick lead pencils and laugh and point. Things don't change much.

181

Title: Pandas of China and Tibet: Where Will They Be Tomorrow? Sub, subtitle. *A Look at the Economical, Political, Sociological Dangers to the Ailuropoda melandoleuca. Pandas: Extinction* mighta been a better title. Jamie flipped a couple cards past that. *Subject: Pandora.* Bingo. He looked on the card in front of it. *Author: Pandemonte, Robert. Cleaning Up America's Rivers.* Then the one in back. *Title: Panegyrics.* Huh? Anyway, that meant one book on Pandora. That was all right.

He flipped back to the card and read it. *Children's title.* It was a goddamn kids' book. The library had a little section of kids' books for people who were gonna work with kids or somethin' when they went to college or got a job. The title was *Pandora's Box.* That made sense, from what Angelo had said. Jamie pulled his pen from the spiral of his notebook and clicked it. He wrote the call number down on the cover of his notebook where he could find a clean space.

CHI over Pan over 1365.872.

He closed the drawer and grabbed his notebook and headed for the children's section. It was more towards the front desk, so he cut through a couple aisles and he passed through the table area. There were a buncha kids there, all at different tables. Some of 'em had their heads bent down over a book or somethin', but most of 'em were sittin' there whisperin' or quiet talkin'. Some of 'em looked towards Jamie when he walked through. People just do that, look to see who's comin' through.

Jamie really didn't look at them. He looked at the call number he wrote on his notebook again and he pretended to be really into where he was goin'. When he passed by the section, he landed himself in the row of kids' books. There really weren't that many. He didn't know why there were so many numbers in the call number. Or maybe that didn't have anything to do with how many kids' books there were, he didn't know.

He found *Pandora's Box*, no problem. It was a big-ass book with that crinkly plastic over its cover and it looked like it had gotten published in the sixties. This girl on the front—must be Pandora—had long blond hair that was cut around her face and this little white dress on up to her thighs and bare feet. She was holdin' a little box, like a music box and sorta peekin' inside. This was who Angelo was talkin' about? She looked like a freak.

When Jamie went back to his cubicle, he cut past the front desk. The line hadn't moved an inch to the computer that you looked books up on. Mrs. Carson was standin' next to Raymond Pepper, Jamie knew his name because he had been in the kid's eighth grade Home Ec. class, when they made yuh take Home Ec. Whenever he saw Raymond Pepper he always thought of that friggin' Home Ec. class and how Raymond never brought his money in for his sewing pattern. Evins would scream at him every day, and the next day he would come in and no money again. Any idiot knew he didn't have twelve bucks to spend on the gym bag pattern. Finally, about midway through the quarter, Evins pulled out a stuffed animal pattern she had layin' around and made him sew a blue bear. He had a thick mustache comin' in when he was in eighth grade and things didn't seem to get much better for him after the blue bear incident. Maybe things weren't so great for him even before that.

Well, Jamie always said hi to him or he always said hi to Jamie. Hey, Pepper. Or what's up, Jamie. He wasn't a bad kid or anything. He hung out with some tough kids. Other people would call 'em the grubs. Guys who worked on cars and whose hands weren't always clean. Yuh know, like grease on 'em or whatever. Some of 'em owned a truck or an old van or somethin' already, and they'd listen to Zeppelin and trip out with a little acid on a piece of paper plate on their tongues.

Yeah, Pepper had a past, and a big blond mustache for tenth grade. He was standin' there now and he had Carson helpin' him find on the computer whatever he was lookin' for. When Jamie went by, Pepper was starin' at the computer. Jamie saw Carson point to the list on the screen and he heard her say somethin' about an inner-library loan card.

It figured. Pepper had that kinda luck that every book he was gonna need was gonna be intra-library loaned. Pepper and his buddies weren't bad kids.

Jamie walked the length of the far wall and he heard Fultoon's herd of elephants streamin' out of the A.V. room. Sometimes a teacher would do that. They'd take kids in there and tell them what to do and then they'd send 'em out and they'd have to go look somethin' up or somethin'. It was a waste of time — for the teacher — because kids in high school know how to look like they're doin' somethin'. Most of 'em would go find a shelf with a friend and pretend to be lookin' for a book or somethin', and they'd stand there and talk until someone walked by. Then they'd kill the period and worry about the assignment the day before it was due.

Jamie sat down and pushed his other books to the corner of his desk. He put his journal notebook down and flipped that open. He figured he might wanna write somethin' down about this Pandora or whatever. He pushed his chair back a little and stretched his legs 'til his feet touched the wall. He rested the book against the edge of the desk and flipped open the first couple pages.

It was one of those books that was all picture and one sentence at the bottom of each page. Jamie kinda tipped the book forward and ran his thumb across the edges of the pages. To count 'em. It had like seven.

The pictures were lousy. Watercolor backgrounds and the people's eyes didn't have pupils.

He leaned it back against his cubicle and for a second he doubted he was gonna find what he needed to find.

Prometheus stole the fire from Zeus and the other gods.

Okay. These guys in white dresses were lookin' all pissed at this other guy—Prometheus, probably—takin' off with a torch of fire.

In return for his bad deed, the Gods sent Pandora to the world.

Jamie's brain kinda tingled when he saw Pandora's name. He didn't bother lookin' at the pictures and he read the next page.

Pandora owned a box. She was told never to open it.

How the hell was he like Pandora? He looked up at the concrete wall that the cubicle was pressed up against. It was a dull yellow color. He stared at it a second and tried to remember exactly what Angelo had said. Pandora looked at the bottom of her box or somethin' like that and that's what you do. That was it. Whatever that meant was the other part to the first part. He looked down again and flipped the page.

Of course, as days went by, Pandora grew more and more curious.

Next page. *What was in the box?*

Years went by. And one day, Pandora opened the box. Jamie looked at the picture on this page. This girl was peekin' into her little wooden box and openin' it up. He looked at the page beside it. It was all dark and all this shit was flyin' out of the open box— like little people with wings and stuff—and Pandora was jumpin' back with her mouth wide open. He read the bottom of that page. *When she did, out came sickness, famine, anger, hate, greed and all the other evils that roam the world today.* That sucked. There was one page left and Jamie went to turn—

"Lotsa pictures in that one, Jamie."

Jamie kinda jerked a little and looked up.

It was Ben, and he was sittin' there smilin', hands on his wheels. He cracked up a little when he saw Jamie jump. Rachel Stappuck was standin' beside him.

"Hey, Ben, what's up." He kinda looked at Rachel and she was like lookin' at the wall and then the bookshelf on the other side of them.

Ben looked up at her, too. "Hey, Rachel, you know Jamie?"

She licked her top lip and looked at him. "Hey."

"Hey."

She looked down at one of her nails and started playin' with it.

Ben kinda looked at her a second and then he looked back to Jamie. "What's up, man. You missed the party." He rolled his wheelchair a little closer.

"Yeah. Sorry." Jamie kinda looked back at the book. He hadn't turned back to the last page. And he looked at Pandora with her hand on her heart and shock and horror written all over her face. Then he looked back at Ben. "I had to work and stuff."

"Work and stuff." Ben was smilin'. "Yeah, right, you're comin' next time if I have to wheel my ass over to your house and get yuh."

Jamie's face got a little red, and he moved in his chair so he could cross his feet that were still stretched out and touchin' the wall. "I will—I mean, the next time—"

"Dude, I'm bustin'." He laughed again. "So what the hell are yuh readin'? Hey, better yet, what happened with that guy you were tellin' me about?"

Jamie looked sorta behind Ben and at Rachel. She had her head tipped and she was readin' the titles of the books on the shelf. "Crazy. You wouldn't believe it if I told yuh."

"Really." If Ben coulda rolled a little closer he would have. You could tell he had just gotten his hair cut like a day ago and it was almost like he'd been to the beach or somethin'. The sun that'd been out had almost given him a tan, well, color, yuh know.

One of Mrs. Carson's staffers rolled a cart past the aisle they were in. She was an old lady who dyed her hair jet black, and she was a nark. She looked right at 'em, and all of 'em looked towards her. She turned into the next aisle and you could hear her and her cart headin' down the opposite end they were at. She'd be sendin' Carson to break up the party in a second without a doubt.

"So what are you doin' in here?"

"I'm in Fultoon's class and we gotta find some crap on the Crusades or somethin'," Ben kinda turned in his chair, "what is it we're lookin' for, Rachel?"

Rachel kept lookin' at the books in front of her face. "I dunno. The Crusades or somethin'."

Ben turned back towards Jamie. "Yeah, the Crusades or somethin'. So what is this?" Ben looked down at the book Jamie had propped against the cubicle. What a bad word. *Cubicle.* It sounds like a place they would keep dying chickens, don't yuh think?

Jamie looked down at the book again. "It's this book about this girl—well, that guy, the one I was tellin' yuh about?"

"Yeah, you started to tell me. What happened?" Ben fixed his pen he had stuck behind his ear.

"He made like some reference to her," Jamie pointed at the open book, "and I didn't have a clue who he was talkin' about."

"So you talked to him again. That's cool. What else?"

Mrs. Nevil—that was Mrs. Carson's stacker—came back into their aisle, she was at the far end and she kinda looked down at Jamie and Ben. She started doin' about as good of a job at pretendin' to look at books on the shelf as Rachel was.

Ben looked up at her.

Jamie turned sorta around and looked at her then back at Ben. "Done for."

"Yeah, we'd better make like eggs, and scramble." He started to back his wheelchair up. Rachel was already standin' at the end of the shelves. Opposite the end Nevil was down, of course. "Listen, you gotta fill me in. You got gym tomorrow or today? I forget."

"Tomorrow."

"I think the swim team's got the pool during eighth all this week—some big meet Saturday or somethin', I dunno—but maybe instead I can get the van for that period to take us bowlin'. Wanna do that?"

"Yeah, that'd be cool."

Ben stretched his arm to do that hi-five, handshake thing again. Jamie was kinda gettin' used to doin' it.

Ben looked down at Nevil, and she was stretchin' her head around the other end of the row, like towards the front desk, gettin' Carson to come over. "All right, we're busted. Meet me at the side door, last period tomorrow."

"Well, I'll see yuh in English anyway."

"Right. But you always fly outa there." Ben was startin' to turn his chair. It was like he knew how long it would take Carson to get from the front desk to where Nevil was standin'.

Jamie kinda smiled. "You're right. Okay, I'll see you eighth tomorrow."

Ben nodded and started wheelin'. "Sounds good. See yuh, Jamie."

"See yuh."

Carson was down by Nevil now, and she was lookin' down the row. Ben had turned the corner before she got there. Jamie just kept his head down at his book, but he was lookin' at her out of the corner of his eyes. He saw the two ladies whisper something to each other and Carson pointed her double-end teacher pen—yuh know red on one end, blue on the other end— down towards Jamie. Nevil nodded, looked down at him, and nodded again. It was like a next time plan.

Jamie looked back at the book. He just kinda stared at it a second. That was cool. Bowlin'. He waited another second and then turned the page.

All the crap had flown off or whatever to contaminate the world and the page was this soft blue. Like the sky on a clear day. Pandora was lookin' in at the bottom of her box, just like what Angelo was talkin' about. At the bottom of the box, there were little lines and yellow light around this really little, winged girl. She looked all beat to hell, but like she was gonna fly off too. Jamie looked at Pandora again, and she was lookin' in the box at this pixie—if that's what you wanted to call her—and she was like movin' her hand to help her out.

He looked down to the bottom of the page and read the last line.

But, there, buried beneath all that was wrong and bad, at the bottom of Pandora's box, she found the start of all good things.

Jamie felt that weird tingle again. It was all over him this time.

HOPE.

Chapter Sixteen

THERE WAS a corral behind the barn where Jamie and his mom would let the horses out in the spring and summer for exercise. In the winter, they let them roam around or they rode them in another smaller building that was just a corral really with a roof and walls.

The whole petting zoo setup was there too, in case you wondered. That was more to the side of the barn and riding ring, though, and they really didn't do much with it until the really nice weather rolled around. But if you're tryin' to get a whole idea about the place, just wanted to mention it.

When Jamie got home from school, it was still warmer out. Not 80 or anything crazy, but he came home and put on just a long sleeve long john shirt and a pair of jeans and he was warm enough. He put his cap on too, he usually wore a baseball cap when he worked. It was a baseball cap, but not with a baseball logo on it or anything, some feed and grain supplier had given him and his dad each one a few years ago for buyin' their stuff and Jamie wore it. It was still a good cap, all worn in with the rim bent just right and stuff, yuh know.

It was still like spring, kinda warm and the corral behind the barn was muddy with some grass that was startin' to get green, but it was also gettin' to be late afternoon in February—yeah, some time had passed since it all started—and winter still held the reins. The afternoon cooled down quick and the sun set soon. So Jamie didn't have much daylight to get outdoors by the time he got off the bus.

First thing he did though today, after gettin' changed and all that, he wanted to spend some time with Puck. His mom had been the one takin' care of him mostly and he knew if the colt was gonna have anything to do with him when it got older, he needed to be around it when it was the age it was now. And, besides that, he just wanted to be outdoors. It was like the air was alive. It like made your nose kinda cold but the sun was warm to your body. He wanted to hear his boots squish in the early mud behind the barn and see if he could smell the grass at all. He just wanted to get outside today.

He went out to the barn and put a halter on Puck, and he led him out into the corral with a rope. A halter isn't a bridle. A bridle is with a bit that you stick in the horse's mouth and all that stuff. A halter you just slip over the horse's nose and ears and you can hook a rope with a snap at the end of it onto it and you can lead the horse around. You've seen like a cowboy in a movie or somethin' stand in the middle of a corral and run a horse in a circle around him attached to a rope? Well, that's what people really do, it's not fake or anything, it's just harder than it looks

192

the first few times you try to do it. Jamie was gonna get Puck used to bein' led and maybe see if he could run him a little.

He took the colt out into the corral. It was wired up to be outdoors. It smelled spring already. It was sorta kickin' its back legs up and jerkin' its head into the air every few steps until Jamie got it out to the middle and kinda stood there with it for a minute. Jamie ran his hand down Puck's back and pet him. Puck had a slick lookin' coat, a good sign he was a healthy animal. Jamie scratched him behind his ears, and said stuff low to him like "Hey, boy" and "What are you doin', Puck, huh" and "Yuh like it out here, don't yuh." You talk to animals like they're kids sometimes.

Puck twitched his ears, and his eyes were watchin' Jamie. His nostrils were flared out a little but he wasn't breathin' as crazy as he had been a minute ago. You could tell he liked it out there, and he liked Jamie. He trusted him.

Jamie held the end of the rope and he sorta moved one of his hands down it so he was holdin' it really close to where it snapped onto the halter. So his hands were sorta at both ends of the rope. "Ready, boy." He kinda pulled at the end closest to Puck's head, and Puck followed. All Jamie did was turn in a circle, standin' in the same place, and he got Puck to walk around him. 'Course, Puck stopped a couple times. An animal is gonna do that. Because it probably seems pretty stupid to them at first. But all Jamie had to do was kinda nudge him by turnin' a little more and pullin' at the rope, and Puck would start up again.

They did that for a while. Just really slow. Jamie talkin' to the colt every once in a while. Like "Good boy" and stuff like that. Some water and mud was sloppin' up from Puck's hooves and some of it would fly up and stick to his legs or land onto Jamie's jeans or somethin'. Jamie looked down at his boots when he saw how Puck's hooves were kinda sinkin' into the ground, makin' a circle of prints around him. He had a puddle formin' around his feet too, and his boots were gettin' muddy and wet. Christ, it seemed good to be outside to Jamie.

He looked back up at Puck and gave him a little more slack. That widened the circle Puck was walkin' around in.

Jamie kept his eyes on the animal. And he watched how each of its legs followed one another, all in sync with one another, and how it lifted its hooves and threw its head a little once in a while to make Jamie think that it was really the one callin' the shots. He watched its muscles all move in one motion, too. Like everything was connected and workin' in one direction, even its ears seemed to be pointed forward. Jamie didn't look at much else while he was watchin' Puck. But it was like—like, how would you describe it? Jamie could feel his feet in his boots, the little room between his warm socks and the end of his boots. He could feel where his boots met his ankles and where he had tied his laces tight around them. He felt the tightness of his long john shirt too and how it kinda shaped around his chest and arms and stuff. He could actually feel a flick of mud fly off from one of Puck's front hooves and splatter onto his jeans. He felt the air and the sun on the tip of his nose and the little flap of hair that stuck out between his cap and that plastic band you use to make it smaller or bigger. He was even, like aware of the Catskills in the distance, like the long, bare trees and the evergreens that sat on them, and where the peaks met the sky.

It was strange. That and the way Puck watched him back,

between the blinks of those big brown eyes. Jamie saw how Puck's stare was on him, too, but like the horse felt what he felt. Not *what* he felt maybe, but the *way* he felt. Sorta, yuh know. It was really strange, but in a really good way.

He started to turn a little faster and Puck watched him. When he picked up his pace, Puck did too and his walk turned into a really slow trot. Puck lifted his legs a little more and bent his knees with this, this — some kinda ability or somethin' that horses must inherit because he trotted and it looked like he'd been doin' it forever. Almost prancin'. Really graceful-like.

Jamie's mom had been in the feedstore when Jamie got home. Things were pretty steady but she usually had everything under control until Jamie got home and changed his clothes and did the barn work and all that kinda crap. Today she needed him though. Farley Westerley, yeah, what a bad name, Farley. Farley Westerley had called and he was all in a huff — like he usually was about somethin', today it was he wanted to pick up a buncha stuff with his pickup and get home in time to milk his cows. Most everybody was pretty cool and didn't act all outa their minds, but Farley Westerley could get outa control. He was type B personality or somethin'. Maybe it was his name. Anyway, he needed like heavy stuff, and odds and end stuff, and Mary couldn't really have it ready and watch the front counter, too. Willy, his cousin, wasn't in today either. So she needed Jamie. She tacked a note on the feedstore door that said "Be right back" and she went to ask him if he would come help her.

She called for him when she came in the barn. And when he didn't answer, she walked down through it. She called him a couple times, but he was outside with Puck, so he couldn't hear her. She followed the barn to the end and then went around the "L" end of it and saw that the colt wasn't there and saw the back doors into the corral sorta half open, and she put two and two together. Mary walked to the door and kinda looked out and she stopped herself when she was gonna say Jamie's name. She stuck her head through the space that the two big barn doors had left and she saw Jamie and the colt.

She woulda said they looked like they were in their element out there that afternoon. Jamie had given Puck a little more rope and quickened the pace a little more and the colt was goin' at a good clip around him now. Pucker-up, that's what Mary had been callin' him, looked amazing. His tail was sorta pointed out and his back was smooth and curved and his hooves seemed to touch the ground and bounce off it with his heartbeats. But it was more than just Puck. Mary moved the door a little, but she was tryin' to do it all quiet when she did, so Jamie and the colt wouldn't see her. She moved it a little so she could sorta stand there, and get a better look. It wasn't just Puck at all. She crossed her arms over her chest—she was a little chilly—and she leaned against the door. She looked at Jamie. She noticed how the cuffs of his pants, just at the very bottom around his boots, were gettin' a little muddy and wet and she saw the way he was startin' to fill out his white long john shirt, and the way his hair curled a little out from under his cap. She saw exactly how he held the halter rope with both hands. The end sorta wrapped around one and the other a little over and under it and up it. Gripped to it. The rim of his hat shadowed his face a little too, but she could see how he watched the colt, or worked with the colt with his eyes, just by lookin' at it he gave it its freedom and taught it at the same time.

Mary and James had been married a couple years before they had Jamie. They got married because they were in love. Well, you know, sometimes people don't get married for that reason, they have a lot of other stupid reasons why they get married and then find out they hate each other like a month or a year later. Mary and James got married and worked together and paid off some loans, school loans and farm loans and stuff like that, and took over the farm from James's parents and expanded it and started the petting zoo and grew stuff to sell. They wanted to have somethin' for their first kid, give him—or her—the life that they had when they were growin' up. Like a good family and bein' able to be outdoors and not have a neighbor's house right on top of yuh. They didn't care or expect him to stick around forever, like they were puttin' money away for Jamie for college if he grew up and decided he wanted to go someday or somethin', but when he was a kid, they just wanted to be able to give him— two parents and—like security. Like barbecues and marshmallows on sticks on hot summer nights, and havin' a pumpkin—the biggest or the smallest one he wanted—to carve on Halloween, or bein' able to pick out a Christmas tree with his dad the first week of December. They wanted stuff like that for him. And they gave him that stuff and a shit load more stuff like that. Then Jamie's dad died. Like outa fuckin' nowhere on this November day before Thanksgiving. Rainy and cold as hell. He died. He wasn't old or anything either. Like 36. An aneurysm. And the doctors told his mom that sometimes things like that happen. Things like that happen.

She watched him, his face under the brim of his hat.

Jamie was turnin' pretty fast now and his arms were stretched out. He'd given Puck most of the rope, and Puck was at a run now.

Mary squinted and each time his face revolved around, she saw Jamie's dark brown eyes on Puck and she saw how he watched him with an intent watch. She noticed how he was gettin' whiskers, shadows now, but whiskers soon, and she saw the color that the sun and the February air had put in his cheeks. She saw something else too. Somethin' she hadn't seen in a long time on his face. He was smiling. Unguarded. It was on the small side and his lips were closed, but it was a smile.

She watched him a second more and kinda turned real slow back into the barn. Farley Westerley could load his own today. Wouldn't hurt him to.

Chapter Seventeen

"Yuh all set, sweetie."

"Yut, I'm all set, Rosie."

"Okay, hold on, honey."

Ben put his hands on the wheels of his wheelchair and steadied it. He woulda anyway, even if she hadn't of told him to, but she always did before he could get himself all on and ready.

Rosemary Lewis hit the switch on the lift and the thing started to hum and move up real slow. "Hold yourself real tight, doll, Milf down at the garage gave this thing a work over and now it's got some real zip." Rosemary bent forward when she said that to Ben and she kinda whacked him on the shoulder and laughed. She was an over-laugher, always had been. Sweet lady, from what Ben had told Jamie, but an over-laugher. Rosemary, or Rosie as Ben had always called her, had been his driver for most of his life. She wasn't the one who dumped Ben off that day in the snow. Remember that day? That was some fill-in. Rosie wouldn't of done that.

Jamie was already in the van-bus. Rosie had already made friends with him, and opened the sliding door for him and showed him where the seat belt was and everything and when he got in, she leaned into Ben and said, "He's a cutie, just like you, Benjamin, where you been hidin' him?" Then she stood up straight and laughed hard. She had asked Jamie things like "What's your name, honey?" and "How 'bout your last name?" and "What's your dad's first name and did he graduate from Coformon High?" and "What year, do yuh know?" Oh, yeah, she knew him, she told him. He was a looker, too. Then came the "Now he wasn't the one, doll, who...?" and "Geeze, honey, I'm sorry to hear that." She even got into what was his mom's maiden name while she was lowerin' the lift for Ben.

Rosie got her hair permed, tight, every two weeks, and it'd been the same dark orange since Ben was about seven. She always wore some sweatshirt or T-shirt from places people take vacations. Disney. Maine. Virginia Beach. You name it, she had one. Today, she had on a pink one that said "I Survived the Comet. The Great Escape, Lake George, New York."

The lift rattled up and stopped about halfway. Ben looked over at Rosie. "Gotcha didn't I?" She put her hand back on the switch and laughed and looked inside the van. "I'm always playin' tricks on this one, Jamie. He ever tell yuh the tricks I play on him?"

Jamie looked at Ben, and Ben was smilin' and shakin' his head. "Rosie's a character, Jamie. She's always full of it like this."

Rosie laughed at that one, too.

The lift had Ben level with the floor of the bus and Ben wheeled himself off it and sorta moved himself next to the seat Jamie was sittin' in.

Rosie folded the lift back up and slid the door closed and came back around the other side and got in. While she was doin' all that crap, Ben had asked Jamie to lock his wheels in place with these things on the floor of the van. Jamie did that for him and got back in his seat right when Rosie was gettin' in hers. She looked in the rearview. "He got you all set, sweets?"

"We're ready when you are, Rosie."

Rosie started the van and pulled from the curb and looked in her rearview again. She was always lookin' in the rearview at whoever was in back. "Buckle up, doll." She was lookin' at Jamie.

Jamie looked down at his lap. The straps of the seat belt were hangin' from the sides of his seat. "Oh, sorry." He snapped the belt across him.

"So, dude, what happened with that guy?"

"Oh, where'd I leave off?"

Rosie stopped at a light and she looked in the rearview. Rosie always wanted in on the conversation too. Not to jump in, just listen in.

"I dunno, you started to tell me how you went back to see him."

Jamie looked up and saw Rosie's eyes in the mirror. She quick looked down at the radio and turned it on real low. Country.

"Yeah, I went back. It's pretty weird. He like knows all this crap about me—I mean he's a really nice guy and everything—

but it's like really strange."

"So he didn't know your dad or anything."

Jamie shook his head. He was gonna tell him about the dream stuff but didn't wanna get into it right then. On the way to the bowling alley and stuff. It was a little out there too, yuh know.

The light had changed and Rosie turned. She had her eyes back in the mirror.

"Maybe he's psychic or somethin'."

They both kinda laughed.

"Yeah, maybe."

Rosie honked and waved at somebody walkin' down the street. She knew everybody.

"Hey, so, how was the party?"

Ben kinda shifted his eyes to the front of the bus, and flattened out his hand sorta on his lap.

Jamie nodded.

"I'll tell yuh, later." Ben said low.

Rosie was watchin' the street and sorta singin' along to Dolly Parton's "Here You Come Again," but she was listenin' all right.

They talked about some neutral topic for a couple minutes. Like the crazy weather they were havin' and stuff like that.

The bowling alley was only about three or four blocks from the school, and Rosemary Lewis probably coulda got them there blindfolded. She had been drivin' buses for Coformon Falls school district for 17 years this coming August. She pulled up in front of Mike and Margie's Hi-Pro Lanes and shut off the van. "One of these days, I'm gonna come in again and bowl with you, Ben." She had done that a couple times, once when Ben was in seventh grade and once when he was in ninth. She was a hell of a bowler, she bowled on the women's league on Saturday nights during the winter months. Knew Mike and Margie, too, real well.

"Anytime, you need me to show yuh how it's done, Rosie." Ben liked Rosie, she was a good lady, yuh know.

She laughed her way around to the other side of the van and pulled open the door and pulled down the lift.

"Jamie, yuh wanna get these again." Ben pointed towards his wheel locks.

Jamie undid his seat belt and got on his knees and undid Ben's locks. They weren't really locks, just these pieces of metal that snapped over the wheels and into the floor of the van.

"Thanks."

"Sure."

Ben did some maneuverin' and was on the lift again and goin' down.

Jamie jumped down after him.

"All set, fellas?"

"Yeah, thanks, Rosie."

"I'll be back in about a half, okay, doll." She put her hand on Ben's shoulder.

"Sounds good."

"Nice to meet you."

"Oh, you too sweetie. I'll see yuh in a few minutes." She leaned in a little to Ben. "I like him better than the other one, that little wise-ass kid." Rosie always let Ben know which friends of his she liked and didn't like. And she didn't like Ron Dychett.

Ben kinda laughed. If he was a kid, it woulda been a giggle. Jamie wouldn't have called it a chuckle because he hated the word chuckle—it was so corny. When Ben said somethin' funny or he kinda thought somebody else said somethin' funny, he usually smiled because this one short laugh was tryin' to make its way out from him. He did one of those laughs when Rosie called Ron Dychett the little wise-ass kid.

Jamie didn't know if he was suppose to hear that, what Rosie had said, and he didn't know which friend of Ben's she was talkin' about anyway, but it's just one of those things that you just kinda looked around at how few cars there are in the parking lot when somebody is sayin' it. So that's what Jamie did.

"Ready, Jamie?"

Rosie was gettin' back in her van, and Jamie turned back to 'em when Ben said that to him.

"Sure. I haven't worn those shoes in a while, so I'm kinda psyched."

"Oh, shit, those half and half shoes." Ben laughed.

"With busted laces. Bowling alleys never buy new shoelaces."

"Yeah, they don't." Ben was still smilin'. He started wheelin' himself towards the ramp into the place.

Jamie picked up beside him.

"And they think a shot of powder's gonna kill the skank from the guy's foot before yuh."

"That is so true, like if the shoe is still sweaty from whoever's foot."

"Now there's one plus to havin' one of these." Ben patted the wheel of his wheelchair and laughed again.

Jamie sorta laughed, too.

Rosie honked when she had put the bus in gear and started to pull out. Ben didn't turn around, but he waved his hand so she could see him in the rearview. Yuh knew she had to be lookin' in the rearview.

"How do you like Rosie?"

"It's like you said, she's a character."

They got to the ramp. "Hey, wanna get behind me and give me a hand, this is pretty steep."

Ben was pretty good at doin' stuff for himself, but the moron who had built this ramp just to meet code had put in more of a mini ski slope.

Jamie got behind Ben, and started to push. Ben was still helpin' with the wheels.

"Yeah, she totally hates Dychett." He kinda looked behind him.

Jamie didn't say anything.

"You know Dychett, right?"

They were almost to the top.

"Yeah, I know Ron."

When they got to the door of the place, Jamie sorta stopped.

"I think this is a push door, Jamie, so you just shove me and my leg rests'll bang it open."

Jamie did what Ben said and the door swung open and they went in.

"Good deal. Thanks."

The place was dead. Nobody bowls in the afternoon, especially on a weekday. Mike or Margie or both of 'em had to be there, though. They lived there. Literally. They had their place above the bar.

Ben wheeled over to the counter and tapped the bell.

A couple seconds later, Mike came out from the snack bar counter, from under the Slush Puppie machine. He was really tall with a mustache and glasses and a balding head.

"Well, hello Benny, how's it hangin'?"

Ben laughed and kinda looked at Jamie out of the corner of his eye. "Same as it always is, Mr. Sims."

Mike Sims had a cloth, and he was wipin' his hands. It was like he had some of the raspberry blue, and cherry stuff on his hands. "That damn Slush Puppie machine is all outa whack again, boys. The interior cooling system under the pressurizer is shot to hell, and the damn flavors are all comin' out at the same time, and they want yuh to call a goddamn Slush Puppie repairman and charge yuh a goddamn arm and a leg to fix the goddamn thing." Half the time he was lookin' at Ben and Jamie, and the other half of the time he was lookin' over towards the big rotating cup on the Slush Puppie machine. At least that still worked. "I shoulda never bought the thing used. Margie told me not to." He looked back to Ben and Jamie. "I think I'm just gonna tell 'em to take the thing and shove it up their asses. Puppie's nose first. Whatta you boys think?" He just kinda looked at Ben and Jamie like he was serious.

Both Ben and Jamie were lookin' at him. Both of 'em were sorta shakin' their heads. They looked towards the Slush Puppie machine.

Mike hit the counter with his hand, and they sorta jumped and looked back towards him. He started laughin'. He could hardly get out what he wanted to say he was laughin' so hard. "Either of you boys know anything about freakin' Slush Puppie machines?"

Jamie just started laughin'. He couldn't help it. And Ben sat there a second with his jaw dropped a little bit, and then he started crackin' up, too.

Mike put the rag in his back pocket. "All righty, Benny. Who's this fella with yuh today?"

"This is Jamie, Mr. Sims."

Jamie reached across the counter and shook hands with Mr. Sims. "Nice to meet yuh."

"You too, Jamie. What size shoe you take?"

"Uh, like a 9, 9 and a 1/2."

Mr. Sims was already reachin' under the counter for that section. A trait of the business, yuh know, knowin' people's shoe size just by lookin' at 'em.

He pulled out a pair of 9s and set 'em on the counter. "We don't have halves, so give these a try and if they're too tight, we'll get yuh some 10s."

"Thanks." Jamie started to get out his money. He'd brought a couple extra bucks along today, knowin' they were bowlin' an' all.

"School gets it, Jamie."

Mr. Sims was already at the cash register, punchin' somethin' in when Ben filled Jamie in. "You're all set, boys. End alley, number 30." Mike Sims prided himself on the fact that Mike and Margie's had thirty alleys, the most alleys in the tri-town area.

"Thanks Mr. Sims." Ben grabbed a score sheet from the counter and stuck a beat-up pencil from the box behind his ear. (No electronic scoreboard stuff on weekdays.)

Mike was still punchin' in the school code and turnin' on the lane and stuff like that. And he gave 'em a wave without lookin' up.

Jamie picked up the shoes and followed Ben.

It was strange to be in a bowling alley when no one was there. The few cars in the lot musta been some people who parked there and worked at the industrial park across the street because the place didn't have a soul in it.

The two of 'em got a couple balls. They separated to do that, one rack never has a good supply of balls, and they met at lane 30.

Jamie put his shoes on. They were cold and stiff and a little tight, but not bad.

Ben stuck the score sheet under the clip on the table and put the pencil there too. "You know how to keep score?"

"No, do you?"

"Sorta, I really don't get strikes or spares anyway, so it won't be that hard."

"Me either, I don't know the last time I bowled." Jamie got up and put his ball in the ball holder.

Ben was sittin' there with his on his lap. "All right Jamie, yuh wanna give me a hoist up there."

Jamie had been movin' to sit at the scorekeeper seat. He went over to Ben.

"Okay, yuh just gotta turn me and tip me back."

Jamie got behind him and turned Ben's back wheels so they touched the step up to the lane. "Like this?"

"Yeah, now tip back and pull."

Jamie did, and Ben was on the lane.

"Thanks." Ben reached over and put his ball beside Jamie's. "You wanna go first?"

"Naw, you can." Jamie went back to the seat and wrote in Ben and put his name under it.

If you've ever bowled, and you're really not that good at it, you kinda know that once you've thrown your ball a couple times and you've gotten some gutter balls and a few splits that your ball goes straight in between on the second roll, or your best frame is a seven or somethin', you know that the whole game is more about the social experience than the game itself. Even Rosemary Lewis would agree to that in a way. Give her a bowling ball and a few of the girls and a longneck Bud or two, and she would definitely agree.

Ben stayed up on the lane because it was a pain to keep gettin' down and then back up that step, so it made it kinda hard to shoot the breeze.

He went and Jamie went, and, honestly, they both pretty much sucked. They were laughin' though, and Ben had to press the reset button a couple times because his ball kept gettin' stuck in the gutter at the end for some reason. Twice Jamie had to straddle the two gutters beside each other and knock it the rest of the way in and that pretty much cracked 'em both up.

Jamie went up and kinda just stayed there after one of his turns, and he sat on the end of the ball holder.

"Do you wanna keep score or fuck it?"

"Do you?"

Ben picked his ball out of the holder. "Not really. We gotta show Coach Martin the sheet, so we'll just write in numbers for two games before we get back to school."

"All right."

Ben put his ball on his lap and wheeled himself up to the line. He tossed his ball, and it rolled down the alley and knocked over a couple pins on the one side.

He half turned to Jamie. "So, what were you doin' with that book yesterday?"

"Book?" Jamie sorta tipped his head.

"Yeah, that big book when I saw yuh in the library yesterday."

"Oh. Yeah. That kids' book."

The ball came rollin' back up the alley and Jamie got up on instinct. It came up the curve and the ball stopper slowed it down. It still clunked into Jamie's. Ben wheeled over and picked it up. "Yeah, that one."

"Remember the guy I was tellin' yuh about?" Jamie sat back down, and Ben sat there with his ball on his lap. "Yeah, you didn't say much about him in the van."

Jamie kinda nodded his head. "Yeah, I know. It's just all pretty nuts that's why. He had said somethin' about this Pandora—"

"Pandora?"

"Yeah, Pandora."

"Oh, I just didn't know if I heard yuh right."

"Yeah, so I didn't know who it was, so I tried to find somethin' about her, and that's the only book the library had."

"Yeah, that place is filled with information, right." Ben started to wheel to the line again for his second roll. "So who was she?"

"She opened this box that was filled with all this crappy shit that came flyin' out of it, but at the bottom of it was hope."

Ben rolled and came back over. "Hope, huh?"

"Yeah. It's a Greek myth or somethin'."

Ben kinda looked down at his lap a second.

Jamie looked at him, and then Ben's ball came flyin' back to

210

'em and they both turned to look at it. Jamie got up and picked up his ball. "So you started to tell me about the party."

Ben watched his ball get slowed down by the stopper. "Oh. Yeah. It was a good time. It gets a little stale though after every weekend. Like I was really fuckin' pissed at Passellow."

"Why?" Jamie sorta held his ball up and tried to line it up between the arrows on the floor. He took a couple steps and let it go.

Ben and him watched and he knocked over like 5 or 6 pins. Jamie turned to face Ben. "Why were yuh?"

"He got a keg."

"You were pissed because he got a keg? I don't think I get it." Jamie sat on the thing. Where the hand fan is.

"Well, I told him no keg, to just get cases. I didn't want things to get too big. Outa control, yuh know."

"Okay, yeah. And he totally got one anyway."

Jamie's ball rolled towards 'em and shot up the curve before the stopper.

Jamie stood up.

"Yeah, they do shit like that all the time." Ben sorta moved his wheelchair so Jamie could get around him, even though he wasn't in the way at all.

Jamie picked up his ball. "Like what?"

"I dunno. Like yuh know how Rosie said Dychett's a wise-ass?"

"Yeah." Jamie was gonna aim his ball and all that crap, but he sat back down on the ball holder instead and put it on his lap.

"She's right, the kid is a complete wise-ass. He's the one friend my parents hate most. You can just tell by lookin' at him that he's practically a punk." Ben kinda looked over his shoulder.

Mr. Sims was polishin' some balls on one of the racks a ways down from them.

"I mean the only thing that separates him from somebody who everybody thinks is a grub is that his parents have a little dough, they get his smart-ass outa trouble when they have to, yuh know."

"I guess, I mean…" Jamie turned his ball over on his lap and found the holes and stuck a couple fingers in 'em, "you'd probably know better than I would."

"Naw, you must see it, Jamie, I mean people gotta see it. Other kids…teachers…even fuckin' Rosie Lewis sees it."

Ben was facin' Jamie, and Jamie shifted his eyes past him just for a second. Mike Sims was sortin' balls out, puttin' the heavier ones on the top shelves and the smaller ones on the bottom. Or vice versa. He looked back at Ben. "I don't know Ben." He was gonna stand up, but he didn't. "Then why do yuh hang out with 'em?"

Ben kinda laughed. "That's exactly it, man. I don't know."

Bowling balls don't bounce, they thump a couple times and roll. That's what this swirly blue one did that Mr. Sims knocked off the rack when he was tryin' to put another one in its place. Ben sorta looked over his shoulder and Jamie looked towards Mike Sims again too.

Mr. Sims looked up at 'em after he sorta scooted after the ball and caught it. He raised his one hand with the cloth and yelled down to 'em. "It's all right, boys, little bastard just got away from me is all."

Ben smiled back and gave a wave too. He turned back to

Jamie. "No, yuh know, it's just like I've been hangin' out with those guys—Passellow, Dychett, Rachel Stappuck, all those guys—" Ben sorta was stickin' out his fingers givin' off the names of his...clique. He had a clique just like most everybody did at Coformon High, and he knew it. "I've been hangin' out with that whole fuckin'...clique, and I don't know why I do. I guess it's just because I always have, like it's somethin' I've always done since junior high, so I just keep doin' it."

Jamie shifted the ball's weight on his lap and he kinda moved his leg. When he did, his ass pressed the reset button and two seconds later that thing that swipes your pins down did and it set up for a whole new bowl.

Ben and Jamie just sat and watched it until the pins were all standin' there. Sometimes there's one that wobbles and there was one this time. It was one close to the one in front and it sorta wobbled a little and then wobbled to a stop and then stood there.

They looked at each other and laughed.

"What'd yuh do?"

"I don't know, I think I sat on the reset button." Jamie looked down to where he was sittin' and then got up and looked behind him. "Yeah. I did."

He looked back at Ben, and Ben was really crackin' up now. "What?" Jamie was really smilin'.

Ben didn't answer. He couldn't.

Jamie was laughin' a little now too. "What?"

"Yuh—yuh shoulda seen your face." Ben was laughin'. "When you did that, you were like—" Ben raised his eyebrows and opened his mouth like he was all shocked and surprised. And he kept laughin'.

Jamie laughed. "I did not."

Ben just nodded.

Jamie shook his head, still laughin'. He walked around Ben and took a couple steps and just flung his ball down the alley. He didn't try to line up with the arrows or anything, he just swung his arm back and gave the ball a toss. It went whippin' down the floor and he turned around to Ben before it crashed into the pins.

"Holy shit, Jamie." Ben stopped laughin' for a second and was lookin' down at the other end of the alley.

"What?" Jamie looked behind him.

The silver lights above their lane were all lit up and flashin', and his pins were all knocked down.

"Holy shit." He turned back towards Ben.

"Staa-rike." Ben raised his arm up and his hand out for Jamie to slap.

Jamie took a couple quick steps towards Ben. They were both smilin' like crazy and they hi-fived.

They were totally grinnin' and half-laughin'. And they hi-fived like they had just won the war or somethin'.

Chapter Eighteen

ANGELO WAS outside the next day Jamie saw him. He was on the backside of the driveway towards the backside of his house. He had a little bed of flowers in front of some shrubs, and he was on his knees with some garden gloves on. It made it a lot easier seein' him out there, yuh know. Jamie was headin' down Rea like he did every day for lunch and instead of stoppin' after he walked to Ray's he kinda wanted to stop before he went up, but it was still kinda weird. When he saw Angelo outdoors though, it wasn't so strange to stop.

Jamie walked up the driveway, and Angelo was scratchin' the round garden with one of those little garden scratchers. He had some bulbs in a plastic bag sittin' beside him and a small spade there too. Angelo was turnin' the dirt over, and it was dark brown and looked like it was prime to be planted in. You wouldn't have thought it was February.

"It's a little early to plant anything, isn't it?"

215

Angelo looked up when he heard Jamie, and he smiled. He hadn't seen him come up the driveway, and, to be honest, yuh know when you're so into doin' something and other things only half register in your brain, that's how it was for Angelo. He was scratchin' at the ground, sorta smellin' the dirt of spring and thinkin' about things, so until Jamie was right there, he hadn't really looked up. And besides that, Angelo was expectin' Jamie sooner or later anyway, so it was no big surprise.

"I suppose it is, but they may just grow."

"You *hope* they grow." Jamie squatted down and he picked up the spade.

They looked at each other, and both of 'em smiled.

"Yes, I hope they do." Angelo started to scratch the ground again.

Jamie reached across the small garden, and he picked up the bag of bulbs too. He put the spade down and got on his knees and untied the twisty tie on the bag.

Both of 'em were quiet a minute, doin' what they were doin'. You could hear Angelo kinda breathin', and you could hear the dirt bein' turned over. Some birds were in the trees across the street and behind Angelo's house and you could hear them, too.

You could hear February.

Just as Jamie got the bag open and was settin' the twisty tie down, you could hear voices comin' down Rea.

It was those guys—Number 10, Rich Passellow and his buddies.

They were horsin' around and talkin' this and that. Jamie kinda looked over at Angelo as they came closer.

Angelo just kept scratchin' away. Like he was on a mission

or somethin'.

Jamie didn't turn to look at 'em when they walked by. They stopped talkin' for a second when they passed, and even though Jamie wasn't lookin' at 'em, he knew why they did. You can just feel when that happens, like on your skin and right through the hollow of your chest. He kept his head bent over the garden, and he set the bag beside him and sorta ran his hand across the dirt and then picked up the spade beside him and kinda got ready to dig a hole.

They passed and got to the corner.

Angelo just kept scratchin' at the ground, and the more he did the more it got softer and more ready to plant.

Jamie sat there with the spade, sorta pokin' at the ground, turnin' its point a little into the dirt. He got a bulb out of the bag and held it in his other hand.

They crossed the street, and their voices sorta faded from distinct words to sounds lost in the air.

"Can I start these?"

Angelo stopped and looked up. He had a little sweat startin' on his forehead. "Phew." He wiped it off with the back of his forearm and set his scratcher down. He put his hands on his thighs and looked at Jamie.

"A work out?"

"Sure was. I got used to doing one thing all winter and anything out of the routine seems harder than it really is." He kinda caught his breath, sort of, he wasn't pantin' or anything but it was like he just ran a little ways or somethin'.

"Guess it's like that with anything." Jamie sorta pointed to the dirt bed with his spade and bulb, and raised his eyebrows.

Angelo gave him a couple nods and stuck his hand out. "It's all yours."

Jamie started away from himself. He looked at the bag beside him, tryin' to figure about how many there was in it. It looked like about seven, so he reached across the garden, mappin' out seven in his head, and dug a hole sorta close to where Angelo was kneeled over.

Angelo liked the noonday sun. He looked towards it and felt it on his already warm face. Then he looked back at Jamie. He reached across the garden to where Jamie had set the bag and he got it. He was gonna hand 'em—the bulbs—to Jamie as Jamie went along.

Jamie had stuck the one bulb in and was shovelin' the dirt back around it, half with his hand, half with the spade. Well, more like pushin' the dirt back around it. When he finished, he dug another hole next to it and reached for the bag beside him, then looked up to Angelo. "Oh."

Angelo handed him a bulb.

Jamie started to plant it.

Angelo watched him. How Jamie set the bulb just so, but without too much thought—not like he didn't give a crap but like it was second nature to him. Angelo watched how he filled the hole back up and patted the dirt lightly up and around it. And how he dug the next hole a little ways from the last bulb he just planted, about the same distance he had just planted the one from the one before that. It was time to give the key another turn.

Angelo handed him another bulb. "Your afternoon with Puck went well."

Jamie stopped and looked up a second. He looked right at

Angelo, and he didn't say anything. Not until he looked back down and started to shovel again. "Whatta yuh spy on me or somethin', Angelo?" He finished the hole and put his hand out for a bulb. He didn't look up, he just reached out for one.

Angelo got one out of the bag and handed it to him.

Jamie started to do his thing with it.

Ever get pissed and it's like—it's like when you pour your cereal and there's not milk and you gottta have a frozen waffle instead? Or you sit down to watch a show and you're sorta into it and then it gets interrupted by an ABC special report or somethin', or the cable goes out. Or your pencil point snaps so you gotta walk in the other room and sharpen it again. You're like pissed, but it's there and gone in about two or three heartbeats. That's how Jamie felt.

"So you have like a crystal ball or somethin' you watch me through?" He kinda cracked a smile so Angelo could see it.

"Jamie, your dream's opening up for you right before your eyes. You're moving along faster than anyone who's ever had one coming. But part of it is accepting some things you can't explain, realizing that today it might not make sense but somewhere along the way it will."

Thump, thump, thump. Jamie patted the dirt with the spade around the bulb. When the little green end of the bulb was stickin' out of the dirt, like it had always been there, along with the other one, he stopped a second, and looked up at Angelo. "Sorry, I didn't mean to get all—"

Angelo always smiled but sometimes his smile was broader or longer or more rounded than it was at other times, and he lit one of his bigger ones across his face when he interrupted Jamie.

219

"That's quite all right, Jamie."

"It's just that this doesn't even seem real—I mean," Jamie looked down at the bulb he just put in the ground and pointed at it with his spade in his hand, "I'm sittin' here plantin' flowers with somebody I barely—some stranger who told me I've got a little pillow with my name on it that's gonna make some dream happen." Jamie kinda took the spade and ran its point across the fresh dirt. He sorta chiseled its point into the soft surface. "Yuh know what I mean? It's just that..." He looked back at Angelo.

Angelo waited for him to finish, but Jamie didn't. "It is real though, Jamie. Maybe a certain kind of real. Just like everything else that happens. A certain kind of reality that you can't make sense out of or figure out yet because you're in the middle of it."

"I'm always tryin' to figure things out, I can't just accept 'em like that, there's gotta be an answer."

"Not always. And if there is it might come disguised as something else. It might not come at all. Not until you've shed one of your skins and grown another or shed that one or the next one and grown a different one."

Jamie looked over his shoulder at Rea Street. He looked at a swing set somebody across the street had sittin' on their front lawn. It was one of those swing sets with the two swings and chin-up bar between 'em and the slide attached to the side. "I had a great afternoon with Puck." He looked back at Angelo, and then started to dig another hole. "It was like—" He looked up for a bulb.

Angelo already had his hand stretched out with one.

"Thanks." Jamie started to plant it. "It's like I—or we— were..." He finished the job and stopped.

"Were?"

He looked at Angelo. "Like we were alive. Really alive." Jamie kinda spread his arms and sorta looked to his sides and up. "Like everything was really alive and we knew it. But at the same time, we were so into doin' what we were doin'." Jamie felt it in his chest when he talked about it. This swelled-up wave or somethin' started there, and it planted a big-ass smile, that he couldn't help or stop, right across his face.

Angelo just looked at him and smiled, too. "The beginnings of the next step, Jamie. You have the beginnings of the next step."

"What?"

Angelo reached in the bag and pulled out another bulb, and kinda nodded towards the little garden.

"Right, right." Jamie started to dig another hole.

They didn't say anything for a couple minutes, they just planted the bulbs. A couple of cars went down Main, but other than that it was pretty quiet. Just some birds, maybe the squeak of the chin-up bar on the swing set across the street as it kinda rocked in the breeze. The sound of Jamie's spade in the dirt or the sound of Angelo's hand reachin' in the plastic bag for another bulb, that was it.

When Jamie packed the dirt around the last one, Angelo was waddin' up the plastic bag and standin' up. "Let's get a few more of these from the greenhouse."

Jamie had set the bulbs in the ground in sort of a design, but there were some gaps here and there, he thought it could definitely use a few more, too. "Greenhouse?"

"Umm-hmm. There's one attached to the back of the house."

Angelo said it like it was some normal thing to have a greenhouse attached to the back of your house.

Jamie looked towards the back of Angelo's house and he saw the clear glass walls of a greenhouse juttin' out from behind it. Like it was a 20x20 addition to the house or somethin'. He kinda lowered his brows. He'd never seen it there until today. Until right now. And he'd walked by this house like a million times.

Angelo had turned, and he was on his way over there, so Jamie stood up. He looked at the greenhouse one more time, kinda wiped some of the wet dirt off his knees, and then dropped his spade by the garden and followed Angelo.

Jamie had a thing for greenhouses. The warm, humid air of 'em. How everything is so green and alive with some kinda smell. He used to go to Diamond's Greenhouse with his dad in Richfield to get flowers for his mom or plants to start the garden with. When he was a kid that was a big deal. Maybe everything has some big impression on yuh when you're a kid, because as he crossed the lawn to the back door of this thing, he kinda wondered why he had been so into Diamond's Greenhouse. It was cool to go into and everything, but when he went last spring with his mom, it seemed smaller in there or somethin'.

Angelo led them to the back door of the thing, so like if you were goin' in with 'em you would be walkin' in and walkin' towards the house. There were some woods that laid behind Angelo's house. Jamie looked into 'em, thinkin' maybe they were why he hadn't seen the greenhouse. Angelo opened the door and the warm air just whooshed out at 'em. They kinda had to go in fast, even though it was a nice day out, it was still cooler than the air in the greenhouse. So Jamie followed Angelo in, and shut the door behind them.

The place was a lot bigger than it looked from the outside. Jamie couldn't even see the other end. He sorta looked for the door that was attached to the house, and he couldn't see it. "Man, this is like a jungle in here. A big jungle."

"It's where I grow some of the more exotic ingredients for the pillows."

There were a couple aisles, maybe three or four, and Angelo went down one of 'em. Jamie just followed him, but he was lookin' around the whole time. There was green everywhere. Like you wouldn't believe. Buds on plants, like bright purple and red and pink. You name it. He looked up and the roof was maybe 20 feet high and the sun was streamin' in through it. There were hanging plants and small, little ones in pots and nursery trays. Even huge cactuses with those little flowers on some of 'em. You wouldn't believe it, Jamie hardly did. His mouth was a little open while he was lookin' at all the stuff.

They cut down the middle of an aisle and went a couple over and went further down that one. Angelo stopped at a counter where it looked like you could plant stuff on it and cut flowers and stuff like that. There was a stack of planting trays and some stray dirt on it and a little shovel. There was a tray that was half full with dirt, like one side had dirt and the other side was sorta empty, like someone had been diggin' around in it. Angelo slid that tray closer to him and set down his bag and picked up the little shovel. It was the tray with the bulbs in it.

"Yuh want some help?" Jamie came up beside Angelo, and he stuck his hand in the bag to like fluff it out.

Angelo dug out a bulb and handed it to Jamie, and Jamie

stuck it in the bag.

"What kinda plant is that?" Jamie pointed to a small plant that was tucked in the corner of the worktable. It was in a little ceramic pot and it seemed like it was set away from the rest of the stuff in there, like Angelo was givin' it some special attention or somethin'. It didn't look sickly or anything, it looked pretty good as a matter of fact, but it was so different from the other ones. That's why Jamie asked him. It had like spirally leaves for one thing. And it was bright green, almost fluorescent green but not that funky color. A nice, tree green, yuh know. And the leaves were almost whitish with streaks of red and violet and yellow through 'em. It had sort of a sturdy stalk with these crazy spiral leaves. Jamie looked back at Angelo.

Angelo handed him another bulb and stopped and looked at the plant. "Funny you ask, Jamie. It's the srepattramer, grown on a tiny island called La Isla Desengelor off from Mozambique. That plant, when it matures, produces the last ingredient I'll add to your pillow before I give it to you."

Jamie stuck the bulb in the bag. "Sree-patram-er? Really." He bent a little and put his elbows on the counter and looked closer at the plant.

"What would you say it's doing right now?"

Jamie stayed how he was, but he looked up at Angelo. "Doing?"

Angelo nodded.

Jamie looked back at the plant. "Uuhhh...I dunno." He shook his head a little. "I dunno."

"What does it look like it's doing?"

Jamie kept lookin' at it, then he looked up at the clear glass of the roof and the bright rays comin' through it. "It looks like it's reachin' for the sun, I guess."

"How do you think it feels?" Angelo started to dig out another bulb.

Jamie kinda laughed. He stood straight again. "I couldn't even tell yuh that one."

Angelo dug a little and looked over at him. "Try."

"It feels like...a good feelin', like it's growin' I guess." Jamie reached for the bulb Angelo had just uncovered. He didn't wait for him to hand it to him. He kinda tapped the dirt off from it into the planting tray and stuck it in the bag. "It's got one thing on its mind, I guess, the sun."

"Do you suppose it feels the same way that you and Puck felt yesterday?"

Jamie looked at the plant again. It caught the sun's light on some of the streaks of colors in its leaves and it looked like somebody had sprinkled glitter on it or somethin'. He kinda tipped his head to the side a second before he answered. "Yeah. It could...it definitely could." He looked back at Angelo. "It's all into the sun and focused on it, yuh know. So, yeah, it could."

Angelo had two bulbs in his hand, and he gave them to Jamie, and Jamie stuck 'em in the bag.

"How many do we have?"

Jamie opened the bag a little more and looked in. "One, two, three, looks like we have five."

"That should be just enough, don't you think?"

"Yeah, it should be."

Angelo set his little shovel back on the counter. Jamie was gonna lead, he picked up the bag and turned to head for the door they came in.

"We'll go through the house, Jamie. I need to add a few things to your dream-way mix."

Jamie turned and saw Angelo standin' there, smilin' as usual, waitin' for him, and pointin' toward the opposite end he had been headin' in, the end connected to the house.

"Oh, okay."

Jamie kinda brushed one of his hands off on his jeans and followed Angelo. They walked down the aisle and it sorta seemed too narrow. Or the plants and stuff on both sides of 'em got bigger and bushier or somethin' because they walked a few more feet and it was like they were walkin' through someplace overgrown with wild green leaves and stuff. There were big round leaves and long thick ones on both sides of Jamie and he kinda put his hands in front of himself to separate 'em and keep 'em from swipin' him in the eye. He could hear Angelo in front of him and he took a couple more steps and could make out Angelo pushin' the door open.

When he got to the door, Angelo was holdin' it open for him. "Geeze, this end really is like a jungle." He stepped from the greenhouse and into the room. He looked up. They were in the dining room where the big table was, and the bowl—the blue bowl with this "dream-way mix"—was still sittin' there on the baby scale, and it sorta glowed in the dim room.

The room was dim, but not dark, and Angelo flicked a switch on by the door they had just came through. Jamie got out of the door's way and Angelo let it go. It was a swinging door, and when Angelo moved towards the table, Jamie looked behind himself.

The door kinda swung closed with a couple swipes of the

door frame like swinging doors always do.

Jamie looked at it and then at the room and then back at the door. It was the same door that—

"You already have the second piece almost in place, Jamie."

Jamie turned, and Angelo was already bent over the table with an opened jar in his hand. He went over and stood beside him.

Angelo must have added a couple things to the bowl since Jamie had last been there. Jamie leaned over the table and looked into the mixture in the bowl. It had turned sort of a midnight blue and had specks of bright yellow sand all through it, the gold sand Angelo had added the other day. It all looked thick and soft.

Angelo was rummagin' through the stuff on the table, under some of that tissue paper you wrap flowers in, and he came up with a wooden spoon. "Here, take this."

He handed it to Jamie. Jamie still had the bag of bulbs and he found a place for 'em on the table, and he took the spoon.

"Hold it out please."

Jamie held it out.

Angelo took the jar he had and held it in both hands. He shook the stuff that was in it onto the spoon. All careful-like.

All it looked like to Jamie was pencil dust. Like the crap you see at the bottom of a garbage pail after somebody empties a pencil sharpener.

Jamie just watched. Angelo seemed to put a good heap on the spoon Jamie was holdin' out, and then he took the jar and capped it and set it on the table.

"Dump it in?"

"No, not yet." Angelo was scannin' the table. "I

neeeed…there it is." He reached between two jars and came up with a little bottle. Like a little perfume bottle, one with one of those tops that sticks in it and you pull it out. It looked really old, all carved glass and stuff. There wasn't any label on it like most of the stuff on the table, and the liquid in it was clear but sorta green.

"I don't get it. What's the second piece?"

Angelo took the stopper out and he turned back to Jamie. Jamie was still standin' there with the spoon with pencil shavings heaped on it. Angelo moved his hand with the bottle up to the spoon. He bent at his knees a little so he was eye-level with the pile of pencil stuff. He steadied his hand with his other hand, kinda holdin' it at his wrist, and he dabbed a few drops of the clear liquid with a green tint onto the pile.

The stuff, when the third or fourth drop Angelo tipped onto it hit, disintegrated. Like that. "What the hell was that stuff?" Jamie looked up at Angelo and then back at the spoon. He held a wooden spoon full of bright yellow liquid now that smelled like…it smelled like the outdoors. Like if you were on a mountain or in the woods and there were pine trees all around you or a wide-open space and a pool of fresh spring water.

Angelo stood straight again and tipped the bottle. "Just some extracts from one of the plants I grow." He set the bottle back in its place. "Harmless stuff." He looked back to Jamie. "You can dump that in there now. Thank you, I always have the hardest time doing that by myself."

Jamie, really slowly, moved his hand across the table and over the bowl. "Just dump it in?" He looked towards Angelo.

Angelo had picked up the bag of bulbs Jamie had set down.

He had them in his hand, and he nodded to answer Jamie.

Jamie turned back to the bowl, and he tipped the spoon.

The liquid poured into the thick soft stuff and kinda laid there on top.

"Give it a stir, would you?"

Jamie dipped the spoon in the stuff and stirred it a couple times. He thought he felt heat comin' off from it. The stuff he had poured in hadn't changed the color or anything. It was still dark blue with speckles of that gold sand. It hadn't made it wetter either. Jamie stirred it a couple more times and tapped the spoon on the edge of the bowl when he stopped. He looked at it and it was dry. Nothing on it at all. "Where do you want this?" Jamie turned and Angelo was—

He turned behind him and Angelo had left the room, he was over in the little room just inside the front door. He had the bag of bulbs in one hand, he was windin' the back of his clock with his other. Jamie sorta yelled over to him. "I'm done. Where do you want this?"

Angelo looked up. "Oh, anywhere there that I can find it. Thank you, Jamie."

Jamie kinda looked across the table. It was a mess. He just sorta set the spoon on top of a couple jars where he thought Angelo would see it if he needed it.

He looked at the bowl one more time and he kinda shook his head and smiled.

Angelo was standin' at the door, with it open, waitin' for him. He crossed the living room. "So you didn't tell me what this second piece that I almost have is."

"You don't expect it to be that easy, do you Jamie?"

Jamie came across the room and into the little room Angelo was standin' in. "I guess not, but I really don't have a clue today. I mean yesterday I, you headed me in the right direction."

Angelo smiled and looked at the clock. "We should finish this before you have to go back." He looked at Jamie and started out the door.

Jamie just stood there a second. Jesus. He looked over his shoulder to the shelf where the clock sat. He looked at it. It didn't even tell the right time for Christ's sake, why was Angelo always windin' it, and lookin' at it like it did? Jamie looked closer at it.

Yup, time was still the same. Maybe the second hand had clicked a couple seconds like the other day. He looked at the girl and that whole scene, that had changed some, he hadn't really studied it too much the last couple times, he hadn't really gotten past the clock's wrong time and the weird phrase thing, but he had a good idea that the scene had changed somehow too since the last time he saw it. Like, that plant, it had grown, it was tall and stickin' straight up, and she—the girl—was wipin' the sweat off from her or somethin' when she had been doin' somethin' else maybe before. The sun was right above them, too, and the little slot that the phrase slipped into had a new one. It said, "When it finds the sun's shine, the seed you've planted will grow in time."

Jamie heard Angelo open the other front door, the one at the end of the hall that went outside. "Hey, Angelo, wait up." He closed the door behind him and went down the hall.

The girl lifted her apron and wiped her warm face. And the second hand ticked another second.

Chapter Nineteen

TRUTH WAS, writing took up a good part of Jamie's time. He wrote in class all day. Takin' notes on a lot of crap like the cell structure of the bamboo shoot, and on the material used to make the variety of *les crèches* that the French set out *pour Noel*. Really useful stuff like that. He wrote vocabulary lists and other stuff for Francis's class, his English class, which could be interesting at times. And he wrote in his journal for that class, which was pretty cool. Francis might give them a topic or he might just say write what you did today. Jamie always kept up on his journal for Mr. Francis's class.

He had his own journal, too. Girls have diaries, guys have journals. Go figure. Well, some guys. What he couldn't put in his notebook for Francis he put in a separate notebook at home. Yuh know, stuff that he didn't want other people to see. At fifteen, you don't write a whole lot of personal stuff, because there's stuff you can't even admit to yourself or you're afraid if you write it on paper somebody's gonna read it somehow and know what a real freak you are. You don't get all philosophical either, because you think you've learned everything you're gonna learn at fifteen and that's the way the world is so why bother writin' about it, yuh know? Especially if you're a guy. Carry the weight. Be a man. Don't wonder. Just work, and sure as hell don't let anybody know what's goin' on inside yuh. Jamie didn't get that crap from his parents, but when you're a kid, your parents aren't the only people who are spoon-feedin' you ideas about what it means to be a guy. In fact, they're probably the last two people who are spoon-feedin' you anything. There's a hell of a lot of other people like teachers, people in school, TV, the president of the United States and whoever else who are shovin' shit down your throat and tellin' you the way things are and the way you should be.

But every night after he did his homework and if it wasn't really late and he wasn't dog-ass tired, Jamie usually wrote, even if it was just the small stuff that he did that day. Like he wrote about Puck the other day and how the weather was so strange. Stuff like that.

It was 10:30 that night. He sat at his desk in his underwear and in an old white undershirt, one like you've worn a few years and it's kinda beat from all the washes and it has real light yellow sweat stains under its arms even though the rest of it is still pretty white. He had brushed his teeth and all that stuff and did as much homework as he could do. He never got all his math done. You could never get all your math done.

He had his own notebook in front of him and a pen. Not the pen he used at school. He had a separate pen to write his own stuff. He didn't want school to rub off on his own stuff. He didn't wanna hold a school pen when he was writin' his own stuff.

His desk was pressed up to the window, and the curtains were open a crack and he could look out 'em. His room was on the back of the house, facin' the barn and the fields, and the Catskills behind them that sorta met the night sky. No lights. Like from houses or anything. It was nice. Peaceful, yuh know. He'd looked out the window for fifteen years, every season, and watched everything pretty much stay the same, sure the leaves would change or the ground and the barn roof would get covered with snow, but that was just the surface. Like the way a person changes clothes.

Jamie held his pen in his hand and before he opened to the next blank page he stared through the space the curtains had left for him to look out. It was night but he could see because there was a moon. A quarter of a moon. The kind that is on its side and you can make out the rest of the moon sittin' on it but it's not lit up. One of those moons. And it was bright white with blue where its crevasses—no, what's the word......craters. Where its craters were. There were a million stars too. He only had the little light on on his desk so he could see them, too.

He just stared out at it for like a minute. Like it put him in a trance or somethin'. Then he opened his notebook and wrote. He wrote about what was out the window, the sky and the stone of the mountains and the outlines of the hills and the barn roof. He wrote about the old chair he was sittin' in. He wrote about at Angelo's today and he wrote about what a weird, strange feeling it was to have a dream, and he wrote about bowling with Ben and how they flipped out when he got a strike. He wrote about how much he missed his dad and what a great mom he had and how he heard her get up at night because she couldn't sleep and how he saw her eyes just all of a sudden get watery when she was makin' out orders or somethin'. He wrote about the horses and how they whinnied and tossed their heads when they watched him break open a bale of alfalfa hay for 'em. He even wrote like he *was* one of the horses, and what it felt like to run with four legs and to be ridden. And then he tried on the coat of one of his goats and wrote how it was to chew on anything from someone's pant leg to another goat's ear. He wrote from other people's skin too and watched himself and told about things from there for a while, and somethin' about that made talkin' about himself a lot easier sometimes. He wrote about writing and about where he went when he did it and about the gold color of his old bedspread.

The ink was blue and it was one of those thick point pens, so it was smudgy and some got on the side of his hand. He wrote in cursive, and his letters and words started out tight and close together and then got bigger, and like somebody had knocked over a glass of milk or somethin', they were like spillin' all over the pages that he wrote on and seepin' in. He bent over it—what he wrote—and his hand was goin' a mile a minute. His longer hair on the top of his head hung down in front of him and almost touched the page because his face was so close to it, so bent over it. His left hand held the notebook like the thing was gonna fly off the table or somethin'. He pressed on it and held it in place, and he wrote.

He didn't know how to describe how it felt. But when he filled about three or four pages, front and back, he dropped his pen from his hand, and he slouched back. He was almost breathin' hard. Well, long, deep breaths. He just looked back out the window, and somethin' inside pushed a smile across his face.

One thing and everything and him at the same time.

When he finally reached over and flicked the light off, he could see a bunch more stars.

He got up and walked the two steps to his bed and got in between the cool sheets. He pulled the blankets around his body and he passed out.

Chapter Twenty

THAT NEXT day—Jamie felt a little different. Yuh can't really pinpoint stuff like that, but it felt different when he woke up that morning and his brain woke up and started doin' its thing. Like thinkin' about the day and stuff. He still had to go to school and the feeling he got when he thought about that would always be there until the day he got the hell out of there—that tightness in his stomach, and kinda the tug it put on some of his muscles towards it, that tight feeling. But there was other stuff for a change too. First thing, he was into his chores a little more this morning. Like takin' care of the animals. He didn't just do it half asleep like he always did it. Like he smelled how good the woody smell of the sawdust was that he bedded the horses with, and he smelled the sweet grain when he poured it from the bag into his bushel bucket and then scooped it to the goats and llamas. And like when he pet the horses that morning, Titania's and Puck's and the rest of 'em too really, their coats were smoother and almost like silk. Titania, when she scuffed her one front hoof on the barn floor and shook her head, kinda cracked him up. Just small stuff like that. On his bus ride he wrote a little more in his journal, the one he used in Francis's class, and he wrote about…like stuff he noticed on the way. People's porches and bare trees and bumps in the road that he knew were there.

He wanted to talk to Angelo. He wanted to tell him what he thought he knew. He would probably run into Ben today, too. Ben had asked him over this weekend when they got back to school from bowling yesterday. He had told Jamie somethin' like, "Yuh know, if you're not doin' anything Saturday night, wanna hang out at my house or somethin'?" And that was kinda cool. The sun was shinin', too, and until today, Jamie almost couldn't enjoy it because he knew that it could end any second. Like some cold front, some normal February weather could blow in at any second and end it all. The air was still chilly in the morning, but the sun was totally doin' its thing like it was July or somethin'. Stretchin' warm rays down on the Catskill Mountains and Coformon Falls, so people could feel it. So Jamie could feel it.

Yeah, things were a little different that morning.

Until he got to homeroom, anyway. When he walked into school that morning, there was a table sitting in the front lobby. Some people were in line and there was a sign that hung there from the table. Somebody had used all different colored markers and wrote:

HAPPY VALENTINE'S DAY
Support the Student Council
Buy a carnation $1

Red: You're hot
White: True love
Pink: Secret Admirer
Blue: Special Friend

Jamie hadn't known the day. Didn't even know the date of Valentine's Day. Definitely somethin' he didn't keep track of. But whatever, that didn't really phase him. He went to his locker and got his books and all that crap and went to homeroom, and homeroom was like throwin' everybody from all walks of life into one room. Because you weren't really with your friends unless your friends had a last name that was somewhere in the alphabet by yours.

Somehow Jamie always ended up in the back row, like in English class. In homeroom, he was in the back row along the wall. He was in the corner of the back of the room, and he liked it that way. Nobody bothered him back there. He could do some homework he hadn't got done or whatever and not have to talk to anyone.

He walked in today and sorta just turned down his aisle and got into his seat. He looked up at the clock and the rip-a-day calendar that said "Today is February 13." Hamner hadn't come in and ripped it off yet. She never came in 'til the second bell.

Kids were talkin', and Jamie just opened his English notebook, not his journal, his regular one, they had a vocab quiz in there today.

Some people had bought carnations or had already had some people give some to 'em. Some people had one or two, or like one girl, Jamie didn't even know her first name, just her last,

238

Baddlesome, she had like maybe seven or eight red ones. She had a boyfriend.

Jamie sorta looked around and saw people with 'em, yuh couldn't not notice. There were some empty desks where kids hadn't come in yet and some of 'em had those pink ones layin' on 'em.

Some desks were just empty though, too. No pink flowers or anything. Hardly anybody had the blue dyed ones.

He looked down at his vocab list. *Scrutinize.* He looked up at the wall above the blackboard and rattled off the definition in his head.

One girl, Gena, had a couple blue ones. She had wrapped their stems in a wet towel that you get from the bathroom. Brown, fold in 'em, scratchy. Yuh never wanna blow your nose with 'em. Those towels.

Gena Barrows was in the back, too. Opposite side of the room from Jamie. She had laid her blue carnations on her stack of books and she was talkin' to the girl in front of her. Jamie didn't even think the girl in front of her liked her, just by the way the girl in front of her sorta only half turned around when Gena was talkin' to her and the way the girl nodded and didn't say much when Gena told her somethin'. She just knew her from a couple classes maybe. But Gena always talked to her. She told her where she went out the weekend before and what concerts she was gettin' backstage passes to because a friend of a friend did lights for so-and-so band. She always had some story to tell. She mighta been one of those kids that are kinda messed up, Jamie didn't like sayin' that, but some kids since elementary school...they're just sorta strange.

Gena had went to Jamie's elementary school. She had sucked her thumb until she was in the sixth grade, and she was always gettin' put in the corner for it or bein' sent to the nurse's office for "talks" about it or gettin' picked on for it. She wore a lot of make-up now, and talked real loud and made stuff up. You could just tell about her makin' stuff up, like about backstage passes and stuff.

Bill Autes came in and a couple other people behind him. Jamie looked down at his notebook. Still sorta studyin'. He mostly knew the words. *Tenacious.* He looked up again.

People were gettin' into their seats. Some of 'em with their flowers and stuff. Aut, that's what most of the kids called him, had on one of his black T-shirts he got at some concert and was sittin' down. Over by Cheryl—that one girl Gena talked to—and Gena, the row next to 'em. He was a druggie. Just a fact. Really fuckin' weird kid. Had sat in front of Jamie in Earth Science last year and had offered him a couple of these little blue pills from the front pocket of his T-shirt. When kids deal they do that, offer yuh a couple free ones at first, then get yuh into it and sell. His eyes were crazy blue and sunk into his head half the time, but none of the teachers ever said anything to him about it or anything.

Everybody talked in homeroom, kinda low—not like Gena—'cause it was morning, yuh know. So there were a few conversations Jamie could hear goin' on. About usual high school stuff. Classes. Other people. Teachers. TV last night.

"Who's the flowers from?"

Jamie looked to the other side of the room. He kept his finger on the next word on his list.

Bill Autes was sittin' sideways in his desk. His back was

towards Jamie and he was talkin' to Gena Barrows.

Gena picked up her carnations and sniffed 'em. "No one *gave* them to me, Bill. I got them for my mother. I get her two carnations every year." They sold carnations every year once you hit junior high. "I spent my last two bucks on 'em, but it's worth it." She said it loud, so everybody could hear her, and she sniffed 'em again like she was really into 'em and smiled and sighed.

Cheryl was still half turned around, but when Bill Autes started talkin' to Gena, she opened a book and tried to pretend she was lookin' at that. Cheryl Banner would never be in a three foot radius of Gena Barrows or Bill Autes if she didn't have homeroom with them.

"Let me see 'em."

Jamie kept his finger on his notebook. He was sorta watchin' what was goin' on. Sorta not turnin' his head towards 'em, but lookin' their way. A couple other people were too. Bill Autes barely ever talked and Gena Barrows was a loud talker, so the combination turned a couple heads.

"Why, Bill?" Gena was holdin' her flowers and she was kinda laughin'. She liked the attention.

"Just let me see 'em." Aut stretched his arm out. "I wanna smell 'em."

Gena was gigglin' a little. In a wary kinda way.

"C'mon."

She leaned towards him and held her flowers out that she had bought for her mother. She wasn't gonna hand 'em over, just put the petals under Bill Autes's nose.

"C'mon, let me see 'em." Bill coaxed her with his hand, yuh know, like if you were behind someone backin' up and they had a lot more room to pull in. "Let me hold 'em."

Jamie was all-out watchin' it all now. He wasn't pretendin' to half look. His finger was pasted to his notebook but his head was watchin' the other side of the homeroom.

Gena Barrows handed her two blue carnations over to Bill Autes. Real slow like, but she did. "Smell 'em, Bill, and then give 'em back." Gena took hold of her thumbnail between her teeth and bit a little.

Cheryl Banner had her head down, lookin' at her accounting book or somethin', but she was kinda lookin' over at Bill.

People were lookin' at Bill.

He took the flowers from Gena, and he was all…like gentle with 'em, yuh know. Like careful to hold the stems so they wouldn't break or anything and had his hand on the wet towel so the towel wouldn't slip off. He looked 'em over, turned the flowers sorta around in his hand and looked at their dyed blue petals, and he smelled 'em. A long, fill his lungs sniff. Then he looked at Gena.

Gena sat there with her arm stretched out, waitin'. "Okay, give 'em back."

Bill started to hand 'em back across the row to her.

Gena almost had her fingertips on the wet, brown towel.

He stopped short of givin' 'em to her and sorta tipped his head.

Gena didn't say anything. She didn't have any time to.

Bill brought the flowers back up to his face, and he stuck the head of one of the flowers in his mouth and he bit it off.

Cheryl Banner turned her head straight at him when he did, and he made eye contact with her. She spewed out a laugh and bent back over her debit and credit columns. A couple other people who were watchin' laughed too.

Aut chewed it a little and made room in his mouth for the other. Then he bit that one off too.

He got a few more spurts of laughs.

He handed the two stems back to Gena and was chewin' on a mouth full of blue carnations.

Gena kinda laughed and looked at the gnawed off stems in her hand. "Biiill." She kinda laughed.

Jamie just sat there. It was like it was some sorta movie. He didn't laugh or anything. He just sat there and watched them and everybody.

Then Hamner walked in. People sorta sat up when she did because she was old school. She liked it quiet when the announcements came on.

Jamie sorta transferred his trance and looked away from Bill and Gena and watched Mrs. Hamner put her attaché case on her desk and set her coffee cup down like no one else was in the room.

Hamner sat down and looked at her watch.

Jamie looked up at the clock. The red second hand was flyin'. He looked back over at Gena Barrows.

Everyone was facin' forward now. Bill Autes. Cheryl Banner. Everybody.

Gena had a book open and she was lookin' down at it. Her two stems stuck in the towel were lyin' there on the edge of her desk.

Jamie just looked at her. She didn't see him.

She had short hair, but she ran her finger above her ear and moved whatever hair there was so it would tuck behind there. Then she put the corner of her thumb in her mouth and bit a couple of times. She blinked really hard. Twice.

Jamie kinda jumped a little when the bell rang. He looked back down at his notebook and his finger was still on the next word.

Serendipitous.

He forgot what that meant.

He started to read the definition he had written down, but the intercom clicked on, and the student of the week came on, and said "Good morning" and "Please stand for the pledge."

Everyone shuffled outa their seats and stood up. Including Jamie. Yuh had to.

"I pledge allegiance to the flag…"

Serendipitous: the act of fortunate discovery by accident. More than a coincidence—in parentheses.

Chapter Twenty-one

JAMIE DIDN'T stop at the front door when he showed up at Angelo's that day. He went into the hallway and he knocked at the inside door. When he heard Angelo yell "Come in" from the other side, he turned the knob and went through.

Angelo was usually busy with somethin' or other when Jamie went there, like sewin' a pillow or mixin' stuff in the bowl on the dining room table, Jamie's bowl, or doin' somethin', but today when Jamie walked in, he looked like he had just woke up from a catnap. He was in his chair in the living room, with his hands sorta folded across his chest when Jamie first saw him, and he kinda propped himself up when Jamie came in, gettin' all situated and stuff like his short sleep was pretty good an' all but he was wide awake now. Ready to shoot the breeze or whatever. He pushed his glasses back up on his nose and moved his arms to the two big arms of his chair, takin' up the whole chair and enjoyin' it. Lookin' like the happy captain of his quarters again or somethin'. Angelo could do that.

Every moment was his own.

"Hello, Jamie."

"Hi, Angelo."

"Make yourself at home."

Jamie sat in the chair that he had sat in the other day. He leaned forward and put his elbows on his knees and brought his hands together in front of him and kinda looked at some of the locks in the shaggy gold rug.

Angelo didn't say anything. He looked at Jamie and turned the air of the room over in his lungs, almost like he was gettin' rid of any nap left inside him.

"It's about focus, isn't it?" Jamie looked up at Angelo. "I mean the next part or step or whatever you wanna call it."

"Right down to business today." Angelo sat up a little more in his chair. "It absolutely is." He looked at Jamie like he wasn't sure why Jamie was all serious or right down to business, but he let him go. He'd see where or why or what the heavy air was about that Jamie had sittin' on his back and that was makin' him lean forward when he talked.

"When I was with Puck the other day—" Jamie kinda shook his head and looked back down, "and last night, when I wrote—" he looked back up, "I write things, Angelo, I guess you probably already know that too."

Angelo nodded and smiled like someone smiles who has caught your mood.

Jamie looked back down. The gold of the rug was the back of some huge Arabian camel and Jamie felt like they were in some camel caravan house in Ali Babba times. If he opened the curtain behind Angelo he'd hear Arabian bells and look out and see a stream of camels before and behind him and ladies in veils and belly dancer clothes and dunes upon dunes of desert sand. Maybe this, all of it was some sorta—

"Focus brings clarity, Jamie. That's what you felt. Or you feel when you do certain things or when you write."

"Yeah. It's only certain things. Like if I'm outdoors. Or if I write and there's no me, there's ideas and words and a pen in my hand and that's it." Jamie kept lookin' down. He usually didn't tell people crap like that, especially in the mood he was in today.

Ever have like—a sad heart? Like your chest feels thick and heavy and you can almost feel your heart beat heavy and sad and slow. That's how Jamie felt.

Angelo saw it. But one thing at a time. "Jamie." He wanted him to look at him when he said what he was gonna say. He needed to know Jamie would remember it, not be lost in the bright gold hair of the Arabian camel that they sat on and that rocked them up and down towards the oasis only a couple miles off.

Jamie looked up at him.

"Write. Breathe in life, focus on living it, all of it. When you do, your senses will come alive, like they did the other day when you worked with Puck and when you wrote at your desk last night."

Jamie looked at him and listened to what he was sayin'.

"Be present in everything you do from the small to the big, and—" Angelo lifted his arms and spread 'em, like he was pointin' beyond the walls on both sides of the room, "this is what will happen." He smiled. So that it vibrated across the room and Jamie couldn't get away from it.

Jamie lifted his cheeks a little but he had to look back down too.

"What else Jamie? It's important that we keep moving toward your dream, and we'll get there. All you have to do is change hope to believe and find the last turn to the key, and it's there." Angelo got up. "But there's room for other things." He walked towards Jamie and the chair Jamie was sittin' in.

Jamie kept his head down and his feet felt Angelo's feet as they came across the soft carpet.

"What else?" Angelo came up to Jamie and he kneeled on one knee in front of him.

Jamie just kept his head down and didn't say anything for a minute.

Angelo just waited for him. He probably woulda waited the rest of the day if he had to, Angelo was like that. He rested his arms on the knee that wasn't on the rug. You could hear the clock and it always reminded Angelo that they were workin' on limited time, but he woulda waited there on his one knee all day if he had to, to find out what else.

"It's stupid." Jamie sat up. Straight, yuh know. And he looked towards the dining room table and took his thumbnail and kinda dug it into the leg of his jeans.

"What's stupid?"

Jamie just kinda shook his head. He really didn't want to get into it. Fifteen-year-old guys just don't like to get into it. They'd rather tell people things like "I'm just tired" or somethin'. "This girl. Today in homeroom. She got a couple flowers for her mom and this stupid kid who's all messed up—ate 'em." Jamie kinda laughed. Not a happy one but one like when you just don't know what else to do. That kinda laugh and he looked at one of the legs on the dining room table. "It sounds really funny when I say it and a buncha people laughed when he did it, but—" Angelo was right there in front of him and he turned his head and looked at him, "but she. This girl, she's like half there anyway. She was almost cryin'. That's all." He looked back towards the table leg.

Angelo didn't say anything.

The table looked like oak or somethin'. Dark grainy wood with swirls in it. Hand-carved.

The blue glass bowl was still on the scale.

And from the chair in the living room, if you looked at the painting behind the dining room table, it really did look like you were lookin' out a window from a balcony out at the night sky.

"I just—I just don't get how people can be so—like the way people are, yuh know…"

Jamie kept his head turned, but Angelo was lookin' at him.

"What happened that day? The day I saw you by the street."

That seemed like forever ago. The snow was gone, Christ, it was like it was spring already. Flowers were almost in full friggin' bloom. Jamie looked quick at Angelo and then away again. Out the painted window. "I'm not talkin' about me. That's got nothin' to do with Gena."

"Why did you act so strangely yesterday in the garden when those boys went by?"

"Angelo, that has nothin' to do with what I'm talkin' about." Jamie crossed his arms and then uncrossed 'em. He tried to look right at Angelo—and he did for like a second—but he turned his head away because he felt his face get warm. "Forget it, okay. Just forget it."

Angelo took his hand off his knee. He held it in front of him a second. And then he put it on Jamie's knee. He didn't say anything, he just put his hand on Jamie's knee.

Jamie didn't flinch or anything, but nobody had...like touched him like that—some touch of concern or whatever you wanna call it—in...he didn't know how long. Even his mom. Well, she had tried but when she did, he would let it go a second and then move or he would like turn or dip to completely avoid it. He wasn't into that touchin' crap. So when Angelo did it, he didn't really like it. "Don't. Just don't. I'm all right, okay." He stood up and walked around Angelo. He walked over to where Angelo had been sittin'. There was a window behind his chair with the curtain drawn. A thick, long velvety curtain. Jamie stood there and folded his arms across his chest. His back was to Angelo.

Angelo watched Jamie get up, and stayed kneeled and watched him go over to the other side of the room from over his shoulder. Then he faced the empty chair Jamie had just got up from. "What's there, Jamie, that you can't say?"

"People are assholes. That's what wrong. That's what I'm tryin' to say." Jamie looked for a crack between the curtains where you could see outdoors. There wasn't one, and he felt his face keep gettin' red and warm. Once you start you can't stop, especially when you don't even know why you're gonna, so he sure as hell wasn't gonna start.

He wasn't gonna start.

He brushed the back of his hand across his cheek just to make sure and looked at it to see if anything was there. There wasn't. "I don't understand how people can be that way that's all."

"What way?"

"Jesus, Angelo, give it a rest." He turned around—looked over his shoulder—to say that.

Angelo had gotten up and it was like he had asked "What way?" to Jamie's back from across the room.

"All right. I'll let it go, if you really want me to." He took one step towards Jamie's back. "Are you sure that's what you want?"

"I dunno." Jamie had a hard time sayin' just that. I dunno. His throat wasn't workin' right all of a sudden. And while it wasn't, his brain fucked with him. Angelo's other question was still out there—about that day those guys nearly hit him and when he practically dug a hole in the dirt that day in the garden to crawl in when Rich Passellow and company passed. Maybe he should just tell him. No one ever knew any of it. Maybe he should just tell Angelo.

About the air that day and how you could feel it behind your ears.

And that fuckin' horn.

And the snow that soaked his jeans like in a second. And his ankle throbbin'.

Maybe he should tell him about Gena Barrows's pasted-on eye shadow and why he thought she talked so loud and told so many lies, and the way Cheryl Banner hunched forward because she wanted to be melodramatic when she laughed at Bill Autes.

About how he hated going there every day.

About "Who? Friendless?" Maybe he should tell him about that and what that felt like in his head and in his chest when they said that.

251

And about how now all of a sudden he was suppose to hope and believe and not think that all this crap he was bein' fed about a fuckin' dream pillow or whatever was gonna be nothing just like everything else.

"I dunno." He said it again. But this time, he really didn't get it all out and he tried to close his eyes but it didn't help. "I dunno." He looked down and he started to cry. Like outa control cry. He put his hands over his face and somethin' from inside him was tryin' to push its way out. He kept his head down and he felt his shoulders movin'. He stood there a second like that, bein' as quiet as he could, tryin' to forget that someone else was in the room with him, seein' him doin' what he was doin'.

Angelo came across the room and he stopped just behind Jamie and looked down for a second. Then he propped himself up, almost like he had done in the chair when Jamie had first walked in. He tried to stand there like that, and he did, but his shoulders wouldn't straighten like they shoulda. They wouldn't help him play the captain of the ship or anything. Somethin' inside got in the way and he buckled under it. He put his hand on Jamie's shoulder.

Jamie felt it and he felt the water streamin' out of his eyes. He could feel the warm wet on his hands, and the tears were leavin' tracks on his face. He knew they were leavin' tracks on his face. He tasted some of 'em and he tightened his eyelids over his eyes to make 'em stop, but they didn't. He just kept sayin' "I don't know, I don't know" over and over.

He turned because Angelo's hand seemed to be turnin' him, and he didn't wanna see him, he didn't want him to see him, but he turned and started wipin' his eyes, still keepin' his head down.

Angelo was quiet when he said it, but he said, "Come here. It's all right." He brought Jamie a little closer to him.

Jamie just kept his head down and kept cryin', and he sorta let Angelo bring him closer and put his arms around him. He stood there cryin'. "I miss my dad, Angelo." He tried to stop cryin' but he couldn't. His eyelashes were all wet and he bit on his top lip to make himself stop but he couldn't. He wanted to keep his hands over his face but he was almost pressed up to Angelo now, and he couldn't. So his arms just went to his sides. He kept his eyes closed and let 'em cry and didn't wipe 'em off. "Sometimes I don't know what I'm gonna do."

Angelo kept his arms around Jamie and didn't say anything.

"Everything hurts so much and they can be so."

Angelo just kept his arms around Jamie and he didn't say anything.

"Sometimes I don't know what I'm gonna do..."

Chapter Twenty-two

JAMIE GOT reminded for a second time that day that it was Valentine's Day.

It was in a better way though than this morning. Remember those boxes of valentines you'd get when you were a kid, and there were like thirty in a box and they were perforated together and had little envelopes to put 'em in? You could get like Looney Tune ones or animal ones or whatever movie was big that year ones. And there would be like one or two really big ones in the box that you gave to your teacher or to the kid you were "goin' out with" and you had to fold it up fifty times to stick it in that dinky envelope they gave you. And if you got a lot of those big sizers in your doily-decorated paper lunch bag you had hangin' on the front of your desk you knew you were big shit. Strange how Valentine's Day could make or break yuh, even in elementary school.

But you remember those, right?

Jamie finished in the barn about quarter of six that night. He crossed the yard to the house and he stuck his work gloves in the back pocket of his jeans and looked up. It was a winter sky. Dark with a million stars. His breath rolled up past his nose and his eyes, and he watched it sorta vaporize into the night. A lot can go on in one day. He kept walkin' towards the house, watchin' his way and watchin' up too. He tipped his head back and stopped. He took off his cap and put it on backwards and looked up. Yeah, a lot can happen in a day. There were a million stars. A few a lot brighter than others, but the others outnumbered the big guys a 100,000 to one—and they were stars just the same anyway, those other ones, just a little, or like a million light years or somethin', farther away, that was all.

Jamie purposely blew some air out of his mouth. Huh. A quick puff into the night again.

The porch light flicked on, and he looked toward the house again. They had a big back porch. Closed in, like some farmhouses do, with windows and stuff, and he saw through them to the back door of the house. He could see the outline of his mom there in front of it. She opened it and taped somethin' to its glass window and closed it again.

Jamie stood there in the yard a second and he could see somethin' hangin' there, stuck to the front door window. And further in, he could see his mom over by the stove cookin'. He breathed in deep. You could smell it. The sauce. The spices or seasoning and the green peppers. You could smell the sauce. No lie. It seeped out the cracks and the wood of the house and window, and worked its way across the yard to Jamie's nose.

When you're fifteen and you stand in the middle of your

backyard between the house and the barn, and it's sorta chilly and it's dark and you're under a billion stars and you've got your insulated leather work gloves stuck in your back jeans pocket, and you breathe in deep and you can actually smell what your mom's cookin' and you can see her through the porch glass and back door window standin' by the stove doin' one of the things she did best, you don't have to be Jamie Auger to know that things don't last forever. They change and go on.

Jamie just stood there a second and let his body do its thing with the February air. And he listened to it doin' it.

Yeah. A lot can happen in one day.

He walked the rest of the way across the yard and up the steps and opened the screen door. It rattled and creaked, and everything always seemed to echo on that big old back porch. Like it was hollow or somethin', but it wasn't. They had the long freezer on one side of it, a couple of plastic chairs, a couple stacks of recyclable paper. Stuff like that.

And Jamie usually kept his boots out there too.

Not a boot room though, his dad didn't like boot rooms—too much of a separation between home and home he'd say. Back porch was okay for boots—if yuh wanted, but no boot room—the truth was his dad didn't care, he was just that way, in a good way. He was like this scholar and farmer and father and husband and…and good ol' boy all rolled up into a man.

Jamie could hear inside. His mom had some music on, a fifties tune. He knew it—"Earth Angel" by…he couldn't remember who it was by, but it was "Earth Angel." It was on this four cassette *Reader's Digest* set called *The Elvis Presley Years* that his mom had picked up at a church bizarre for a

couple of bucks one year around Christmas time. She loved
Tape One because it had all these be-bop songs on it. Not just
from Elvis, it had a buncha songs from the time he first started
makin' music to the time he got all messed up and died. So he
heard "Earth Angel" playin' and he could see his mom stirrin'
her spaghetti sauce and he could tell from her back she was
singin' along to it.

He thumped across the wooden porch floor, that's how your
steps sounded on it, and he looked at what his mom had put up
there. It was a small see-through envelope and she had written
Jamie Auger on it. He kinda smiled and bent down and unlaced
his boots and took 'em off and set 'em by the door and then he
peeled the taped envelope off.

He held it in his hand a second and then he looked through
the window again. His mom had this plastic fork-spoon in her
hand and she had turned around and she was lip-synchin' into
it and pointin' at Jamie. Bein' a real geek on purpose, yuh
know.

Jamie shook his head and had one of those tryin' not to smile
smiles on his face. He looked down and flipped the envelope
over and ripped it open. It was a folded up valentine. One of the
big-ass ones. He unfolded it and there was a bird, like a parrot or
a toucan, it looked like Toucan Sam—the bird on the Fruit Loops
cereal box—with his wings spread and holdin' up a huge heart.
Happy Valentine's Day.

Jamie looked up again and through the front door window.
His mom had went back to cookin'. She was cuttin' up some
garlic in a saucepan and her back was to him again. He looked
back down at his valentine and turned it over.

To: Jamie

From: Mom

Happy Valentine's Day

P.S.—Hope you're free for dinner

Jamie kinda smiled and went in. "Cute, Mom." He took off his cap and hung it on one of the backs of the kitchen chairs.

Mary kept cuttin' up a thing of garlic she had in her hand and she looked over her shoulder at him and smiled.

"Thanks." He held up his valentine.

"You're welcome." She put her knife down and lowered the flame under her saucepan.

"Smells good in here." Jamie took his gloves out of his back pocket and set 'em on the counter by the door and then he walked over to the stove and looked into the pot of spaghetti sauce. There was some basil sprinkled on the top, and his mom had cut up some mushrooms and peppers in it and had added the meatballs already. It was poppin' with slow bubbles. He picked up a spoon lyin' there on the stove and stirred it.

When they had spaghetti at the Augers', it was sort of an event. His mom usually cooked the sauce all day and put like canned tomatoes from the garden and some tomato paste and a buncha crap into it. It wasn't like a couple jars of Prego or anything.

"It's almost ready. I just have to pour this over the bread." Mary pointed to the saucepan in front of the pot of sauce. It had some melted butter in it and the pieces of garlic she had cut in there. A long loaf of French bread cut in half the long way was sittin' on the counter.

"I'll go change and wash up."

"Should be ready when you come down." Mary was all into what she was doin'. Gettin' plates out of the cupboard and stuff like that.

Jamie went upstairs and took care of his valentine. He put it on his dresser where everything that he just got and that was very important always went. There was loose change up there. A couple pictures from Christmas. Letters. Mail. Stuff like that. He tossed the envelope in the can and propped the valentine on this old bank he had gotten for his birthday when he was about six. It was a turtle on his hind legs with a top hat and a cane. His grandmother had bought it for him from the fair that was down at the fairgrounds every year.

He looked at the big red heart that the bird was holdin' up. Bright red with gold letters written on it. The bird was all smilin' too holdin' it up.

Valentine's Day. Who knows.

Jamie changed out of his work clothes and put 'em in the hamper. He got into some sweats and pulled a sweater from a drawer and put it on, thinkin' he'd dress up a little, and then he washed up. Like his hands and stuff, and went back downstairs.

His mom had went all out. She had the table set and had made a salad and put that on the table. The spaghetti had been in a strainer in the sink, and she put that on a plate and put it on the table too. Sauce in a bowl. Dinner was on and it looked really good in an informal kind of way. Corelle dishware with the blue design on the edges and stuff, you know the ones.

Mary was gettin' out a couple wineglasses from the cupboard too. They were nothin' fancy, a couple mismatched wineglasses from his grandparents' house that they didn't feel like havin' around anymore so they brought 'em over to Jamie and his mom. But they were wineglasses.

"What can I help you with?"

"I think we're just about set." She looked at the table. "Maybe get the salad dressing."

"Okay." Jamie went to the fridge. Viva Italian and some creamy blue cheese were in the door. He got 'em and sat down.

Mary had turned down the music a little and Elvis was on now croonin' away.

"Well, I got us some wine." She came over to the table with the glasses and a bottle she had got from a cupboard that was the closest thing to the liquor cabinet you were gonna get in their house. "White. Is it white or red you're suppose to have with pastas?"

"I didn't know there was a certain kind you were suppose to have." Jamie was dippin' out some salad for them into their salad bowls.

"Well, that's what they say. Somethin' with fish and meat and another for pastas. I never remember." Mary set the glasses down and opened the bottle. Twist off. Nothin' fancy. She poured it.

It's not like she let Jamie drink wine all the time, in fact they rarely had a bottle of anything sittin' out, but it wasn't like a condemned thing either and Jamie wasn't like "Oh, please, I'll drink water or milk" when it was bein' offered.

Mary set a glass in front of him and moved the other one to her place.

"Thanks." Everything was pretty much on the table, and Mary sat down.

Jamie went to take a sip and stopped. He lifted his glass. "Okay. Happy Valentine's Day."

Mary got her glass and ting'd Jamie's. "Cheers."

"Cheers."

They both took sips.

"Not bad, right."

Jamie took another quick sip. Wine always had this strange taste to him. Like it made a top part of his tongue taste that never really got used and it traveled different pipes when he swallowed it. It was sweet and dry, not like he knew anything about wine or anything, but it did taste good. "Yeah, it tastes good."

Mary took another sip.

They didn't say anything for a couple minutes. You know how it is. When there's really good food in front of a couple people and they're hungry, they get all quiet and dish their stuff out and get all base instinct. It doesn't matter if it's two or ten people. Everybody just sorta shuts up and starts to eat. That's what Mary and Jamie did.

Salad. Spaghetti. Wine.

It was really good. Jamie had knocked back about three-quarters of his glass of wine and that was probably the first thing that he came up for air to say. He reached for the bottle for a refill. "Yuh want a little more?"

Mary kinda swallowed some salad she had in her mouth. "Yeah, just a little more." She had slugged down quite a bit too, but not as much as Jamie.

Jamie filled 'em. "This is so good."

"I got it at Wellman's. Joyce recommended it."

"No, not the wine—well, that's good too—but this dinner—"

he pointed to his food in front of him with his fork, "it's awesome."

"Thanks."

They ate a little more. And drank a little more.

The wood stove was crankin' from the other room and the whole house was pretty warm. And Jamie had a sweater on besides.

"Joyce said she's run the liquor store by herself for almost three years now since Al left her." Mary picked up her glass and took a sip. "And they owned it for fifteen before that."

"Really."

She nodded and drank and then put her glass down. "Yeah. She said now after almost twenty years she's thinking of takin' some classes over at the college."

Coformon Falls had a community college just outside of town.

"That's cool." A lot of people did that in Coformon Falls. Like if they got divorced or lost their job or they wanted to do somethin' else, they went to C.F.C.C. "She's a nice lady." Jamie remembered Joyce Wellman. She used to be a lunch lady part-time when he was in elementary school.

He rolled some spaghetti around on his fork and ate it. He ripped off another piece of bread and followed it up with that.

They were quiet a second. You could hear the one tape finish and another one start up. Yeah, their stereo had continuous play. His mom had put *The Drifters Greatest Hits* in and not rewound it or anything, and they came on with one of their songs.

"I've been thinkin' about doing that." Mary reached for the wine and filled her glass. It was a big bottle. Jamie kinda pushed his glass towards her and she gave him some more.

"Takin' some classes?"

Mary nodded and sipped. "Yeah."

"Really? Wow. I didn't even, I didn't know you wanted to do that." Jamie drank some of his wine.

"Well, it'd have to be part-time. I've always wanted to work towards vet school and I'd have to start somewhere."

"Mom." Jamie set his glass down. "I didn't know that."

Mary got a little, well, she was like blushin' a little. She looked down at her plate and got a piece of meatball and a mushroom and ate it. "You think it's a bad idea?"

"No. No way."

"What do you think your father would have said."

"I thing he would have dug it, he would want what you want."

Mary set down her fork and she picked up her wineglass and held it in front of her with both her hands. "Yeah, Jamie, I just…I don't know. You're gettin' older. You'll probably be goin' off to school somewhere in a few years and…" She took a sip and then kinda whirled around the wine left in her glass and looked down at it. "I saw an ad in the Richfield paper for someone to work a few hours a week with the horses up in Saratoga this summer on some type of intern or training program and it got me thinking I guess." Mary looked up.

Jamie was listenin'. He had his fork in his hand and his piece of bread in the other and he was lookin' at her.

"I would love to do something like that—I mean, I would never let go of this place. I love this place, but I would love to try something like that too."

Jamie smiled back at his mom and he put down his piece of bread on the side of his plate and refilled his wineglass. It was kinda scary, in a way. How different things were gonna be. And his stomach felt a little funny, but he hadn't seen his mom look the way she looked right now in forever. Her eyes were bright green. Something inside had sparked 'em back to life.

He tipped the bottle towards Mary and raised his eyebrows.

"Sure." She put her glass out and he filled it.

"So why don't you. Take a crack at both the track and school."

Mary didn't say anything for a second. She took a sip of wine like she was taste-testing it. "I think I'm going to. If it doesn't work, it doesn't work."

"Gotta try."

"Um-hmm."

They got quiet again. Not a heavy silence or an I'm hungry silence. Both of 'em were thinkin' about stuff. The stuff they'd just talked about.

The tape went quiet, yuh know between songs, and when Jamie noticed that all that he heard was them chewin' and the clankin' of their forks on their plates and bowls, he looked over at his mom. She had a piece of bread in her mouth and she stopped mid-chew and looked at him.

They started cracking up.

The wood stove was blastin' heat and Jamie could feel how red his cheeks were.

Mary put the back of her hand on her cheek like she knew what he was thinkin'. "It's hot in here."

"Yeah, it is." Jamie flapped the front of his sweater. He felt a little bead of sweat where his hair met his forehead. "Holy shit, it is."

They were laughin' then. Full, big laughs. Like when you look at somebody and your eyes are all squinty and your laugh is pushin' a huge smile across your face.

They had eaten like there was no tomorrow and Mary had put a buncha wood on the fire before Jamie had come in.

The bottle of wine from Wellman's Corner Liquor Store was sittin' there on the table. It had maybe enough for a half of glass each left in it. They had pretty much kicked it.

They were laughin' and The Drifters were still singin'. And if they had a camera sittin' on the table, they probably woulda got together and pointed it at themselves and taken a picture. That's what it felt like right then.

Valentine's Day…Happy Valentine's Day.

Chapter Twenty-three

JAMIE DIDN'T go to Angelo's house for a few days. It mighta even been a week or a couple weeks even before he went back to see him. It wasn't like he was embarrassed or anything. He wasn't embarrassed. It was just sorta strange, that's all.

But it wasn't that he was embarrassed.

And besides a lotta other stuff was goin' on, so he really couldn't have gone if he had wanted to. And he did want to.

What stuff? Well, for one thing. Mr. Francis had assigned this big unit on poetry, and everybody had to partner up (well, except Harold Forrests, he was the only one who wanted to work alone) and they had to analyze five or six poems from some poet they drew from a hat. Tell about his life and stuff like that and then present it to the class and do a paper on all of it. How does the guy or girl's life relate to their work. Or vice versa.

Jamie and Ben partnered up. They had drawn out Robert Frost, and they considered themselves pretty lucky for it. The guy was American, and he wrote in this century, which—for the most part—meant that you could pretty much understand what he had to say without a whole lotta translation or anything. Other kids got like Shakespeare and they had to read some of his sonnets. Which were just about like his plays—impossible to understand without *Cliffs Notes*. Or, or they got like Emily Dickinson. She was this lady who locked herself away and wrote all this crazy stuff about God and dying and used a buncha dashes and capital letters and made no sense at all. There were a buncha different poets that were in this classy-lookin' thirties felt hat that Francis had stuck the names in.

Ben had drawn out Robert Frost when Mr. Francis had come around to him. Mr. Francis said somethin' like "Oh, he's a good one. Who are you working with? Oh, Jamie. Great. You two look at 'Desert Places' and 'Birches' and his big one 'The Road Not Taken.'" He said "Pick out a couple more on your own" while he was writin' *Jamie and Ben—Robert Frost* down on a pad that he was keepin' track of who was partnered with who and who was doin' what. Jamie had jotted down the ones Francis said to look at while he was listin' 'em.

Anyway, Jamie had to catch the bus after school and had to work besides, so him and Ben started gettin' together during study halls. And lunch. That's the main reason why Jamie hadn't been to Angelo's, he'd been meetin' with Ben to figure out what Robert Frost and his poetry was all about.

Truth was, they started hangin' out a little bit too. Like Ben had asked Jamie over when they went bowling and Jamie went over to his house for supper the Saturday night after Valentine's Day. They hung out and ate with Ben's folks—who were pretty cool people, too. Ben's mom kept loadin' Jamie's plate with potatoes, and his dad loved the fact that Jamie was composition extraordinaire and had helped Ben out. They ate and shot the bull, and then Mr. and Mrs. Callihan went out, and Ben and Jamie watched some HBO movie with Matthew Modine in it and then some MTV. They half watched the tube though, mostly they talked about whatever and laughed or made fun of whatever was on.

They talked on the phone, too. Like they had to sorta plan their presentation and stuff like that, but they started talkin' on the phone about different shit, too. Jamie went bowlin' again with Ben and they went in the pool again, too. And they checked out a movie at the Dual Cinema in town one night besides.

They were hangin' out over the couple of weeks that Jamie didn't get to Angelo's house. Other stuff kept him pretty busy too. Like that time that he didn't see Angelo, the days seemed to fly. He worked at the feedstore a lot. People just seemed to come in more in the nice weather, gearin' up for spring and all. And the weather said definite early spring now. Jamie had Puck or one of the other horses out as much as he could, takin' advantage of the sun and soft ground.

But all of it didn't mean he had stopped thinkin' about the dream stuff and all the stuff him and Angelo had sorta talked about. Not at all. It was sorta funny, because it did just the opposite, he thought about it a lot. Not like obsessive or dwellin' on it. But he might be ridin' home on the bus, lookin' out the window, or stackin' seed bags or workin' with Puck in the corral and he'd remember somethin' Angelo had told him or he'd go over "the combination" in his head.

He couldn't have said exactly how things were those few days in late February and maybe early March, but the sun felt different and the bus ride home seemed shorter.

It was a Wednesday afternoon when he was leanin' against the boards of the corral. He had led Puck around for a while and then unhooked the rope from the halter and let him wander around by himself. Jamie walked to the back end of the corral and hung Puck's walkin' rope around a post and he put his arms on the top board and looked out at the mountains behind their fields. The sky was like Easter egg blue and there were a couple of those puffy clouds, but it was a clear afternoon. The sun was really warm. He had a T-shirt on.

He could hear the colt walkin' around behind him. He looked over his shoulder and behind him and it had stopped and was tryin' to eat some grass that was startin' to grow. It looked up at Jamie when Jamie turned around to see him. Yuh could see how Puck had grown a lot already. His legs were way ahead of the rest of him, but he was gonna be a beautiful horse. Jamie looked at his tail. Puck was swishin' it. Just for the hell of it because there weren't any flies or anything around him.

Jamie turned back around and leaned on the corral again. The grass in the hayfields were tryin' to green but the trees on the mountains were still bare. Maybe there was a shade of green on 'em. Jamie squinted. Maybe.

Ben had to retake a math test so they weren't gonna meet in the library for lunch tomorrow. Their project was pretty much done anyway and their turn to go—to give their presentation— was Friday. They were ready.

Jamie knew he was goin' to Angelo's.

He lifted one of his feet and set his boot on the bottom board of the corral. He watched himself do it and then looked back out there.

His stomach felt a little strange, like it flip-flopped or somethin'.

It wasn't like Angelo wasn't gonna remember who he was or anything.

He had his arms on the top board of the corral and he put his chin down on where his hands were.

Change hope to believe. Angelo had said that.

He kinda tipped the brim of his cap up a little so he could see better.

The mountains were straight in some places and peaked in different spots, and they looked silvery today in the sun.

Chapter Twenty-four

EVERYTHING SORTA happened pretty fast from that day 'til it was all over. The next day, Ben went up to Mr. Rayner's to do his math retake, which he didn't think would take the whole lunch period. He had completely bombed his first test, some short thing on proving somethin' about the radii of a circle. Really useful stuff in the real world. Most of Ben's class were in the same boat as he was, so they convinced Rayner to let them retake it. Rayner was old, kind of a real unlively kinda guy, used an overhead projector all the time, and cursed at the thing when the bulb blew during class, but he was fair enough, so he let 'em redo it. Ben had met Jamie just after fifth period, before lunch, and they decided to meet outdoors. It was like 70 that day. Crazy sunny and warm. They were gonna hang out and just run through any wrinkles in Robert Frost that they still had. Ben told Jamie he'd meet him out by the bleachers by the field in about 20, 25 minutes.

That gave Jamie plenty enough time. He coulda waited 'til

the next day to see Angelo, but it was in his head to go, yuh know. He was ready to see him, fact was he kinda missed him, not seein' him. He missed him a lot.

When he went into Angelo's house, he went through the first door like he had the last time he was there and when he got to the second door, it was open. Just a crack. He lifted his hand to knock, but he waited. He sorta leaned his ear in, and he could hear Angelo hummin' from his chair and the quiet of the house and the tickin' of that clock on the shelf by the door. Yeah. He had missed goin' there. "Angelo." He knocked and the door kinda opened a little more, and he went through.

He glanced at the clock on the shelf and it still read the same time. 5:59. The second hand had moved a couple more ticks though, he was definitely sure of it this time, and there was this huge sunflower beside the lady now. He looked a little closer at it. "Angelo," he said again, just so Angelo knew he had come in. The sunflower was really the sun too, and a bird had come and sat by the lady, sorta lookin' up at her. The slot above her read, "Earth and sun, air and water, celebrate your grown gift and nourish the others."

The second hand ticked and moved. Almost to the XII it was. Jamie had never seen it move, and he sorta cocked his head back a little when it did—like a chicken or a duck or somethin' woulda when it got surprised by somethin'. The sunflower—the sun— was bright yellow with a golden brown face and its petal rays looked painted like they were real in a painted world. If that makes sense.

Jamie went into the living room and Angelo was there in his chair.

"Just in time." Angelo looked up from what he was doin'.

"Hi, Angelo. Sorry I haven't..." Jamie's sentence sorta trailed off. Not so much because of what he wanted to say or didn't know how to say but—well, he walked in the room and he was gonna sit in the chair he had first sat in when he went to Angelo's. As he did, his eyes sorta wandered to the dining room. They just did. Habit or whatever. He kinda looked at the crap on the table and stuff and then at the scale. On top of it.

It was empty. The clear blue glass bowl was gone. His bowl with all that stuff in it, for his dream, wasn't there. He tried not to be obvious when he noticed and kinda scanned the table for it. Maybe Angelo had taken it off for some reason or another. Maybe he thought he wasn't comin' back.

He sat down in the chair across from Angelo and when he looked at him, Angelo was smilin'. "What?"

Angelo had some fabric in his hand. A greenish pillow with the topside half sewn and the other half unsewn. Like a sack you could stuff.

Eyes are funny things, they get drawn wherever there's movement or color or where you think somethin' should be and it isn't or whatever. Angelo was smiling. He had already turned the pillow right side out—when you sew somethin' you sew it inside out—and he reached his fist into the stuffing hole and sorta poofed the sides out. Like he was makin' room for what was goin' in there. It was a small pillow, not like a pillow you'd sleep on at night, not that big. It was more like maybe a quarter that size. Jamie asked "What?" and he watched Angelo with the pillow, but he looked down to beside Angelo's chair. Somethin' there, the color hollered up to his eyes, and he looked down.

There was Angelo's basket there with all that stuff. Like there had been from day one. But sittin' on top of it. Sittin' on top of it was the blue bowl. It was heaped to the top with a buncha stuff and it sat sorta crooked on the wads and the rolls of fabric and stuff, but it was sittin' there beside Angelo's chair.

Jamie stared at it for a second and he felt his face get warm and his feet and his hands get light. Then he looked back at Angelo. "That's. Isn't…"

Angelo had looked down beside him because he knew why Jamie was sittin' there like he was hypnotized or somethin', and then he looked back at him.

They sat there a second. Jamie waitin' for Angelo to say somethin'. And Angelo was half expectin' Jamie to spit out what he was tryin' to say.

But neither of 'em did. Instead, Angelo lifted the pillow a little and sorta looked down at the bowl.

Jamie got up and he went over to him. "This is it?"

"This is it." He held out the pillow again. "You should have the honors." Angelo tipped his head after he said that. Like what he said wasn't exactly right. It was the first and only time Jamie ever saw him do that. "Well, to be honest, I have the honors, too."

Jamie came over in front of him and he kneeled down on both his knees. He let his eyes do the talkin'. He looked at Angelo and then at the bowl.

Angelo nodded his head, and Jamie reached for the bowl and picked it up.

It smelled like a forest or the ocean or the outdoors, and it went straight in your nose like some smells do, and it was almost like Jamie could feel it hit his lungs and then spread to his limbs

and his brain and even out his skin. It smelled like the first time
Jamie walked into Angelo's house, but stronger. Jamie looked
closer at it. Dried-up weeds and pine needles and a bunch of
other stuff like that, like whatever had been in those jars on the
table and then some. Spurts of blue color like the last time he'd
seen it and that gold sand too. He kinda lifted it a couple times.
It weighed like the bowl was empty.

"How's this work?"

"Do you doubt it?"

"No. I don't." Jamie shook his head. "I think this is crazy
and I don't have any idea what's happened or what's goin' on
lately." He nodded his head towards outside. "Even the weather.
None of it makes sense. But somethin's different, Angelo. I
don't know what it is and I don't care." He looked down at the
bowl with the buncha stuff that mostly looked like it coulda came
from somebody's front lawn after they mowed it. "And I don't
doubt this."

"I know you don't. But it's a technicality. I have to ask that."
Angelo put the pillow down a little so Jamie could start to sorta
pour the stuff or use his hands to put it in the cloth. "You want
to know the ground rules is what you mean."

"Yeah, that's what I mean. The ground rules."

Angelo brought the empty pillow back a little to his lap, and
Jamie stopped his pour midway and looked at him.

"All right. That's easy enough. First, this is a one shot deal.
This pillow will work, Jamie," Angelo looked down at the
unstuffed pillow in his hand, and then back at Jamie, "but it only
works once. And only for you."

Jamie nodded his head. "Okay."

Angelo nodded his head too. "Secondly, you pick whatever dream it is that you want to dream."

"I don't get it." Jamie kept one knee on the carpet and brought his other knee up so he could set the bowl on it. "How do yuh mean?"

"It's the dream of your choice, Jamie. Whatever it is you want to experience in those seventeen and a half seconds is up to you—although you do have to run it by me before you walk away with this. But it's basically that easy…you provide the framework and the pillow will do the rest."

"I pick the dream." Jamie said it more to himself than back to Angelo. Like repeating it would sketch it somewhere on his brain so he would remember these couple of rules.

"When you leave with this and you tuck it beside the pillow you sleep on or somewhere in the sheets or wherever you decide, and you fall asleep with it there, the dream," Angelo held the empty pillow out to him again, "is yours."

Jamie just sat there, steadyin' the bowl on his knee.

"Oh. And it's real, too. Everything that happens will be a reality." Angelo smiled. Everything about him smiled. His mouth. His eyes, gray-blue like an ocean sky. His whiskers even sorta shined. "So should you decide to include another person, or people, in your dream, then it becomes their dream too. And—" Angelo bobbed his head to the side like the rest of his idea was a cat sittin' on the arm of his chair beside him that he was referrin' to, "their reality."

Jamie just shook his head. He couldn't do much else.

Angelo gave him a second. He looked past Jamie's shoulder to the chair he had been sittin' in. The foot with the wing caught

his eyes, and he looked at that then, and that made him think of
the small paper bag that sat in his basket and he looked down at
it. He could hear that clock ticking from the shelf in the foyer,
and he looked back at Jamie. "Jamie."

Jamie looked up at him like he had been dozin' off or
somethin' and Angelo had given him a nudge.

"Still no doubts?"

"No doubts." Jamie straightened his shoulders and propped
himself up. He was back from where he had went. Sometimes,
with anything, you need a second to let somethin' seep in, and
when it does, it either sinks your shoulders in or it straightens 'em
out. Jamie didn't force 'em out or anything, he just sorta filled
up with it, or with somethin'.

"Before we really do this though, know that there's more to
it all than just the basics, behind what makes it work."

Jamie brought the bowl to the hole. "More than the ground
rules?"

"Yes. A lot more." Jamie had the bowl tipped a little and a
few beads or seeds of somethin' slipped off from the top of the
heap and bounced off the edge of the bowl and dropped into the
pillow.

Angelo felt them land in the bottom seam.

Jamie kept the bowl where it was, but he tipped it back some
and put one of his hands there so nothin' else would fall out. He
didn't say anything. He waited.

"Everything is connected, and I think you already know that.
But with your newfound faith comes a trust in believing in
something you can't see or explain or prove. That's what faith is,
and, with it, things can still surprise you or unfold into something

277

else. Are you ready to accept that?"

Jamie kept his hand where he had it, and it was so quiet in there he heard himself breathe a long, steady breath.

"Am I reminding you of Kwai Chang Caine yet?"

Angelo never said stuff like that, and Jamie laughed. They both did.

It wasn't 'til way after that that Jamie figured out why Angelo decided to say that right then.

Jamie was still kinda smilin' when he finally did say somethin'. "In other words, there's things you're not tellin' me."

"Not just me, Jamie." Angelo didn't quit smilin' either. He sorta rolled his head to include the sky and the room they sat in and a city or somethin' three continents over. "It. All of it."

Jamie shook his head. "Yeah. I know. Just before." He looked down and his eyes focused on this little red pedal or somethin' or other. He could make out its veins and the end that had been stuck in the round part connected to the stem. "Before I couldn't admit that. I know now though."

They looked at each other.

Gray-blue and dark brown. An ocean, sky, and a sure ship?

Life is strange like that.

"I think we're ready."

"We are."

Angelo stuck his finger in the hole one more time to kinda widen it, and Jamie took his hand and started to sorta help the mix of stuff into the pillow.

There had to be a hundred different things Angelo had mixed up in that bowl. Jamie couldn't say what they all were, but while he was pushin' 'em all into the pillow, he could feel some soft leaf once in a while or some prickly piece of somethin' or the cool damp of somethin' else. His hand even brushed against a really small pebble. Smooth like it had laid in a creek for a century or somethin'. It had a hot feel to it too, like it had laid in the sun all summer on a shore.

Jamie worked about half the bowl in, and Angelo sorta shook the pillow, like he was makin' some room for the rest.

Not much dropped onto Angelo's lap, even when Angelo kinda did his shake thing. Jamie was pretty careful. Maybe a small half of a twig or shaving of somethin'. But if one of 'em saw it drop and land on Angelo's pant leg or the seat cushion of the chair, he picked it up between his fingers' tips and dropped it in the pillow.

The whole project didn't seem like it took a lotta time, but they had probably worked at it a good fifteen minutes or so. When Jamie scraped the last of it into the pillow, the thing was full. Its sides were bulging and it didn't have a soft look to it at all. Angelo had stopped Jamie a couple times to press the stuff down in there. Packin' it in. And it was heaped to the hole and you could see the little shapes of the stuff in there pressin' against the sides. You know. Like a bean bag stuffed to the max, and you can make out all the little beans in there. Same thing with the pillow. The thing wasn't at all soft and its sides weren't smooth and cushy.

Jamie tipped the bowl all the way and brushed his hand one more time on the bottom of it. "I think that's it."

"All right then..." Angelo was holdin' the pillow right up by the hole and he squeezed the opening together a little bit, "set that down over here," he kinda looked to the other side of his chair that didn't have the basket by it.

Jamie reached around and set the bowl down, and started to get up.

"Wait. One more thing." Angelo set the pillow standin' up so nothin' fell out, between his legs. He reached beside him in the sewing basket and felt around. He was sittin' still, facin' Jamie, so he wouldn't move the pillow while he was doin' whatever it was he was doin'.

Jamie looked at the basket and watched Angelo move around some pieces of cloth and other stuff like a pincushion and one of those long yardstick tapes that fashion people drape around their necks, the soft ones you can roll up. He heard somethin' sorta crinkle and Angelo pulled up this paper lunch bag. It was sorta wrinkly and beat-up and it was rolled at the top to keep whatever was in it in it.

"Here. Take a few of these and put them in." Angelo handed the bag to Jamie and pressed the stuff in the pillow a little more and lifted it back up.

Jamie took the bag. "Feels empty."

"Light, isn't it." Angelo had one of his quiet smiles goin'.

Jamie unrolled the mouth of the bag. "Yeah, light as a—" he looked down inside.

If was half full. With small, fluffy white feathers. They looked like a handful of fresh snow, the light, big puffy kind that sorta stacks real high on itself when it's really cold out. And they kinda sparkled too, the feathers did, like that kinda snow does when it catches the sun the morning after a storm.

"Feathers."

"Well, not quite feathers as we know them." Angelo nodded slow-like. "Remember the srepattramer plant we looked at in the greenhouse?"

"Yeah. Yeah, I do." Jamie looked back in the bag. "These come from that?" He looked back at Angelo, and he kinda pulled his head back, givin' himself a double chin thing for a second.

Angelo nodded again, this time a little more with fervor (vocab word Jamie'd picked up from Francis's class).

"From that island." Jamie was bringin' back to his brain that conversation him and Angelo had had in the greenhouse that day about the plant and how it would give the last ingredient to the pillow and stuff.

"Yes, La Isla Desengelor." When Angelo said that this time, he had that look on his face for a second like the one that somebody gets when they think about home when they've been away for too long.

And Jamie saw it, so much that he sorta shoved aside what was goin' on in front of him with the feathers. His brain had sorta arranged the words of the question he was gonna ask Angelo, somethin' like "What, do you live there?" or "Where is that place exactly again?"

But Angelo came back to the living room too quick. A quick wink and he smiled at Jamie. "Anyway. Take as many of those or as few of those as you'd like and put them right here," he nodded to the opening, "and we're done. Your dream pillow is done."

Jamie kinda shook his head a couple times and looked at the opening in the pillow. Angelo had tried to pack everything down in there some, but all of it was tryin' to take up as much space as it could and kinda rose to a mound where the two sides of cloth separated. He smiled and looked up at Angelo. "It's done?"

"I just have to sew up the mouth, and, then, when you've decided on your dream, you can come back and take this." Angelo brought the pillow forward a little more. "But first those." He looked towards the bag in Jamie's hand.

Jamie looked down in the bag again, and then he stuck his hand in it. It was like sticking his hand into nothing. Softer than the cotton stuffing his grandmother would use when she made pillows but with a little more feel to it than a bag of air. Like a cloud or somethin'.

He put his hand in until it touched the paper bottom of the bag and he got a handful. He could just make out the thin shafty things or really the main vein that they'd have been when they were leaves on that plant, but mostly it was like holdin' a handful of silk or somethin'. They were warm too, not oven warm or sunny day warm, but they had this warm to 'em that seemed to come off... he didn't know...sometimes smells or tastes or somethin' you see will spark somethin' else in your head. Like the smell of a candy apple will remind you of the time you threw one up on the Super-Loop when you were eight at the county fair and your stomach kinda flip-flops just thinkin' about it. Things like that. Well, the warm from the feathers in that bag did that. They were the kinda warm that came from his dad when he had a bad dream when he was little and his dad would come in his room and look under the bed for him or out his window and then sit with him for a while. That kinda warm came from them.

He pulled his hand out and when he did, a bunch more came out with it, like when somebody smacks open a feather pillow and the feathers fly out and float around. A bunch came out when Jamie pulled his hand out. He looked at Angelo and his jaw dropped a little. "Sorry, Angelo."

Angelo didn't say anything, he just smiled and held the pillow out for Jamie to put the feathers in.

It seemed like a hundred or so little feathers slipped out with his hand and they swirled around the two of them until they hit wherever they were gonna land. The sewing basket. The gold carpet. The chair's arm. Jamie's arm. Angelo's beard.

Jamie set the bag down beside him and he pressed the mix with his free hand back in the pillow one more time. It didn't do much good, but it gave him a second or two of room to put the feathers there on top.

He got most of 'em in there, but a few slid out and whirled around with the other ones.

When Jamie finished, Angelo took the two flaps of cloth and kinda squeezed 'em together. "I believe we're set, Jamie."

Jamie was closin' up the bag of feathers. "Angelo..." he got up from the floor and put the bag back in the sewing basket.

Angelo watched him and he waited.

"I don't even know..." Jamie kinda moved his hands out from his sides. "I don't even know really who you are." He shook his head and smiled. "Or where you came from or why you did this for me."

Angelo sat there with the pillow on his lap and with his hands keepin' the cloth closed. He was lookin' up at Jamie.

Listenin'.

Jamie stopped a second again. Then he shook his head up and down. Instead of the other way that he had been shakin' it. "I do know—I mean—" He looked down quick and then back at Angelo. "Thanks."

Angelo wasn't a hard person to read, and he always told it like it was. But that day, with the dream pillow in his hand and lookin' up at Jamie, Jamie wasn't sure what to think. Angelo still had some of those feathers on him and in his beard and even a few of 'em were still in midair or landin' around him. His eyes always shined, and they did right then too, but Jamie kinda thought that the corner of his left...it shined...it shined the way dew does or a raindrop does when sunlight catches it a certain way.

Angelo gave a bigger smile, and took one of his hands off the pillow and held the sides shut with his other. He looked down into his basket and got his pincushion. "I'm glad our dream paths converged, Jamie." He looked up then and his smile made his cheeks and his eyes smile too. "And I thank you just as much."

Jamie wanted to hug him and he did take a step closer to him, but he stopped. And just kinda put his hand up in a wave and smiled back. "I gotta meet Ben."

Angelo found the needle he was lookin' for in the cushion and took it out. "I know you do." He looked up at Jamie and smiled and then pulled the dark blue thread that hung from it tight, so he could measure the length of it with his eye. To see if he had enough on there to finish the job. "Come back when you've chosen your dream." He eyed the thread one more time and decided it would be enough, so he started to get to work.

Jamie just stood there a second. Angelo was all about business now, but he looked up one more time at Jamie.

Jamie couldn't help his lips from turnin' up again. "See yuh, Angelo."

Angelo gave a goodbye kinda nod. "See you soon, Jamie."

✦ ✦ ✦

Metal bleachers heat up fast in the sun. Jamie sat on the bottom tier and sorta leaned back on the one behind him and spread his arms out. He had beat Ben to the meeting spot, well, he had sorta booked down Rea so he would be there on time. Not like Ben woulda minded him bein' late or anything. He wouldn't have minded at all. But when Jamie left Angelo's, he kinda jumped down the three front steps, and he felt like runnin'. Just takin' off. He woulda put his arms out too, like he was Laura Ingalls runnin' down that hill at the end of *Little House*, but he knew he woulda looked like a complete moron if he had done that, so he just ran instead. That was good enough anyway. He took off and he had this energy that started right below his ribcage and above his stomach and it was bouncin' off his insides. It woulda hummed like power runnin' through a radio that wasn't turned to a station but had its speakers cranked, if it had a sound.

He sat there only like a minute or two, catchin' his breath and feelin' the heat through his jeans from the bleacher underneath him. He could feel some sweat, too, on his forehead, where his hair started. Coulda ran further if he had had to. He kinda jumped up then and walked the length of the first row of bleachers and then he stepped up to the next one when he got to the end and started across that one. That's when he saw Ben comin' down the paved walk that led to them.

Jamie lifted his arms and spread 'em out. "'Two roads diverged in a wood, and I—/I took the one less traveled by'—"

He was sorta yellin'. Or kinda talkin' loud and all fake stern, tryin' to be kind of a geeker, yuh know. And, man, he was smilin' like crazy, almost crackin' himself up kind of smile.

Ben could appreciate it. He was about halfway down the walk, and he stopped his wheelchair. He had some sweat around his hair and forehead too and he had his book bag on his lap. And he was smilin'. One of those tryin' not to smile smiles.

Jamie knelt down on one knee and put one of his hands over his heart, "'And that has made all the difference.'"

"Okay. You're on crack." Ben started comin' the rest of the way to the bleachers, and he laughed a couple short laughs and shook his head.

Mission accomplished.

Jamie laughed a little too and stood up and wiped the hair off his forehead. He stepped down to the first bleacher. "Yuh want some help?"

"Naw, I got it." Ben wheeled himself closer to the bleacher Jamie was standin' on and he gave himself a good push and let his wheels coast the rest of the way. "Never a borrower nor a lender be because yuh 'could do worse than be a swinger of' birch."

They started crackin' up.

"Yes!" Jamie stepped down beside Ben, and he put his hand up for a hi-five.

Ben slapped Jamie's hand. "Didn't our man write that too?"

They were laughin'.

"Sorta."

"We are gonna rock this tomorrow." Ben put his bag on the bleacher.

"Yeah, we are." Jamie went to sit back down.

286

"Yuh know what. Yeah, you can help me." Ben sorta pulled his chair in and angled in towards the bleacher. He put his brakes on his wheels. "I wanna get out of this fuckin' chair."

Jamie had hung out with Ben enough by now to know what he had to do to help him out. He got back up and stood behind Ben's chair and held the handles. Just kinda steadyin' it.

Ben lifted himself up and moved onto the bottom bleacher. Beside his bag. "Thanks."

Jamie came back around and sat on the other side of the bag. "How'd the make-up go."

"Not bad. I had to do better than I did on the last one." He kinda laughed. "Anything's better than a 30."

They just sat there a second. The sun felt so damn good.

Ben was catchin' his breath now. He had wheeled a good distance. "Man, this sun." He tipped his head back a little and shut his eyes 'cause it was so bright. "So awesome."

Jamie looked over at him and then up at the sun, too. It was warm on his face.

They sat there another couple of seconds. Puttin' off the inevitable. If you've ever worked with somebody on a speech or a group project or somethin' like that, the last thing you really do is work on it. You sit and you bullshit or you get the stuff out and have it in front of you both, but you wait 'til the last five seconds to really do anything with it or you say somethin' like "We're pretty much set on it anyway, right" and the other person says "Yeah, we're pretty much set."

"You ever been up to the falls?" Ben looked behind him and then sorta wiggled on the bleacher that he was sittin' on so he could lean back on the second row.

"Coformon Falls?"

(The falls really didn't have a name, just when Edgar W. Coformon named the town after himself, the falls got the name too because they were like a few miles up Route 47 from it. Then the town, about a hundred years later, got Falls tacked onto it because the falls had outlived Edgar's great legacy of why ever he was so famous to think he should have a town named after him.)

Ben nodded.

"Yeah, I usually get up there at least once or twice a summer." Jamie leaned back too and looked up at the sun and spread his arms out like he had had 'em before. "What makes you ask that?"

Ben had his head tipped back again, like somebody was pourin' the sunshine down his throat and he was drinkin' it nice and slow. "I dunno. This freakin' Robert Frost poem. 'Birches.' Since we started messin' around with it, I can't get outa my head that trail that leads into 'em."

"Yeah, you're right. All those white birches."

They sat there. Probably both of 'em in the same place right about then. You had to hike a good three or four miles up this footpath to get to the falls, and on both sides of it were these big round white birches. Hundreds of 'em. Naw, even more than that. And they gave you the strangest feeling. Like it was bright white in the woods and all quiet and the sun came down through the leaves, which were all green. It was a really cool place to go.

"That's why my parents wanted me to go to the Y." Ben looked towards Jamie. Movin' his eyes, yuh know, and keepin' his head how it was.

Jamie felt his skin twitch a little. Not like Ben coulda seen it or anything. It was like when somebody comes up behind you and you don't know they're there and they say "Boo" or somethin', and you kinda flinch. That's what Jamie did when Ben said that, only a real mild flinch. Thing was, neither of 'em had mentioned those days at the Y until right then, and it just, well, it just seemed like a world ago to Jamie, yuh know. But that didn't stop him from lookin' over at Ben. Not at all.

"Yeah, you were in my Y class, remember?"

"Yeah, I remember."

"Well, I'd been up to the falls all that summer before we started, and I had it in my head that I was gonna jump from 'em and swim around in that huge pool at the bottom." Ben kinda shook his head. He was lookin' up again. "Man, I was not lettin' it go. Like cryin' and shit all the time."

"Really?" Jamie was still lookin' towards Ben, and he had his face crinkled a little on the one side 'cause he was squintin' from the sun.

"Yeah. So to shut me up, they told me if I went to swim class and got really good, they were gonna let me do it the next summer."

Jamie kinda kept his head turned toward Ben. Thinkin' there mighta been a little more to the story.

Ben didn't say anything though. He swiped a bug that was tryin' to land on his eyebrow, and then just kept his face in the sun.

Jamie looked back up too, and they sat there. You could hear the bug like zzzzzz-in' away.

"I still would like to do that. Yuh know...just stand out there and then dive." He used his hand to show his jump. "Then I'd swim around in the whites and then out to the calm part."

Jamie didn't look over, but he saw Ben sorta look at his wheelchair that was sittin' cockeyed to the bleachers with its little brakes pressed against the rubber tires.

"I'd do it butt-ass naked too. As planned." Ben pushed himself back up so he could sit up straight. He kinda laughed. "I think my folks were more worried about that. That I kept sayin' that I wanted to do it with no bathing suit on and with it hangin' out and stuff." He looked over at Jamie. "They probably thought I was gonna grow up to be a flasher or somethin'."

Jamie had turned his head towards him, and Jamie was kinda smilin'.

Ben was too. He reached for his bag. For the project stuff. Then he stopped. "What about you? Isn't there like some crazy-ass thing you've wanted to do since you were a kid?"

Jamie stayed how he was, sorta stretched out.

Now Ben was lookin' over at him and he had the side of his face all squinched up on the one side the sun was on.

Jamie kinda laid there, maybe a second or two. "Yeah, yuh know. It sounds cheesy, but I wanna write somethin'." He looked over at Ben. "Somethin' really fuckin' good."

"That's not cheesy." Ben kinda bobbed his head a couple times and looked out at the football field, which was just a big green lawn without any chalk lines or boundaries or anything this time of year. "That's actually pretty cool. Like a poem or a play or somethin'?"

Jamie looked out there too. The mowin' guy hadn't cut anything yet, and the grass was really green and sorta all different lengths and stuff. Untrimmed, yuh know. "Yeah, everything and anything that came outa me, I guess. Shit, I'd even write a couple pages like our boy Frost writes his stuff, yuh know," he kinda bobbed his head, too, real slow-like, and then cracked a quick smile. "But whatever I wrote, I'd want it to be really fuckin' good...and I'd want it to last forever."

Ben got this huge smile on his face, and he looked around to Jamie. "I can see you doin' that—givin' the world a lifetime supply of movie material and then some."

Jamie looked over at him and raised the corner of his mouth. A sorta big smile too. He sat back up straight. "And you're a crazy enough bastard to jump off Coformon Falls. Wheelchair or no wheelchair."

Ben's smile sorta got smaller. But it was still there. He looked down and started unzippin' his bag. "No hope for that, man. Maybe skydivin' or somethin' un-water related." He kinda laughed. A humph laugh. One that sorta makes your shoulders bounce once. Then he pulled out the folder that had all the Robert Frost stuff in it.

It was one of his folders. Plain red. Two pockets on the inside and labeled *ROBERT FROST PROJECT* in capital letters on the front of it.

Jamie looked at the straight lines of the letters and how Ben's *E*'s and *F* were perfectly cornered. Then he looked at Ben—he was openin' the folder, lookin' down at it, and his eyes were squintin' a little from the sun but you could see how bright blue they were. This kid had the brightest blue eyes. And this little scar too on his chin, just above his cleft. He had told Jamie one night when they were sharin' scar stories—you know everybody shares scar stories sooner or later when you're friends with somebody—that he was flyin' down a hill when he was a kid, no hands on a 25 cent bet *slash* dare, on his banana bike, and he nailed the curb halfway down and took a hell of a spill. The scar was a little zigzag thing that you could only see once in a while, but you could right then. Maybe the sun or somethin'.

Who knows.

Strange.

Life is so damn strange.

Jamie stood up. "Ben, you're gonna kill me, but I gotta go."

"What?" Ben looked up. He was pullin' out the notes on Frost's life. They had to include a little bio too in their presentation.

"I know. I'm sorry." Jamie took a couple steps back, like he was gettin' ready to go.

"You're jokin', right?" Ben had the couple sheets of loose leafs.

"I'll catch up with you later today, or I'll definitely call yuh tonight." Jamie was still facin' Ben, but the next couple steps back he took were a little quicker. Like he was gonna run backwards to where he was goin'. He pointed to Ben's chair. "Can you get back okay?" He knew he could.

Ben looked quick over to his chair then back at Jamie. "Yeah, of course, I can. Jamie what the hell are you doin'? I'm leavin' school early. I got a doctor's appointment in the city and I don't know what time I'm gettin' back. Remember? That's why we were into meetin' now."

Jamie was still leavin'. "Ben, we're so good on this, you know we are. This other thing can't wait."

"What other thing? Where yuh goin'?" Ben was talkin' to Jamie's back now though.

"I'll tell yuh tomorrow. I promise." Jamie yelled from over

his shoulder. He was runnin' at a good clip now.

Ben looked down at the Robert Frost notes. *Robert Frost was born in*—he looked back up. "You'd better, you bastard."

Friends call each other names like that. Bastard and stuff.

Jamie lifted his arm. And took off down Rea.

Chapter Twenty-five

I FELT someone poking my shoulder, and I woke up slowly from my sound sleep.

There's a certain subtlety to the woods in the morning, a quietude that walks hand in hand with the break of a new day. It is just as you would expect it to be. Streams of sunlight wash through the treetops and give the leaves an emerald green glow. Rays splash past and through the limbs and onto the quiet places of the forest's belly. A raccoon scuttles for bed while a deer and her fawn stretch their heads and stand. The owl stops hooting and a morning dove begins her soft coo. It may be here, deep in the woods of a high mountain, that day and night make love rather than do battle.

Stillness, peaceful dream, and daylight intertwine into one.

And that *one* rocks and sways you like you are its newborn, giving truth to tale that someone could sleep for some twenty years or more in the forests on top of a Catskill mountain...

When I felt the finger on my shoulder, my eyelids barely opened. The ground I was on was soft, covered with fallen leaves and patches of moss, so my body, with the two, had generated a sleepy warmth, and had imprinted itself there, on them, nestling without any intention of leaving soon.

But the finger I felt jabbed again.

It was an old finger. That I could tell without seeing it. Hard and crooked with a little longer nail. It knew the mountains and hard work, and I opened my eyes a little more to its persistence.

The rush of sun and bright white watered my vision some and I squinted, blinked, and finally focused to see around me a field of white birches. Tall trees with thick trunks, as thick as trunks that white birches can have, surrounded me. They stood dignified and straight and their coats were pure white with streaks of gray. I stared at them and tilted my head up and followed one's body, the one closest to me, to its top where it burst into a thousand branches and leaves that connected with the branches and leaves of a thousand other white birches. I just stared and traced the design they made above me, and watched how light rippled through in a hundred different places. I'd forgotten all about the finger that had brought me to, and I sat and stretched at the same time and couldn't help but look out and up, and listen to the morning's low lull.

The finger turned into a hand though, and I felt it on my shoulder. Callused and old, but with a warmth to it.

I turned, and he took it away and stood there only for a second in front of me. He was short and half bent over and with a beard from a fairy tale. Long and to his knees. He held a knotted old walking stick made from the root of a tree, and it wound around itself until it curved at his weathered old hand, a hand that looked as if it had been part of a tree once itself. He'd worn the knees and the cuffs from his pants and the sleeves from his shirt, and his coat was more like a cloak. But he wasn't dressed in rags. His forehead crept back to above his ears, and he looked happy to see me, judging from the way his eyes sat on his cheeks.

When he had my attention, he winked and nodded his head to his side, as if he were pointing to something or somewhere behind him. And with that, he turned and began through the trees, weaving between them, his wrinkly leather boots stepping in turn with the tip of his walking stick.

I stood and moved to follow him, and it was then that I noticed my feet were bare. I looked down at their pale white skin that rarely sees sun, and I could feel the soft prickle of pointed moss on my arches and between my toes. Beside them, lay a notebook and a pen.

I looked up and he had stopped, waiting for me to follow. He pointed with his stick to there beside my feet, and turned and went on. He was a good distance from me by now already, and I bent for my new pad and pen, and took off after him.

The morning air of the woods was a cool-warm, but you could tell that, above the trees, the sun already burned hot and bright. It was a summer day. Late June or better. And I followed after the old man at a quick pace, a comfortable run that resembled a sprinting walk. The fabric of my faded Levi's rubbed gently across my legs, moving with my movements and lightly tapping my ankles at its bottom seams. The latter sticking most in my head, having never jogged barefoot in the woods before. The fear of poison oak or poison ivy or snakes or broken glass never entered my mind because there was nothing ominous in this place that I was. Had I wanted to spread my arms and fly, it was here that that could have happened. That is the feeling that whispered from the trees and ground and air around me.

I wore an undershirt too, and, as I passed through the white birches, trying to keep the old man in sight, I could feel the air between where the loose cotton touched against me and where it didn't. It seemed most present on the tender beneath my upper arms and in the short, fine hair of my underarms.

The quiet mountain I was on let me hear my heart. It didn't seem awkward or out of place to hear it in sync with the long steps I ran or in accompaniment with the chirp of an early bird or the bass string notes of a bullfrog. It sounded in my ears and I felt it in my chest, and it beat differently here, with more force and more ease. Beyond agileness, its rhythm sent the mountain air undiluted to my blood and body, and I breathed steadily and with an incredibly pleasant purpose. Energetic peace I would call it.

We continued on this way, I would guess for the shorter end of an hour, with him just ahead of me, and me trailing not far behind, the distance between us barely ever changing. I had my notebook and pen in my hand, and small beads of sweat began to form on my forehead, in the center of my chest, and in the hairs of my thighs and lower legs. They were welcome as they rolled down my body parts, because I felt natural here, between the trees, chasing after this little man.

I partly wished we wouldn't reach our destination, for the travel to it was like none other that I have ever experienced. My limbs were loose, and the thin layer of my skin that separated me from where I was and what was around me did not seem to exist. For the first time in my life, my body was my spirit. And my spirit was all.

The old man stopped. I wish I could give you more of him. His bent bones and back and crooked nose and curly gray brows. His smile hidden behind the wisps of wooly beard. He was an antique from an old world. And he turned just once more and nodded and stepped to his side, where a birch blocked my view of him. And that was the last I saw of him. Ever.

My feet stopped then too, and they sent sensations of the soft forest ground, cool from the shade of the birch I stood beside, to my brain, and something told me that he and I still stood on a common vein of mountainside.

I stood and I looked through the trees.

And there, where he had disappeared, was an opening. I could make out places of blue from the sky and bright light from the sun.

He had led me to this place. The place.

I began to walk forward, and with each step I took, the sound grew louder. I heard, soft at first, the easy pour of water over rocks. Falls tumbling over an edge with a frolicking force. The trees began to separate, and the welling rush of water filled the spaces. Its voice took over my ears and my insides. Its rumble felt there within me too, and I quickened my last few paces to the edge of the white birch woods until it was there before me.

The white and the clear water of the vast gorge. A theater of water and rock, high on this mountain, spread to touch the sky and the flat of slate and grass I now stood on. Sweat trickled down my brows and from my back and chest and body, and the way the sun sat and reached down, he was looking to quench his thirsty outstretched tongues with a few more licks of me. I took a few more steps out onto this stage and, beside a small tree, one that looked like an overgrown bonsai, I dropped my notebook and pen on some warm slate and pulled my shirt off in one motion. I dropped that down too, and I took another three steps to the edge and looked down. I was at least eighty feet up and level with the top of the falls. The pool at the bottom was deep and wide and it mirrored everything above and around it, and I wanted to jump.

I went closer to the edge and, again, I could have spread my arms and flown. There was no fear in the thump against my rib, it was only freedom. I bent at my knees and I brought my hands straight behind my back and tipped my head forward. I was ready to jump. I could feel the hot sun and the cool watered air, and I could feel first my longest fingers and then my body in the cold summer water. I stepped a little closer to the edge and I curled my toes over the slated edge. I stretched my arms back to be sure my dive would be out and I—I felt the tap of a walking stick on my bare shoulder.

I stood straight and I looked behind me.

He wasn't there. But a breeze off the ledge flipped open my notebook, and I just watched as a few of the pages turned with its invisible fingers. I think—no, I *believed*, truly *believed*, then that I knew. I knew what it meant.

I didn't need to jump. I already knew how it felt. Like so many things that I hadn't witnessed or touched or experienced, I only had to imagine it, and it would be mine. I could imagine it and feel it because I could write it, and somehow, in doing that, it would become a reflection of me or me a reflection of it.

Someone else needed to jump here. Now. In this place and in this time. And I would be jumping with him.

I felt the misty spray from the falls as the breeze shifted and sent speckles of water across my face and arms and chest. I took my hands and rubbed my face as if the small droplets of water were a washcloth, and then I pushed my moist hair from my forehead. I breathed the air like it was my last breath and I smiled. Until I could feel the creases in my face from what had caused them from the inside.

A smile seems to be even more when no one else is there to see it or call it a smile.

I walked over to where my undershirt and my notebook and my pen were and I sat down, Indian style, a foot or two from the tree. My neck tingled, right then, just as I found my place, and, as customary when it sends such a signal to me, I could not help but wonder if another's eyes were upon me. So, once more, I looked behind me and, of course, only the stillness of the birches stared back. But I let my instinct guide my head, and I found myself looking up toward a higher limb of the tree beside me. Sure enough, I could vaguely see the outline of some kind of smaller-sized bird hidden there in the green. Although I could not completely see it, I knew its small eyes were upon me. I studied its whereabouts more intently, just enjoying the moment for what it was worth. But the bird stayed completely motionless, so I returned to my matter at hand. My new company would be far from a distraction, and, in fact, as strange as it was, I felt somewhat that much more inspired in its presence — yes, a bird I couldn't even see — and even ventured to guess it was somehow connected to what I was about to do. I reached over and picked up my already opened notebook, and I found my first blank page. I picked up my pen, and I began to write. I began to write and I waited...

I heard his whistle first. Sharp and shrilled. The finger and thumb stuck in the mouth and pressed to the tongue. A maverick's whistle.

I don't know how much time had past. I had kept my pen moving and had looked up from time to time to breathe in what was before me or check in on the quiet bird above me, but there seemed to be no time in between anything because here, where I was, and when I was, everything was happening. My writing had become some magnetic force, and what was around me, the falls, the slate I sat on, the sun and the sky, seemed to cipher through me and onto the paper in front of me. When I looked up and around, it was as if I were looking within. I had lost track of the number of pages I had written, and I had even forgotten what I had put there upon them. Those details, at the moment, becoming far secondary to the process and action of this all. Insignificant to my transferal and unification of myself with everything into the notebook before me.

My head was bent over the notebook, and my hand was sprawled across it, guiding the words that came from the pen's fine tip, when I heard his whistle. I looked up and across then. Across the falls to the other side where a flat bluff, much like the one I sat on, stuck out and over the water.

When he had my attention, he lifted his arm and waved. He used his body when he did this, almost jumping up and down, swaying side to side, and, although he was a ways off and the water gushing over the base drowned out the words that he yelled out and over to me, I knew what he was saying by the smile that took over his face, the type of smile that I could have seen from anywhere.

I waved back to him, and I smiled back to him.

He looked at me, making eye contact the best one could from such a ways off, to make sure I was looking at him. Then he looked down at his feet and I could tell by his standing in place movement that he was wiggling his toes inside his sneakers. And then he did just one more thing before he seemed to enter his own world and forget that I was there watching him from the other side. He looked back across to me and pointed down to his legs.

Because he was standing on them.

He pointed at them and then he felt of them. He cupped both of his hands on the thighs beneath the khakis he had on. He squeezed the legs he felt beneath and worked his hands down to his calves and his shins and then his ankles, taking his time along the way. When he was bent and his hands were wrapped around his ankles, he stood there for a moment like that. Letting them seep in. He didn't want to shake his head, but he did. In disbelief. He shook it and he dropped to his knees, taking his hands from his ankles and pressing his open palms and stretched-apart fingers on the rock that he now kneeled on.

He shook his head from side to side, burying his face between his arms at first, and then looking up. He had never cried in his life when he had been happy or thankful, and he started to laugh at the idea that he was now. His tears seeped from his eyes and ventured down his face, passing lines of upward curve rather than those of down that they had traveled so many times before.

He stood back up and spread his arms out and laughed. Big, resounding laughs from inside of him. With them, and somewhere between, his head slowly went from shake to nod and words like "Yes" and phrases like "Thank you, God" formed across his lips. He jumped up and down and spun around, his arms still out like wings. His fingers spread wide and his hands held stiff. He jumped and spun and even ran the longer length of the bluff a couple of times, turning full circle sometimes in the middle of a lap or bending to feel one of his thighs again or one of his knees.

Then he walked to the edge of the rock and looked down into the waters. He looked at the calm of the pool and followed the waters to the whites and up the falls. He hadn't quit smiling, and at the sight, his smile, if possible, grew a little more.

He began to unbutton his shirt. It was a dress shirt, solid dark blue, and neatly tucked in his pants and under his belt as it always was. He undid his top two or three, and then, rather than finishing, he undid his cuffs, and pulled it over his head. His V-neck undershirt came off in one swipe too, and he tossed it in the vicinity of where he had flung his shirt. He untucked the end of his belt from the buckle and took the thick brown leather from around his waist, pulling it from his pants loops until it hung like a dead snake from his hands. He took his sneakers off with each of his feet, while he unbuttoned and unzipped his pants and worked them down off his legs. He used his feet again, this time to take his pants all the way off, and he bent and pulled both of his socks off. He stood now only in his bleach white boxers, and would have gotten dressed again, just to feel how he had just felt. How quickly he had undressed, and with as many body parts as he had done it. And all while standing up too. Could anyone know how good that felt besides him?

He looked up again. This time directly at the sun. His eyes squinted, but he looked at its white heat. He could feel it instantly warm his face, and his body's skin exchanged it for clean sweat. He stuck his thumbs in his waistband, at each of his hips, and he pushed down. His boxers slid around him, still making use of their elastic, until he had worked them low enough so that they slipped past his thighs and lower legs and he could step out of them and to the side as they landed to the hard rock surface he stood on.

He looked down. At his legs again. And they matched the toned muscle of his upper body. The bones were surrounded with flesh and sinew and there were no sores or red, festered blotches from sitting too long. He took both his hands and cupped his left thigh, and he flexed the muscle there. He rubbed down and then up it and then did the same to the other. The heads of his thousands of tiny light-colored leg hairs sent signals to his brain. They could feel the tug and the touch and the squeeze of his warm hands that they had hardly ever been permitted to feel.

He moved his hands up his right thigh and he let them cross over. He ran his hands and his fingers through the soft bristly hair there, and he let his right hand rub down and around and touch until it reached his tip. Not ashamed. Not sexually. He watched himself as his body responded with a flush of blood inside. There had always been feeling there, sensitive reaction. But often times not without soreness and pain. He looked at the small slit and it looked human, not irritated or red from the entrance and exit of a catheter, not humiliated by the handling of another whom he didn't want there.

Here and now it was different. Pure and alive.

He would have let himself do it, and he promised himself he would later, but there was something he wanted even more than that at that very moment. He breathed in and he let his hands hang at his sides. Shoulders back but not forced. Arms loose but not careless or clumsy. He took four steps to the edge of his platform, feeling every joint and muscle coordinate and work from his feet to his hips. The sockets in their grooves and the solid of his bones in use.

When he could curl his toes over the rounded, weatherworn rock, he looked out and over. The water burst from the bed above, and reminded him, strangely enough, of fireworks in a world where water is divine and where people sit in awe of it and are able to see the array of silvers and blues and clears as it explodes over a gorge. Where they see the water as he saw it...as he felt it.

He sensed his body change, thinking of entering it. Submersing himself in its wet manifolds. Goose bumps peppered the insides of the soft of his arms, and his toes and fingertips connected themselves with a whirling reflex of adrenaline that zipped around each notch of his spine before splintering into pulsating ends of his body. His heart beat with a steady thump, his chest felt light.

He was ready.

In one flow of motion, he stretched his arms above him, lifted the heels of his feet so his toes would be a pushing force, tucked his head in his biceps, and sprang. Out, and aiming for the whites of the falls.

Midair lasted only the short of three and a half seconds, but, had he really known what flying was like, he would have said that, when his feet left the rock and he was only a body suspended by nothing but the experience itself, he felt as if he were really flying. Soaring, as he spread his arms out and arched his neck and back, almost cresting himself on a wind the way the eagle and the hawk do. Feeling weightless and unattached, from land and from himself. Unknotting some thick, wound rope inside of him that he had walked around with for years. Sun doused his back and sprigs of cool water bounced and then clung to his skin.

Here, his element appeared, and, oddly enough, as life often does when exposing such things, it served for a more practical purpose. This brief glide would insure that he was as far from the edge of the gorge as he could be.

So no sooner had he spread his arms, did his eyes and his instinct, both wide open and focused on the tumbling waters below, tell him he would be safe from the rocks that jutted out from the walls and hid themselves beneath the water's surface.

His dive was a dissension and impossible to halt, but he savored each minute particle of time he was given to it. He transformed himself from one stage of it to the next with an ease and unintention. With a nature of not doing, but letting it happen. Of letting him happen with it.

From pointed to spread, his arms readied with his body for the submersion. They bent back, staying stiff and straight, and then rounded over his head again, to poise and point for the destination once more. His body followed their lead, and he felt his muscles tighten for the breaking of the surface. A phase of the course, no longer than the previous ones, he transfixed all that he was onto and into it. His body fell faster with its final arrow-like metamorphosis, precise and prepared for the realm it was about to enter. The sound of water rolling and turning grew. It gained his being, and overtook his ears until it was all that they heard. He had kept his breath steady, but now, only three lengths of himself above the water, his lungs gripped around the last mouthful of oxygen he sent down to them. Sharp splashes and slaps of water extended from their source toward him.

His fingers, flat and pressing close, extended to them. To it.

Perhaps, he penetrated the white, hurling waters or they consumed and swallowed him, but it may be best said that, when his body touched the wet and it enveloped him, there was more of an embrace than anything else.

His fingertips guided him and he broke the base of the falls. The round curving lines grooved at each of his fingers' ends, nature's coded key of only his identity, shot a web of alive from his hands to his feet, awakening every area of his exposed skin there and in between, and wiring the forthcoming immersion throughout his body.

There was no dark, hesitant interval. Instantaneously, he was part of the rush of cold, thrashing water, and his body shot past the tosses and hurls of Catskill water whitecaps until it wrestled with the ripples of current beneath them. With a natural reaction, he had closed his eyes upon entering, but here, underneath, as he continued deeper, unable to stop if he wanted to, he desired sight of what was around him. He opened his eyes to the clear murk of mountain water, and he listened to the muffled crashes of breaking water above him. He allowed himself to travel farther down, keeping his arms in front of him, driving and directing him forward, protecting himself, to an extent, from a misinterpretation of the gorge's bottom. The dark and degree of cold took greater control, and his body, which had been drubbed and drummed closer to the water's surface, only swayed as it went deeper down and now regained full navigation.

He didn't desire to touch the bottom, he only wanted to surround himself with the quiet and the dark and the frigid waters of it. So when he dove as far as he could, without the pressure drilling his head and ears too hard, he spread his arms and stroked himself upright. Then worked, reversing his strokes to keep himself under, for a moment or two. To remain here. Below. Allowing himself to suck *here* and *below* in. Feeling his hair flowing from his head, weaving and waving slowly like seaweed at the base of a pond. Looking up and seeing only the faint light from the sun outside, its heat and rays turning the surface to a watery slab of marble. Feeling the winter of a summer's stream as it surrounded his every body part and shrunk his rigid sack. Every sense acute, slipping three bubbles from his mouth, he recorded their quiet release.

Soundless, they rose above him and disappeared.

And he followed them, dismissing his arms from pumping, and now using them to control his rise to the surface, in unison with the water's push and his body's urge to institute its floating birthright.

When he buoyed to the surface, he had flowed with the waters and was now a good distance from the falls, out of the harder water, but still in a current. The hot air of the gorge invited him back and, partnered with the coolness of the water his body was in, it concocted a vast smile across his face. He gave the stream reign and let her take him to her soft belly and her restful waters.

As the rippled surface changed to a calm liquid sheet of glass, he watched the images of the trees and rock and sky smear themselves across it. And he was there, dressed in his bare wet skin, in the midst of this natural canvas. A part of it.

The jump and the water still registered heavy in his breath and his chest and his spirit, and only until he began to propel himself along (relying less on the water's work because she had brought him as far as she was going to) did the motion of his feet fluttering at his command, his action, and his capability fuse an additional charge to his being.

He hollered. "Hhh-hhhhaaaa!" Laughing and yelling from the crevice inside his gut that he hadn't hollered from or laughed out of in forever.

Echoes off the high rocks around him. "Hhh-hhhaaaaa!" and "YES!" and a rolling, schoolboy laughter.

He dove beneath the surface. Swimming underwater and then popping up, resurfacing with the ideal and sport of a smiling dolphin...

I had jumped up and ran and leaned out to see him land after he dove. I watched, for what seemed like several minutes, to see his head or a sign of his white skin contrast with the whites of the water. I lost sight of him, however, and I jogged the length of short ground I was on to scan below for him.

When I finally saw, first his blond hair, and, then, his upper torso bobbing and bouncing down the stream, I watched intently, sure he was fine, but drunk in the experience with him. My eyes followed him as the waters gave him back his way, and I heard him yell, or I saw him tip his head back and lift his arms and turn full circle in the water and cry to all that surrounded him, and I imagined the sound of his yell and laugh.

I laughed out loud and cheered to him then, I even jumped up and down for him, with my arms above my head and my hands clenched in fists.

He had been a man and a bird and a fish all at once, and I had been part to it.

Of course, he did not hear or see me, because he was a distance from me now, and that was all right. I watched him a minute more as he did somersaults and dove under and swam strokes and floated on his back, his arms fanning out from him and his legs flapping water in buckets above him. He was as naked and as natural there in the pool below as a child is in his mother's womb, and I folded my arms across my chest and stood and smiled, delaying my turn from him, sharing a last transmission of his sheer bliss. And while I could have stayed there on the edge peering down and out at the water and at him and his acrobatics, I knew, even by my arms tucked neatly across my sticky chest that I had to turn away, back to where I had been sitting, beside the tree and with my notebook...my notebook and my pen.

I sweat, and the sun sprayed more rays across my shoulders and back, and had done his job heating the slate I had crossed in a hurry (and had paid little heed to, in regards to its warmth) only a minute or two ago. I eased my arms again and walked a few feet, and I looked down and then forward, my mind quietly encountering everything, what it'd seen, what it was seeing, and what it was about to see.

While I had been away, the bird so quietly sitting above me earlier had hopped from our tree and landed beside my notebook.

How long it had been there I couldn't say, but, now fully visible to me, I easily identified it as a red-winged blackbird. I paused in my steps when I saw its bold black. Its bright strip of red and sprig of gold across the wing it faced me with elevated the flood of energies that had now cascaded my already diminished human dam within. It was no less grand than the crashing falls near me, and had eyes no less clear than the calm waters I had been looking down at. Brilliantly ordinary and ordinarily brilliant. And like me, it may have come out of its resting spot to see the cavorting white naked human otter below, because it too radiated, and held in common with us, that one same sheer bliss.

The bird sat there, strangely seeming to be waiting for me now. It watched me, and I returned the concentrated tilt of its head and stare of its careful eye with an intent gaze of my own. The interest had become mutual. I began to move as slowly as I could to get back to where I had been sitting and, hence, closer to it, the two destinations somehow tied together now.

I took long and prolonged steps, my bare feet pressing a path of conscious civility. One step and another, and then another, it watched, blinking only once and opening its beak, as if trying to speak or form a word rather than talk the tongue of a bird.

Two and a half steps to home, I began to notice even more its sleek feathers and tender skin of its legs. As if it had felt my finger rub its ringed, almost scaly foot, it skipped backward from me, closer to the trunk of the tree, and I stood still, breathing lightly through my nose and feeling a trickle of my sweat drip down my side from below my arm.

I waited. And watched.

It seemed to open and close its pearlish-yellow beak. Asking me a question or priming its tiny vocal cords for something other than a typical birdly hymn.

I took another step. Then one more, and it stayed. I settled for this side of my notebook and, with my eyes still on the bird, I bent, first at my knees, then following with my body. Slowly.

It flicked its wings once, standing there, and then with half a thought, it snapped them up and down again, and turned and flew away and into the birches. I watched it easily, its black vivid against the trunks of the trees, until it darted up into the millions of overlapping leaves and left my eyesight.

I sat then and put my legs out, crossing them at my feet. I looked over my shoulder and behind me, sure the bird was looking back. It would trade wisdom for its untimely timidness, and I knew. I turned and looked out across the gorge, and the sun hadn't seemed to move in the sky. I looked at the crooked trunk of the big bonsai tree beside me as it swayed to catch a light breeze and toss it over on me. I picked up my notebook and my pen and put my point to the space between two lines that I had left off at.

I hardly dismissed presence behind me, a guardian, a mentor, a winged messenger waiting to make its appearance when fitting. Glowing and real. I began to write again.

Hours or a minute, or it could have been a whole summer that passed by this way, with me, here, writing. And the falls and the sun and the birches and the old man who led me here…and Ben…had etched themselves into me.

And the red-winged blackbird, too.

All, through the movement of my pen.

The soft breeze the bonsai had started, multiplied with its cousins' help, and I set my writing down, having nearly come to the bottom of a page, and I reached for my shirt beside me. The cotton fabric slid freely over me, my skin no longer moist from the sun but cool now from the moving mountain air.

I looked up and out one more time, and I sighed. I sighed as if I had swallowed everything before me or it had swallowed me.

It was one of the best sighs I have ever experienced or will again in my life.

When I returned to write this time, it came back. The red-winged blackbird. It flew and landed under the tree beside me, and it took a few short steps to sit closer by.

I stole glances between words from my pen and pretended it wasn't there, and it returned these favors by staying. Not pecking at the ground or walking around in place as birds sometimes do, or even singing its song, though I had begun to completely doubt it had one. It stood there, moving nothing but its beak, as it had done before, giving me the strange feeling it was trying to talk...trying to speak my language. If only I could decode its quiet speech.

I came to the bottom of the page I was writing on, and I moved my hand carefully to flip the sheet. The bird just stepped closer then and it now was nearly touching my left leg. I felt the paper between my thumb and forefinger, and I rubbed.

It was my last page.

I thought I heard a sound. A low peep.

The cool breeze turned to a quick chill.

I looked beside me, at the red-winged blackbird, and then I turned the page and wrote...

You sit.

In the circle of shade beneath a tree.

Bright colored wings unable to be seen. You stray

*from your brother and sister's ways. They perch on a
     tall,*

tall piece of canary grass that bends and blows

*in the breeze in the center of a farmer's sunny
     hayfield.*

There they bob and bounce and reign

and sport to be kings and queens.

*Their nation's flags flashing, embroidered upon their
     wings.*

How come you are not like your two regal siblings?

Nothing is left to chance.

The cool is good for now

in this dimmer sphere of my tree.

It's needed and welcomed, and,

if only you look harder,

you might see my rose red and golden seam.

But look even more,

with a stronger and newly fixed eye,

and see that what is attached to my glorious seal is me.

*You see, I sit in this circle of shade beneath a tree, far
     from foolish or sad.*

I know that, because of the here and now,

*that in good time, when I will fly to a field of growing
     hay,*

the sun's rays will be that much longer and warmer

and brighter.
The sway of my perch will be that much more free,
and beholden that much more to the black and
*   red-winged bird*
that I deem myself to be.

Small goose bumps on my arms and the sun is settin'.
My pen's goin' dry, but I got one more thing to get down.

Then again...life is strange, isn't it. Or somethin' like
*   that.*

Chapter Twenty-six

His hand was movin', like it had a pen in it and stuff, and there was a breeze too, chilly as all get-out. He reached down to scratch his nuts. Guys do that before they even are all the way awake. His eyes were still shut, followin' images in his head or wherever. Life is strange. Somethin' like that. He kept sayin' that and he could feel his lips formin' the words, but no sound was comin' out. So he made sure he was writin' it down. Life is strange. Life is strange. Life is strange. Damn it, somethin' like that. The birches were all sorta blendin' together now and he saw himself lyin' back down in 'em. In the same place where he was when, when…when he turned over on his side in bed, he stopped writin' and he crossed his arms over his chest 'cause the forest or his room, it had gotten really cool in there. He felt somethin' hard on his cheek. And he sniffed.

That's when he opened his eyes. When he sniffed. They say your smell is the strongest sense and stuff when it comes to stuff like that. Rememberin' or puttin' it all together. His room was dark, but you can see things in your room even when it's dark. His curtains were kinda almost straight out from his window and they were filled with wind, like parachutes are, yuh know. He watched 'em flap and fill up and go down a little and then catch another gust of air from outside. When he went to bed, he had left his window open 'cause his room had been stuffy and warm. Now his eyes were open and it had gotten really cool in there, and he watched his curtains for like a minute or so, just lyin' there with his arms across his chest.

He sniffed again. Twice. It was lumpy and kinda hard, and.

Holy shit. He sat up, and he flicked the light on by his bed. He shut his eyes, all blinded for a second, and he blinked hard a few times. But the whole time while his eyes were adjustin' or whatever to the light, he was reachin' for it.

He picked up the little pillow that he had rolled over on and landed his cheek on a couple of minutes ago. Holy shit. He put it up to his nose. Holy shit! Holy shit!

He looked down at himself and he had on a white T-shirt and a paira jeans. No fuckin' way. The wind kinda whistled and his curtains sorta snapped instead of flapped, and he looked over at 'em and then stood and went to shut the window.

The air had like changed overnight.

He set the pillow on his desk on top of his books and notebook. This big thick notebook. He looked down at it, but he musta been like still half asleep or somethin' because he just went to close the window.

It was one of those old kinda windows, and he had to take the prop stick out and lay it between the screen and window and then

317

push a little to get the thing shut. The wind wanted in, and he kinda shivered while he was standin' there tryin' to take care of closin' things up.

Damn. It felt like mid-March again.

He reached on the back of his desk chair and got a sweatshirt and pulled it over his head. That's when his eyes caught the pillow—while he was shovin' his arms into his sleeves—and he couldn't help pickin' the thing up again.

And that's when *it* registered. The big notebook.

It was so damn quiet in his room, he could hear himself lookin' at the thing. The big spiral and the black cover with a red and gold border. He lowered his eyebrows, just lookin' at it. He had the pillow in his one hand and he took his other hand and rubbed down it. Like it was...like he didn't think it was real and he wanted to make sure that it was.

He swallowed and could feel his Adam's Apple (that was startin' to poke out some, like he said before) go up and then down with the spit.

He sorta squeezed the pillow without really knowin' that he was doin' it, and then he flipped the notebook open with his other hand. Some page, halfway in the middle, maybe. And it was filled. Filled with writing. His writing. He didn't get lost in one particular word or phrase or anything, he just looked down at the page and the ink all over it from top to bottom.

He turned the page and looked.

Same thing. Completely filled, no margins or anything. His handwriting.

He turned another page and then another. Looked at 'em and then looked down at the pillow in his other hand.

It worked. It had really worked!!! He wanted to go ape-shit. He started to laugh and then he caught himself, and looked behind him at his closed door. He started jumpin' around. Smilin' like crazy and laughin'. Bein' quiet the whole time. Yes, yes. Holy shit. He jumped up on his bed and he started jumpin' up and down. It worked. He still had the pillow in his hand and he held it above his head and then held it with both his hands. Like that guy does with that baby in *Roots*. And he was lookin' up at it too. Jumpin' up and down, and he kissed it even. Angelo, thank you Angelo. He turned around a couple times on his bed until he was almost a little dizzy. He was goin' nuts and he reminded himself of…of Lenny maulin' the shit out of a puppy or somethin', but he didn't care. Thank you—

He stopped and he looked at his alarm clock. Red digits with the two blinkin' dots stared back at him. 3:17. Naw, he was asleep. He had to be.

He got down off his bed and set the pillow down and picked up off his floor another sweatshirt. He didn't care. He pulled it over his head. He was goin'. He grabbed a pair of socks, too. That took a second, he saw one right away and picked that up, then he got down on his knees and looked under his bed and one was wadded up under there. He got 'em both and sat down on his bed. He took the one and put it on. Then he unwadded the other and started to put it on. He sorta curled his toes to stick 'em in when he did, and he stopped. He held the sock just in front of his foot and he looked at his toes and he curled 'em up and then uncurled 'em and curled 'em again.

Ben.

He whipped his sock on and picked up the pillow and stood up.

His sneaks were around somewhere.

* ✦ *

On his way out the door, he'd gotten his cap—the one he wore when he worked—off the back of the kitchen chair he'd hung it on. He wished it covered a little more of his head because the walk was gonna be a little longer, well, kind of a lot longer than he had thought it was gonna be. And it was cold too. His body was all outa winter mode, and whatever it was out now felt like tundra cold to him. He tugged it over his head a little more, even though it wasn't gonna do anymore good than it was already doin'. And he kept walkin'. With his arms across his chest, almost like he had had 'em when he woke up, and for the same reason, but out here he had the pillow tucked in there with 'em. He didn't know why he'd brought it with him. He just did.

Route 47 was bare. Not a car on it. It was a main drag into town, but no one was out this time of night or on a weeknight, especially. Jamie had to get to the other side of town practically. Long walk or cold, didn't matter. He had it in his head he was goin' to Angelo's to thank him. He musta been half asleep too, even though he didn't feel it, because he told himself after he went to Angelo's he was gonna walk to Ben's house and see him too. He pulled his hand from the warm armpit he'd tucked it under and he wiped one of his eyes. He wanted his body to be as awake as he felt he was. Everything was so awake. Christ, he woulda ran like Rocky, if that part of him was awake like the rest of him was.

A dog barked, and he looked up the driveway he was passin'.

He could hear a chain rattlin' and the dog flippin' out, and he thought he could see the thing runnin' back and forth in the people's yard. But he couldn't make it out for sure. He wasn't afraid or anything. It was just one of those walks he sorta just let his head think its own thoughts. Everything was a detail, yuh know.

Like the driveway he went by. It led up to a farm that had been in the family for like six generations and they bottled their own milk or somethin'. He didn't even know the people but *The Coformon Falls Daily Record* ran a story on them almost every year just because. It actually was kind of a cool little gig the Grangers, that's who they were, had goin' on. But *The Record* doin' so many stories on 'em? He wasn't so down with that.

He could smell the sweet stink of cow shit too in the damp air. It wasn't nasty or anything. Jesus, yuh probably think he had some obsession with crap or somethin' by the way he already talked about it that night when he went to the barn to deliver Puck, and with him mentionin' it now. But it's not that way at all, it's like…well, if you lived on the other side of town you smelled the leather mills, and they sorta smelled like rotten eggs so bad it could make yuh sick, but if you were used to it and you grew up your whole life on that side of town, it was sorta what reminded you of goin' home.

Man, the air was damp too. He looked up and the sky was dark, but he couldn't see a star. All overcast. He looked down to watch his step on the loose gravel on the side of the road and then he looked back up. Gray night clouds were floatin' in and out of each other up there. If he didn't know any better, he woulda said that it might even—

He looked back in front of him and moved closer to the guardrails, 'cause a truck was comin' from town. It came over a small knoll he was about to hit, and the guy had his high beams blastin'. It was a big-ass truck by how it sounded. Rumblin', gears shiftin' to get over the hill. Like a work truck or a dump truck or somethin'. Jamie kept walkin' but he put his head down so he wasn't lookin' straight into the headlights.

When it was just about to roll past him, he looked up a second at it. Instinct, yuh know. At the windshield. The color of the truck he could make out. Pine green, or somethin', yuh know. And the emblem on its side. The emblem on its side. Shit.

He pulled his cap down over the front of his face and kept walkin'. Maybe it was somebody else.

He heard the truck slow down real quick and pull off to the side of the road. Onto the loose gravel he had just walked on about five seconds ago. He heard the air brakes and all that stuff behind him.

He had been takin' big, long steps the whole way so far, not strollin' or anything, but he was takin' even bigger ones now. Even though he knew he was busted.

He heard the door open. It was an old truck and the hinges were creaky.

The quiet of somebody lookin' at him.

A couple more steps.

"Jamie?"

He stopped and turned around. He saw the ass-end of the truck and the red break lights. One of 'em had black tape over part of it where some crewman musta backed up too close to somethin'. Or somethin'. He saw the outline of him standin' on the truck floor and hangin' out the open door, and he saw the lit end of his cigarette. "Hey, Barry," he hollered back to him.

Barry started laughin' and went into a cough.

Jamie could see him turn his head and cover his mouth with the hand he had his Marlboro in. Jamie kinda just stood there and scuffed his sneaker on a couple of stones.

When Barry caught his breath, he yelled back to Jamie. They were maybe fifty feet from each other and the truck was still runnin'. "Whatta yuh doin', kid? Christ, it's three somethin' in the mornin'." He laughed a little again and stuck his cigarette in his mouth.

"I'm goin' to a friend's house." God, that was stupid, but he couldn't think of anything else.

Barry just stood there a second leanin' out the driver's side door. He looked down at the road.

Jamie could see him a little from the lights on the inside of the truck. He saw some of Barry's smoke, and he thought he saw him nod his head.

Barry looked back up and out at him. "Well, at least, lemme give yuh a lift, partner."

They stood there, half seein' each other, out there on the side of Route 47. It was at least another seven or so miles to Angelo's.

"Okay." Jamie tipped his cap up a little, off from his face, and jogged to the truck.

Barry was already behind the wheel and leanin' across the seat, openin' the door for him when he got there. He was smilin' with his cigarette hangin' out of his mouth.

Jamie climbed up and got in and closed the door. He had kinda kept the pillow on his one side, away from Barry. He wasn't tryin' to be sly or anything, but, well, it wasn't like he could get into it, yuh know. So when he got in, he kinda made like he was gettin' situated and he tucked the pillow pretty good into the crack between the seat cushions on his door side.

They didn't say anything at first. Barry musta figured Jamie's *friend* lived in town because he did a Uey and headed back that way.

Yuh sit way up when you ride in a county truck, and Jamie hadn't been in one in a while. He used to ride once in a while when his dad helped Barry out when Barry was in a fix or somethin' and needed him to drive. To salt the roads. But that was rare, and that's why Jamie would be ridin' with him. Because it was a big deal to ride in one of these when you were seven or eight and your dad was drivin' and you never got to ride in one that much. The seats were squishy as hell and the springs were all worn out. Just like he remembered. Barry's salt and sandin' truck.

The heat was on kinda low and it took the chill off in a nice way. Barry had the radio on real low too and it was Patsy Cline singin' on some country station comin' outa Richfield. The ashtray was heaped with butts, and smoke had penetrated every friggin' corner and piece of vinyl and plastic and metal in that thing. The dash was dusty and some wise-ass had fingered out "WASH ME" on it. There was stuff on the floor. Tools and stuff. Empty boxes of Marlboros down there and some on the seat. Leather work gloves that had seen better days. And the stick shift stained from dirty, workin' hands. Smudges of grease and stuff, yuh know. This was Barry's home away from home. Kinda cool.

"Thanks Barry."

"No problem, kid. Where am I headed?" Barry was shiftin'

up, gettin' them goin' along. You bounce along in a truck like
that when you get goin'. No joke.

"Rea Street."

Barry butted his nub and reached in his front flannel pocket.
"Yup, we paved that last summer." He pulled out a cigarette and
stuck it in his mouth and reached over and pushed his truck
lighter in. "Helluva hot summer it was last year doin' that.
Weather's all nuts in the Catskills these days."

"Sure is." Jamie nodded. "Yeah, whatta yuh doin' out in the
sander?"

Barry leaned forward a little so he could look out and up at
the sky. "Believe it or not, they say maybe snow tonight."

"No kiddin'? I thought maybe by the way the air was, but…"
Jamie leaned forward too and looked up. You really couldn't see
much up there through the windshield though.

"Yeah, crazy stuff, don't even seem real." Barry was shiftin'
again and you could hear some grindin'. "Third's just about shot
in this thing." Under his breath and through his cigarette. With
half a smile.

Jamie bounced up in the seat a little when the truck jerked
because of the rough gear switchin'. The seat was like an old
mattress that if you jumped on it enough you could probably get
some height goin'.

When he bounced, somethin' landed in his lap. Like it had
fallen from the ceiling of the cab or somethin'.

The lighter popped and Barry reached over and pulled it out.
He lit himself up and put the thing back in the hole in the
dashboard by the radio. He inhaled and kept his cigarette in his
mouth and exhaled. He sorta looked over at Jamie. "Now what

the hell was that?" He kinda chuckled. That's a really bad word. *Chuckled.* But that's what Barry did a lot.

Barry was always a good-natured guy.

The thing was a picture and it had landed face down on one of Jamie's legs. "Looks like a picture." He picked it up and was gonna stick it back in the strap on the visor where there was a buncha papers and ripped-open envelopes and stuff stuck there.

But Barry flicked on the interior light. "Oh yeah?" He looked down at the radio and then he turned it up a little. It mighta been Conway Twitty or somebody. "What of?"

"It's of…" Jamie flipped it over and looked down at it, "wow, it's of you and my dad." He looked over at Barry.

They came to the four corners, where all of Coformon Falls sorta spread from, and Jamie looked up at the light. Just 'cause yuh do that even though you're not drivin' or anything. It was green and Barry went through.

Jamie looked back over at Barry, and Barry was smilin'. "Let's have a look." He took one of this hands off the wheel, and Jamie handed him the picture.

He took his cigarette from his mouth with his other hand, and for a second the steering wheel was just wobblin' along. Not long, but it was empty for maybe a second until his hand with his cigarette went back on it and went back to steerin'. Barry looked at the road and then down at the picture and started crackin' up. Chucklin'. Whatever. "Holy Christ, Jamie I ain't seen this in— in," he looked back up at the road and handed the picture back to Jamie, "a good ten years, it's gotta be."

Jamie looked at the picture again. A little closer this time. You could tell it was taken up at the falls, like at one of the campgrounds up there, the trees had changed, and there was somethin' goin' on because there were a buncha people roamin' around in the background. His dad and Barry were standin' next to each other, like with their arms around one another's shoulder. They looked like they were, man, maybe seventeen or eighteen. Like young guys. Both of 'em pretty good-lookin', too. Barry, well, he hardly had a wrinkle on his face compared to now—not that he looked like an old man now or anything, he just, yuh know, looked kinda older than he really was, like he'd seen some cold winters and some hard work, yuh know. He was grinnin' ear to ear though, and he had—Jamie lifted the picture up a little—a socket wrench in his hand and was kinda holdin' it up, like he was shakin' it or somethin'. When Jamie looked over at his dad, he had to look up. The picture was kinda beat-up, but it was colored. So—and—it was like—when he looked right at his dad, it was just that his dad's eyes were...so alive. Dark brown and lookin' right back with his smile lines around 'em. It just took Jamie a little by surprise is all. He looked out and at his side mirror for a second. There wasn't much to see in it, nobody was behind 'em or anything, and the street they were on was sorta still outside of town. So there were a couple street lamps shinin' maybe and that was about it.

He looked back down. At his dad.

He kinda half laughed, 'cause his dad's hair was a little longer and you could tell by the way it was he mighta had it in a ponytail or somethin'. Jamie'd seen a lotta pictures of his dad when he was younger, but this picture kinda seemed different, for some reason. It was like his dad was so...Jamie didn't know what—the way he was standin' there with Barry, with that look on his face, smilin' like he was, and with...he had somethin' in his hand too. But he was holdin' it to his chest, like you'd see a preacher do or somethin' with his Bible. Yeah, it was a little red book.

Jamie felt himself blink. Like his eyes were all dry, probably from the smoke in there, and he felt his lids moisten them, and, and he even felt the second of dark that goes along with a blink. His spine and stomach sorta melted into one for a heartbeat or two. He knew what book was in his dad's hand.

He looked up and out the front windshield. Barry had turned onto Main. Jamie's jaw mighta been a little dropped even.

"What's a matter, chief, yuh ain't never seen a paira aces like them before?"

Jamie kinda tried to laugh...that was the book...yuh gotta look over at Barry. He made like a laughin' sound, but he just kept lookin' out the front window. Say somethin'. Anything. "Where are you guys? The falls, right."

"Yup," Barry nodded and shot some smoke out of the corner of his mouth, "they called it Senior Year Dream Day."

"Huh?" Jamie looked over then.

"Yeah, they don't have that anymore?" Barry was lookin' at the street. Main ran a long ways, from one end of town to the other. They hadn't hit the main Main part yet.

He musta saw Jamie shake his head no. "They took yuh up to the falls the first Friday in October and you had a picnic and all that happy horse shit," he chuckled a rattly chuckle and planted his cigarette back in his mouth, "and you were suppose to bring up somethin' that had to do with what you wanted outa life, and they took your picture for the yearbook—'course Char took that one of us." He tossed his head towards the picture in Jamie's hand. Charlene was Barry's wife and had been with him since like eighth grade. "No more Dream Day?"

Jamie shook his head and kinda turned his lips down like yuh do sometimes. They were drivin' past Doogles' Auto Body Shop and Used Car Sales, and he couldn't help but think of Justin Doogle and the closest thing they had to this Dream Day thing now. Around the end of September they pull the juniors and seniors outa study hall, and they take 'em one by one into the guidance counselor's office and ask them what their plans are for the future. Justin's mom cut hair at The Clip Wizards on Humbs Street, and, 'course, his dad had the mechanic business. They wanted Justin to be the first generation of Doogles to go to college and Justin wanted to go too, so he said that to Mrs. Darwins, the guidance counselor. Justin wasn't a smart kid, he wasn't an idiot either, yuh know, he was really good with cars and you could tell he helped his dad a lot...by his hands, yuh know. But Darwins took a look at his grades and told him he'd be better off gettin' a full-time job that had benefits than goin' on in school. Jamie only knew all this because he was in study hall with him and Justin came back almost cryin' and Francis—Mr. Francis— happened to be in there talkin' with the homeroom teacher, Mrs. Wilkins, and he knew Justin from English and went back to Justin's seat and talked with him.

Jamie craned his neck as they went by. There was still a light on in the shop part, not like a thief light, but a light light, and he could make out somebody workin' under a raised up car.

Then he answered Barry. "Naw, no more Dream Day."

"Well, like I said, they'd take your picture and you filled out a little card with what you planned on doin', and then some of 'em would land in the yearbook." Barry laughed and ashed his cigarette. "'Course, we didn't end up in there, you had to want to be a lawyer or somethin' like that back then too."

"What'd you guys put?"

Barry took a breath. "Lemme see. I think I wrote down I wanted to own my own truck service. Marry Char. Have a shit load of kids." He was usin' the hand with his cigarette in it to sorta check off what he said on this list in the air. "And." He stopped his checklist in the air and he sorta held his hand out there and then brought it kinda slow back to the steering wheel.

Jamie was lookin' at him and he looked over at Jamie for a second. And Barry smiled. "And I wanted to be a character in one of your dad's plays." He looked back at the road. "That's what Jamesie wrote. He hadn't dated your mom yet, and all he wanted back then was to write a play like that one that was in that book he was holdin' there—" he ran his finger and thumb down his scruff, "his favorite, what the hell was the name of it...*Midsummer Night's Dream*."

Jamie kinda mouthed it along with Barry when he said it, and looked back down at the book in his dad's hand and at his dad's face. *Midsummer Night's Dream*.

Barry snapped his fingers. "That's it. *A Midsummer Night's Dream*." He shook his head, like you do when you can't believe time has passed like it has, yuh know. "Weren't too badda dreams for a couple boys from outside of town."

Jamie let out a little puff of air and "hmph" kinda thing. Weren't too badda dreams for a couple of boys from outside of Coformon Falls.

They were gettin' down to the three or four blocks, to where what people really called Main. There were stores like you would expect to see up there, like Clayborn's Hardware Store and a Rite Aid pharmacy and a photo place. Big old buildings with maybe like the Catholic Family Crisis Center or Planned Parenthood offices in 'em or people's apartments or somethin'. Some buildings though were just empty. The stores had closed down, and there still might be like a sign or somethin' in the storefront, but nothin' would be inside 'em anymore. It—the town—stayed alive somehow though.

They passed the old Coformon Falls Hotel. Closed before Jamie was born. But still standin' because somebody wanted it there.

Barry looked over at Jamie.

He was just starin' out the front windshield.

"Why don't you keep that, Jamie. Put it in an album or somethin'. Where it belongs."

Barry flicked off the interior light, and Jamie looked back down at the picture. It was dark, yuh know, but he could still see it there, in his hand.

There were a couple potholes on Main, and they hit a few of 'em. All the lights that usually stopped people during the day, they were all just blinkin' yellow and you could go through 'em at night.

"You—you believe...in dreams, Barry?" He looked over at him.

"How do yuh mean?"

"I mean, like, do you think there's any—like—truth to 'em, yuh think they can be real in their own way?"

Now it was Barry who kinda turned his lips down and tilted his head. "I think we're talkin' about two different kinda dreams here. Dreams like goals and what you want outa life, and the dream I think you're talkin' about—dreams you have at night." He glanced over at Jamie, then back to drivin'.

"Aren't they kinda the same though? If yuh think about it, both kinds are things inside of yuh that you're tryin' to get out. And some people get the chance," Jamie sorta moved his feet, and his sneakers rattled some tools and some stuff down there, "and some people don't. Yuh know?"

They passed through the first intersection. Barry turned his lips down again, but this time he was noddin' his head up and down. "Yeaaah, I think you got a point there. But it makes me thinka somethin'. The wife and me went up to Auriesville a couple summers ago for this Indian festival, she likes lookin' at all the, uuh—crafts and jewelry and things, and I like the trip up there," he flicked his wipers on 'cause the air was gettin' wet outside, "you know, right up the Thruway, Exit 26, then hop on Route 5-South. You been there, right?" He looked back over at Jamie for a second.

"Naw." He shook his head. "Never been there."

"Nice place. Get your mom up there. Anyway, I got talkin' with this old Indian man who was doin' a dance—you can watch 'em dance and so on—and for some reason, I think because he was doin' some sorta dream dance, we got talkin' about it, and he told me some Indians think that your dreams are what's the real, and the real, the day and everything else, could just be what we'd say is the dream. Who knows? If yuh look at it that way maybe…" Barry took a long drag on his cigarette, and raised his eyebrows and tilted his head again.

They were gettin' closer to where Main hit Rea.

Jamie was kinda quiet and he looked back down at the picture in his hand. He still held it there like he could see it if he wanted to look at it even though it was too dark.

They both kinda sat there, not sayin' anything for a few seconds. They passed the bank and went through another couple of intersections.

Barry had both his hands on the wheel and he had his cigarette danglin' out of his mouth. He took it out, and Jamie looked over at him.

Barry nodded. "So yeah, to answer your questions, yeah, I s'pose one way or another, sooner or later a dream'll turn out true," he kinda bobbed his head back and forth, "or truth or whatever yuh wanna say."

"Yeah," Jamie moved his thumb over on the picture to about where he thought he could feel the cover of his dad's book, "that makes sense."

Rea was just ahead. On Jamie's side. He was about to say somethin' 'cause the truck seemed to be barrelin' down the hill end of Main, but Barry hit his blinker just as he turned to tell him.

"It's this one on the corner."

Barry pulled over and slowed down. "Looks like your friend left their light on for yuh."

"Yeah." Jamie had his hand on the door handle and the picture in his hand. He could see a dim light through a crack in Angelo's curtains in his living room. That was kinda strange. "It does."

They stopped.

"Thanks, Barry. For the ride," he held up the picture, "and the picture."

"Anytime, chief."

Jamie opened the door, and he was gettin' out.

"Hey, Jamie."

Jamie was half out, standin' on that running board thing that trucks have. He looked at Barry. "Yeah?"

Barry was grinnin' ear to ear. "Do you?"

Jamie just kinda tipped his head.

"What you asked me? 'Bout dreams?"

He nodded his head and smiled. "Yeah. I do."

Barry smiled too and he butted his cigarette. "You're a good kid, Jamie," he winked, "your father's son."

"Night, Barry."

"Stay outa trouble."

Jamie climbed the rest of the way down, and shut the door. The air was pretty cold after bein' in the truck, and he could feel the dampness draw into both his sweatshirts. He waved to Barry as he drove around the corner and onto Rea. One of those arm straight out and up kinda waves. He knew Barry probably didn't see him but he didn't care.

He turned around and ran across Angelo's lawn. There was the dream, and the book now, his dad's book. He ran to the house and stuck the picture in his back pocket so it wouldn't get any more bent than it was and he wouldn't lose it. Maybe he'd even show it, show his dad, to Angelo.

When he jumped onto the front porch, he skipped the steps altogether, and he felt a flush of heat go over him. His chest tightened, and he stopped.

The door was open a crack. Angelo had left his inside door like that before—but not this one. And at night besides?

He felt his heart start to race a little. Nobody gets robbed in Coformon Falls, but there were a few weird things that had gone on since he was a kid, like in any town. He looked behind him and sorta around him. Like that was gonna do some good. Or to see if somebody was out there or somethin', he really didn't know why he did.

He looked back at the door, and he pushed it open really slow the rest of the way. The hall was pretty dark, and he could see the crack of light from inside the living room.

That door's open too? "An-Angelo?" His throat kinda cut him off.

Nobody answered. It was quiet.

He swallowed and walked into the hall, and tried again. "Angelo?"

Nothing. Nobody.

He went down the hall and looked through the crack. He could see the shelf of the little foyer room through it.

It was empty. No books. No Hawaiian girl. No clock.

He shoved the door the rest of the way open and went in. "ANGELO!"

When he went around the corner, he saw Angelo jerk awake in his chair.

"What are you doing? Why are your doors open?" Jamie ran his hand over his head and down the back of his neck. "Christ, Angelo, you almost gave me a heart attack."

Angelo reached one of his hands behind his glasses and rubbed one of his eyes a little. "Hello, Jamie." He had on that

335

sweater from the day when he fell off that ladder and Jamie had helped him, and he ran his hands down the front of it and sat up a little more. "I must've dozed off, just as I thought I would."

Jamie could feel his body gettin' back to normal. Like when he pushed the door open, everything in him was like a board. He walked over to the chair he always sat in and sat down. "Your doors are wide open."

"I know. I was expecting you, and I didn't want to miss you."

"You were expecting me," Jamie kinda shook his head and laughed sorta and looked down at the carpet. "You're somethin' else."

Angelo smiled. He took off his glasses and huh-huh'd some of his breath on one of the lenses and rubbed it on his sweater.

Jamie looked back over to the shelf. "Where are all the books and stuff. And that clock." He got up and walked over there again and looked.

Shelf was bare.

Angelo held up his glasses, looked at 'em, then put 'em back on. "First tell me how things went."

Jamie's face—the whole dream thing lit back across it. He turned back to Angelo. "It worked." He walked back in the living room and he smiled and Angelo was smilin' too. "It worked Angelo!" He started laughin'. "I mean I knew it would, but it, it was amazing—" He couldn't even finish what he wanted to say.

Angelo was noddin' his head up and down. Jamie could see his chest bouncin' up and down too.

They were both laughin'. Jamie walked over to Angelo's

chair. He tried to get serious a second behind his smile. "God, Angelo, I don't know how to thank you." He bent down beside Angelo's sewing basket and in front of the chair Angelo was sittin' in. He put one of his hands on the arm of Angelo's chair when he did, and Angelo moved his hand and put it on top of Jamie's.

"You're a good kid—young man, Jamie. Your father's son."

Jamie tipped his head a little when Angelo said that. And a strange thing happened. He happened to look back down beside him, and the sewing basket was gone.

"What's goin' on, Angelo? Did you know my dad?" Jamie stood up and sorta backed away. He felt that board growin' in his body again.

"Stay calm, please Jamie, or you'll wake up right away." Angelo got up too.

"What?" Jamie started breathin' kinda crazy heavy and bumped into the chair he usually sat in. He looked behind him at it. The woodwork framing, remember with the winged foot and all that, it looked even more poofed out or somethin'…and the wings…they were feathery.

"Now, you've trusted me this far, haven't you?"

He looked back around to Angelo. "Yeah, of course," he nodded and tried to catch his breath, "of course I have."

"All right, then. And you trust me now?"

Jamie nodded.

Angelo came closer and he took Jamie's hand. "Sit."

Jamie nodded again and he sat.

Angelo bent down, beside Jamie, at his feet. He still had his hand. "Let's enjoy the end of this, Jamie. There's still more, and

337

I don't want you to miss a wink of it." He smiled.

"End of what, Angelo?" He could feel his eyes start to water and he didn't know why.

"This was my dream, Jamie. I shared mine with you."

"Your dream? What—nothin's been—" Jamie went to get up, but he sat back down, he had that feeling like he didn't know what to do with himself, he felt sick to his stomach and maybe even he was gonna throw-up. "You shoulda told me that, Angelo, you shoulda." He yelled at him, right at Angelo's face, and then he looked down at the carpet.

"I'm sorry, Jamie. I think you're right, I should have, but I didn't want to risk this," Angelo tried to get Jamie to look at him. He got down on his knees even, and tried to look at Jamie's face, "your reaction. You might have woken up if I had told you. Do you see?" He had kept his hand on Jamie's the whole time.

Jamie was still lookin' down and the brim of his hat was doin' exactly what he wanted it to do. But even that feeling was fadin'. Truth was, usually he didn't get mad like that, but when he did, it came and went in flashes anyway. He nodded his head a little.

"It's all been a dream, my dream, but it's all been real too, just like yours was. And now…it's served its purpose. It's ending, we're waking up."

Jamie was gonna start to sob. He had to press his lips together and bite the inside of his cheek. That's about all that separated him from losin' it, that and what Angelo said. He was tryin' to do what Angelo said, about stayin' calm. His voice, well, he was practically whisperin' now. "Why?"

Angelo squeezed Jamie's hand. "Why what, Jamie? You

need to say what you have to. This could end any moment."

Jamie looked up and the same damn face Angelo had had on since he first met him was right there. He could feel a little pulse in part of his upper lip, and his voice was still low. "Why…me?"

"You're the messenger now. You have something to say and people are going to listen." He looked right into Jamie's eyes. "That's why I picked you."

Jamie just sat there a second. He swallowed some spit in his throat, and just sat there a second lookin' at Angelo. Christ, his hand seemed big. And strong. Angelo's did, and he just kept it there on his hand. "How did you know me, from my dad?"

"Yes."

"I don't," Jamie shook his head, "remember ever meeting you. Or, or him sayin' anything about you."

"I didn't know him here. I met him—"

Before Angelo could finish, the room got brighter. Like this light was comin' from the dining room, not blinding or anything, but like someone was slowly turnin' on one of those dials that controls a mood light or somethin'. They both looked in that direction. The long table with all Angelo's stuff on it was gone. All that was left was the painting that used to be behind it, but it had changed or was changing. The blue colors and the dark and stars were washin' away, and the moonlight was comin' from a different angle, further off to the one side, and it was makin' room for the sun over to the other side. It had come to life sorta, more than it had been to begin with. You could see the sun's white rays and part of its globe way off and to the side, and it was makin' its way from the horizon real slow, like it does…when it rises. A cool wind started to blow too. It was comin' from the painting or the window or whatever it was now.

Jamie looked back at Angelo.

"Be true to yourself, Jamie." Angelo looked like the captain of his ship, he was all stern, but he was full of heart too when he said that. God, what a lousy thing to say, or way to describe him. Full of heart. But he was. He could make you believe.

"I'm not gonna see you again, am I?" Jamie lost it then, he knew his face was all red, and the valve popped in his head and he started to cry.

Angelo took his free hand and he brought it up with his other one on Jamie's. He shook his head a couple times. "Jamie…" Even if he had known what he was gonna say, his words wouldn't have come out right then. He moved his lips, and then stopped, and started again. "Jamie, even I didn't know how it all was going to completely turn out, but all seventeen and a half seconds of it have been worth it. You're a character, Jamie Auger, and you're right here," Angelo took one of his hands and fisted it and put it over his heart. "We have that."

Angelo watched one of Jamie's tears leave a streak down his face and drop off onto their hands. He took a deep breath, and put his hand back with his other one on Jamie's. "Now aren't you ready to see what's around the next corner?"

Jamie nodded his head and kinda wiped his face. "I'm just sick of people leaving me, Angelo."

"But no one ever goes that far." Angelo shifted on his legs and he took one of his hands and reached behind him, like into his back pocket or somethin'. And while he was doin' that, he tipped his head back towards the dining room, and smiled. Jamie looked back in there, and…and it wasn't the dining room anymore.

He looked back down to Angelo. But he was gone.

In his hand though was the book. *A Midsummer Night's Dream*. He held it in both his hands and looked down at it. He rubbed its red cover with his thumbs.

A horse whinnied, and Jamie looked back over to where the dining room had been. It was a stable stall from their barn now.

He heard the horse whinny again from behind the stall door.

Everything was like he was lookin' at it through a crystal ball or he felt like he was inside of one. It was like he was watchin' himself now, at certain times, from some other place, but he could still, like, sense everything even when he was. The air was still cool and wind was coming from somewhere. He still had the book with him and he got up and walked over to the door. The gold carpet was golden hay, and he looked down at it when he heard it sorta crunch under his feet. He unlatched the door and opened it and walked in.

The creak of that door was crystal clear, and everything else was quiet, so quiet, and sorta bright.

The stall was like a hundred times bigger than any of the ones in his barn were, and it didn't have a roof or ceiling or anything — that mighta been how or where the light was comin' from.

Puck was in there, he sorta came runnin' out of nowhere. He was runnin' around and whinnyin' and tossin' his head. He was sleek and his coat was wet like he'd been gallopin' around for a while. He looked right at Jamie with his huge brown eyes.

Jamie stood there and watched him.

Man, that horse was gonna be a runner, and he rounded by one of the walls where his bridle was hangin', and he just stopped short.

341

Jamie squatted down. He could hear himself breathing, and he heard Puck too. He watched him.

Puck lifted his front legs a couple times and stomped 'em off the stable floor. Then he shot up on his hind legs and wagged his front legs, like yuh see horses do. The whole time he was watchin' back at Jamie.

Those dark brown eyes.

Jamie stood up.

He saw his dad then, standin' there, in his work clothes, his jeans, and a T-shirt and boots and his cap. He was lookin' straight at Jamie, and he smiled, and he winked. He took his cap off and mussed his hair up a little because it looked like he had been workin' and he was a little sweaty. Then he hung his cap on the peg where the bridle was hangin'.

Jamie took a step towards him.

But, it was over in a second.

Puck dropped back down on all fours and he walked over to Jamie.

Jamie had the book in his one hand and he stuck his other hand out and Puck's nose was right there. All funny feelin' like.

Puck's ears were pricked up and he shook his tail and clacked one of his front hooves on the ground. Jamie pet the side of his face, and Puck moved in closer beside him.

Things shifted when Puck took a couple steps, but Jamie didn't really notice. Or care.

They were outside now. In the corral. Jamie felt chilly, and bright had turned to twilight too, dawn's twilight because the sun was sneakin' up from behind the eastern range. Jamie and Puck just stood there though, Puck sorta with his nose real close into

Jamie and Jamie's arm sorta around him and runnin' his hand across his smooth coat. Everything was so damn quiet.

A good quiet.

Snow started to fall. Just one and then a million more. Big, thick flakes.

Like angels' feathers.

It was so quiet. Just the sound of the snow fallin'.

"What do I do now?" Jamie whispered.

"You'll know," they told him.

Both their voices, just as quiet as he had asked, answered him.

"You'll know," they said.

Chapter Twenty-seven

WHEN HE woke up, he was in his long johns, and his blankets were all off from him. He was lyin' on his back and he had one of his arms across his chest. And the book was right there, risin' up and down real slow with his breathin'. That was probably the first thing he noticed when he was wakin' up.

He reached down and stuck his hands under the elastic band of his long johns, and he scratched. Then he grabbed a couple of the blankets from around his feet and pulled 'em back over him. He did it all eyes closed and half asleep and with *Midsummer* strapped across his chest like it was a fuckin' teddy bear or somethin'.

He wanted to slip back to where he had been for a second. Just a second more. Christ, just a second more. He went to where he left off. Probably the easiest way to go, he put himself in the corral and he put Puck beside him and he—he...he was awake. His goose bumps sent a chill up his arms, and he wrapped himself tighter in the thick blanket he'd fished up from around his feet.

It was cold in his room. Really cold.

He rolled to his side, and opened his eyes. The wind was whippin' through his window that he'd left open about halfway.

Have you ever seen snow blow and whirl around into your room and land on your rug? Curly long flakes in the dim of morning? And in your room? Jamie hadn't either. It kinda makes you wanna laugh or feel somethin' good, yuh know. Because it's like it seems so outa place there, tryin' to make a bank on your floor. He kinda stretched his neck and looked down. His paira jeans and sweatshirts and work hat were all there in a pile, and the snow was blowin' in and landed on 'em and on his rug around 'em.

He woulda laid there all day. Watchin' it come in and cover his clothes and his floor. It coulda stacked up to his bed if it had wanted to, he wouldn't have cared. His blanket was already warmin' him now and he still had the book pressed up close to him, and everything was there, fresh and, and so alive in his head.

But the damn red eyes of his alarm clock glared at him. Like a dragon through the snow.

5:59.

His alarm was gonna go off at 6:00. He got out of bed and clicked it off. He didn't wanna hear it. He just wanted to wake up quiet, and on his own.

His feet melted some of the snow that had started to layer there on his rug, and he left footprints when he turned around and looked down. He wondered if he was still dreamin'. Or he kinda wished he was still dreamin'. But he knew he wasn't.

He had the book in his hand, and he went over to his desk

and he looked at the cover one more time before he put it down. Thinkin' about who had held it. Oh, shit. He set the book on his open black notebook in sort of a hurry, and he bent down on his knees to the clothes he'd worn last night. He shook some of the snow off his hat and put it on. It wasn't wet or anything—the air was that cool in there, so that the snow wasn't gettin' wet while it landed. Then he found his jeans and he reached in his back pocket. It was there. He pulled it out and looked at it.

When he did, it's kinda hard to explain how he felt. If you've ever taken a really cool vacation or you've had the summer off from school, and then you hit the night before you have to go back…that's sorta how he felt. Somethin' behind him was big, but that's just what it was now. Behind him. And when he looked at that picture, he didn't wanna feel the way he did, but he did.

He stood back up and opened his dad's book and stuck the picture there inside it. Then he closed the cover back up, and he spread his hand out over it, his palm coverin' most of the thing.

He stood there in his long johns and his cap and bare feet and without a T-shirt on or anything, and he had his hand on that book. He bent his head and he closed his eyes, almost like he was prayin' or somethin'. Even he didn't really know what he was doin'. It was just makin' that heavy feelin' that shoved into his heart go away.

Outside was still comin' in, and his skin bristled for a second when some flakes hit him in the face and melted on his lashes. He opened his eyes, and reached over to the window.

Morning was makin' its way. Snow and wind were blastin'

on his bare chest. But it wasn't a bad thing at all. It was…alive and the air was alive. And he was alive or awake or somethin'. Alive, that's all he could think. He stood there with his hand on the sill for a minute and looked out. Their fields and the barn. The mountains. The snow comin' down.

Christ, everything had seemed so messed up. He shivered and he smiled. But maybe everything was the way it was suppose to be.

The sun was comin' up. Even though nothin' was clear, you could tell where it was. And that it would be up in a couple minutes. He'd watch for it, then he was gonna do his chores and get the bus. Like he did every morning.

＊ ✦ ＊

His mom's bedroom door was open when he came down the stairs and went into the sittin' room to put some wood in the wood stove. That was nothin' new, about his mom. She was usually up before him, doin' her part of the barn work—they shared it—and doin' early store stuff and things like that. But when he walked by he saw that the bed was all made. Kinda strange, not a big deal, but strange enough, because that was usually the last thing she did in the morning, after morning chores and breakfast and before she opened the store.

Jamie went over to the stove, and it was peddlin' a little heat. He guessed his mom had thrown a couple sticks of wood on when she got up just to take the chill off, and then figured Jamie could stoke the thing when he got up. He opened the door and he was right. A couple small sticks, with small flames jumpin'

347

from 'em. He picked up the poker beside the stove and poked at
'em and rustled at the ashes under 'em. He could feel some heat
shoot up when he did that. He threw on a couple more thicker
chunks they'd brought in the night before, and closed the door.
He stood up and turned around. That's just how people with
wood stoves do it, they put their back to it first and get warm,
then turn and face it.

He still only had on his long johns and he'd left his hat on,
and he stood there and let the heat get goin' and warm him up at
the same time. He folded his arms across his chest. Man. He
kinda shook his head and smiled. Nobody but nobody was gonna
believe it.

Nobody...

His brain woke up in intervals or somethin' because as soon
as he said that, another holy shit came across his lips.

Ben.

Ben would.

He was about to turn around, his back was gettin' too warm.
It was like he was on a rotisserie or somethin'.

Yeah, he could not wait—as he turned, he happened to look
out to the kitchen—that's how it was at their house, the rooms
were more or less connected—and, anyway, he saw a piece of
paper taped on the kitchen door.

He went out there and flicked the lights on. The heat from
the sittin' room hadn't made its way out there yet and the brick-
patterned linoleum really did always feel like cold brick first
thing in the morning. He went over to the door and pulled down
the note.

ANGELO

Morning Jamie,

I got up early this morning. I couldn't sleep anyway, I've got that interview for the intern at nine this morning in Saratoga. Wish me luck.

Good luck, Mom. You'll get it.

Anyway, I was so wired, I did your chores and mine, so maybe you can go back to bed for a while if you want. There's a new box of Lucky Charms in the cupboard. Have a good day at school, and please lock the door before you go.

Love, Mom

P.S. You left your hat hanging out in Puck's stall, so I brought it in and hung it on your kitchen chair.

Jamie reached up and felt his hat on his head. Yeah, he'd put his—he shot a look over to his chair. On the back of it was a cap. He set the note on the kitchen table and he walked over to it. He stood there starin' at it for probably ten minutes or somethin'. It was—he knew it was. He kinda went for it slow, yuh know. And he picked it up and looked it over. It was a little beat-up. Diamond Grains logo on it. Just like his. And it smelled a little. Like work and like the barn some…and like his dad.

He reached with his other hand and he took his off and went to hang it on the chair. The other hat was still in his other hand and while he was hangin' the one, he slipped the other on his head.

⌐ He took both of his hands and sorta fit it on there. He squeezed the brim and rounded it out a little more, and he pushed the cap on again. He kinda laughed.

Man.

He laughed again, and he kinda embarrassed himself smilin' like he was when nobody was around. He went to the cupboard for the fresh box of Lucky Charms. He opened the door, and the box was right there, next to his mom's Frosted Mini-Wheats.

He pulled it out. All still kinda smilin' and stuff.

He got in the other cupboard for a bowl.

Frosted Mini-Wheats.

Frosted…Frost.

"Shit." This time he said it out loud.

Him and Ben had that Robert Frost thing today.

◆ ✦ ◆

First period wasn't that bigga deal about bein' late for. He looked out the all fogged-up window and swiped his hand down it and looked out.

His bus waddled over the speed bump.

He started gettin' his books together that he had sittin' beside him. No, thank God, he didn't have to share a seat today. Sometimes—most of the time—he did.

Homeroom was definitely over. It had to be around twenty after or so, and he could just say the bus was late—which it really was—when he went straight to class. And because nobody else in there, his first period class, rode his bus, he could show up even a little later.

And the weather was snowin' and stuff…fuck it, he didn't even know why he was makin' excuses, he was just goin' down there. He had to know. Well, he was almost sure, but it was one of those things.

"Si'down!" Kurt the bus driver was lookin' up at his big mirror over the steering wheel. "Si'down 'til I stop!"

The kids who were already standin' up sat back down and cursed him out a little bit, and Kurt just glared back at 'em until everyone was sittin' half on the seat they were on. Kurt and the pre-seatjackulaters went through the same routine every morning while the bus made the loop over to the front of the school.

Kurt pulled up and stopped and pulled the door open and everybody stood up and started to file outa there. Jamie sat towards the back and he got up, and where there was a gap he filed in too.

Small steps. Shuffle, shuffle. Eager beavers behind yuh, steppin' on your heels.

He wasn't even gonna go to his locker. He had the shit he needed for first period and for English. He looked down at his books and notebooks in his arms. Yeah, he had everything. Only problem was he wasn't sure what time it was exactly, like how much of first he had missed already, he just didn't wanna miss any of second, yuh know, with it bein' presentation day and all. The bus ride had seemed like it took forever, but it always seemed like it took forever when you rode the bus, so you really couldn't go by that.

He wasn't gonna be that long anyway.

He got to the front and stepped down the bus steps. Snow was flyin' around. Another bus had pulled in behind 'em and kids from that one were gettin' off too. Instead of headin' for the front doors like the rest of 'em, Jamie just did a beeline. He put his head down a little and tucked his books beside him and started walkin' at a good clip. He figured no one was gonna say anything to him anyway, but he just wanted to be sure. When he was past the fence and around the corner of the school, he slowed down a little. That length of the school didn't have any windows. It was just a long, tall wall of bricks. With one door in the middle there. The door he tried to help Ben out with that time and ended up pushin' him around front.

He walked past it. Man, he couldn't wait to catch up with Ben. He had to do this first though. Somethin' inside of him secretly hoped, yuh know...even though, even though, further down than that, what was left of his Lucky Charms in his stomach told him the truth.

He passed the teachers' parking lot and the ass-end of the school and those goofy steps, some builder's attempt at style and class that didn't fit at all and kinda came off, as, well, goofy.

Jamie kinda shook his head and smiled. All just part of Coformon Falls High School, yuh know.

His nose started to run a little, from it bein' pretty cold out, and he wiped it on his coat sleeve.

He crossed over the speed bump and he was on Rea. Some cars were still rollin' in. Students, probably. Kids who were gonna take full advantage of bein' able to say they were late because of the weather. Some staff workers, like the lunch ladies and people like that, people who normally didn't come in right when school started anyway.

Nobody looked twice at him. He had his collar up, keepin' his neck warm, and he was walkin' in the opposite direction they were goin'. But no one looked twice or said a damn thing to him, they were all on the same mission.

Jamie looked over at the fields and the bleachers. Yesterday, or was it yesterday? Him and Ben were sittin' on the bleachers bullshittin' in the sun. He looked up to the sky when he thought about that and instead of lookin' at all the flakes flyin' down at him, he tried to look at the spaces between their paths. The snow was those big fat snowflakes and they were fallin' like crazy, but if you zigzagged up between 'em you weren't like somebody drivin' with their high beams on in a snowstorm. It wasn't blindin' like that at all. Fact was, you could see the blue of the sky if you followed far enough up.

He crossed the culvert and the little patch of woods behind the house, and his heart started to beat a little faster. He sniffed to try to get the wet that was startin' on the end of his nose, and he fixed his books again.

He slowed down when he got to where the driveway woulda been, and he stopped and just stood there.

Nothin'.

No driveway, house, flower bed, nothin'.

He looked the lot over. A thin layer of snow was startin' on it, and you could see where kids were cuttin' the corner from Main to Rea on their way to school. Some mud and green grass and fresh snow, a sloppy footpath diagonal across Angelo's front lawn.

His ears were cold and his hands were too. Funny thing was though, this morning, he'd thrown on that pair of boots that he hardly ever wore, he didn't know why, one of those just because things, yuh know. He had saved 'em for good, and he hardly ever wore 'em, but he put 'em on today, so everything had a good chill goin' on except his feet, they were all warm and dry inside his boots.

He stood there.

His breath rolled outa his mouth and he didn't feel like cryin'. Or smilin' really either. Ever feel like that? Your chest sorta feels empty and you wonder if your head is gonna let you think some other thought or feel somethin', anything, but nothing comes. Well, that's how Jamie felt, standin' there.

He musta been there a good fifteen minutes or a half hour watchin' the snow fall down on where Angelo's place had been. He could feel snowflakes meltin' in his hair and startin' to get little icicles in it. He even squatted down when he didn't wanna stand anymore and he just looked there in front of him.

"Angelo." When he said it, he barely heard himself. It was less than a whisper. Only his lips moving, really. He had just raised up one hand, not the one holdin' his books, the other one, to his mouth and blew warm air from inside him on it, and he was gettin' up to stand because his ankles and calves were about to bust from squattin' down as long as he had. He sorta stomped off the snow that had started to stay there on his boots, and he had said it. "Angelo."

When he fixed his books one more time and was about to turn and go back down Rea, he didn't. Instead, he yelled it. He spread his damn arms, with books in one hand and everything, and he looked up. He yelled as loud as he could. "ANGELO!"

But this time, when he said it, he knew that at least someone heard his voice.

Chapter Twenty-eight

"THIS WORLD is an extremely morbid place. Death. Greed. Wars that people don't under—" Harold stopped mid-sentence, and turned and looked towards the door. He was one of those kinda people that wouldn't have, he woulda just kept right on talkin', but the rest of the class was more interested to see who was comin' in than what he had to say about Emily Dickinson and her poetry. So he turned around with a real pissy look on his face and stopped rattlin' from his stack of 3x4 index cards.

Jamie was openin' the door real slow, and only part way, and was comin' in as quiet as he could, yuh know. First thing he scouted out was Mr. Francis, which he had a pretty good idea that he was in the back of the room because that's where he planted himself when people were doin' presentations. Jamie was real late, and he knew it. Well, not real late, but pretty late. He had figured that he'd make it at least to the end of first, but he had figured wrong. Turned out the bus ride really had taken forever

355

and he was late for second.

When he closed the door behind him, he figured he could head straight for his seat. No big deal. Francis wasn't a hard-ass like that as long as you didn't show up like that every day, and Jamie'd get to his seat and pass his excuse over to him without a to-do, yuh know. But the room was all silent and it was mostly because Harold was makin' such a big production about bein' interrupted. So when Jamie turned around and shut the door, he glanced over at Harold. Just to be polite, yuh know. "Sorry."

"Tsst."

A couple people tee-hee'd. Not at Jamie, but at how Harold got so lunatic about the whole thing. His face was like, yuh know, his jaw down a little and his bottom lip jutted out and his eyes rollin' when he couldn't help the tsst slip off his tongue.

Jamie looked like a drowned rat. He had to of. His hair was all wet and he ran his hand through it on the way to his seat. His jeans were dark denim from the snow that soaked 'em. Even his eyelashes looked like they had mascara in 'em or somethin' the way they were so dark from wet snow. His face was pink from the cold and it made his eyes a darker brown or somethin'. Yeah, he had come in from the cold and the snow and he looked it. And his boots were meltin' a little snow too on the rug, they had to have been. It was like he was trackin' in on someone's living room carpet or somethin'.

Sandy Khatz perked up when he walked by or whatever, her eyes traced him from head to foot and back up. She stopped scribblin' flowers in her notebook—today it was flowers—when he passed. But he just kinda kept his head down, until he got to his seat. He didn't really care what or why she was lookin' at him.

Harold didn't miss a heartbeat. He cleared his throat and picked up where he left off. "And again, to conclude, wars people don't understand. Emily Dickinson led a lonely, desolate life, and her poetry…"

Jamie got to his seat and set his books on his desk. He peeled his excuse off his top book, it'd gotten wet from the book's cover, almost soaked through. The secretary's writing was still there though. *Please excuse James Auger. Late bus.*

Francis was two rows over on Jamie's left and he passed his excuse to the kid next to him to hand it over. When the slip got to Francis, Jamie made sure he was lookin' that way. Francis took the note and looked at it and then looked over at Jamie and winked and gave a nod. Jamie mighta been Francis's pet.

Maybe Jamie could stop by after class and tell him, or after school, maybe. It might take a while to tell him, and somethin' between his lungs and his ribs told him to take the time.

"…indefinitely hollow and sad. Alone." Dramatic pause. "Her strongest poetry by far is that which rejects faith and…"

Jamie got out his English notebook and he opened it, and then he sorta looked outa the corner of his eye to the other side of him. Three rows over. At Ben.

There was a kid and an empty desk between 'em, but Jamie could see Ben hunched over his notebook, usin' his pen like a madman.

No way could he be takin' notes like that from this numb-nuts up there. Jamie sat up in his chair a little more and he pulled his pen from his spiral, and leaned up some. Tryin' to get Ben's attention.

"…her obsession with death was boundless, the world so

357

full of it…"

Jamie tapped his pen on his desk a little. The kid next to him, between him and Ben, looked over at him, and Jamie gave a quick smile, and clicked the tip of his pen out. Then he bent over to pretend to write, and he turned his head again. He could see Ben over there.

Ben had on one of his button downs, but it wasn't all buttoned up or tucked in either. It had a T-shirt underneath it too, that you were suppose to see, and it hung over his jeans.

Jamie could make out Ben's notebook too. There were some words down. And they looked pretty neat, but there was somethin' else too. Jamie focused his eyes a little more.

Ben was streakin' his pen down the margin of his notebook.

"Morbidity,"

Ben…Ben was doodling.

"morbidity,"

Jamie saw Ben wispin' streaks of ink down his notebook.

"morbid—"

"Thank you, Harold," Mr. Francis cut him off right when Harold had one fist clenched and his stack of index cards in his other sorta up in the air, "you can take your seat." Harold stood there a second.

Mr. Francis gave a nice smile and gave Harold a nod toward his seat. "I'd like to give Jamie and Ben enough time to speak."

That's when Ben finally looked over at Jamie. He smiled over at him and he sorta held up his notebook, so Jamie could see what he'd been doin'.

"…they've prepared a presentation on…"

Jamie saw this title *Emily Dickinson/her poetry* on the top and there were some notes there. But to the side of it was this crazy waterfall Ben had detailed with his pen. It had whitecaps at the bottom and it looked all dimensional and stuff the way Ben had shaded it. Jamie didn't know if he was seein' things or not, but written down it, almost like hidden or somethin' in the rushin' water, in capital letters, was the word BELIEVE.

"…and it will be interesting to see what they've done with one of his most famous selections 'The Road Not Taken,' so without further…"

Jamie looked up at Ben. And he smiled at him and he nodded. Ben set his notebook down and picked up their presentation folder, and he gave Jamie a thumbs-up.

"Gentlemen. It's all up to you."

Jamie clicked his pen a couple times and then stuck it behind his ear. Then him and Ben went up to the front of the room, and started in on Robert Frost.

✦ ✦ ✦

When he finished, he took another last swig from the can of Sprite I'd bought him from the teachers' lounge. We had moved up there when the janitor kicked us out of the empty classroom he'd found me in, and we sat at a table in a room where the soda machine was brighter than the three lamps they had set on some of the end tables. Teacher lounges are always dim like that.

It was after six, and he had by far missed the late bus, so I drove him home, of course, without thinking twice. We didn't say much on the way, not while we were flicking the lights off, or going down the stairs, or going to my car or on the way home.

There are good quiets though, and this was one of them.

Coformon Falls at dusk earns a certain reverence from anyone who passes through it, especially as you take the four corners and start heading out of it. I had never really been to his side of town, to be honest, being that I was relatively new there, and he pointed out a few landmarks and told me when to slow down as we got closer to his house.

His mother, Mary, happened to be outside talking to a woman in a pickup. Probably her last customer for the day. She pulled away, and Mary started over to us.

He opened his door and the car light came on, and when she saw it was him she continued over, but with a walk of family instead of work. She started with questions, like mothers do, when she was close enough, and he answered without an answer, like kids do, and introduced her to me. He opened the door wider, and when she bent to look in and greet me, I noticed right away the way her loose ponytail fell just so over her shoulder, and how she crossed her arms across her chest to keep the cold from her body. I could tell she had worked a hard day and thrived on it. It was in the bright hazel of her eyes. Such bright hazel was there in her eyes that when she smiled and thanked me for bringing him home and then invited me in for dinner, I had to glance away and turn the radio knob lower, even though it wasn't on.

He looked down at the radio when I did that, and then, with a smile just at the one corner of his mouth, he looked over at me, as if he almost knew.

There was talk just between them at first as we walked around the store to the house. Talk about Saratoga and how it looked pretty good. And a question about Barry stopping there today with a small pillow left behind in his truck. Then the conversation included three, and we went inside for dinner.

Don't wonder a whole lot about what happened after that night because I think you probably already know. And if you are one of those people who is uneasy with that or you just aren't ready for such liberty, I can give you just a little more without betraying too much of a part of what he hopes you haven't missed.

He went on to write books, good books.

And he and Ben, they remained good friends, the best of friends—because people who share dreams usually do.

Me? I suppose he wouldn't mind me saying that I developed a sudden interest, and later on a passion, for horses right from there on out.

Yuh see, truth is, days pass, then months, and then years, and, you'll find—like he did—that, as they do, they have a way of tying up the loose ends.

Then again…life is strange, isn't it.

Or somethin' like that.